***"You're a handsome man. Surely you've
bedded your share of women . . ."***

Catriona hadn't just startled or confused him,
she'd stripped the words from him. For a long
moment, Mark could only stare at her.

"Are you asking what I think you're asking?"

She nodded.

Every thought flew out of his mind. He remained
silent, too fascinated by her proposition to move.

"You would have to keep it a secret, however,
and leave Aunt Dina's employ soon after."

"You don't wish to be reminded of your mistake,
is that it?"

She shook her head. "You aren't a mistake, footman. You're a temptation."

He had to leave now, before he took her up on her
invitation. His body, long celibate, was warming at
her words.

"I've never been offered such an interesting
proposition."

"Are you going to rebuff me? If you are, I wish
you'd do so quickly, before I humiliate myself further."

"Frankly, I don't know what I'm going to do," he
said, spearing his hand through his hair.

"What do you want to do?"

"Take you to your bed and keep you there for a
day or two."

Romances by Karen Ranney

KAREN RANNEY

The Lass Wore Black

AVON

An Imprint of HarperCollins*Publishers*

This book is a work of fiction. The characters, incidents, and dialogue are drawn from the author's imagination and are not to be construed as real. Any resemblance to actual events or persons, living or dead, is entirely coincidental.

AVON BOOKS
An Imprint of HarperCollins*Publishers*

Copyright © 2013 by Karen Ranney
ISBN 978-1-62090-805-1

Avon Trademark Reg. U.S. Pat. Off. and in Other Countries, Marca Registrada, Hecho en U.S.A.
HarperCollins® is a registered trademark of HarperCollins Publishers.

Printed in the U.S.A.

Chapter 1

July 1862
London

"**M**iss Cameron, are you ill? You've grown so pale."

Mrs. Smythe-Anderson stepped toward Catriona. Her hostess was an older woman, her long, lean face equipped with a pointed chin, aquiline nose, and a series of wrinkles radiating out from her brown eyes like the rays of the sun. Those eyes were now narrowed in concern.

Catriona blinked. She stood in the doorway of the Smythe-Anderson parlor, unable to move. She licked her lips, took a deep breath, and tried to form some type of answer.

Not one word came to mind.

"My dear, come with me," Mrs. Smythe-Anderson said, leading her out of the dining room. "We'll find a place where you can compose yourself."

Please. Dear God, she was going to faint, and she'd never fainted in her life.

"You look pale, as if you've seen a ghost," her hostess said.

Yes, a ghost, that's what it was. Not a ghost like the ones that fascinated her sister at Ballindair, but a ghost from her past. A substantial ghost who'd stared at her from the doorway with the same shocked recognition.

Dear God, what was Andrew doing here?

"You said your aunt was ill?"

She nodded. Because her hostess was considered a doyenne of society, and this dinner an important introduction to some people, she'd come anyway.

"I do hope it's not catching," Mrs. Smythe-Anderson said, leading her up the stairs. "We've already lost one guest this evening. Mr. Prender just this minute left. He, too, was suddenly taken ill."

She halted on the stairs, grabbed the banister and looked up at the older woman.

"He's gone?"

Mrs. Smythe-Anderson nodded. "Perhaps it's just as well. Andrew is such a charming man, but I daresay not a good companion for my unmarried female guests." The other woman leaned down and whispered, "He's quite a flirt, my dear. He has a reputation that might be considered a trifle risqué, especially for a young girl like you."

Wordlessly, she followed her hostess to a guest room.

"Would you like me to send your maid to attend to you, my dear?"

"No," she said. "If I could just sit here for a few minutes, I'm sure I'll be fine."

"Of course, but if you want to loosen your clothing, just pull on the bellpull. I'll alert the staff that your maid might be needed."

"Thank you," she said. "You're very kind."

"Nonsense," Mrs. Smythe-Anderson said. "What kind

of hostess would I be if I allowed my guests to become ill? I do hope it's not catching."

Since smallpox was known to occur in London periodically, she hastened to reassure her hostess. "I'm only feeling a little chilled," she said. "My aunt has a cold. No doubt that's all it is."

A few pleasantries later she was alone in the bedchamber. She walked to the window, parted the curtains and looked out at the rainy night. Was he there? Was he spreading tales, even now, of their liaison?

She could barely breathe and her stomach was in knots.

Tonight, the Duke of Linster had paid court to her. She'd laughed with several people, told stories of her shopping expeditions in London, listened intently to boring discussions of politics. Everyone had smiled at her. She'd been complimented about her dress, her hairstyle, and her smile.

What would the guests say if they knew that the woman at the center of attention, the sister-in-law of an earl, had once been a maid?

Wouldn't they gossip to know that she was the daughter of a murderer, and that her father had killed his own wife in an act of love? An act that had resulted in him being hanged and she and her sister nearly starving to death?

But most of all they'd all be in a tizzy if they learned that the virginal and chaste Catriona Cameron was anything but, and that she'd bedded Andrew Prender not once but many times.

She should never have come tonight. Why hadn't she stayed at home? Why had she listened to Aunt Dina and attended this dinner party?

Disaster loomed as sure and certain as the sunrise.

She'd never told Aunt Dina about Andrew. Yet she

should have planned for him to be here. London society was smaller than she'd thought, with everyone knowing everyone else.

The better for gossip to spread quickly.

She'd been a fool.

Perhaps he wouldn't speak because of the affection he'd felt for her. Perhaps he would remain silent for the sake of Morgan, her brother-in-law and once Andrew's friend. Perhaps they'd even mended their rift after her departure for Edinburgh. Perhaps he was kinder than she thought and didn't want to destroy her chances in London.

Perhaps the moon would turn purple and birds fly backward, too.

What was she going to do?

She couldn't hide in this room. She twisted her hands together, released them, and gripped them tightly again. Her stomach was icing over and the back of her tongue felt odd.

He'd been startled to see her. Was that because he'd known her as Catriona MacDonald? She'd gone back to her real name of Cameron after she and her sister decided it was safe enough to use again.

He'd fallen in love with her, something she'd not anticipated. When he offered her a position in London as his mistress, she agreed.

Would he remember that? Or just that last day, when she'd been given another choice by her brother-in-law? A chance to start again, become someone else, Catriona Cameron, the woman she was now. A woman who was being courted by a duke.

What was he going to do? Tales of bedding her would only add to his allure while destroying her.

She walked to the fireplace, pulled the bellpull and went to the door and waited.

The woman who responded was an older, settled sort, with gray hair beneath her cap and a square, matronly shape.

"Would you please tell Mrs. Smythe-Anderson that I'm going home," she said.

"Yes, miss."

"Could you send my maid to me?"

"Of course. I'll also ask that your carriage be brought around."

She nodded in thanks, walked to the dresser and surveyed herself. She was too pale, and looked decidedly ill. Good, that would explain her haste in leaving.

A few minutes later she and Millicent were tucked into the carriage, her farewells to the rest of the guests being made by her hostess. She wouldn't get to say good-bye to the Duke of Linster, but mystery never hurt in the chase. The duke had hinted he might join her on her morning ride. To be seen in public with him panting after her would be a great advantage.

Please let Andrew keep silent.

"Was it a good party, then?"

She leveled a stern look at Millicent.

All Aunt Dina's servants were lacking in decorum. They didn't know their proper place, witness the girl's curiosity. She was not going to discuss her evening with a maid.

What would the girl say if she told the truth? Most of the entertainments in London were exceedingly boring and ponderous.

Couldn't Prince Albert have died a few years ago? The whole of society seemed to be in mourning, even though it had already been months since the man died. Was she supposed to spend all her time in London pretending a downcast air and speaking in a subdued whisper?

After tonight, she might well have to.

"Is the duke still interested, then?" Millicent asked.

She frowned severely at the girl. Were they talking about her in the kitchen? Her campaign to interest the Duke of Linster had been a closely guarded secret, or at least she'd believed so until this moment.

"You'll not talk about my personal business with other people, Millicent," she said.

"No, miss."

"Anything you happen to overhear, or see, for that matter, should never be discussed with another servant."

"No, miss," the girl said meekly. She didn't look the least chastised, however.

Catriona plucked at her loose-sleeved cloak, feeling the material cling damply to her exposed skin. If Aunt Dina had come with her, she would've been doubly horrified. How would she have explained Andrew?

How did she explain Andrew?

Aunt Dina knew her as the Countess of Denbleigh's sister and was ignorant of everything else she'd done.

After patting an errant blond curl back into place, she adjusted the fit of her gloves and smoothed her hand over the cloak that protected her gown.

Her stomach still rolled.

Before she'd seen Andrew, the Duke of Linster had smiled at her. Twice, he'd sidled up to her, and twice she'd moved away. She wanted him to lust after her. After all, lust had proved to be an ally of hers.

Would Andrew say anything?

The duke, although Irish, was her best chance at a titled marriage. Twenty years her senior, he nonetheless considered himself a roué, a word she'd learned from Dina's whispered warning.

Millicent was snoring.

She didn't wake the girl. Instead, she bit her lip, turned and raised the leather shade, hoping that the passing scenery would take her mind from Andrew for just a moment.

Fog obscured her view, but at least it was a white, shrinking thing, tendrils floating off into the air like ghost fingers. She didn't mind the fog at night, but the yellow thickness of it during the day made her feel as if she were wading through soap. More than once she'd had the disconcerting sensation of seeming alone as she made her way to the carriage, yet able to hear the voices of Aunt Dina or her maid.

In this section of London, not only were the streets lit by gas lamps, but some of the shop owners had mounted gaslights behind large bottles of liquid. The result was blurry balls of pink, blue, or green in the shop windows.

As they turned, shadows lingered at a corner. No doubt a beggar stood there, hoping the carriage would stop rather than simply slowing. Another thing about London she'd not expected. Beggars were everywhere, either claiming that they were veterans or impoverished tradesmen. She'd seen whole families, the children dressed neatly, their faces washed, standing next to their parents, hands outstretched. Other beggars had hidden their faces; some had claimed to know no English, while others shuffled right up to her, murmuring about how hungry they were.

She'd starve, too, if she didn't find a husband.

She couldn't live forever on her brother-in-law's generosity. Not when she had her beauty as a tool and passion as a skill. She might have to, however, if Andrew started talking.

Once, she'd had such high hopes for this time in London. But the truth was, she wasn't all that enamored of the city. London stank. She'd been told it was due to the open cesspools or the sewers that ran to the Thames. At times the breeze carrying the river's stench was overpowering. On a calm day soot would linger in the air, causing her nose to itch. That, or the ever present odor of horse manure, made any outing hideous.

But inside, too, she was subjected to the most ghastly odors. The corridors in even the most luxuriously appointed home smelled of unwashed servants and cooking. At a ball, the scent of a dozen perfumes was not enough to mask either body odor or bad teeth.

No, Edinburgh smelled a great deal better.

The window suddenly exploded.

The cloud of glass shards illuminated by the carriage lamp looked like yellow diamonds. She had barely registered the sight of them when a protective impulse made her throw up her arms to protect her face.

Too late, however, to save herself.

She felt each separate shard as it sliced into her skin. A surprised gasp of pain accompanied each, along with a surge of terror.

Millicent screamed. The coachman shouted in the distance. Wheels screeched against the cobbles, and horrifyingly, another window shattered.

As the carriage rocked, she blindly reached for the strap above the window. In a motion so slow it felt part of a dream, the carriage rolled, tossing her to the far side of the vehicle in a shower of glass and metal.

Her leg was twisted beneath her, and she pushed against Millicent in panic. The maid was silent, the girl's composure a lesson. If Millicent could be brave, so could she.

Her face felt heavy, something cold and sharp cutting her. Warm liquid flowed into her eyes and she knew it was blood. She raised a trembling hand and found a large triangle of glass where her cheek should be.

Where was her face? Dear God, where was her face?
Blood was choking her, and she wiped it away from her mouth, her breath coming in heaving gasps.

Her gown, her lovely gown was ruined.

Her face was gone.

Chapter 2

January 1863
Edinburgh

Dina MacTavish stood in the foyer of her Edinburgh town house, clasping her hands tightly before her. For the first time in a long time, she wished her husband were still alive. The man had been a wastrel, however, a horrid manager of money. Because of him, she was dependent on her sister's child for subsistence.

Why was she even bothering to think of Harold? He wouldn't have been any better at this situation than he was at providing for her. In fact, he would have layered his own impatience over her fear.

No, she should count on her own common sense. Praying wouldn't hurt, either.

The man coming up the steps was her last resort. She had to believe that Mark Thorburn would be able to accomplish what no one else had been able to do.

How quickly life changed from an agreeable existence to one fraught with endless drama and doubt.

Of course, she'd had money troubles. Who didn't have money troubles, unless they were as rich as Croesus, like her nephew, Morgan? Thank heavens no one wanted to quit imbibing whiskey, especially MacCraig whiskey, the basis for his fortune. More than once, she worried about that. Should she feel more guilty that her existence was dependent on the drunkenness of others?

Yet when she worked in Old Town, she never saw empty MacCraig bottles. No, MacCraig whiskey was expensive enough that it wasn't responsible for the destruction of lives and families. At least, that's what she told herself.

The young man coming to the door was nearly as wealthy as Morgan. Rumor had it that he'd inherited a great sum of money from his grandmother, a woman who'd doted on the boy.

Not quite a boy, though.

The housemaid opened the door, and she steeled herself.

Seven months had passed since she'd seen him last. What was he, thirty-two? A question that made her feel even older than when she'd awakened this morning.

With his antecedents, his family's wealth, and his exceeding good looks, he was a package to turn any woman's head—regardless of her age.

Mark Thorburn was tall, possessed of long legs and broad shoulders. His face was perhaps on the stern side, except for that mouth of his, that beautiful, and surprising mouth. Full and mobile, it was almost always curved in a pleasant half smile, as if he anticipated life would be agreeable. She knew that wasn't correct. He'd seen the misery the world had to offer only too well.

His eyes, a dancing blue, could become serious all too quickly. She'd seen him level a look at a neglectful mother and lecture her about feeding her child.

His cheekbones were high, his face hinted at Roman ancestors, and his black hair fell down to brush against his brow. His eyebrows, another arresting feature, could alter his entire expression in a moment, make it questioning or communicate disbelief, depending on the look in those blue eyes.

His nose was long, but fit the rest of his face. That was the riddle when looking at Mark Thorburn. Separately, none of his features were remarkable, but put together and they created a more than acceptable mien. He was handsome without being pretty. Striking, perhaps, would be a better word. He commanded attention when he walked into a ballroom or into his surgery. Look what he'd done to her foyer. He'd taken it over.

Worse, when he removed his coat, it was to reveal formal attire. The black of his short-tailed coat was a stark contrast to the crimson silk vest and snowy ruffled bib of his shirt.

She stepped forward, unclenching her hands and extending both in a welcoming gesture.

"Dr. Thorburn," she said. "I've taken you from something. I do apologize."

"I'm due at a function this evening, Mrs. MacTavish," he said, removing his hat and gloves and placing them on the sideboard. Only then did he reach out and grab her hands in his, the grip steady and reassuring.

For a second she wanted to be a younger woman. If she were his contemporary, she might have thrown herself in his arms and wept against his shoulder. Gentleman that he was, Dr. Thorburn would no doubt have set her gently away from him, sparing them both embarrassment over her histrionics.

"You wanted me to see your niece?" he said, effectively banishing any silly thoughts about throwing herself on his mercy.

She moved aside, leading the way to the front sitting room.

"She's not actually my niece," she said, taking her place on the settee and gesturing to an adjacent chair. "However, I've come to think of her as one. Or even my daughter, if I had been blessed enough to have children."

My recalcitrant and troubled daughter.

That part, however, she kept to herself for the time being. If this meeting followed the tenor of the other ones, Mark Thorburn would find out just what kind of patient Catriona was soon enough.

She was running out of physicians. She'd consulted the most famous ones in Edinburgh and none of them had been willing to treat Catriona. If the girl hadn't been so badly injured, she would've lost patience with her weeks ago. As it was, she could only offer Catriona her pity, along with a determination that matched the girl's own.

Catriona would get her treatment, even if she objected every hour of every day. Yet that's exactly what the girl was doing, and effectively.

Dr. Thorburn's stubbornness might help him succeed where others had failed.

"Catriona was in an accident in London," Dina said. "She was grievously wounded," she added, staring into the distance. "My maid, Millicent, was killed in the accident."

She looked over at him.

"For a few days I was not even certain that Catriona would survive. She had lost a great deal of blood, you see." The explanation had taken longer and been framed in more delicate terms with the other physicians. She knew Mark, however, and had even served as his assistant on more than one occasion in Old Town. Besides, she was a contemporary of his mother's. If he couldn't deal with plain speaking from a woman, she'd selected the wrong candidate for this task.

"But she didn't die," he said, urging her along.

"No," she said. "She didn't die. We convalesced in London until Catriona was well enough to travel. The journey home was done in stages, in a conveyance suitably fitted to accommodate a patient."

Once again, her nephew, Morgan, had provided the funds, if not the emotional energy, to bring Catriona back to Edinburgh. He'd been all set to take her home to Ballindair, where she would have been cared for by her sister, but Catriona abruptly and unexpectedly refused. Instead, she'd remained for a month in her suite of rooms upstairs, transforming them into a luxurious hermitage.

When Dina explained that to Mark, his mobile brow arched upward.

"I don't think it's out of the ordinary, Mrs. MacTavish, that she not want to see visitors while she is recuperating."

"She has been recuperating for five months, Dr. Thorburn."

The brow stayed in place. "In all that time, has she not had the care of a doctor?"

"In London, yes, but not since we returned to Edinburgh. In fact, the only person she has agreed to see is her sister, and Jean, being in the family way"—another indelicacy there—"will not be able to visit her for at least several months."

"Yet something has happened to make you summon me," he said.

She sat back and folded her hands on her lap. He was an intelligent young man.

"I'm concerned about her," she admitted. "She doesn't seem to be improving."

"I'm not the only physician you've summoned, am I, Mrs. MacTavish?"

Yes, he was an intelligent young man.

"You are the sixth, Dr. Thorburn. Everyone else was summarily dismissed."

In actuality, Catriona had threatened them with bodily harm.

He didn't speak, didn't question her, simply waited, a patience she would have admired if it hadn't been directed toward her.

"She throws things," she said after a suitable moment of silence.

"She's spoiled, then."

Dina shook her head. "Not spoiled. Troubled. She does come out of the room, but only at midnight. She takes the back stairs to the kitchen and out to the courtyard and walks the square. I've seen her myself."

"I don't know how you want me to help her," he said.

"She was badly injured, Dr. Thorburn. Her face was cut by shattered glass. The physicians in London said there was nothing they could do."

"She was scarred, then."

She nodded. "Would you not look at her and see if there's anything to be done?"

Somehow, she needed to give Catriona hope. Perhaps, then, the girl wouldn't just sit at the window and stare out at the world like a prisoner trapped in her own body.

The tears came abruptly, but not entirely unexpectedly. Whenever she thought of Catriona, she became weepy.

"She was such a beautiful girl," she said. "But she'll never be beautiful again." She composed herself, then frowned down at her clasped hands. "The first time I saw her face, I recoiled. To go from what she looked like to what she looks like now would be a difficult journey for anyone."

"I cannot perform miracles, Mrs. MacTavish."

His voice had altered, taken on a stern tone, as if she were one of those Old Town mothers guilty of drinking too much and neglecting her children.

She tapped her foot against the carpet.

"You have always struck me as an intense young man," she said. "Someone who would not accept a barrier. You crawl over it, or walk around it, or perhaps you would even break through it."

Still, he remained silent, that look in his eyes warning her that she had only a few minutes to convince him. Otherwise, he would claim the press of his social obligations and leave.

"Will you not at least try, Dr. Thorburn?"

"I have never had to convince a patient to allow me to treat them, Mrs. MacTavish."

She nodded. "Ordinarily, I would agree with you. However, Catriona has always been extraordinarily stubborn. Both of the Cameron girls are, I daresay, each in her own way."

"Catriona Cameron?"

She nodded. "No doubt you've heard of her. She was renowned for her beauty. Quite popular in London, as well. A duke was about to make an offer." She sighed, bit back that thought and concentrated on the present. It was never good to weep over what could not be changed.

For a moment he sat there, frowning at the floor, his hands loosely joined between his open legs. He made her substantial chairs look tiny, as if he sat in a dollhouse of her making.

"Very well," he said, and stood.

Surprised, she stood as well, looking up at him. "You'll see her, then?"

"I will attempt to see her," he said. "I can promise nothing, especially if five other doctors have tried and failed."

"Oh, but you are not like the others, Dr. Thorburn," she said. Less a compliment than the truth, but he waved off her comment impatiently.

A few moments later they were outside Catriona's suite, a lovely set of rooms comprised of a sitting room, bedroom, and a small bathing chamber. Her nephew had ordered it refurbished for Catriona's stay.

Beside the door was a long sideboard, and on it a tray with Catriona's evening meal, still untouched.

"Does she take her meals in her room?"

Had he not been listening?

"She doesn't leave her room, Dr. Thorburn. Not during the day, at least. She will not even allow the maids into her room. We have to leave her tray outside the door. If she's hungry, she'll eat. If not, she won't."

"She hasn't been eating?"

Dina shook her head. "Another worry," she said, and then told him the truth, the reason she'd asked him to call. "I'm afraid she's willing herself to die."

This time his expression of concern was the mirror of hers.

Chapter 3

Mark knocked firmly on the door, but received no response.

He glanced at Mrs. MacTavish. The woman made no effort to conceal her worry. She bit at the knuckles of one hand, the other supporting her elbow. The foot that had tapped so impatiently in the sitting room was now beating a rhythm on the green runner before the door.

"Are you certain she's inside?"

The woman nodded.

He knocked a third time and heard movement on the other side of the door. Was Catriona standing there, listening to their discussion?

"I wish to see you, Miss Cameron," he said.

His voice carried well enough, but he might as well have been whispering, for all the response he received.

If Catriona meant to annoy him, she was succeeding. He was expected at his parents' home in a quarter hour. Even if he didn't attend his grandfather's birthday ball, he could always find something to do that was a damn sight better than standing here waiting for a spoiled miss to answer the door.

"Miss Cameron," he said, "I must insist. I'm not leaving."

"Go away." The voice sounded husky, as if she didn't often speak. He pressed his fingers against the wood of the door and turned to Mrs. MacTavish.

"Does she admit any of the servants?" he asked.

She shook her head.

"Even to clean her room?"

"Only for her earth closet and chamber pot," she said, looking away. "She cleans her room by herself."

"What does she do during the day?"

Surprisingly, she sent him an irritated look. "My dear Dr. Thorburn, I don't know. She won't even admit me. The moment we returned to Edinburgh, she decided that she was going to be a hermit, and a hermit she has been."

"She can't be allowed to continue such behavior," he said. A comment that earned him another annoyed look.

He removed his coat, handing it to her without a word. She looked startled, but not as much as when he removed his vest, cravat, bib, and collar. She stood there blinking down at her armful of his clothing, then back up at him.

"Do I look the part of footman?" he asked.

She shook her head slowly from side to side.

Ignoring her, he moved to the sideboard, peered beneath the napkin, then put it back into place. Hefting it in one hand, he knocked on the door with the other.

"Miss Cameron," he said. "You need to eat."

"Go away." This time the already resolute voice was stronger.

He sent Mrs. MacTavish a look of apology, drew back his right leg and slammed his foot into the door beneath the latch.

The door swung open, bouncing against the wall. He'd have to send a workman over tomorrow to repair the door frame. But for now, still hoisting the tray in his left hand, he entered the room.

When Mrs. MacTavish would have followed him, he shook his head slightly, stepping into the darkness alone.

Immediately overwhelmed, he took a step back toward the open door. As he did whenever he was reminded of his intolerance for small spaces, he made himself stop, look over his surroundings, and take a deep breath. The room wasn't that small. The darkness merely made it feel suffocating. Another deep breath, another step away from the doorway, and he'd mastered the sensation.

The room smelled of potpourri, something like apples and cinnamon, but it was much too cold in there, as if she'd recently closed the window.

Was she trying to freeze herself to death as well?

"Get out."

He turned his head toward the voice. In the corner of the sitting room sat a shadow, darker than the gloom. As his eyes adjusted to the lack of light, he moved to the window.

"If you open the curtains," Catriona Cameron said, "I shall scream."

That was unexpected.

"I doubt you have the strength to scream," he said. "How long has it been since you've eaten?"

"Get out."

He made his way carefully to a large circular table in the middle of the room and placed the tray in front of a chair.

"Would you like me to light a lamp?" he asked.

"Get out."

"Or a candle, perhaps?"

"Who are you?"

"I'm the new footman," he said, wondering if she'd believe him.

"I'll have you dismissed."

"I've just begun this position."

"You've just ended it," she said. "Get out."

"Are the other servants afraid of you?"

She didn't answer. Nor did she move. No doubt she was glaring at him from her position in the corner.

"I was hired for my tenacity," he said, a true statement, if she only knew it.

"Get out."

"You should find another command. That one is growing old. You need to eat."

"Get out."

"Not yet," he said. "After you've eaten, I'll take my leave. Your dinner is cold, but perhaps something is still edible."

"I'm not hungry."

"I find I don't care," he said. "You still need to eat something."

"Is that why you've been hired? To be obnoxious and irritating? If so, you've done your duty," she said. "You can leave. Tell my aunt you did everything within your power to get me to eat. Including violating my wishes. If nothing else, perhaps she'll give you a bonus."

"Are you angry at her?"

"No."

"You're not punishing her by refusing to eat?"

"Why should I answer a footman?"

"Because I'm curious," he said. "Because I genuinely want to know why you intend to starve yourself."

"Whatever I do," she said, "it's none of your concern. Now leave."

"One bite," he said. "One bite and I'll leave."

"I'm close enough to the bellpull," she said. "I'll summon my aunt."

"She's right outside the door. Shall I call her?"

"I doubt if Aunt Dina would allow you to break down my door."

"Shall we ask her?"

She remained silent.

"No doubt it's hunger that's making you so quarrelsome," he said.

He removed the napkin from the tray, placing it beside the plate, and picked up a pastie.

"One bite and I'll leave."

"What I eat or don't eat is none of your concern."

"I'm new here," he said. "I've been put in charge of your eating. It seems to be my only task. You wouldn't want me to fail at it, would you?"

A pause stretched between them. Just when he thought she wasn't going to answer, she said, "I don't care if you lose your position or not."

What was he doing here? Why was he catering to a woman's moods? In his practice, he saw many hysterical females, a variety of wealthy women sent to him by his mother. Women who were too intent on the slightest ailment. Was the irritation on her finger a cancer? Was her spring cough a sign of consumption?

Each of these irritating patients was surrounded by luxury, servants, and wealth. If they'd had to endure only a few of the conditions he found in Old Town, they'd spend every day on their knees in thanks to God for their blessings.

Catriona Cameron had turned into one of those.

Besides, what recourse did he have against a woman's stubbornness? Most of his patients agreed to listen to his advice. They didn't require that he carry trays and pretend to be a servant.

He turned and was at the door before realizing he still had the pastie in his hand. He turned back and retraced his steps, continuing on to the corner where she sat. She was draped in a widow's veil, or perhaps more than one. How did she see?

He held out the pastie.

"One bite," he coaxed. "Only one."

"If I do, will you leave and never return?"

"I'll leave," he said. Beyond that, he wouldn't promise.

A gloved hand slowly emerged from beneath the veil.

He put the pastie on her palm and watched as her hand retreated. In the confusion of shadows, he wasn't certain if she took a bite or simply dropped the pastie to the floor.

When he turned, intent on the door, her voice called after him.

"Go away and don't come back."

"When are you going to return?" Elizabeth asked her husband.

Andrew Prender looked up from his notes, facing his wife of a dozen years or more. The time spent being married hadn't concerned him. Until this moment, Elizabeth had been a conformable spouse, a biddable woman.

She'd never asked him about his schedule.

"You're leaving tomorrow. When will you return?"

"Soon enough," he said.

"When is soon enough, Andrew?"

He was surprised at her tone if not the question itself. In all these years, she'd never said a word about his living arrangements. Not once had she demanded that he spend more time with her and the children.

He studied her, wondering at her daring.

Her narrow face was nearly gaunt and her nose long. If she would have listened to his advice, he would have suggested that she not scrape her black hair back in such a severe bun. The style did not flatter her nor give any softness to the severity of her face.

She was not, however, given to any type of fashion advice, or she would have padded her flat bosom or done something to spare him the sight of her angular hips.

Elizabeth had never been beautiful, but the expression she wore now made her ugly. As a rule he preferred to surround himself with attractive people.

She'd borne five children, and for that he was suitably grateful, especially since all of them were hale and hearty and seemed to take after him in appearance more than after their mother.

Now, however, she was being remarkably grasping, and at the worst time.

"Why do you suddenly care, my dear?"

"It's a Scottish bitch, isn't it?" she asked, taking a few steps toward him. "You've been different ever since you came back from Scotland. What happened, did a woman reject your advances?"

He'd been known for his flying visits to his country house periodically to inspect the children, all five of whom were growing at an alarming rate. But he'd erred when returning from Scotland. Instead of nursing his wounds in London, he'd come home. Evidently, his actions gave his wife the impression that she had the right to comment on his behavior.

She had nothing to complain about. He didn't challenge her expenditures on herself, the house, or the children. If she needed more money than he had allocated for her, she had only to go to his solicitor.

"I never minded all the other women," she said. "But this one is different, isn't she?"

What a remarkable change had come over his wife. He regarded her steadily for a moment, wondering what would teach her the fastest and best learned lesson. To cut off her money? Doing so might harm his children, and he did love each and every one. Giving her a few lashes? Surely he could obtain a whip from the stables.

He decided that he didn't have the energy for corporal punishment. Perhaps the truth would be the hardest lesson of all.

"You know my friend Morgan?" he asked her amiably.

"The Earl of Denbleigh?"

He nodded.

"The man who got a divorce?" she asked. "Is that why you bring him up now? To warn me?"

"I can do the same, Elizabeth."

She startled him by smiling. "She doesn't want you, though, does she?"

The next time he returned home, he would have to do something to punish her for that remark.

"Where I'm going or what I'm doing is none of your concern, Elizabeth."

"Go after her, then, and I wish you good luck," she said, leaving the room.

Perhaps it was a good thing this new task of his would take some time. When he returned home, his temper would have cooled.

The Scottish bitch, as his wife had so richly described her, was living in Edinburgh. After he dispensed with that matter, he'd school his wife in the proper way to address him.

Catriona sat with the pastie in her hand, and because she'd taken one bite, she took another. Her stomach clenched. How long had it been since she'd eaten? Long enough that she was suddenly ravenously hungry. Another irritation to lay at the feet of that footman, odious and arrogant as he was.

What had Aunt Dina been thinking to hire someone to coax her to eat?

She moved to the ruined door, pressed it closed, and arranged a chair in front of it for good measure. Only then did she walk to the table and sit. Slowly, after a glance at the door, she removed her veil and ate some of her cold meal.

She'd send Aunt Dina a note complaining about the new footman's behavior, insisting that he be dismissed immediately.

She required absolute privacy, and if Aunt Dina couldn't give that to her . . . Her thoughts trailed off. Who could? Where could she go in all of Scotland, or England, for that matter? Anywhere she went, people would turn and stare at her. Unless she was heavily veiled, she'd send young children screaming for their nurses.

She would not think such things.

Moving to her secretary, she opened it and sat down. Her right hand shook as she withdrew a sheet of stationery. To properly write the note, she would need to light the lamp. If she lit the lamp, she'd see a sitting room with pale gold and white wallpaper, a damask-upholstered settee, a large table and adjoining chairs. A self-appointed prison she'd endured for a month.

Would she be able to remain here for the rest of her life? If not, what other choice was there? She fingered the brown glass bottle in her pocket but did not retrieve it. Instead, with great care, she took the glove off her right hand. The left remained shielded from her sight. With bared fingers she rubbed the smooth mahogany, trailed them to the leather blotter and hesitated before touching the lamp a few inches to her left.

Her heart beat in her ears, and her breath was painfully tight. Darkness was not a friend, but a less abusive enemy than daylight. Candles were an abomination, because they reminded her of laughter and kisses, baring her body in the flickering light, smiling in that certain way at a lover.

The crystal lamp sat accusing her, the chimney hardly darkened by soot.

Slowly, she put the glove back on, then stood, moving to the chair beside the window. The note to her aunt would have to wait until later.

Besides, her left eye was bothering her, tearing too much. That was to be expected, she'd been told by learned men with somber expressions. They had kept their eyes carefully averted from her face as they addressed her.

"Miss Cameron," each of them had said at various times, "we've done the best we can." Another of the physicians had nodded at her enthusiastically, the tip of his beard pointing at her like an arrow. "Indeed, you are a lucky young lady, miss."

When he left the room, closing the door behind him, his words had hung in the air like sodden gauze.

She didn't feel especially lucky.

How strange, that she'd never thought of herself as separate limbs. She'd never been Catriona Cameron, of two hands, two feet, two legs, two arms, a torso and a head. She'd been herself, a combination of all of these.

A woman who'd driven men to lust.

Now, having eaten, reattached her veil and ensured that it was properly in place, she slowly opened the draperies, revealing an Edinburgh evening the color of ashes. Still, the view granted her some freedom. A moment later she opened the window and eased into the chair next to it, folding her hands on her lap.

She'd always loved the sun, but Edinburgh had forbidden her more than a watery glimpse of it since returning from London. She'd always loved the bright days of spring, when she pinned the newest flowers in her hair. She'd always loved laughter and the appreciative looks of young men. More than once, in violation of propriety, she'd grabbed her skirts with both hands and run for the simple joy of it.

The accident had stripped her youth from her and made her a cripple. No man would ever open his arms and sigh in welcome when she embraced him. No one would care that Catriona Cameron had once been a harlot.

She raised the veil high enough so the chilled breeze could sweep up and caress her heated cheeks.

Reaching into her right pocket, she withdrew the bottle, holding it tight between both hands.

Another ritual in her new dark life.

The icy wind made her shiver. She held the bottle, praying for courage to light the lamp, to face herself or take the laudanum.

Chapter 4

"Catriona Cameron?"

His mother wrinkled her nose, an expression that meant she was trying to remember.

While his father had grown increasingly bloated over the years, his jowls reminding Mark of an English bulldog, his mother had become more delicate, her apparent fragility masking a constitution as hearty as any he'd seen. She was never ill, and was impatient with sickness in others, a fact he'd discovered as a boy.

More than once he'd gone to his studies with a fever, and on one memorable occasion, knew he had the measles before the family physician had diagnosed him.

Even as a boy he'd been curious about medicine, an interest that was never encouraged. Instead, he was coached in the duties of being the heir to the heir of an earldom, no matter how far away that earldom seemed.

His grandfather was as hale and hearty as his mother, though only marriage connected them, not blood. The Earl of Caithnern was thin to the point of gauntness, but religiously advocated his routine of eating and exercise.

"If you'd have your patients eat as I do, my boy," he

said on every meeting, "they wouldn't have any problems with corpulence. Have them walk while they're at it."

Since his grandfather was seventy-two, perhaps he had the right prescription for longevity.

The earl abstained from sweets, using William Banting's diet as a plan for eating. He walked each morning and evening around the house he'd recently purchased outside of Edinburgh. He laughed a great deal, and he was rumored to have more than one mistress after his beloved wife of thirty years had died three years ago.

He had never questioned his grandfather as to his mistresses, but he wouldn't have been surprised. The old man enjoyed all the passions of life.

"Oh, I remember now," his mother said, interrupting his thoughts. "The Earl of Denbleigh's sister-in-law. That's the one." She lifted a finger and pointed at him, as if he'd deliberately withheld that information.

"As lovely a girl as you've ever seen. And her gowns? I understand the earl paid for an exquisite wardrobe as well." She frowned. "Wasn't there some scandal about her?"

Gently placing his hand on her elbow, he led her away from where the orchestra was tuning their instruments. He hoped they played substantially better than they practiced.

"There was an accident," he said, hoping to stifle her curiosity about Catriona's past.

"What's that?" She wrinkled her nose again. "I don't remember hearing anything about an accident."

"It was in London, Mother," he said.

"Still, I should have heard."

He was curious why she hadn't. His mother was very involved in Edinburgh society. Perhaps the Earl of Denbleigh still had some power to silence the gossips about

Catriona. Or, perhaps simply disappearing from the social scene had something to do with it. His mother, however, always on the lookout for a suitable match for his two younger brothers, should have known if anyone did.

He'd managed to dissuade her from matchmaking on his account by veiled hints about Anne Ferguson, a perfectly acceptable girl who'd charmed his mother and flattered his father. The former was easily done; the latter was a triumph.

"There you are, Rhona," his father said, marching toward them with a look of determination in his eyes. Everything Kenneth Thorburn, Lord Serridain, did was accompanied by that same look.

His father's face was florid, his eyes narrowed, his mouth pursed in a grim line. If anything, he seemed to have gained more weight in his midsection in the seven weeks since he'd seen him last.

If his father didn't calm himself, he'd collapse of a stroke, a premature death putting an end to his lifelong ambition of becoming the Earl of Caithnern.

"We need to lead the procession," his father said, barely sparing a glance for him.

His mother patted her husband's arm as if to calm him. The gesture, often repeated, never appeared to have any effect.

A pity the man didn't listen to anyone—not his father, the earl; and certainly not his son, a physician. Mark had given up trying to dispense medical advice when the only reaction was a dismissive gesture or a cutting remark.

"Are you ready?"

His mother smiled and nodded, moving toward the ballroom.

"The Duke of Linster," she said, glancing back at him. "He was rumored to be courting her."

Mark's father frowned at him, as if he'd deliberately taken his mother's attention away from the festivities for some selfish purpose. He only nodded, having had years to come to grips with his father's antipathy.

He had a great many faults, according to his father. He didn't value his unique position of being in line to inherit an earldom. He didn't appreciate the family reputation. Nor did he attempt to comport himself with dignity.

As far as his curiosity, another besetting fault, he should leave that trait to other men, those who didn't have a certain position in society to maintain. Instead, he seemed to enjoy getting his hands dirty, or even worse, trafficking with derelicts and the unfortunate unwashed.

Poverty, according to Lord Serridain, was an affliction, one that was contagious.

Once, he asked his father if he wanted him to be more like his brothers, inveterate gamblers and drunkards, neither of whom showed any desire to grow up and make a life for himself.

His father had sent him a cold look and said, "Neither Jack nor Thomas has gone out of their way to humiliate me, Mark. You can do a great deal for the poor of Edinburgh without touching them."

Now he watched as his father and mother greeted their guests, his father inclining his head in a royal nod. His mother was more egalitarian, stopping from time to time to make a comment on a woman's appearance or to share a word.

The feeling of alienation was so familiar, he didn't even note its presence. He didn't belong here, and hadn't, for a long time. Each time he made an appearance at his parents' home, the gulf seemed to have widened between him and his father.

"Are you concerned about one of your patients?"

He turned to find Anne Ferguson at his elbow. His smile came naturally, both in appreciation of her appearance and the compassionate look in her warm brown eyes.

"You were frowning," she said, smiling up at him.

Her brown hair was arranged in a complicated style, with little pink pearls entwined in it. Her dress was pale and pinkish, and he made a mental note to compliment her gown, something he often failed to do. Women liked that sort of thing, he'd been told.

"My mind was on other things," he admitted. "You're looking lovely this evening."

Her cheeks turned rosy as she touched his arm in the same soothing gesture his mother had used earlier. Did women think men were fractious cats?

"You look tired, Mark," she said, her voice low so as not to be overheard. Calling him by his first name was an intimacy brought about from their long acquaintance. It also hinted at their future alliance, but so did her fluttering lashes.

"It was a long day," he conceded.

"You have to rest more. What good would it do for all your patients if you allowed yourself to become ill?"

"I'm not ill, Anne," he said. "Nor am I that tired. It was simply a long day."

She looked surprised at his tone. He didn't need to be managed, or treated as if he were five and had played too long with his tin soldiers.

"What have I done?" she asked, dropping her hand and taking a step back.

"Nothing," he said.

She was sensitive and he'd been curt. He picked up her hand and kissed the tips of her fingers in apology.

Such a gesture in a crowded room was tantamount to a declaration. He realized it the instant she did. While she wore a radiant smile, he felt a sinking sensation in his stomach, as if he'd fallen from a great distance.

She patted his arm. "Dear Mark."

Her next words would be something to the effect that her father approved of him, and how delighted her mother was that they danced so often together. He didn't believe in precognition, only recognized the pattern of similar evenings.

"I've made the final arrangements," she said. "As well as sending out the invitations."

He stared at her. "For what?"

Anne sighed. "I knew you would forget. The party we discussed. You are going to come and greet our guests with me."

He remembered now and nodded.

"I'm sure it will be a wonderful entertainment," he said.

Before she could tell him any more about the party, he stepped away, bowing slightly and mumbling some excuse about having to attend to his grandfather.

A cowardly escape, and as he left, glancing back at her, he realized she knew it as well.

Catriona sat watching until, as the hours passed, the clock's ticking grew monotonous and strangely reassuring. When all was quiet around her it felt as if only she were awake, a creature caught and held by midnight.

Standing, she made her way to the bureau, pulled out a drawer and withdrew the heaviest of the veils she'd had made, replacing the shorter veil she wore during the day.

This one covered her to her waist and was so impenetrable she could stand beneath a gas lamp and not be seen. Viewing the world through gauzelike lace was a difficulty she'd learned to accept.

She'd been told, by a well-meaning fool in London, that she would forever walk with some difficulty. Her left leg had been deeply cut, the damage in the muscle causing her to limp. She was counseled to accept the disability as a price for her survival.

When she hadn't responded to that absurd statement, the physician left the room, no doubt disappointed that she hadn't complimented him on his wisdom.

Had her own father talked to his patients in such a way? She doubted it. Her father had been kind but not given to false good cheer. He'd been compassionate and loving, and only once intensely cruel.

She pushed thoughts of her parents from her mind, went to the door and removed the chair. When she was satisfied that none of the staff was abroad and Aunt Dina had retired, she slowly left the room.

The gaslight at the end of the hall was at the lowest setting. The flame lent the air a yellowish hue as well as a noxious smell. If she asked Aunt Dina to extinguish the lamps, she'd have to give her a reason, which is why she kept silent. These nightly walks were private, and belonged only to her.

She slipped down the back stairs, halting at the landing.

Was the obnoxious footman somewhere around? She didn't want another confrontation with him.

She rarely saw anyone when she left the house. Once or twice she'd narrowly missed Artis locking up for the night, but she knew the maid's schedule now, and adjusted her own to it.

Number 17 Charlotte Square belonged to her brother-in-law, and was, she'd been told, among the most prestigious addresses in Edinburgh. Charlotte Square consisted of four long buildings facing each other like the sides of an ornate crown. In the middle was an expanse of mature trees and landscaped lawn. The building facades were ornamented like palaces, with Corinthian pillars, pedimented centerpieces, and steeply pitched roofs guarded by sphinxes.

Each town house was fronted by a black lacquer door, a wide series of steps, and topped by a fan window that let in the light on sunny days. Iron railings sat on either side of the steps, ending in graceful inverted trumpets. In front of each residence was a gas lamp on a fluted column, its square base mounted to the pavement.

If carriages passed this way at this late hour, they did so in reverent silence. Not for Charlotte Square the rowdiness or the drunkenness of other Edinburgh neighborhoods.

Occasionally, the residents of the square entertained, and when that occurred, she postponed her walk, unwilling to take the chance of being seen. Tonight there were no parties, no well-attended dinners, simply the gas lamps shining over frosted grass and trees that remained still and arthritic in the cold night air.

The square was draped in a blanket of cold and silence. A quiet winter night that echoed only her footsteps. The sky wasn't truly black, but a strange gray, illuminated by the streetlamps. A snow sky, perhaps, with hints of more storms to come.

Two of the gas lamps had been extinguished by the wind. She walked, staying away from the remaining lamps when she could, keeping to the deep shadows around the trees.

At first she limped, but that was to be expected. She'd

done nothing more today than sit in place or walk around her rooms. If the weather held, she would walk around the square four times, as usual. This midnight regimen gave her something to do and perhaps even extended her life by one more night.

When her mother died, she'd wanted to curl up in a ball and simply sleep the day away. Her sister, Jean, pelted her with sayings of a positive nature, until she had no choice but to rouse herself. Her sister always believed in good outcomes, even in the midst of dire circumstances.

Perhaps she ought to adopt Jean's attitude. After all, her sister had acquired an earl for a husband.

What would Jean do in her situation?

Your beauty is not all you have to offer the world, Catriona.

She recalled what Jean had said a month earlier, on her arrival in Edinburgh. She hadn't bothered to comment, because doing so might hurt her sister's feelings.

Ever since she was a child, people had come up to her mother and said such wondrous things. "Oh, isn't she a beautiful little girl!" "What bright color hair she has!" "What an exquisite face!" "She'll melt the lads' hearts, she will."

How could Jean understand? Her sister had always been plain. People had never gasped aloud at her appearance in a doorway. Nor had men danced attendance on her, in hopes of winning a smile or more.

Yet marriage had somehow enhanced Jean's looks. Her smile was always present and her eyes sparkled, no doubt because Jean was with child.

She was going to be an aunt, Catriona thought.

If they trained the child from birth, perhaps he or she might not scream at the sight of her.

Should she be grateful she'd survived? Why, to spend

her days in seclusion? To be nothing more than the odd woman down the street, the one about whom they warned their children: "You'll be good, Robbie, or the monster will get you."

To go from Catriona Cameron, beautiful girl and daring temptress, to someone swathed in black, was a journey everyone seemed to think she should travel without difficulty. But the abyss between who she'd been and the person she was now was too large and empty. It left her flailing alone in the dark, just like now, a solitary figure looking for answers on a winter midnight.

Mark instructed his driver to pull to the curb. The Mac-Tavish home was out of his way, but the minute he saw the movement on the other side of the square, he knew why he'd returned. He sat in the darkness, watching the solitary parade of a shrouded female, all the while calling himself a fool.

Why was he so curious about Catriona? Because he remembered the girl he'd seen years ago? A girl with dancing blue eyes the shade of the Mediterranean Sea. A face as beautiful as any ever painted or sculpted, and hair so brightly blond it seemed to mimic the sun.

He'd known it was her, from her voice. A voice didn't change all that much. Not even hers, overlaid with anger and sorrow.

Curiosity niggled at him and made him wonder how injured she'd been in the accident.

Why had she refused to see another physician? Earlier, he'd acquired the address of the London physician who'd treated her. He would write the man and discover what he could about her condition.

When she walked below the overhanging branches of

a tree, he lost sight of her and waited for her to emerge on the other side. When she did, he felt oddly relieved. Her progress was slow. She evidently had some damage to her left leg, because she favored it when she walked. She also held her arm oddly, but it might be simply the swath of material around her.

Would she have agreed to see him as a physician if he'd told her the truth?

I knew your father. A confession he should have made. *I visited him on more than one occasion. You never paid me any attention, which was just as well.* He might've become besotted, and there had been no time with his studies.

Perhaps that's why he was here, after all, in gratitude to the man who'd spent time with him. From Catriona's father, a popular physician in Inverness, he'd received encouragement and approbation, more than he ever received from his own father. There, that explanation sounded as reasonable as any. He felt as if he owed her father a debt, and treating his daughter would be one way of repaying him beyond the grave.

More likely it was simply his curiosity again and the memory of a shining smile and a quick, mischievous look. The woman was not the girl. But who was the woman?

He realized he wanted to know.

Chapter 5

As Catriona placed her breakfast tray back on the sideboard, she heard the sound of weeping.

"Stupid girl!"

A muffled scream held her immobile, both hands clenching the fabric of her skirt. She turned in that direction, hearing Artis's low voice.

"Shut up now and do as I say."

That command only generated more crying.

She frowned, took a few steps down the corridor, then stopped. Whatever was happening was no business of hers.

Artis suddenly appeared at the end of the corridor. Everyone else skittered out of her way. The maid stared straight at her then, as if able to see through her heavy veil.

"You done?" she asked, stomping toward her.

Artis had a face like a horse, long and narrow with a wide-bridged nose. Between her brows were twin frown lines, even though she was a young woman. Nothing in her flat brown gaze revealed appreciation, gratitude, or that she even liked what she saw.

Catriona reflected that if Artis was acting as housekeeper, Aunt Dina had evidently given her the power to do so. Yet it was entirely possible that Aunt Dina didn't know that Artis was terrorizing the other maids.

And then there was the footman she'd hired. Look at his behavior.

Could someone be too kind? Dina was forever rescuing people, giving them opportunities they didn't deserve. Had the footman been destined to a life of drunkenness? Had he beaten his wife? Was he a thief?

"Are you acting as housekeeper now?" she asked Artis. "Does Aunt Dina know you're punishing the other maids?"

Artis didn't answer, but her mouth turned up in one corner in an expression of contempt.

"I'll be taking the tray," she said, circling her. She grabbed it, and without another word walked down the corridor.

"I'm going to tell her."

Artis stopped. Slowly, the maid turned and walked back to her, the tray in front of her like a weapon.

"Are you now?"

She nodded. Artis didn't have the power to intimidate her. No one did.

"I'd not be doing that if I were you."

"Leave the maids alone," she said.

"Who are you to be telling me my business?"

Whatever happened with the maids was not her concern. The same was true of the footman, as long as he didn't enter her rooms.

Why did she even care? Perhaps because she'd once been a maid herself. However, she'd never been defenseless or subjected to bullying.

The memory of what she'd done once to another girl had her face turn warm.

"You'll leave them alone," she said to Artis. "Else I'll be reporting you to Dina. I'll have you dismissed."

Artis walked so close, the tray bumped her in the arm. Was the maid going to strike her?

"I think you should go back to your room and stay there, miss."

All her life she'd charmed people. Artis was the first person who actively disliked her, and it was such a disconcerting experience that she almost backed down.

Doing so would give the maid the impression she'd won this skirmish.

Perhaps Artis had, because she turned and walked away, leaving her to return to her room, closing off the rest of the world when she shut the door.

Mark stood at the doorway of the servant's room on the third floor of Mrs. MacTavish's house. The room was so small that if he extended his arms on either side, he'd be able to touch two walls. The bed, with its sagging mattress, looked barely long enough to fit the petite Mrs. MacTavish. He was certain that his feet would drape over the end if he ever chanced to sleep here.

The miniature window, set up high in the wall, barely allowed in the morning light. Of course, if he were a real footman, he wouldn't be returning to his chamber for anything but sleep.

The air smelled strongly of starch. No doubt the residue from a previous occupant. Either that or the pillowcase and sheet were starched, which couldn't mean a restful night's sleep.

He was a fool to consider doing this.

The picture of Catriona walking alone at midnight disturbed him more than he wanted to admit. He couldn't rationalize that image with the laughing girl in his memory.

If he was going to play a part in order to get closer to her, he needed the trappings of a servant, and this room was merely a prop. If he didn't have quarters in Mrs. Mac-Tavish's home, the other servants would know something was amiss. Yet even though he wouldn't be sleeping here, he couldn't tolerate this space. He could barely breathe, and hadn't yet stepped inside the room.

"This won't do," he said. "Haven't you anything . . ." His words trailed off. What was he going to ask? Anything larger? Anything more spacious? Anything less stifling?

He turned to Dina MacTavish and said, "Do you have anything closer to your niece?"

"Closer?" she asked.

"You said yourself that your niece was not amenable to strangers. I merely wish to observe her comings and goings."

"There's a room over the carriage house," she said. "My driver doesn't use it, but has lodgings in town. It has a view of Catriona's window. Will that suffice?"

"Is it larger than this room?"

She nodded.

"Then I'm sure it will be fine," he said.

"I'll see to it, Dr. Thorburn."

"Another thing," he said. "You shall have to call me Mark. After all, I'm your servant."

Another nod.

"I'll show up every afternoon," he said. "I can at least monitor Catriona's lunch and perhaps her dinner. In that way I might be able to gain her trust by seeing her each day."

Mrs. MacTavish nodded. "I appreciate this more than I can tell you, Dr. Thorburn. Mark. To give up your practice so."

"I haven't given up my practice, Mrs. MacTavish. I've just abbreviated it by an hour or two each day. Of course, there are times when I'll be gone, but you can always say that I've been sent on an errand."

She nodded once more. "It shouldn't take more than a few days. Don't you think, Doctor? Mark?"

He only smiled at her, knowing from previous experience that it was best not to limit treatment to a certain period of time. Healing happened when it would, and not when doctors wished it.

Was he engaged in healing, though? Or simply assuaging his curiosity?

"I pity her so, Mark. She was such a beautiful girl."

"Pity will not do her any good, Mrs. MacTavish."

"No, you're right, of course." She sighed. "Catriona won't be happy about my interference, Mark."

"We aren't here to please Catriona," he said. "She's been entirely too willful as it is."

That, at least, hadn't changed.

He smiled. He'd declared war on Catriona Cameron, only she didn't yet know it.

"What do you mean he'll oversee my meals?"

Catriona sat in her usual chair beside the window. Dina stood facing her, arms wrapped around her waist, her expression lost in the dark of the room. She would have offered to open the curtains on the window, but it was not yet evening.

The veil shielded her, an article of fashion that had become a shroud. Her heart still beat, her breath still caused her chest to rise and fall. She was without excitement, or fear or any emotion at all except, perhaps, acceptance. A placid and endless acceptance that was now being burned away by anger.

"If I promise I'll eat, will you keep that odious footman from my door?"

To her amazement, Aunt Dina shook her head.

"No, Catriona," she said in a firm tone. "I'm afraid it's gone too far for that."

"You don't trust my word?"

"Oh, my dear, I do. But my concern for your well-being is greater than my concern for your feelings. I'm afraid I will be more reassured when . . ." Her voice trailed off, and then abruptly reasserted itself. ". . . when the footman reports to me."

"Is he going to watch me eat?"

Dina's chortle of laughter had a surprised edge to it. "I wouldn't be the least surprised if that's exactly what he did, my dear."

"He wasn't here this morning," she said.

Dina nodded. "You can eat your breakfast alone, but he'll be here to monitor your lunch and dinner. Beginning tomorrow, Catriona."

"I'll eat what I wish to eat when I wish to eat it, Aunt," she said.

"No longer, Catriona. He is to report to me each day. I shall not be swayed on this."

Aunt Dina's voice trembled just the slightest bit, enough that Catriona suspected the older woman was near tears. She didn't want to witness Dina crying yet again.

"What does it matter?" she asked.

"It matters because there are people who care about you," Aunt Dina said. "Jean writes me every week, wanting to know how you are. I haven't told her the truth, but I've decided to do so now."

Irritated, Catriona sat back in the chair and folded her arms, staring at the other woman. For the first time in a long time, she wished the lamps had been lit. She wanted to see if Dina was bluffing or not.

"My sister is with child, she isn't to be bothered."

"You think your death would not concern her?"

She almost smiled at that comment. "I'm not close to death, Aunt Dina." She was hale and hearty and would, no doubt, live to be an old woman.

"If you don't start eating more, you'll grow increasingly weaker, Catriona."

"Then set your footman on me, Aunt Dina," she said. "But you'll not write Jean and bother her, especially now. Do I have your promise?"

To her surprise, Dina stepped away, walking back to the door. There, the older woman turned and faced her again.

"We shall see," she said. "If I have good reports, perhaps I won't tell your sister the truth."

When the door closed behind Dina, Catriona grabbed the arms of the chair, squeezing so tightly her left hand hurt.

After seeing his last patient of the day, Mark entered his carriage, giving Brody instructions to return home.

The house where he lived had been his grandmother's family home and part of his inheritance. Located near the edge of Old Town, it was too large for only one person, but was ably managed by his housekeeper. Sarah Donnelly also occasionally served as his nurse and welcomed those patients who called on him at home.

He had two distinct groups of patients. The city paid for him to care for thousands of patients in Old Town, ostensibly on a part-time basis. In addition, he had hundreds of society patients.

What made him think he could spare the time for Catriona Cameron?

On arriving home, he said good night to Brody and made his way through the house to his apothecary, where he unpacked his bag. Each night, he performed an inventory before restocking his supply of medicines, most of which he mixed himself.

He'd read once—either a philosopher's teachings or something he picked up from a physician with whom he'd studied—that a man who works at what he enjoys never truly tires. Ever since he was a child, he'd wanted to be a doctor. He'd wanted to know, to understand, to explore the mysteries inherent in the human body. Because he loved medicine, he only rarely felt fatigue, even after twenty-hour days.

Today, however, was proving to be an exception.

He heard a sound, glanced toward the door, but returned his attention to the task at hand.

By her look, Sarah was evidently annoyed at him.

Access to this room was restricted. Besides himself, only Sarah was allowed in, due to the danger of the medications stored here. As it was, his staff only numbered three: Brody, a young stable boy, and Sarah, along with a woman who came in twice a year to help with the heavy cleaning.

He finished corking the bottles and put them in the bottom of his bag. Only then did he turn and face his housekeeper's wrath.

"You're late," Sarah said, both hands fisted on her hips, a frown transforming her genial face. Her white hair gleamed in the lamplight, looking like a halo. She was short and nearly child-size, but filled with such energy that he rarely noticed her stature. Lines crisscrossed her face, mapping the toll of poverty and suffering of her early years.

However, her brown eyes were warm and filled with good humor. Not unexpected, since she was one of the most generous and compassionate people he knew.

Sarah had been one of his patients in Old Town, and when he'd moved here, he offered her the position. Not once had he regretted it. In addition to keeping him in clean clothes and a tidy house, she also advised him of his Old Town patients, having kept in touch with her former neighbors and relatives.

"Did I miss dinner?" he asked, knowing he had.

"You're forever missing dinner. I've learned to put it back." She folded her arms, studying him. "You're tired," she said.

"I am at that."

"You work too hard."

He only shrugged. They'd had this conversation before, many times.

"I might be missing dinner in the next few days," he said. "I'm about to do something foolish." It was better to be honest with Sarah from the beginning.

She only lifted one eyebrow, regarding him steadily.

He told her about Catriona. When he was done and she still didn't speak, he folded his arms, one of his eyebrows mirroring hers.

"You're right," she said in that lyrical accent of hers. "You're being a fool."

She was old enough to be his mother, and he felt as chastised as when he'd been a child.

"You don't approve, then," he said.

"I think the girl needs a good talking to," she said. "Not

you flitting about, pretending to be a servant. Anyone with half a mind could see that you're no servant."

"That's the point, I'm afraid," he said. "She's not looking outward. She's focused too much on herself."

"You think to fix that, do you? It might not be an illness," she added. "It might be character instead."

"You could have a point," he said.

The stiffness of her expression eased. "I'm right more often than I'm wrong."

Since that was a comment she made at least once a day, he only smiled.

"Will they put you to work?" she asked. "Polishing the silver and the like?"

"I suppose they will," he said, realizing he hadn't thought about it. "If I'm to masquerade as a footman, I suppose I will have to act like one. At least for a day or two."

The corner of her mouth quirked up in humor.

"I'd have them teach you to pick up your belongings," she said. "Maybe be neater when you shave."

He sent her a look, but she only smiled at him, suddenly looking pleased about his masquerade just as he was beginning to doubt the wisdom of it.

Chapter 6

When Catriona first returned to Edinburgh, she'd given instructions that all her new gowns were to be dyed black. The only exception was a lovely dress she'd never worn, a pale yellow confection that made her look like a flower or a sunbeam. She'd laughed in delight when Aunt Dina made that comparison, but it was a flattering gown nonetheless, with tiers of fabric, each a different shade of yellow.

She couldn't bear to have it turned black.

Now, she withdrew it from the armoire where it was tucked behind the rest of her clothing and laid it on the end of the bed, looking at it in the dim light of her chamber.

Here, too, the curtains were closed against the afternoon light, but it was a gray winter day, chilly and unappealing, a perfect accompaniment to her mood.

Her hand reached out and she touched the fabric of the dress, feeling the delicate softness. She could see herself in it, dancing and laughing, flirting with a handsome man.

Her partner would compliment her on her dancing, and she'd smile at him, teasing him with a look. His gaze would grow even more intense, darkening with lust.

Men were so easily charmed.

In those enchanted months in London, she'd learned the full extent of a beautiful woman's power. She could smile, flirt, and say nearly anything, forgiven simply because of her appearance.

Those moments were gone.

She'd never go to another ball, never listen with delight to rumors of an appearance of a high-ranking member of court. She'd never make an entrance again, standing at the door, her eyes scanning the crowd as she drew everyone's attention. No more listening to the excited whispers and the speculation as she slowly entered a room.

"That's her, isn't it? The Earl of Denbleigh's sister-in-law."

"I wonder if his wife is as beautiful?"

From now on no one would ever beg for a dance or whisper a shocking suggestion in her ear, only to be treated to her chiding glance. Not one daring suitor would suggest a stroll on the terrace and kiss her hand with fervency while declaring her lips were his true target.

Instead of tears, which might have been a remedy for the pain inside her, she felt a vast emptiness.

She could live without dancing again. She enjoyed the visits from other women, but she could endure never talking to a contemporary. She loved flirting, teasing a man into smiling at her, having him besotted with her. That, too, was something she would miss, but it would not be the source of her greatest grief.

At Ballindair she'd been a foolish girl, seeking affection from anyone who would offer it, believing that fondness from men would end the ache of loss. None of the men she'd bedded had ever eased her heart more than a few hours. They couldn't bring back her parents or give her back her life in Inverness.

Yet she still missed passion.

How did she survive for the rest of her life without the touch of another human being? How did she live without pleasure, kisses, or the stroke of trembling fingers on her bare skin? Those learned men who'd treated her, the ones who hemmed and hawed, never looking at her, wouldn't have had those answers. For that reason, she'd never asked the questions.

The knock on the sitting room door made her glance toward the mantel clock. She knew who it was immediately.

She walked from the bedroom into the sitting room and stood there for a moment, waiting. When the knock came again, she slowly opened the door.

The footman stood there staring at her. Must he be so tall?

"You're an hour late," she said. "My lunch should've been served an hour ago."

She moved to close the door in his face, but he elbowed it open, turned and grabbed the tray on the sideboard, and simply marched into her sitting room.

He neither offered an apology for barging in or for being late. Instead, he went to the table, placed the tray on it, turned and regarded her with folded arms. In a gesture surely meant to be mocking, he pulled a chair up to the table. When she didn't move toward it, he moved the plate, cup, teapot, and silverware from the tray and set it down on the table, arranging it with some dexterity, then put the tray aside.

"You can eat now, though, can't you? Or have you already eaten?"

He knew she hadn't.

She folded her arms beneath the veil.

"I'm not hungry."

Instead of bowing, saying something conciliatory, or simply removing himself from the room, he did something shocking. She should have expected it, truly, especially in light of Aunt Dina's words the day before. The man took a seat on the opposite side of the table, leaned back in his chair and drummed his fingertips on the tabletop.

"I'm waiting," the boor said.

"You can wait until there are icicles in August," she said, as pleasantly as possible. "Or until you can milk a bull. Or until St. Agnes returns. Choose one. Choose them all."

"Here, people were telling me you were unreasonable."

"Who said that?"

He shrugged. "I'm not at liberty to say. I will, however, trade the information for one bite of salmon, I think."

Was she supposed to play some game with him? Who did he think he was?

"I have no intention of eating on command," she said. Her throat tightened. Her voice would not tremble. She wouldn't give the man the satisfaction of knowing how upset she was.

"Pity," he said. "I'm not leaving until you eat something."

"Leave the food here. I'll eat when I'm hungry."

His chuckle startled her.

"I'm sure that your manner has been off-putting to some people, but I'm not impressed. I'm not leaving until you've eaten something. If we must spend the night together, we must. Do you snore?"

She walked to the table. Could he see that she limped? Did he watch her with contempt?

"I'm certain you weren't hired to be insulting."

He didn't respond to that, and his lack of comment

bothered her more than anything he might have said. He sat back, arms folded, seemingly at home in the shadows.

Odious man, to have invaded her sitting room. Even after he left, the room would smell like him. Something pleasant, which was just as irritating as if he had a sour odor. Was he smiling at her?

"All you have to do to rid yourself of me is eat something," he said, his voice even, his tone moderate.

"I don't like being commanded."

"Pity. Each of us has someone we must report to."

"I'll have you dismissed," she said, grateful to realize that her voice had lost its quaver.

"You would have to leave the room to do that," he said. "I'm the only one allowed to serve you, Princess."

"Princess?"

"What would you prefer I call you? Empress? That might work as well."

She couldn't believe his effrontery. No one had ever treated her with such disdain.

"If you must address me at all, you should call me Miss Cameron."

"I don't think so."

"Why not?" she asked, unwillingly curious.

"Because that would be respectful," he said. "You haven't earned my respect."

She moved toward the bellpull.

"Everyone has orders to ignore your summons, Princess. As I said, I'm the only one allowed to serve you."

She hated him in that moment. She hated Aunt Dina as well. Add to that the coachman, the horses, the accident, and every physician who had so ineffectually treated her. What good was saving her life when she must live the rest of it in Hell?

She was so filled with hatred it sickened her.

Turning, she reached the table, grabbed the tray, and threw it at him. He'd lifted one hand, as if he knew what she was about to do, easily batting the silver tray away. It fell with a solid thunk to the carpeted floor.

"How mature you are. You're three, are you not? Is it not having a nap that's made you querulous?"

"Get out. Get out now."

"No," he said calmly. "Eat something."

She went to the door and held it open, only too conscious of the bright afternoon light streaming into the corridor.

"Will you leave, please," she said, gripping the frame of the door tightly with one hand.

"No," he said, still with the same annoying calm. "I'll leave after you've had five bites."

"I thought it was one," she said.

"That was for information. I've decided not to share anything with you. But the price for my departure will be five bites."

She slammed the door and marched back to the table.

"I haven't been trying to deliberately starve myself, you idiot," she said. "I haven't been hungry."

"Is that what you told everyone else?" he asked. "I'm not as gullible."

He surprised her into silence.

"Of course you're sad about your changed circumstances," he said.

"What do you know about me, to be able to judge my circumstances one way or another?"

She pulled out the chair, only too conscious that he didn't stand and offer to do it for her. He was a rude and annoying boor. She sat and glared at him.

"From what I hear," he said, "you were a beautiful woman. One who led your suitors on a merry chase. Now, all of a sudden, you've retreated to your suite of rooms. One can only surmise that you're no longer beautiful. Either that, or you've found God, but since you're a mean and surly hermit, I doubt that's the answer. "

She didn't know what she wanted to do first, call for Aunt Dina or hit him over the head with the teapot.

"I've heard about the carriage accident. Would you like to tell me about it?"

"Five bites, you said?"

If that was the only way to get rid of him, she'd do it. She would pretend some interest in the salmon before her and eat.

Didn't he realize how difficult eating was with her veil? If he expected her to remove it, he was doomed to disappointment.

"You are appallingly bad at dealing with people," she said. "I can't imagine how you ever got hired."

"I'm rather good with people, actually. Women, especially."

In the half-light coming in from around the curtain, she could see him well enough. He was handsome. No doubt a woman only saw his appearance and not his abysmal character.

"Very foolish women, I daresay."

He propped one elbow on the table, and studied her. "I find myself partial to younger women," he said.

She raised her veil enough to slip the fork beneath it. The salmon was good, and the sauce tasted like Hollandaise, but without a light, she couldn't be sure.

"Why? The better to mold them to your liking?"

"No, because they haven't been molded by others. They're fresh and innocent, and have an eagerness for the world."

She took another bite, wishing she could block the

sound of his words. She didn't want to think of her own life, a scant three years earlier, when she might have been considered as fresh and innocent as he'd described.

"What you're speaking of is naiveté," she said. "We're all naive at one time or another. I daresay even you."

His chuckle was warm, but he made no further comment.

She concentrated on the second bite, then the third. She was more than halfway through. In a moment she could banish him from the room and wouldn't have to see him until the next meal.

"I promise I'll eat from now on," she said, hoping to forestall that moment. "You don't need to watch me."

He shrugged, a gesture she was beginning to suspect meant nothing.

"You're going to be here anyway, aren't you?" she asked.

"Yes," he said in that same annoying manner. "I've been hired to ensure that you eat. That means three meals a day, and perhaps a dessert from time to time."

"Are you so desperate for a position that you would hire yourself out to be a nanny to me?"

"Let's just say you pose an interesting challenge."

"You don't speak like a footman."

"I was well educated for a footman," he said. "It's an interesting story. Would you care to hear it?"

"No," she said.

"For some reason, I knew that would be your answer. If you ever do want to hear it, let me know. I'd be more than happy to regale you with my personal history."

"Go away," she said, putting the fork down on the edge of the plate.

"Two more bites and I shall."

He had been counting.

She took one more bite of the potatoes. There, four bites. One more and he could leave.

A moment later she was done.

"Six bites. I congratulate you, Princess. You did well. Five plus one."

"I know how to count," she said.

"Do you?"

Abruptly, the footman stood, retrieved the tray from the carpet and placed the dishes on it. Before he left, however, he poured her a cup of tea.

"Sugar?"

She shook her head. "What is your name?"

"Do servants even have names? Why are you suddenly curious, Princess?"

"If you won't tell me, I shall call you Footman," she said.

"It doesn't matter, does it? I might call you Princess, for example. Although it's not your name, I'll wager it's close to your temperament."

"Then I shall call you Mr. Boor, or Mr. Irritating, or something equally rude."

"Whatever you wish, Princess."

She didn't like him.

"How long must you monitor my meals?"

"Until your aunt is no longer concerned about your health. How long is up to you, I think, Princess."

"Are you going to call me that forever?"

"Yes," he said, picking up the tray. "I think I am."

With nothing more than that, he walked out of the room and closed the door.

Andrew Prender looked over the documents his solicitor proffered for him to sign. He didn't give a flying farthing about the property in Charlotte Square or how much it cost. His fortune was such that he was normally spared the knowledge of those details or any concern about them.

"You have kept this confidential, I hope," he said, signing all the necessary pages with a flourish.

"Of course, Mr. Prender. As per your instructions."

If his solicitor was curious about why he'd bought a property in Edinburgh, especially one in such an expensive neighborhood, he didn't ask. The man's tact was one of the reasons why he'd employed him for years. Another was that the man had the ability to deal with his wife, thereby sparing him the necessity of doing so too often.

He watched as the solicitor took himself off, closing the library door behind him.

This London house belonged to his father. A series of mistresses had been housed here, each one lovelier—and younger—than the one before. By the time the old man died, tucked away in his bed, he'd had a dozen or so illegitimate children, none of whom, thankfully, were mentioned in the will.

The library in which he sat was for show, books purchased by the meter, their spines all shiny and barely creased. It was a gentleman's library, and that's all his father had cared about. The elder Prender believed that the conventions should be observed.

They were only one generation removed from tradesmen, after all. If he bothered to do anything in regard to the family soap factories, he would be engaging in trade as well. They didn't, blessedly, require his assistance, and so he did what his father would have been pleased for him to do—spend his money and consort with the titled and the rich.

Everything about his life had been nearly bloody enchanted. Granted, he wanted to be taller than he was, but nothing could cure that. He enjoyed his life. He'd lived a hedonistic lifestyle, and it pleased him, for the most part. He devoted himself to those pursuits that interested him for the moment. Each year, he chose one separate task or trait to learn.

He'd taken up painting just before meeting Catriona Cameron.

He'd loved the bitch.

For the first time in his life he'd fallen in love, enough to put his world at her feet. He might have even gone so far as his friend and divorced his wife. He would have abandoned his children for her. He would have given her his money. He would have gladly begun another family as long as she was at his side. He would have lived with her day in and day out, hours upon hours, and found himself complete.

Instead, she'd smiled prettily at him and walked away. She'd tossed her radiant hair and without a backward glance left him on a road in Scotland.

Tomorrow, he would travel to Edinburgh and temporarily take up residence in Charlotte Square. Once there, he would accomplish what he hadn't been able to finish in London.

He would kill the woman he loved, the only woman who'd ever walked away from him.

Chapter 7

"I've received a letter," the Countess of Denbleigh said when her husband joined her in the library.

Jean had appropriated his desk in the last few weeks, since it was one of the few places where she was comfortable. He'd arranged a footstool for her use and she could sit at the massive desk and pen her book, the story of William Seath, Steward of Ballindair, and his contributions to the castle. When that was finished, she'd vowed to write a definitive work about the myriad ghosts of Ballindair.

Morgan MacCraig, the Earl of Denbleigh, only smiled when she said such things, kissed her, and thereby changed the subject for a long time.

Today, however, he was carrying a cup, which he placed in front of her. "A restorative," he said. "Your aunt swears by it."

"Speaking of aunts," she said, waving the letter in front of him, "I've received a letter from yours."

He sat beside the desk and pointed to the cup. She looked at the ceiling, then drank half of the bouillon, only making a face once.

"I haven't the slightest idea why I have to drink beef broth every day."

"Our son will thank you," he said, staring fixedly at her stomach.

She was round. Rotund would perhaps be a better word. She could no longer see her feet when she stood.

"I need a hammock," she said. "Or a sling. Something to hold my stomach up when I walk. I'm getting entirely too large." She stared down at herself and made another grimace. "I could loop it around my neck, then place it below my belly."

"You look beautiful," he said, smiling.

She appreciated his kindness, but she didn't feel beautiful. She felt large and ungainly.

"It might well be a daughter," she said.

"Then we shall simply have to keep trying for an heir," he said. "Now, tell me what Aunt Dina wrote. Is Catriona causing problems?"

She frowned at him. "No, and she hasn't ever since the accident. Well, not that kind of problem, at least."

Once upon a time her sister obeyed whichever rules of society she wanted, without regard to what people might think. She'd had affairs, even as an unmarried woman, the last one with Andrew Prender, a friend of Morgan's. It hadn't ended well. Morgan had given Catriona a choice to either go with Andrew to London as his mistress or be schooled by Aunt Dina in Edinburgh before taking her place in society.

In one of the most intelligent decisions her sister had ever made, she chose Edinburgh. But then disaster struck, and Catriona's life had been changed.

"Drink the rest," he said, pointing to the cup again.

She finished the rest of the cup and made another face, just for good measure.

"Catriona isn't eating, and she isn't seeing anyone, and she's become a hermit in her quarters."

"She could come home to Ballindair," he said.

She looked over at him, loving him for that comment if for nothing else. Catriona had been a trial to both of them. Yet here Morgan was, offering her a home. He'd welcome her back to Ballindair without another thought, if only for her sake.

"She won't come," she said. "I tried to convince her to come to Ballindair when I was in Edinburgh."

"Is the situation worse than it was?"

She read from his aunt's letter.

I have solicited the help of a young physician with whom I am familiar. He and I have worked together in Old Town. I have expressed my concerns to him, and he agrees that Catriona should be examined. However, she has refused to do so. We are taking other steps to ensure that her health is maintained.

"I wonder what other steps they're taking," Jean said, looking over the top of the letter at her husband.

Morgan shook his head. "My aunt is an extraordinarily resourceful woman. Whatever she deems necessary, she'll do."

"I do wish I could go to Edinburgh and see Catriona."

Before she could clarify her comment, Morgan got the most mulish look on his face. She held up her hand in an effort to forestall his lecture, but it didn't do any good.

"I refuse to hear of you even contemplating a journey to Edinburgh."

"I wasn't, Morgan. I love my sister, truly I do. But my child comes first. At least right now," she said, patting her stomach reassuringly.

The mulish look vanished, replaced by a half smile.

"Good, as long as you remember that. Catriona has a way of pulling you into her plans."

"Perhaps once," Jean said. "But no more. She is part of my family, yes. But so are you, and so is our child. You have no need to worry that I might put her above you."

"I wasn't jealous," he said.

"I know, dear," she said, hiding her smile.

Catriona walked to the door and checked the lock to ensure it was working correctly. This afternoon she'd been forced to hide in her bedroom while a workman repaired the door.

She wouldn't put it past the footman to break in again if she didn't open it at his knock. He wasn't here now, however. It was dinnertime, and he was late again.

What was she supposed to do, wait around for him? He was the servant, she wasn't.

She went into the bedroom, to the vanity she rarely used, and picked up the hand mirror. Returning to the sitting room, she lit the lamp on the desk. There, enough light to see the truth.

Returning to the table, she pulled out a chair, placed the hand mirror facedown on the table, and sat, composing herself.

In the first weeks after the accident, she'd examined herself both in the morning and at night, telling herself that the damage to her face would fade. Gradually, she'd become the beautiful girl who'd traveled to London with such high hopes and dreams.

She'd been like Jean, believing that good things would always happen. Gradually, she realized that she'd been right all along—people who only looked at the good side of life often got a rude shock when things didn't turn out.

As she'd told her sister once, hope was just another name for wishing. Wishing never made anything better.

No, the best way to handle a situation was to stare it in the face.

A year ago she'd looked at herself realistically. She hadn't anything other than her appearance. She wasn't exceptionally intelligent, not like Jean. She wasn't witty. Instead of inciting men to laughter, she had the ability to make them think of lust.

She'd come to Edinburgh, studied under Dina, learned what she needed to know, and transformed herself from a hoyden and someone who occasionally shocked others to a respectable Scottish sister-in-law of an earl. She'd learned the rules: how to address anyone, how to converse in polite and titled society, and how to comport herself so that not one person would be shocked at her behavior. She'd become proper and restrained, moral and demure.

The Duke of Linster had paid court to her. She'd been whispered about, complimented, and courted until a night in July when the world changed.

After the first weeks, she'd dispensed with looking at herself, knowing that nothing would change. Nothing miraculous had happened. Instead, the scars seemed to sink deeper into her skin, rivers of red and bluish lines on the land of her face.

A strange thing had happened in the intervening months. She'd forgotten exactly what she looked like.

Would the scarring be the same? Would she still be as monstrous as before? Or would something have changed?

Slowly, she slid her fingers over the hem of the veil, then raised it. Without the concealing lace, the air felt cool on her face.

For a moment she kept her eyes closed. Stretching out her hand, she felt for the mirror, grabbed the handle and pulled it close. Pressing it against her bodice, she took several deep breaths, gathering up her courage from where it had scattered. Months had passed since she'd seen herself.

The knock on the door saved her.

With trembling fingers she placed the mirror back on the table and restored her veil.

"Who is it?" she asked, hearing the quaver in her voice and hating it. Who was she to be so afraid—not of the person on the other side of the door, but the reflection in the mirror?

An image she blessedly didn't have to see at the moment.

"The footman," he said.

She stood and extinguished the lamp before making her way to the door. She unlocked it and moved into the shadows.

He entered the room, carrying her dinner tray. Something smelled wonderful—soup with chicken and onions?—making her realize she was hungry.

"You're late again."

"Yes."

That was it? A simple yes? He wasn't going to explain?

"Where were you?"

"I had other duties to perform," he said.

"I thought your duty was to monitor my meals."

He didn't answer, merely put the tray on the table. He picked up the mirror, turning to look at her. There was just enough light in the room to see his face. His handsome appearance made her feel even uglier.

"Inspecting yourself, Princess?"

She didn't answer him, merely jerked the chair some distance away from him, sat, and pulled the tray over to her. The sooner she ate, the sooner he'd be gone.

"Are you hungry?" he asked.

She studiously ignored him, concentrating on her meal. He sat on the other side of the table, just as she expected.

"Are you a drunkard?" she asked, pouring herself a cup of tea.

"Why would you ask that?"

"Is that why you have difficulty being on time?"

He smiled, and she looked away, uncomfortable with his amusement. Or perhaps it was simply that the smile made him even more attractive.

She hated him for the power he had over her, granted him by a woman for whom she held some affection. She hated him because, once, even a man as handsome as he would have vied for her attention. She hated him more than any human being she'd ever known. She hated him more than any circumstance she'd ever endured, including her father's death and the carriage accident that nearly took her life. She hated him because he'd come into the place she'd made her sanctuary and changed it.

He reminded her of what she'd never have again, what would now always remain just outside her grasp. If she'd still been a maid, she would have flirted with him. In London, she would have ignored him for fear someone would think her interest shocking.

Now, she was only a chore, a duty, and perhaps an object of derision.

"Do you talk about me to the servants?" she asked. "Do you laugh about me?"

His smile abruptly disappeared.

"Why would I do that?"

"No comments about the woman in black? The hermit in her room? The monstrosity?"

He pulled the mirror closer to him, held it up and

stared into it. "Is that what the mirror tells you? That you're a monstrosity?"

"What it tells me is that I don't belong anywhere," she said, then wished the truth back the moment she spoke it.

"You're only seeing a part of you."

How easy that was to say, especially looking as he did.

"You cannot see a person's character," she said. "Or view a soul. All we have is a person's appearance by which to judge him."

"Foolish, if that's all you use. I've known my share of ugly saints, and beautiful sinners."

That's what she'd been, once. A beautiful sinner, a woman who'd taken a lover—three, to be exact—in violation of her upbringing, society's rules, and, no doubt, common sense. She hadn't found herself with child, but she had discovered that she enjoyed lovemaking.

If she'd waited, if she'd been as pure and virtuous as she should have been, she would never have known that.

What man would want her, damaged and scarred as she was now?

Did he have a great many lovers? Aunt Dina only employed three maids, and all of them were plain. Is that why he was late? Had he seduced one of them?

She concentrated on her meal, pushing away any thoughts of the footman, annoying as he was.

A moment later she put her fork down, blotted her lips with her napkin, then stood, walking to the door. She held it open for him, and without a word spoken, he gathered up the tray and followed her.

"How are you feeling?" he asked.

"Is that part of your new duties? Not only to monitor my meals but to engage in conversation? I would much rather we talked about the weather than my health."

"Do you always limp?"

When he didn't leave, she brushed the air with her hand, as if to banish him. When he still didn't move, she glared up at him, then realized he couldn't see her expression.

"Yes, I always limp," she said, annoyed that she had to divulge that bit of personal information.

Now would he leave?

"Have you tried any liniment?"

"Liniment? As in what you use for horses?"

"I found it's efficacious in certain circumstances," he said.

"What, you learned that from a groom friend of yours?"

"My quarters are over the carriage house. I can't help but learn something there."

That was a surprise.

"The servants' quarters aren't good enough for you?"

"Perhaps Mrs. MacTavish is worried about my proximity to the women servants," he said.

There was that damnable smile again.

She grabbed his arm, conscious of two things: the material of the shirt seemed finer than most footmen would wear, and his muscles flexed at her touch.

After guiding him out the door, she closed it, turning the lock, and hoping he wouldn't try to test either the repairs of the door or her resolve.

Now all she had to do was worry about tomorrow.

Chapter 8

Because he called on patients in Old Town every day, Mark didn't need to give his driver instructions. Brody pulled the carriage to the side of Lothian Road as he did each morning. Certain areas of Old Town could only be traveled on foot.

As he had all week, Brody frowned down at him when he left the vehicle.

His driver was tall and angular, reminding him of a heron. He also walked with his long nose jutting forward as if searching for food.

Sarah's mission on earth was to fatten Brody up, but it didn't seem to be working. No matter how much the man ate, it didn't add anything to his frame. Mark had several patients like that, all of them healthy. His corpulent patients had most of the medical problems.

"Sir, do you think it's safe?" Brody asked.

Last week a man had been garroted not far from there in another robbery. His attackers succeeded in strangling him, but not to death, since the man was still recovering from his injuries. Gangs of youths were also known to shoot randomly throughout Old Town. Even though they were occasionally arrested, others took their place.

"When has Old Town ever been safe?" Mark asked.

Crime had been on the rise lately. A certain element in Old Town preyed not only on those who strayed too close to their borders, but among themselves. The poor were often victims of the poor.

He tried to remain as unobtrusive as possible when walking into certain areas to treat his patients. He had more than one set of clothes earmarked to wear in Old Town. Nothing fine that would immediately label him a mark.

Handing his gold watch to Brody for safekeeping, he took what medicines he would distribute from his case and shoved them into the inside pockets of his coat, along with what diagnostic tools he'd need. He never carried his bag into Old Town. Doing so was an invitation to be robbed.

The majority of Edinburgh society believed that the inhabitants of the slums of Old Town were poor because they wished to be. It was said that they were shiftless, addicted to drink, or simply lazy. He knew, however, from witnessing the conditions and knowing the people, that circumstances, more than inclination, kept people here.

The family he was visiting this morning was one of those cases. Edeen MacDonald had been abandoned by her husband a year ago. Without family or prospects, she'd been forced into prostitution to support her children, at least until Mrs. MacTavish interceded. Dina had obtained a piecework job for her, where she could make lace during the day and be able to attend her daughter Christel when the girl's medical condition warranted it.

Still, she lived in abysmal conditions that would probably result in the death of one of her children and grant a dreary future to the other.

He bid Brody farewell, gauging the time he'd need to

visit Edeen. If he didn't return in a timely manner, Brody would go in search of him.

He began walking, keeping his focus on his destination and not the poor souls lying slumped against the brick walls. Gaunt faces and soulless eyes were the uniform of Old Town. The smell of cooked cabbage overlaid by the stench of urine made his eyes water, but he kept on, down into the deepest part of St. Agnes' Close.

Here, death waited, lurking over a slumped body nearly devoid of life. A woman cringed in the corner clutching a threadbare shawl, her face grimy and slack.

For centuries, there had been nowhere to build but up. Consequently, Old Town was constructed of tall buildings sloping together at the top.

A man's worth and wealth were determined by where he lived. The poorest always lived on the ground floor, where broken sewers made life miserable. Those with some funds had their homes on the top floor, where traces of sunlight entered the windows. For a while they could forget where they lived.

The gaslights were still lit, and in some places they were never extinguished because sunlight never reached these narrow streets. Black was the predominant color, with varying shades of gray the only accent. The cobblestones glistened wetly, the smells ripening, causing his stomach to clench. Even being a physician didn't prepare him for some experiences. He carefully avoided the worst of the puddles as he followed the street downward.

So many people were living on top of each other that he could witness all of man's depravity, and only some of his virtues, within one block.

If he lived here, would he spend all his money on whiskey or gin? Possibly. He'd like to think that he'd survive, and leave Old Town as quickly as he could, but these people had probably once felt the same optimism.

The passage grew increasingly constricted, the cobblestones slick.

When the bridge between Old Town and New Town was built, huge vaults had been constructed below the span. Originally planned as warehouse space for the shops located on the road above, the vaults had been transformed into living space by the desperate and the homeless.

Edeen had claimed one of the vaults as her home. Here, the stench of effluence wasn't as strong, but the cold, damp stone created an unhealthy place to live all the same.

Three vaults down a fire was lit. While it did little to chase away the cold, it pushed smoke into the space, which wasn't good for Christel's cough.

As he walked deeper into the gloom, he could feel the rumble of the traffic in the stone beneath his feet. Not far away he heard high-pitched laughter and a drunk whining about losing his bottle.

In the flickering shadows, he could see James sitting on the end of his sister's cot. Edeen was nowhere to be seen.

Some children had been cowed by Old Town with its army of prostitutes, thieves, and drunkards, growing wide-eyed and silent. James, however, hadn't yet succumbed to hopelessness. He was curious and inventive, asked questions incessantly, and was a handful for Edeen, who was already worn down with Christel's illness.

Both children were too old for their years, their father's abandonment affecting them more than their living conditions.

When James saw him, he grinned, turned to Christel and shook her leg. The little girl roused with a moan and a cough.

"Where's your mother?" he asked, taking the ebony stethoscope from his pocket and kneeling to examine the little girl.

"She said she'd be back soon and I was to see to Christel."

He bent and listened to her chest. Like her brother, she was small for her age. At six years old, she was too pale and thin, but he marveled at the strength of her frail body. Long after she should have succumbed to the asthma that made her life miserable, she rallied. A lesson to him that, while he might think he had some power over illness, the human will was sometimes stronger than disease.

Catriona was going to have to eat her noon meal without supervision. No doubt he would hear about his dereliction of duty later, but he wasn't going to leave the children alone.

For the next hour he played a game in the dust with James until the boy, with the uncanny instinct of children, suddenly jumped off the end of the cot and headed for the shadows.

"Mam, the doctor is here!" he said, his voice echoing through the vault.

Edeen came into view, clutching her shawl around her shoulders. She looked tired. No, beaten down was a more apt description. He stood, giving up the only other place to sit, a small trunk that held their meager possessions.

Even under these conditions, Edeen was a beautiful woman. Tall, willowy, with a striking grace, she had bright red hair and a complexion that rivaled any London beauty. Her eyes were a soft green, and the expression in them inspired his compassion more often than not.

He waited until she greeted James, went to check on Christel, then moved to his side.

"What happened to the lace making?" he asked.

"They've no need for more work at the moment," she said, her voice soft, because of James's eternal curiosity. "We can't wait on their needs to eat."

"So you sell yourself," he said, biting back his anger.

Her smile surprised him.

"I've something of value, at least."

What she didn't realize was that she could easily become diseased like any number of women he treated. What good would she be to her children if she was struggling for life herself?

They'd already had that discussion too many times to count.

He pulled out a few bank notes and reached for her hand. She stepped back, shaking her head.

"Don't be proud, Edeen," he said, forcing the bills into her palm. "Take it for Christel and James."

"I don't need your charity," she said, her voice husky.

"Get the children some food, and some warmer blankets."

He would have taken them to his own home, but he knew Edeen wouldn't allow it.

Edeen was as stubborn as the princess. She wouldn't apply for poor relief, and she wouldn't accept money from the churches that regularly ministered here. The only assistance she'd taken was when Mrs. MacTavish had recommended her for a job. Even here, in Hell's foyer, she'd created lovely pieces of lace for which she earned some pennies, yet not enough to afford decent lodgings or as much food as they needed.

James and Christel weren't the only children desperately in need of help. He did what he could, but it was never, and would never, be enough. Today, however, he wasn't in the mood to tolerate Edeen's pride.

"Please," he said, when she looked as if she wanted to throw the money to the ground. "For them."

She frowned, glanced at her children, and finally nodded.

A few minutes later he left, dissatisfied with her future and with Christel's health. He called on one more patient, Robert MacNair, an elderly man who grumbled incessantly and reminded him of his grandfather.

He had to keep all the appointments he'd scheduled before agreeing to attend to the princess. The rest of his patients were all wealthy matrons, most of whom had fewer true ailments than querulous complaints. They were lonely, bored, or wanted to flirt with him.

Catriona was most definitely not in that category. She didn't want to flirt with him. Instead, she wanted nothing to do with him. In addition, he'd seen her limp and observed that she had some difficulty with her left arm. He wondered at the damage done to her face.

To a beautiful woman, any mark would be a disaster. What was the meaning of ugly to a princess?

In the month since she'd returned from London, Catriona had grown accustomed to her prison of rooms. After all, the suite of sitting room, bedchamber, and bathing room was substantially larger than the childhood room she'd shared with Jean, the maid's quarters at Ballindair, or even the suite she'd occupied once Jean married her earl.

At first, when her leg was still healing, she could barely walk. She'd exercised by trodding a path from one side of the bed, in front of the armoire and vanity, around the end of the bed to the door, out to the sitting room, circling the large table in the middle and then the chair beside the window, the settee in front of the fireplace, and back to the bedroom.

In this way, she'd strengthened her leg, even though

those fools in London had said she might not regain the use of it. They were as pessimistic about her left arm, and she'd gradually made it stronger through lifting heavier and heavier objects.

Even after she'd walked through her rooms for an hour, she still felt restless.

Today was an anniversary, of sorts, one she didn't truly wish to recall.

On this day, three years ago, her father was hanged. Her papa, who would sit by her bed when she had night-mares, and told her stories about his patients, making them sound like animals, like Dora Duck with her sore throat, and Maisy Mouse, who had an infection in her left ear.

Papa, who always thought she was the sweetest girl, who'd showered her with smiles and made her believe the world was a lovely place, had chosen to do what he did.

She would not cry.

Her mother had been dying, and her father, a physician, chose to end her life rather than see her suffer. He had gone to his death, if not gladly, then at least with an unburdened heart.

She and Jean had paid the heaviest price for his actions.

Shunned by their neighbors, called the Murderer's Girls, they nearly starved in the months following his death.

Her sister had been resolutely optimistic, believing in better days. Better days? Jean's solution was for them to become maids at Ballindair, where their Aunt Mary was housekeeper. They'd scrubbed and waxed and buffed and dusted until their hands were black and their backs ached.

From the beginning, she'd plotted to be something more than just a maid.

Through it all, Jean had been determinedly cheerful.

Perhaps she should emulate her sister. After all, Jean had gone on to become the Countess of Denbleigh, while she was a scarred hermit in a lush Edinburgh prison.

She told herself not to look back. Nothing in her past would make her hopeful. She would simply get through this day and all the rest.

Perhaps she simply needed an occupation, an interest other than her hermitage. She had no skill at needlework. She didn't have a pianoforte in her sitting room. After the interlude with Andrew Prender, she didn't want to have anything to do with painting or drawing. Not that she wouldn't have as much talent as he'd pretended to have, but even looking at a painting brought Andrew to mind.

Sometimes she wished she had the courage to venture outdoors during the day.

Her midnight walks would have to suffice.

Catriona picked up one of the books Jean had sent her. A few chapters in, she rolled her eyes at the foolish predicament of the heroine. At least the woman had a face. At least she wouldn't terrorize children. At least she didn't have to be swathed in veils to shield others from a sight that would make them gasp in horror.

But even bitterness became tiring after a while.

In this new and solitary world, she missed people the most. She'd always been surrounded by people. Women had sought her out for help with their appearance. In Inverness, she'd been popular. At Ballindair, she'd genuinely enjoyed the company of the other maids. She'd laughed with them, and gossiped, and told tales that weren't kind. She'd also been silly, unwise, and even mean at times.

Catriona Cameron, for all your sins, I banish you from the world.

Was this isolation punishment for everything she'd done wrong?

She sat at the window as afternoon turned into gloaming. Did anyone ever see her sitting here? Did they remark on her silence and her motionless pose?

She angled her chair, the better to see the carriage house. What was the footman doing? Why hadn't he appeared at lunch?

Her scars were beginning to itch, as if demanding her attention. She raised the hem of her veil, allowing air to touch her face.

When it was time for the footman to appear at dinner, he was again absent. Annoyed, she opened the door to find that while the footman hadn't appeared, her dinner tray had.

Her lunch tray had arrived in the same fashion.

Had she gotten her wish? Had he been dismissed?

She closed the door without retrieving the tray from the sideboard. What game was he playing? Whatever it was, she refused to participate. When she realized, an hour later, that she was hungry—all the pacing she'd done had worked up an appetite—she peered around the door again to find that the tray was gone. She closed the door harder than necessary, turned and leaned against it, folding her arms and frowning toward the window.

The footman had probably taken the tray, just as she did not doubt that he was at the root of this game. Did he intend to starve her to prove a point? She had to address the issue with Aunt Dina, certain that her aunt didn't know what her newly employed footman was doing.

Putting on the heavy veil she used for her walks, she left the suite, intent on Aunt Dina's room. But Dina wasn't there. Nor was she in the parlor or the upstairs study. For twenty minutes she roamed through the house, unable to find a single maid or her aunt. Only when she descended to the kitchen did she discover all three of the maids sitting at the kitchen table laughing, drinking tea.

Each of Aunt Dina's servants had been hired from Old Town. It wasn't an act of charity, Dina had explained, as much as a training program. What they learned in her household would equip them to take other jobs elsewhere.

When she questioned the three of them as to Dina's whereabouts, Artis responded with a barely repressed sneer.

"She's out," she said.

Her Aunt Mary, the housekeeper at Ballindair, had an expression for people like Artis: *Aye reddin the fire.* She was always stirring up trouble.

Isobel reminded her of a question mark. Skinny, she seemed to fold over herself and rarely spoke.

Elspeth was Isobel's opposite in every way. Her figure was firm and full, her nose upturned at the end as if to call attention away from her tiny rosebud mouth. Her soft blue eyes were always lively, as though she had just heard a jest and repeated it to herself so as to not forget it.

"Where has she gone?" she asked the three.

Artis shrugged and looked away. "I didn't ask."

In London, the maids were a great deal more respectful. But there, she'd been the sister-in-law of an earl. Here, she was an oddity, a hermit, a strange woman dressed in black.

Nor had she attempted to befriend the servants. She didn't speak to them, and they remained silent as well. At this moment, however, with all of them looking at her, she wished she'd done more to curry favor.

Rather than ask about the footman or grab something to eat, she turned and walked away.

The night was freezing, sleet icing the street. She decided not to walk, but to retire early, wishing she could command herself to sleep. Where were the footman and Aunt Dina?

The woman was devoted to helping others, but for the past six months she'd done nothing but attend to her. No, Dina had been that way from the beginning.

When she arrived in Edinburgh a year ago, it was with certain expectations. She'd thought Morgan's aunt would be a stuffy woman who disliked the duty foisted upon her. Dina would teach her what she needed to know to take a place in society but nothing more.

Instead, she'd gotten a warm and loving woman in Dina MacTavish, someone who had become her second mother. They'd spent hours talking and laughing together. Dina had shared anecdotes with her as she taught her the finer graces. She'd sailed into society feeling a confidence that had its roots in Dina's praise.

In London, in the early days after the accident, she'd existed in a haze of pain and fear. Dina had been there as well, sitting at her bedside, holding her hand, talking or reading to her, and keeping her calm.

Where was she now?

Had the older woman gone to dinner with friends? Or to one of those lectures she was always attending? If so, it was strange that she hadn't mentioned it. But then, she hadn't been open to conversation with anyone lately, had she?

Well, it was a good sign that Aunt Dina didn't worry as much about her and was pursuing her own life.

Catriona bit back her envy.

Where was the footman? Perhaps Dina had fired him, and he would never again bother her.

It wasn't disappointment she felt, she told herself, but relief.

Chapter 9

"**W**hat do you mean, you haven't fired him?" Catriona asked. "He's surly, insulting, and rude. Is he another one of your good causes? Is that why you've employed him?"

Dina was still dressed in her wrapper, her hair braided for the night.

Catriona, however, hadn't been able to sleep well, appearing at Dina's door barely past dawn. Not acceptable behavior, most assuredly, but she had been pushed beyond her limits.

"Oh dear," Dina said. "Is he all that, truly?"

Catriona sat on the end of the bed, hands twisting the swatch of her veil.

"He's the rudest servant I've ever known," she said. "He goes out of his way to bedevil me. He insists on calling me 'Princess' in that insulting way of his, and looks as though he's laughing at me."

Dina didn't turn to look at her. Instead, she sat at her vanity and began to undo her braids. There wasn't a touch of gray in her dark brown hair. Her face was unlined, if plump, but the whole of her body was like that. Dina reminded her of an overstuffed pillow, one that was comforting yet attractive.

"I don't know why I need him," she said. "I've already
eaten my breakfast. Why does he never appear at breakfast? Why do I not see him around the house?"

"You never leave your room," Dina said calmly.

That was certainly true.

"Then why does he never bring me my breakfast tray?"

"I have him doing something else," Dina said, standing.

Before she knew it, she was being walked to the door
of Aunt Dina's sitting room.

"Dismiss him. If you won't dismiss him, then at least
trust me to eat, Aunt."

"I did that," the older woman said, her face firming
into a stern expression. "I will not have you winnow away
to nothing because of your grief."

Startled, she pulled back. "I wasn't starving myself,
Aunt. Nor was I grieving."

"Don't be foolish, child. Of course you were. You still
are."

"I wear black for an entirely different reason. It's less
transparent. Would you have me walk around in a red veil?"

"Yes," Dina said, to her surprise. "Anything but grieve
for your former life. If we can admit something between
us, let us do so, child. You are not the girl you were when
you first came to Edinburgh. At first I thought it was just
because of the accident. Lately, however, I'm beginning
to think that the change in you isn't simply physical, but
emotional. You are hiding from the world, dear Catriona,
and, I suspect, from yourself."

"For that reason, you've appointed a footman as my
keeper."

"I would have hired anyone who was your match in
temperament," Dina said. Another surprise. "Mark is
your equal in stubbornness, I think."

"Mark?"

"I believe you simply call him Footman."

Abruptly, she was on the other side of the door, staring at it.

For a few long minutes she didn't move. Should she argue her point more vigorously? Or simply admit that Aunt Dina had won that battle?

The footman didn't look like a Mark. He looked like an Alistair, Hamish, or Douglas. A name that matched his stern jaw and blue eyes that were the equal of hers in shade. Had she ever looked at anyone with such a penetrating gaze?

She didn't trust Aunt Dina's assertion that she had Mark doing other duties first thing in the morning. Her aunt was protective of her servants, only reluctantly divulging their backgrounds.

What was Mark's secret?

Aunt Dina had looked away when she'd spoken, a habit she had when she didn't wish to discuss a matter. She would be the last person to call Dina MacTavish a liar, but the other woman had a way of skirting the truth, avoiding it, or simply ignoring it at times.

What was she hiding about Mark, the footman?

When the odious man arrived with her noon meal, Catriona refused to leave her bedroom.

"Just place it on the table," she said through the door. "You can come back later for the empty dishes."

"Must we discuss this again, Princess? You know my orders."

"What do you think I'm going to do with the food? Place it in the bottom of the armoire? Hide it in one of the fern pots?"

"There are enough of them," he said.

How dare he discuss Aunt Dina's decorating? She frowned at the door.

"I can eat easier without an audience."

She hadn't meant to tell him the truth, and from the resultant silence, he evidently hadn't expected to hear it.

"Because of your veil?" he said. "You don't have to wear it."

"Yes, I do," she said.

"Then I'll turn my back."

"Why not just leave the room?"

When he didn't answer, she sighed. What an exceedingly stubborn man. Was he being loyal to Aunt Dina? Or was he simply intransigent by nature?

She rearranged her veil and slowly opened the door. Gripping her hands tight, she willed herself into composure.

"You're a bad footman," she said. "Where were you yesterday?"

"Perhaps you could teach me how to be a more proper servant."

"What does that mean?" Did he know that she'd once been a maid? If so, was that comment his not-so-veiled attempt at sarcasm?

"You seem to know a great deal about what I'm not doing correctly," he said, after setting the tray on the table, sitting down and leaning back in his chair. "Is there anything I'm doing right?"

Sunlight stole in on either side of the draperies, casting a gray, pearly light over the room. He sat at his customary place at the table, his right ankle resting on his left knee, relaxed and at ease. A man who was supremely confident in himself. His white shirt was open at the collar; his sleeves were rolled to the elbow, revealing strong, muscular forearms.

All her life people had turned to look at her, commenting on her blond hair or the color of her eyes. But this footman had blue eyes that were even more striking.

She wanted to sit and study them for a moment, in order to discover what it was about him that was so arresting. Maybe it was the jaw hinting at stubbornness, or his mouth, quirked even now in a half smile. He sat with nonchalance, one arm resting on the table, the other at his side.

At an earlier time, she might have lusted after him. She might have even taken him to her bed and enjoyed him.

She'd had three lovers in her life. The first, a footman like this man, had offered comfort at a time when she needed it. Although he had been more excited than skilled, she still felt some affection for him. The second was a coachman, an older and much more experienced lover. But for all his talent on the mattress, she'd left him after one night. He'd smelled of something sour.

Andrew Prender had been her third and last lover.

A question occurred to her as she studied the footman. Would she ever have another lover?

Aunt Dina said she was grieving. If she was, this grief was nothing like the mourning she'd felt for her parents. What had she learned from that? How to endure, perhaps. Time hadn't lessened the sense of loss, only rendered it bearable.

How, then, did she learn to live with no face? Or with a body that didn't work as it should?

She folded her hands before her, wishing she weren't so warm in her veil. Her face had begun to itch, a discomfort she normally tolerated. Now, it seemed to abrade on her nerves. Or perhaps it was just the footman doing that.

"Where were you yesterday?"

Instead of responding to that question, he said, "Have I nothing to recommend me? Isn't there anything I do correctly?"

"No."

"Surely there's something."

She inspected him. "You're always dressed neatly and cleanly," she said. "You don't smell of the stable." In fact, he smelled good, something reminiscent of sandalwood or spices.

"You speak well, perhaps too well for a footman. Hold up your hands."

"My hands?"

"Another thing, you dispute me entirely too much. You should never question your betters."

"Are you one of my betters?"

"See? You're doing it again. You should simply accept what I have to say as the truth."

"You are a princess, aren't you?" he asked, holding both hands up, palms toward her.

She couldn't see from where she stood. Impatiently, she motioned him toward her. He stood, walked around the table and held out his hands.

To her surprise, they were hard, not soft. The hands of a working man. Still, she shook her head.

"You don't have the hands of a footman."

"Oh? If I'm not a footman, what am I?"

"One of my aunt's causes, I think. A confidence man, perhaps, one she wants to see lead a more honest life. Or a gambler."

"A gambler? I've never been considered a gambler."

"But you have been considered a confidence man?"

"I suppose I have, in a great many ways."

"I will not allow you to take advantage of her."

"Are we talking of your aunt? I can assure you, I have

no intention of taking advantage of the dear woman. I have a great deal of fondness for her, as a matter of fact. If I didn't, I wouldn't be here now, talking to you."

He returned to his chair, reprising his earlier indolent pose.

"What does that mean?"

"I'm doing a favor for her, you might say."

"By being an irritant?"

He startled her by laughing, such an alien sound in this room that she frowned at him.

"I don't believe I said anything that amusing," she said.

"Oh, Princess, you are the first truly amusing thing that has happened to me all day. Perhaps for two days, actually."

She didn't know what to say to that comment, so she remained silent, walked to the table, and sat in the other chair. When he would have stood, she waved him back into his seat.

"Don't try being polite now. I'm afraid it's too late. I know your true nature."

"I do apologize, Princess. I usually do not foist my true nature on people until after they've gotten to know me better."

"I can assure you," she said, picking up her fork, "I have no intention of getting to know you better."

Alone, she would have dispensed with the veil. Because he was there, she had to use one hand to lift the bottom of the veil away from her face so that she could accommodate the fork.

When she was done with her meal, she said, "There, you can tell my aunt that I've eaten. There's no need to remain here."

"Why deny myself the pleasure of your company?"

His voice held a note of humor. Was he ridiculing her?

"You can leave now," she said. "You've done your duty."

Surreptitiously, she raised her hand beneath the veil and gently patted her cheeks. The itching was nearly unbearable. Once he left, she'd raise the veil enough to cool her face.

"I'll build up your fire before I leave," he said.

She was adept at maintaining a fire herself, as well as being skilled at blacking the bricks, but she didn't tell him that.

"It looks like snow again today," he said, tending to the fire.

Once again she patted her face. Would he please hurry?

"What about the fireplace in your bedroom?"

"Leave it."

"It's a raw day. Don't princesses ever get cold?"

"Would you please go?"

He stood, walking back to the table, stopping beside her chair.

"What is it, Catriona? Is something wrong?"

She wouldn't tolerate this. She pushed back the chair and stood, making her way to the door. Because she was conscious of his gaze on her, she tried not to limp.

She held the door open, gripping the edge of it tightly with her right hand.

"Get out," she said.

If he didn't leave now, she would take the poker and use it as a weapon against him.

He went to the table, gathered up the dishes, and placed them on the tray.

"Leave them," she said.

"I'm trying to be a good footman," he said.

"Leave them," she repeated. She made a fist of her left hand, concentrating on the pain in her fingers.

He stopped what he was doing and turned to look at her. The expression on his face was one she couldn't decipher: a combination of interest, compassion, and something else that reminded her, oddly enough, of her father.

"Shall I call your aunt?" he asked. "Would you tell her what's wrong?"

"No," she said.

He nodded, as if unsurprised. "Why not tell me? I'll swear myself to secrecy. No one need know."

"Tell any of my secrets to a confidence man? No."

She waited, impatient and near to screaming, as he walked to the door.

"Perhaps I can help."

"I don't think so." Did he have the power to roll back time itself? Could he prevent an accident? Or change that hideous night?

"Please, just leave."

Her face felt as if it was on fire, each scar burning into her skin.

She closed the door after him, then jerked the veil off, threw it on the table, and walked to the window, opening the sash a few inches. The bitterly cold air cooled her skin, easing the discomfort. A cold compress would help as well. Then there was the laudanum if the pain increased. But she tried not to use it, keeping it for a time she might need the whole bottle.

"How do you find her, Dr. Thorburn?"

Mark closed the door on Catriona's suite and faced Mrs. MacTavish.

Her brown hair was in a bun at the nape of her neck, her dark brown dress properly somber, given her status as a widow. She held her hands tightly clasped together in front of her. But it was her eyes that gave her away. Large, warm, and brown, they held a world of compassion.

"I wish I could say that she's fine," he said. "But the truth is that I don't know how she is, Mrs. MacTavish. She seems to have taken a dislike to me. I'm no closer to examining her than I was at the beginning."

She exhaled a sigh. "I'm so glad," she said.

"Glad?" he asked, surprised.

"Oh, don't you see, Doctor? If Catriona hates you, at least it's some emotion. It's better than what she's been like all these months. She's never expressed a dislike about anything, not even tomato aspic, and she hates that. She doesn't dislike anything, but she doesn't like anything, either. But she hates you. Don't you think that's a good sign?"

His not wanting Catriona to hate him was as disturbing as the realization that he'd given her every reason to do so.

He'd never known a woman who confounded him as much as Catriona Cameron. But then, perhaps he'd been incorrect in his assumptions about her from the beginning. He'd only seen her a few times in Inverness. On those occasions, he'd developed an impression of a girl of exquisite beauty, one who was aware of it as well. She flirted with impunity, laughed with abandon, and wasn't as demure or proper as she should have been.

Once, she'd come into her father's office, a flurry of skirts and lace-trimmed petticoats. She'd flown to where her father sat behind his desk and hugged him, leaving as quickly as she arrived, never once sparing a glance to where he sat facing the desk.

That's how he thought of Catriona, never noticing anyone but herself.

Except something was missing.

Something was there he should have seen or understood. He was a scientist; he sought answers when most men were satisfied with the questions.

Why did he have the feeling that he was watching a play, one in which he was being led to believe one thing while something else was happening?

What, exactly, was he not seeing?

Andrew watched the house for several days before making a decision. The minute that one particular maid closed the door, bundled against the weather and holding a basket, he approached her.

"Miss," he said, stepping out from around the corner.

She jumped, startled, then immediately gained her composure and frowned at him.

He tipped his hat and smiled in his most charming manner. "I apologize for frightening you."

"What do you want?" she asked.

She didn't possess a servant's demeanor, but that could prove to be advantageous.

"Do you work for Mrs. MacTavish?" he asked, knowing the answer before he asked the question.

"Why would you want to know?"

She adjusted the handle of the basket on her wrist but didn't move away.

A good sign, one he rewarded with another smile.

"Is she a good employer?"

"Again, I'll be asking why you want to know my business?"

"An attractive woman such as yourself deserves to have a fair employer."

She narrowed her eyes. Perhaps he'd overdone it.

"Does she pay well?"

A flash of interest proved he'd adopted the right course of action. She was evidently more greedy than vain.

"Why would you want to know that?"

"I have a proposition for you, if you'd like to earn more money. If you're not interested, I apologize again for waylaying you, miss."

He tipped his hat again, bowed, and stepped back. He turned, smiling to himself and counted the steps. He wasn't a gambler, considering it a waste of time and money, but he bet himself that she would stop him before he was ten paces away.

"Wait!"

She'd waited for seven steps, which indicated a stubborn personality. He could deal with stubbornness. But if she was also stupid, that might prove to be a hindrance. Time would have to tell.

"Are you interested?" he asked, turning.

She nodded.

"Finish your errands, then," he said, pulling out his card and approaching her. "That's my address. It's across the square. Come and see me before you return to the house."

"You're not a slaver?"

He shook his head, allowing himself a warm, reassuring smile.

"Or a murderer?"

Since Burke and Hare had made themselves infamous in Edinburgh, he understood the question and smiled fully. Fool that she was, she looked reassured. Why would a simple expression assure her she wasn't going to be murdered for her body parts?

Perhaps she was stupid, after all.

She stared down at his card and nodded once. Enough to let him know that he'd trapped the crow.

Dina MacTavish stood in the parlor, watching as Dr. Thorburn left the house. His coachman had parked the carriage around the corner, and he was forced to brave the cold and walk the block because of her.

Still, she wouldn't change anything she'd done.

A movement to her left caught her attention. She moved to the side of the window, frowning at the sight of Artis standing at the end of the alley. What on earth was the girl doing?

Dina walked through the house to the kitchen door. She hesitated, hand on the handle, about to call Artis when a stranger approached the maid, handed her something, then tipped his hat to her. Artis preened, silly girl, and watched as the man walked away and out of sight.

Artis was one of her trials. Not everyone wanted to be saved. Sometimes, she came up against a stubbornness that made charity difficult. Artis had once been an unfortunate woman as well as a pickpocket, and God knew what else. Life in Old Town had not been easy for her. The girl had been mistreated and beaten nearly to death.

Most of the women who came into her home did so with gratitude, knowing it might well be their last chance at a happy life. Each was trained well for her position, enough to advance to another, larger, establishment.

Artis had been different from the beginning. She wasn't adverse to communicating her dislike of a certain chore with a roll of her eyes or a sneer. Because of her attitude, she'd not recommended Artis for any other job or advancement.

In the two years that Artis had been with her, she had never once said thank you. Gratitude, however, was not necessary. Obeying the rules was.

Male visitors were not allowed in the house. Only on her half day off was a girl allowed to see a suitor, but the relationship must be serious, and destined for the altar.

When Artis returned, she'd question her about the stranger. Until then she would occupy herself by writing her nephew and his wife, telling them about the exciting developments in Catriona's care.

The girl was becoming angry, and wasn't that a lovely sign?

Chapter 10

Instead of the footman Catriona had been expecting, Aunt Dina arrived at her door with dinner, Isobel behind her holding a second tray.

"I thought we'd eat together, my dear," Dina said, placing the dishes on the table and directing the maid to do likewise.

After Isobel left, Catriona lit the lamp, placing it in the middle of the table. Because she had few secrets from the older woman, she removed her veil.

For the next hour they engaged in a pleasurable meal. Aunt Dina kept her entertained with stories of her friends.

Not once did she ask Dina about the footman. Not once did she complain about him.

Only one time did the conversation become uncomfortable, and that was when Dina insisted on talking about the future as if nothing had changed. As if she had only taken these months as a time of reflection.

"You cannot remain in these rooms for the rest of your life, my dear. You must choose what you mean to do, and continue on that path."

She put her fork down, folded her hands together, and

looked at the other woman. It was all too obvious that she had become Dina's good works project.

"I don't know what I want to do with the rest of my life," she said, feeling helpless in the face of Dina's insistent good cheer. She and Jean would be great good friends. Both of them had a penchant for looking at the best in any situation.

Aunt Dina nodded. "Which is to be expected, I think, given that you've been a hermit for months."

"Hardly months," Catriona said.

"Five weeks since we returned to Edinburgh," Dina countered.

"What would you have me do, join you in Old Town?"

Dina sighed. "You should, you know. Your own plight might be a great deal more acceptable if you knew how other people lived."

How on earth could a ruined face and body be more acceptable?

She stared without speaking at the older woman. Aunt Dina looked away.

"If you do nothing else, then cease wearing nothing but black. You're entirely too young to be in mourning. No," Dina added, waving a hand at her, "don't tell me you're in mourning for your lost youth or your beauty. We all know that. You can grieve without being dressed like the Grim Reaper."

"What would you have me wear?" she asked.

"Blue," Aunt Dina said without hesitating. "You'd look good in blue. A dark blue if you must. If you insist on wearing a veil, we can dye the lace a beautiful blue."

"If I wear blue instead of black, will you be happy?"

"Enough to stop haranguing you?" Aunt Dina smiled. "Absolutely not. I haven't decided what your life will be like yet, child, but I know you were not destined to be a hermit. I miss your laughter. You had such a sparkling laugh, as well as a great wit."

She wished she hadn't removed her veil. She blinked rapidly, willing herself not to cry. The tears weren't for herself, but in gratitude to the lovely woman who'd been as kind as a mother to her.

For a long time she hadn't wanted to live, having lost herself in those agonizing months in London. First, the pain had stripped the humanity from her. Secondly, without being herself, without having a face she recognized, she was left floundering for an identity.

Dina had held fast to her, refusing to let go.

She cleared her throat. "Very well, Aunt Dina, I'll wear your blue."

"Excellent," the other woman said, smiling brightly. "I'll summon the seamstress tomorrow."

She hadn't considered a seamstress. But looking at the happiness on Aunt Dina's face, she knew she'd have to suffer another person's invasion of her sanctuary.

Once Dina left, she occupied herself with straightening her rooms, reviewing her wardrobe, and repairing the lace on her shift.

Jean would laugh to see her chores, each and every one of them tasks she'd managed to avoid at Inverness and Ballindair. She'd grown accustomed to people caring for her, taking up the duties she'd not wanted to do. Jean had been her greatest defender, loyal and caring even when she'd not returned the emotion.

Not having walked the night before, her legs felt even stiffer than usual, particularly her left knee. The pain was a constant reminder that however optimistic Aunt Dina was, she still had physical limitations.

Catriona dressed and readied herself for her walk. A few minutes later she stood atop the kitchen steps, looking out over the alley. Even with her heavy veil, her eyes stung with the cold and the tip of her nose tingled.

She stepped out onto the snow.

Tonight, she limped badly. Her body, in all its separate parts, was making its displeasure known. *You think yourself above pain, Catriona?* Here, a headache to make even blinking a chore. *Nothing is beyond you?* Let's see how well you do in boots and a knee that refuses to bend. *You are above such petty things as loneliness?* Here's a memory for you, of sitting and laughing with other girls. Or being kissed until your body feels on fire and your heart beats so hard you can barely breathe.

Try and forget those memories. Try not to long for those days.

Mark was tired after a full afternoon and evening of calling on his patients. For some reason, tonight he'd been stopped by relatives. Mr. MacNeil's wife wanted the truth about her husband's difficulty swallowing. A mother needed to be given guidance about her son's vision. Two sisters listened with intense regard and barely subdued grief when he told them their father would probably not live to see the end of the week.

Why, then, was he here? Why was he standing in the shadows on a cold winter night, watching for a woman who didn't need his help, didn't want his help, and rejected him at every turn?

Because she wasn't his patient. Because she made him forget his worry and his care. Because she made him smile when so much of his day—especially today—made him want to imbibe too much whiskey and forget about the despair he sometimes witnessed.

The night was bitterly cold, so much so that his eyes

stung. He was wrapped in his greatcoat, a garment more luxurious than a footman could afford, but since he was draped in night, he doubted she would see him.

How strange that she was part of his past, but only because she was Dr. Cameron's daughter, a man he'd greatly respected. She didn't know him, didn't remember him, and had never truly seen him.

What he'd learned at her father's side had augmented his university education. He'd called on patients with Dr. Cameron, learning something each time. The advice he received had made him a better doctor.

"The patient will always know more than we do," Dr, Cameron had once said. "They don't know that they know, but listen to their complaints. That will tell you as much as your examination."

Dr. Cameron had also insisted, unlike some of his peers, that he write out his notes within minutes of visiting a patient.

"Don't wait until the next day. You won't remember the details that can make the difference between life and death. Write down the patient's color, his demeanor, whether he talks about other things or only his health. Is his aspect good, or do lines form on his face? Are his pupils expanded? Is the sclera white or gray? Are there dark circles beneath his eyes? Is his breath foul? Your words might prove invaluable to a physician who comes after you."

He attempted to write his notes after each visit. Some nights, like tonight, he was forced to write them in the carriage, using the carriage lamp as his only illumination. Now, Brody waited patiently around the corner, no doubt freezing like he was, and wondering as to his sanity.

Dr. Cameron had not been the only physician with whom he'd studied, but he was the most memorable. Not because of his daughter, although Catriona had remained fixed in his mind for a long time, but because of what happened to him later.

Mrs. Cameron had developed a cancer of the breast. Her dying had been by inches, and when he could no longer ease her pain, Dr. Cameron had simply administered an overdose of morphine. He'd heard that the man went cheerfully to the gallows, not attempting to rationalize his decision or his act.

Had he ever thought of his daughters? Only Dr. Cameron could answer that.

The man was a great believer in the human mind being responsible for many illnesses. He'd recounted a tale of more than one matron who, once her children were grown and gone from home, became sickly.

"Women, especially, need to feel useful," Dr. Cameron said.

He'd found that true as well in his own practice.

What would Dr. Cameron have said about his own daughter? He could imagine the man's words: *She needs a purpose, a place in the world, somewhere to belong.*

That sentiment could be applied to his own life. Other than Sarah, he had no friends, unless he could count his grandfather among them. He was too busy to form relationships. Even his friendship with Anne was one more of convenience than a genuine melding of minds. He and his brothers didn't live similar lives, and his father would never understand his need to be a physician.

His purpose was solid and immutable: medicine. He had to heal or at least try. Sometimes his intentions were blocked by the patient. Sometimes he lost the battle no matter how arduously he fought.

But where did he belong? He'd asked himself that question for years.

His stomach growled, reminding him that he'd missed dinner again.

The sleet had increased in the last hour or so, seemingly intent on peeling the skin from every poor soul abroad tonight. He spared more than one thought to his patients in Old Town.

He leaned his shoulder against the doorway, watching as Catriona, swathed in black, emerged from the house and slowly descended the kitchen steps. She turned right, heading for the square.

The night was silent but for the wind, carrying the bitter cold to his face and neck. The tall oak trees lining the square did so in military precision, their ice-bedecked branches throwing dancing shadows on the snow.

Catriona slowly walked along the square, obviously favoring her left leg.

Strange, that he'd never heard her complain.

He knew too many young women who thought a bruise was a reason for whining and a turned ankle cause for histrionics.

Catriona hadn't mentioned her leg or arm, and had attempted to hide her injuries from him. Her determination, witness her walking at midnight, was another surprise.

The snow started again, the slow descent of the snowflakes lit by the gas lamps. The only living creature in this midnight landscape was Catriona, limping around the square, half hidden by the trees and the darkness.

Did the night sadden her? Did it somehow mirror her mood?

He stayed where he was, thrusting his gloved hands into his coat in order to stay warm as he waited for her. He sincerely hoped that what she wore was substantial enough.

She turned back toward the town house, her footsteps slowing as if she were reluctant to come home. He watched as she walked down the alley, her limp less pronounced than when she'd began.

Just when he thought she was ready to climb the stairs to the kitchen, she turned and faced the carriage house.

"Why are you spying on me?"

"Do you have eyes like a cat?" he asked through lips that were cold and numb.

"Isn't it enough that you make my mealtimes miserable? Must you spoil my walks as well?"

"You interest me," he said, unwittingly giving her the truth.

"I haven't the slightest idea why," she said. "I'd prefer you showed more interest for your duties."

"You are one of my duties," he said. "My most important one."

For a moment she didn't say anything. Just when he thought her rejoinder would be cutting and sarcastic, she shook her head.

"You mustn't say things like that, even if it's true. It implies too much intimacy."

"Are you training me in my duties as a footman?" he asked, smiling.

"Someone needs to," she said.

"Have you always been so dictatorial?"

She made a dismissive movement with her right hand. "I'm not at all," she said. "Everyone knows that footmen don't lurk in carriage houses at midnight."

"Do they?" he asked, amused.

She folded her arms on the outside of her cloak.

"My sister always said that, too. As if she doubted what I said."

He'd heard of her sister from Mrs. MacTavish, but she'd never mentioned her before now.

"Do you miss her?"

"With all my heart," she said, surprising him. "She's a much better person than I am." Another bit of honesty he hadn't expected. "Being around Jean was like having the voice of a conscience always near."

"That sounds miserable. No one wants to be reminded of their failings."

"Have you no one better than you in your family? Or are you the most perfect one of them all?"

He smiled again. "I have two brothers," he said.

"Are they paragons of virtue, then?"

"I wouldn't say so. They don't spend their time in worthwhile endeavors."

"So you are the most perfect one."

"I wouldn't say that, either. But why waste your time in drunkenness?"

"It's a problem in Scotland," she said. "If the newspaper accounts are to be believed."

"So you read the newspaper."

She studied him, and he wished the damnable veil didn't hide her expression.

"Do you think me stupid?"

"No, just insular," he said. "Not caring about the world outside this house."

" 'The world is too much with us,' " she murmured.

"Wordsworth?"

"I've been reading books, too, footman. Are you doubly surprised?"

More than he would admit.

"It's cold tonight," he said. "Are you warm enough?"

"My nose is cold," she said. "Although, I suppose my veil keeps me warmer than wearing nothing. You, however, should be frozen. Have you been watching me the whole time?"

He didn't want to answer, but he nodded.

"Have you no other interests than me?"

"Scientific pursuit," he said, treading too close to the truth. "Perhaps politics, and you?"

That question startled a chuckle from her. "I have no interest in either," she said.

"Gardening?"

"Are you trying to say you've an interest in gardening? I don't believe it."

"I could have," he said. "How do you know what a footman is interested in?"

"Very well, scientific pursuit, politics, and gardening. What else?"

"Bread," he said.

"Bread?"

"I think bread is miraculous."

"Miraculous?" she asked, sounding bemused.

"It grows. It swells. Yes, I'd most definitely add bread to the list of things that interest me."

"Could it be because you're hungry?"

"I am, by the way. Very hungry. I've missed dinner. Do you make bread?"

"I have, yes," she said slowly. She turned and looked at the darkened kitchen. "Are you asking me to make bread for you?"

"If I knew how," he said, "I would, but I haven't been allowed access to the kitchen."

The idea of her cooking for him was intriguing. Would she do it?

He should leave, wait in the darkness until she'd reached her room, then go in search of Brody. Sarah would have left a filling dinner for him. Instead, the singularly implausible idea of Catriona baking for him kept him motionless.

"I can't bake bread for you," she said, glancing back at the kitchen again.

"Why not? Perhaps if you bake bread for me," he said, "I'll remain in the corridor while you eat your lunch. Or take a walk while you eat dinner."

"You won't sit at the table and watch me as if you're a hungry jackal?"

He laughed. "What do you know of hungry jackals, Catriona?"

"You shouldn't address me as Catriona."

"Another lesson in my footman duties? Perhaps I won't do that, either."

"There shouldn't be a price for your propriety."

He didn't comment, merely waited for her to make up her mind. Would she surprise him and say yes? Or do what he expected, leave in a huff, with a threat to have him dismissed yet again?

"If I do," she said, "do you promise to not speak to me? You won't badger me or tease me or ridicule me."

"I don't think I've teased or ridiculed you," he said in his own defense. "Perhaps I have badgered you. I promise to remain silent."

She turned and walked toward the house.

"Well, come on, then," she said, neatly surprising him. "It's too cold to argue the point out here."

Chapter 11

Catriona heard the crunch of his boots on snow and knew he was following her. She opened the door, turned to the left and entered the darkened kitchen. He would insist on light. Indeed, she would need it. But she would dictate how and where. Instead of lighting one of the gaslights on the wall, she went to the pantry and withdrew a lamp, placing it on the end of the table.

She motioned to one of the chairs. "Please sit there," she said.

"Would you like me to light the lamp?"

"Yes," she said, "but keep the wick low."

"You're going to make bread?"

He sounded so surprised that she remained silent for a moment.

"I'm not sure I remember how," she said. "I made it when I lived at home with my parents, but it's been a few years."

She couldn't believe she was considering cooking for him. No man had ever suggested such a thing.

As if he knew she was wavering, he said, "I haven't eaten dinner, and on my salary, I can't afford a meal at a tavern."

"Bread is not enough for dinner."

"It will do for now." He smiled at her. "If I could make it myself, I would, but I doubt I could eat the result."

She felt a burbling gathering in her stomach, a feeling so akin to amusement that it startled her.

After locating the flour and sugar without much difficulty, she was stumped when it came to finding the muriatic acid. When she said as much to him, he sat back in the chair, his forearms on the table.

"Muriatic acid?"

She nodded. "That's what my mother used. It helps the dough to rise."

"Must we wait for that?" he asked. "Isn't there some bread you can make that's faster?"

She turned to look at him. By the soft lamplight he was a study of shadows. He'd removed his coat, revealing a jacket and a vest over his white shirt.

"Where were you, to be dressed so fine?" she asked.

How much did Aunt Dina pay him? If he couldn't afford a meal, then why was he wearing a silken vest?

He only shrugged, but his gaze didn't move from her, as if he could see beneath her veil.

She'd removed her own cloak, draping it over the bench closest to her. Now she turned back to the pantry.

"I can make bannocks," she said, studying the shelves, then glancing back at him.

"That'll do," he said, smiling like a mischievous boy. *"Bannocks ar better nor nae kin o breid."*

She turned at that comment, surprised. How thick his burr sounded at times, while at others he sounded English.

"Are you sure you're from Edinburgh?" she asked.

"Did I say?" He looked toward the storeroom. "There'll be jam and butter, won't there?"

She glanced at the stove, grateful that it was never allowed to grow cold. The heat was such that it would cook the bannocks in no time at all. A few minutes later she'd located two bowls, pumping water into the first while she filled the second with oats. Reaching into the cupboard, she located a saucer.

"What's that for?" he asked.

"It's a template," she said, not turning toward him. The less she looked at him, the better. "I like my bannocks to be the same size."

"Do you like to cook, Catriona?"

There was his use of her name again. Instead of correcting him, however, she simply let it pass without remark. Perhaps if she didn't allow him to upset her, he would revert to more proper behavior.

How proper was it to be cooking for him?

Yet it was the first improper thing she'd done in over a year, and with it came a curious sense of freedom.

"I haven't cooked that much," she said. "This is the first time I've made bannocks in three years."

"Then I sincerely hope you remember how," he said. "I'm very hungry."

She patted the oatmeal mixture between both hands, wishing she could fully straighten the fingers of her left hand. Still, she made do without him noticing. Using the saucer as a guide, she shaped the bannocks, placed them on the griddle and then into the oven.

For the next few minutes she checked them often to ensure they weren't browning too much.

The smell of cooking oats brought back memories of her childhood, days laced with joy, now remembered in a haze that made them appear as if they weren't memories at all, but dreams.

"What duties do you have that make you so hungry?"

she asked, preferring to discuss the footman than think of her past.

"I have a great many duties," he said.

"I haven't seen you perform one of them," she said. "Other than ensuring I eat."

"Curiosity again?"

She placed a jar of butter and one of jam on the table, then returned to the stove.

"Should I not be curious?" she asked, carefully withdrawing the bannocks from the oven. "You certainly ask enough questions of me." She placed the pot holder to the side, took a fork and gently peeled the first bannock from the griddle. She'd always been good at bannocks and was pleased that her efforts had been successful.

She withdrew a plate from the cupboard, put the bannocks on it, and placed it on the table before the footman. An exchange of roles so easily done she marveled at it.

"I wasn't always the sister-in-law of an earl," she said, sitting opposite him. "Once, I was a maid, employed at Ballindair."

The moment she said the words, she wondered why she'd confessed such a thing to him, especially since she'd kept the knowledge carefully hidden for nearly a year.

Perhaps because it was late and she had just cooked for him, or because he had such an expression of bliss on his face as he took the first bite of her bannocks. She propped her elbows on the table and watched him, wishing she could remove the veil to see him more clearly.

"I'd heard that," he said after his first rapturous bite.

Now, that was a surprise.

"I didn't think anyone here knew it," she said. "Other than Aunt Dina, of course."

"I don't remember who told me," he said. "But I think it's common knowledge."

She nodded. That would explain the antipathy of the maids toward her, especially Artis.

He was making noises as he ate, little sounds of enjoyment that made her smile. She couldn't remember cooking for anyone before tonight. Even as a child she'd been more concerned with her own appetite than anyone else's. The act of doing so was oddly intimate, as if she'd performed a personal service for him.

He finished off all four of the bannocks, a compliment to her cooking that kept her smile in place.

"You've never been a servant before, have you?" she asked.

His smile abruptly disappeared. "Why would you say that?"

"You don't have the demeanor of a servant."

"What is that?"

She didn't know, because she'd always been told that she didn't have the demeanor of a servant, either. But she made it up as she spoke.

"A subservient air, I think. You should never look at me directly, but always avoid my gaze. It's a mark of respect. You should most definitely accede to my every wish."

"You don't want a servant, Princess," he said. "You want a lackey. Or a beaten down dog."

What a pity he couldn't see her frown through the veil.

"What would you say," he asked, as if he knew she was annoyed, "if I said that I hadn't always been of service, that I've fallen on hard times?"

"Is that the truth?"

"No," he said. "So you needn't try to find the right words to soothe me."

She bit her lip. How could he take her from amusement to irritation and back to amusement again so easily?

"My sister used to say I was lacking in empathy for others."

"Are you?"

She sighed. "Perhaps I am. My aunt says I should accompany her to Old Town. She does a lot of good works there. She distributes clothes and food, and counsels women on the evils of alcohol."

He didn't say anything.

"Even though I don't go with her, I'm not devoid of compassion. If that truly had been your story, I would've been sorry for you, but I would also have been surprised."

"Surprised? Why?"

"You don't seem to be the type of person who would allow something like that to happen to you. You're too determined. Too stubborn. Besides, I suspect the only reason you would tell me a story like that would be to solicit my sympathy, and I don't see you doing that, either."

"Is that why you never talk about your injuries? Because you don't want to solicit anyone's sympathy?"

The question startled her.

She decided that it would be best not to answer that question. Instead, she said, "I can see you becoming a majordomo in a household much larger than this one. Perhaps even working for an earl."

He smiled. "I could see myself doing the same," he said, as if they were in perfect accord.

What a strange meal. What a strange man.

"Is that why you wear a veil?" he asked.

Had he returned to that subject again?

"I think it is," he said, not waiting for her to answer. "I think it's because you don't want anyone's pity."

"Perhaps it's because I can't bear the sight of myself," she said softly.

"Does wearing a veil help to pretend? I think that it would be a constant reminder."

"It doesn't matter if I wear a veil or not," she said. "I'm constantly reminded."

"I wouldn't say anything if you dispensed with it."

"Why are you so eager to see me?"

He shrugged, a curiously insouciant gesture that didn't match the intensity of his look.

"Curiosity?" she asked. "You'd be better served to be curious about something else. Your science, perhaps. Or your gardening."

He smiled, such a charming expression that it hurt to witness it.

Somehow, remarkably, insanely, this footman's smile seemed to bring forth the feelings she'd not had for a great many months. She felt warm, heated inside.

If the accident hadn't happened, she might have gone over to him, sat on his lap and intertwined her arms around his neck, smiling up at him with a coquettish look. The idea of her doing that now was not as shocking as it was simply impossible.

She grieved for the girl she had been, unwise and im- provident. Had she somehow realized that she quickly needed to taste all that life had to offer, because it would one day be cut short?

She'd never be a lover again. She would never be a wife. She would never be a mother. Laughter would be beyond her. Joy would be felt only through memories.

"Could you leave now?" she said, her voice raspy from unshed tears.

He glanced at her.

"Please," she said. One word she'd not expected to say. She reached out and grabbed the edge of the table with both hands, her fingers drawn up into fists, knuckles pressing into the wood.

If you have any compassion, leave me. By all that's holy, leave me.

She, who had never wanted pity, who had eschewed it, who had known nothing but contempt for it, wanted it now from this man, someone who'd annoyed her and irritated her from the beginning.

She forced herself to look at him. He was standing and coming around the table.

Please do not touch me. Don't let your hand linger on the sleeve of my dress so that I can feel the warmth of you. Please do not say anything kind or gentle, because I will begin to weep.

Once, she would have enthralled him. She would have caused him to dream of her. She would have teased him and toyed with him and left him needing her. Now, he was doing the same to her yet without a word spoken, without a gesture, and without a touch.

Did he know? Is that why he suddenly left the room without saying anything? She heard the click of the door latch and only then carefully pushed away the dish, lay her head on her folded arms, and cried.

Chapter 12

A hundred years ago Mark's ancestor, a man known for his idiosyncrasies, developed and manufactured bleaching powder. The formulation was so inventive and popular that Mr. Thorburn was made an earl in dutiful appreciation of his expertise, not to mention making his fortune. From that day forward the Thorburn family was exceptionally grateful for the first earl's chemical genius and ignored rumors of his personal oddities.

Mark's grandfather was as much a character as the founder of Thorburn's Bleaching Powder. As his father would have said, "The damn fool doesn't have the sense God gave an ass. He's spending a fortune."

The fact that it was his grandfather's fortune to spend never occurred to Mark's father. Nor did it register that most of his purchases would ultimately benefit the family in some way.

Take this house, for example, some five miles from Edinburgh. His grandfather had purchased it from the original family after his wife died. In the intervening three years, he'd spent what his father would have called "a bloody fortune" on the initial restoration. Kingairgen was a reddish brick house with numerous turrets and walls, reminding him of a tumor that had grown amok.

His mother was kinder. "Kingairgen is a house that thinks it's a castle," was how she had put it.

His parents, along with his two brothers, rarely made the trip from Edinburgh to visit his grandfather. He did often, because he admired and liked the old man. In addition, he served as Douglas Thorburn's doctor, since the Earl of Caithnern refused to see anyone else.

Today, he elevated his grandfather's left foot back onto the stool and shook his head.

"It's not gout," Douglas said, waving a hand to forestall the lecture Mark had no intention of making. "It's a sprain."

"You don't get gout on the Banting diet?" he asked. For years his grandfather had eschewed any other form of eating, and consequently ate meat and whiskey to the exclusion of most everything else.

"I do not. It's a sprain," his grandfather said.

"What were you doing to cause a sprain?"

The old man looked away, causing Mark to smile.

"Dancing again? Or more strenuous exercise?"

Douglas glanced at him out of the corner of his eye before resuming his far-off stare. "You and your mother. She'd have me be a monk."

He laughed. "I doubt my mother knows anything about your proclivities," he said. "Don't tell her. But you are in your seventies, sir. Perhaps restraint wouldn't be amiss."

"Your mother is more worldly than you know, my boy. My son made a fine decision marrying her. She made the most of him."

Since he'd heard a variation of that comment for most of his life, he remained silent. It wouldn't be fair to call it enmity between father and son. Perhaps discord would be a better term. His grandfather believed in living life to the fullest, while his father was more circumspect in his actions. One didn't care what the rest of the world thought, the other cared too much.

"Still," he said, standing, "I can't think it's good for you to consume all that much whiskey."

"Nonsense, my boy," his grandfather said. "It thins my blood and heats it as well." Douglas smiled, and wiggled one of his bushy white eyebrows at him. "I wouldn't mind a nip of it now, as a matter of fact."

"You expect me to dole out your poison?"

His grandfather shook his head at him. "It was just a country dance, my boy. A reel we were practicing. It would have gone fine if I hadn't miscalculated Mary's zeal."

"Mary?"

Douglas frowned. "You'll not be carrying that name back to Edinburgh."

"Of course not. She'll be a secret between you and me." Despite his earlier words, he walked over to the credenza along one wall and pulled the door open on the lower cabinet. He'd never noticed before, but his grandfather's choice of whiskey was MacCraig. Morgan MacCraig, Catriona's brother-in-law, was the scion of the family.

A hint of Catriona, as if he needed to be reminded. Last night she'd cooked for him, and he couldn't forget their amity, the moments that felt as if they were tinged by humor and friendship. Her sudden sadness still disturbed him. Or more properly, his ruse disturbed him as much as his curiosity.

She fascinated him.

He poured his grandfather a restrained measure, carrying the crystal glass back to him.

"To Mary," he said.

Douglas took the glass, hoisted it in the air, and smiled.

"To Mary," he said, before drinking nearly all of the whis-key in one gulp. "You realize, of course, that she's only a passing fancy of mine."

The last thing he wanted to discuss was his grandfa-ther's mistress, but he remained silent. He learned a great many secrets being a physician, most of which he didn't want to know.

"I'll be joining my beloved Dorothy soon enough. Mary's just a stop on the road."

Mark sat on the adjoining chair, lifting his feet to share the ottoman. The day had been raw, the travel time ex-tended because of the blustery storm and the icy roads. If it weren't for his patients, he would have stayed overnight. But Mrs. MacAllister had a burn that wasn't healing as well as it should. Tommy Sanderson had a nasty boil that he might need to lance again, and Fanny MacDougal was near term. She refused to be seen by anyone else, even a midwife, claiming that they didn't offer nearly a pain-free delivery.

He was a great advocate of chloroform, having seen the difference in a woman fearing the onset of childbirth and one anticipating it.

Then there was Catriona.

"A woman is a confusing creature," he said, staring at the portrait over the fireplace.

His grandmother had been thirty-three when her por-trait was painted by Christina Robertson. She'd been smiling at the time, an expression he remembered often. Her face was, perhaps, not conventionally attractive, being pointed at the chin and wide at the brow, but her joy made anyone forget her appearance and concentrate on the feeling they experienced in her presence. People wanted to be around her.

From his earliest days she was one of his favorite

people. As an infant he'd reached as often for her as for his mother. He'd confided his greatest dreams to her, and she, above anyone else, had believed in him.

When she'd fallen ill, she consulted her doctor, then came to him for a second opinion. He'd had no good words for her. At that moment he would have given up the practice of medicine in order to save her.

But he was not God, and his powerlessness was something he realized each day. Despite his desperate wish and deep need, there were some things he could not prevent or cure. Still, when she died, it seemed as if a light had gone out of the world for a while.

She'd left him a fortune, including his house in Edinburgh. Every day, he was grateful for the independence she'd given him.

He saluted the portrait, smiling up at his grandmother.

His grandfather had refused to have the portrait moved anywhere else. Instead, it remained above the mantel here in the library where Douglas Thorburn spent most of his day.

Each generation of his family, despite their individual idiosyncrasies, had been blessed by good marriages. His parents adored each other, and even years after her death—and despite his grandfather's many bed partners—his grandmother was still mourned.

"I wouldn't think that Anne would be all that confusing," Douglas said now.

He pulled himself back to the present. "Anne?"

His grandfather sat back in his chair, eyeing him sharply. "If she's not confusing you, who is?"

"A patient," he answered. Not a patient, though, was she? He'd never examined her, never advised her. Nor had he ever told her he was a physician.

"Is she ill?"

He shook his head. "She's recovering."

"Yet she still troubles you? Why?"

That was the question, wasn't it?

"Are you going to offer for the girl? For Anne?"

Another question he hadn't expected. Mark directed his attention to his grandfather and met the other man's shrewd gaze. He could change the subject, pretend a need to return to Edinburgh this moment, or answer the question honestly.

"I don't know," he said, choosing the truth.

"Do you like her?"

"She's a fine woman," he said.

His grandfather only nodded.

"She's beautiful."

Another nod from his grandfather, this one accompanied by a slight smile.

The uncharacteristic silence from his grandfather annoyed him, made him feel as if he were taking his orals at university.

"I don't know," he repeated.

"Well, you better damn well know," his grandfather said, glaring at his empty glass. "Is what you feel for her strong enough to make it through the bad times? They'll come, you know. You'll lose a patient or a child. You'll make poor decisions or bad judgments. You'll need someone strong enough to stand by your side, someone who'll push you when you need it, and pull you when you can't move another inch."

Before he could speak, his grandfather continued. "Don't think you won't be doing the same for her. You'll hold her when she cries, and try like hell to understand why she's angry. You'll coax her and reason with her, and stand shoulder-to-shoulder with her. You better damn well like her, my boy, because love is ninety percent like and ten percent passion."

"Is that how it was with you and Grandmother? You liked her first?"

"Hell no," his grandfather said with a laugh. "It hit me, pure and simple. I had to have her. Reason didn't have anything to do with it."

He wasn't going to lie to his grandfather, but he'd never felt overwhelmed by passion, at least not with Anne Ferguson. The closest he came to that feeling was the excitement he felt about medicine. Every day brought a new challenge, a new way of battling the odds. He pitted himself against sickness and disease. Romantic entanglements paled beneath the daily life and death struggle.

When he said as much to his grandfather, the older man laughed heartily.

"You haven't met the right woman, my boy."

Unbidden, the sight of a veiled figure came to mind, a woman who seemed to be coaxing him too close to the edge of impropriety. He should tell her who he was. He should demand that she allow him to examine her, instead of continuing this charade, one that had become strangely exciting.

He wasn't about to tell his grandfather about Catriona. The older man would immediately assume there was more to their relationship than physician and patient. That's all it was. If he liked picking at her temper, that was simply a character flaw of his. If he spent too much time wondering at her appearance, that was merely the curiosity that he'd been blessed with since birth.

"Have you heard about the new plan for the Glasgow factory?"

His grandfather hadn't been actively concerned with

the Thorburn business in many years. His father thought it beneath him. Consequently, he'd delegated the authority to a team of excellent managers. Because of them, the company was growing and expanding.

The newest plan, however, concocted by his father, was to put his brothers in charge of the factory.

His grandfather nodded, then stared at his empty glass again.

"I've often heard it said that a fortune will only last three generations," he said. "If your father insists on your brothers taking their places at the factory, I would give it a year before we lose everything. Those fool brothers of yours will make us all bankrupt. I won't be living to see it, thank God."

On that cheery note, his grandfather thrust the empty glass at him. The physician in him measured the whiskey against his patient being seventy-two, and decided that his age alone deserved a celebration.

Dina MacTavish stood in the doorway, staring out at Charlotte Square.

The wind had eased since the night before, creating a calm she didn't trust. Although the air was cold, the day was bright and sparkling. However, the minute she believed winter was done, it was back with a vengeance.

Artis was late again. Where could she be?

Something must be done.

For the longest time, Artis considered herself above the other girls because of the length of her employment. Yet the other girls knew that Artis was no better than they and resented her bossiness. When Artis wasn't complaining to her, the other two were, and the resultant discord among her servants gave her a constant headache.

In the last week, however, Artis had ceased being difficult and had, instead, become invisible. She spent too long on her errands and, worse, was absent from the house on two separate occasions.

When she'd demanded to know the reason, Artis only shrugged and claimed she needed air, that the house had been stifling and her head needed to be cleared. Nor had the girl purported to know why the man had stopped her several days earlier. When she asked what the man had wanted, Artis only shrugged again.

"I can't remember what he said."

"Who was he?"

"I don't know."

When it was evident that was the only answer she would get, she excused the girl. Now, Artis was late again returning from her errand.

What was she going to do about her? She certainly couldn't return her to Old Town. Nor could she recommend her to friends for employment. She was going to have to get answers from Artis.

The day was too busy to have another worry heaped on it.

She needed to fold all the donated clothes and apportion them for various stops throughout Old Town. She promised Reverend Michaels that she would put together a list of names for the newest campaign. She wanted to reserve her seat at the new symposium, a series of lectures on the evils of drink. In addition, she needed to plan for some time to attend to other relationships.

She also needed to write Jean and inform her about Catriona's progress. But what on earth could she say? That things were odd in Edinburgh?

Dr. Thorburn was still masquerading as a footman.

Catriona was still wandering around in a full veil,

when she wasn't sneaking into the kitchen to cook at midnight. What on earth had prompted her to do that?

Perhaps it would be best if she waited to write Jean until there was something good to say. Or, if not something promising, then perhaps less strange.

Chapter 13

True to his word, the footman left her alone. For a week he did exactly as he promised.

At lunch he entered the room, placed the tray on the table, and saluted her smartly before occupying her chair by the window. He opened the curtains, pretending an interest in the view of the carriage house and stables. He remained silent, which grew more onerous as the days passed.

She wanted to hear him talk. Or disturb the tenor of her thoughts, most of which were focused on him and how he looked in his plain white shirt and black trousers.

Today she was even more attuned to his appearance, a fact that irritated her. What was there about him that interested her? He was a handsome man, but she'd known many handsome men.

No doubt he knew his own appeal. However, men with an awareness of their own attractiveness tended to be self-ish lovers.

She almost asked him that question, then remembered that she was Miss Cameron, the poor unfortunate lady struck down in her youth by tragedy. Not Catriona Cameron, tiptoeing on the edge of shocking behavior.

"Aren't you going to speak?" she asked, turning to where he stood beside the window. "I believe the agreement was that you were going to leave me alone while I ate. I've eaten."

He turned his head and studied her as if he could see through the layer of lace shielding her face. What would he say if he could see her?

Looking away was easier, toying with the hem of her veil much more preferable than wondering at the footman's bedroom achievements, lack of them, or his thoughts.

He stacked the dishes on the tray, still speechless, honoring the agreement they'd made. She'd made him promise to be silent, and silent he was.

Why on earth had she insisted on that? She missed his conversation, and wished he would talk to her.

Was she lonely enough to want to converse with a servant?

Yes.

He left, easily opening the door with one hand while supporting the tray with another.

She heard voices and wondered if he'd engaged one of the maids in conversation. Was he flirting with one of them? Were they exchanging stories of their day? Was he as charming to them as she suspected he could be?

Standing, she moved to the door, one hand raised, fingers resting against the wood. She opened the door to find the corridor empty.

He was gone, and so was the opportunity to talk to him.

Someone screamed, the noise so unexpected that she jerked in surprise. She walked as quickly as she could down the corridor to the servants' stair.

To her horror, Isobel lay crumpled at the foot of the steps, moaning.

Artis stood above her, her face expressionless.

"How did this happen?" she asked, passing Artis on the stairs. Because of her knee, she held on tightly to the banister, taking each of the steep curving steps with care until she reached the fallen maid.

Because of the weakness in her leg, she couldn't kneel, but she sat on the lowest step and reached out to the young girl.

"What happened, Isobel?"

The girl's eyes flickered open. "I fell, miss, that's all. I'll be fine in a moment."

She doubted the girl was telling the truth. Isobel was cradling her arm, evidently in pain.

Looking up, she discovered that Artis had disappeared.

She hated feeling helpless. She shouted for help, hoping her aunt heard. Instead of Aunt Dina, however, the footman suddenly appeared from around the corner. He took in the scene with a glance and knelt at Isobel's side.

"Where are you hurt?" he asked.

"I don't know," the girl said weakly. "My arm, I think."

"Did Artis do this to you?" Catriona asked.

The footman sent her a swift look, and she bit back another question. When Isobel looked away, however, she knew the truth.

"Can you sit up?" he asked.

Isobel nodded.

He gently helped her move until she was propped up against the wall. Carefully, he unbuttoned her cuff, then pushed the sleeve up to her elbow.

Isobel cried out only once, when he touched a place on her arm that was rapidly swelling.

"I'm afraid your arm is broken," he said. "I can help you if you'll let me."

Isobel nodded.

"Charm only goes so far, footman," she said, annoyed at the worshipful look Isobel was giving him. "She needs a doctor."

"Why?" he asked, glancing at her. "You won't see a doctor."

She frowned at him. "I don't need one."

"I don't need one either, miss," Isobel said, smiling at the footman. "Mark will help me."

"Mark can hurt you," she said. "What if your arm is not set properly? You won't be able to use it."

"I'll set it properly," he said, standing.

He bent and scooped Isobel up in his arms, her uninjured arm looped around his neck. Before Catriona could voice an objection, he'd disappeared around the corner with the maid.

She sat there for a few moments, uncertain about what she felt. Despite her objections, the footman had taken charge. Isobel was at his mercy, and he arrogantly thought he could fix the girl's arm. Add to that her suspicion that Artis had pushed Isobel down the stairs.

The entire household was in a state of chaos. Things had to change immediately.

She stood and went in search of Aunt Dina.

"**S**he wants you gone," Dina said, sighing. "I'm afraid she was adamant about it."

"I don't doubt she was," Mark said.

They sat in the drawing room, Mark nursing a sherry because Mrs. MacTavish thought he'd looked cold when he arrived from calling on a few patients. The room was blessedly warm, as opposed to the night outside. He was surprised his skin wasn't a shade of blue, and he thought Brody must be near frozen as well.

He paid his driver twice what he could make elsewhere, because of his odd schedule and constant travel, but money couldn't make up for the miserable weather Brody had to endure.

"How is dear Isobel?" Dina asked.

"She's doing fine," he said, putting his glass on the doily on the table and leaning forward.

He laced his hands together loosely, regarding Dina with intensity.

"Her arm will heal quickly," he said. "She'll need to be put on light duty for a while, I'm afraid. A month, at least."

Dina nodded. "But that's not what you meant to say," she said, placing her cup of tea next to his glass. "What is it, Mark?"

"I believe you have a viper in your nest of maids."

She nodded. "Catriona thinks Artis was responsible for Isobel's accident."

"Isobel said that Artis was annoyed and pushed her. Whether the fall was intentional or an accident, the result is the same. Isobel was injured."

"I shall have to do something," she said.

He nodded. "Not everyone can be saved."

"Regrettably, you're right," Mrs. MacTavish said, sighing again. "I can't send the girl back to Old Town, and I can't advance her, either."

She picked up her cup again and took a delicate sip. She frowned at the fireplace, evidently in deep thought. "However, Isobel is a different matter. As soon as her arm has healed, I can go about finding another position for her."

"Kingairgen," he said. "My grandfather's house. They're always looking for staff, and the housekeeper is a kindly woman."

He'd send her there with the proviso that the girl be warned about his grandfather's lecherous impulses. He'd have a word with Isobel himself.

"Are you certain, Mark?" she asked, blinking rapidly.

He looked away, took a sip of his sherry, and fervently prayed she wouldn't begin to weep.

"Reverend Michaels will be glad to know the situation has a happy ending."

"I urge you not to tell him," he said, concerned now.

She looked surprised. "Why ever not?"

Most of the relief given to the poor in Old Town was organized through churches. He'd managed to remain secular for the most part. A great many of his patients didn't like being preached to as payment for a blanket or a hot meal. If Reverend Michaels believed he was a convert, the man would never leave him alone.

"I'd prefer to be anonymous in this instance."

"You're too modest," she said.

"I might say the same about you."

Mrs. MacTavish's good works consisted of not only being excellent at soliciting donations, but in putting that money to the best use. A word to a friend over a pot of tea, and the coffers of a certain church were suddenly larger. A gathering of friends, and two maids had been hired, their prospects significantly better than a month earlier.

She waved away his comments and said, "However, perhaps it was a blessing that Artis did come here."

At his quick glance, she smiled.

"Don't you see? It's Catriona. A month ago she would not have noticed the maids, let alone Artis's behavior. Nor would she have cared." She tapped the tips of her fingers together. "She certainly would not have demanded that you be dismissed."

"Will I be?"

"On no account," she said cheerfully. "I can't wait to see what happens next."

The very reason he should leave as quickly as possible.

Catriona couldn't believe it.

Not only had Aunt Dina refused to dismiss the footman, but the older woman laughed gaily when she insisted upon it.

"Oh, my dear," she'd said. "I couldn't possibly dismiss Mark. He's been too valuable."

Not only that, but she also refused to dismiss Artis.

"If what you say is true," Dina had said, "then I need to counsel the girl."

"You need to send her back where she came from," Catriona told her.

Dina looked shocked.

"You can't be serious, Catriona. That would be tantamount to a death sentence for the poor girl."

She doubted, frankly, that things would be so dire as that. But it seemed as if Dina was determined to retrain Artis.

The maid's new task was to inventory and clean the attic, a duty that evidently didn't please her at all. One morning, she opened her door to find Artis arriving with her tray. The maid slammed it down on the sideboard, scowled at her, and stomped off.

The footman had treated Isobel adequately enough. Her arm was bandaged well and she wore a sling made of soft yellow flannel. The girl spoke of him in a rapturous voice, her eyes misting and an otherworldly smile on her lips.

It was exceedingly annoying, especially since the footman was still bringing her meals, but maintaining his silence. He wouldn't even look at her, but left the moment she finished eating.

Yes, it was exceedingly annoying.

What a strange household they had—misfit maids, an arrogant footman, a too kind employer, and a woman who dressed in black from head to toe.

Perhaps she was the oddest of all of them.

Tonight, the trees stood stiffly beneath the mantle of snow like a forest of guards. The wind snapped at her veil and iced her face. Her lips were nearly numb, but she pressed on, intent on her walk. Her knee protested, stiff with cold, but she determinedly placed one foot in front of the other, wrapping her arms around her waist beneath the cloak.

As soon as she turned the corner, she wouldn't be walking into the full force of the wind. All she had to do was continue a few more steps, twenty at most.

Where was the footman tonight? Was some other woman cooking for him?

She began to count. Numbers were preferable to thoughts of that odious man.

A minute later she'd reached the corner. In spring the trees, with their lush growth, provided a leafy and cool canopy. Now, the icy branches clicked at her like a dozen disapproving maiden aunts.

The night was moonless. The gas lamps had been allowed to go dark, or hadn't been lit this evening. Only a few lights dotted the square, and she wondered what kept people awake.

Did they, too, have servant problems?

As she rounded the next corner, she could see the carriage house. The window of the footman's room was dark. Was he standing there, watching her?

Did he know she was thinking of him? Had Aunt Dina told him that she wanted him dismissed?

"Why can't you simply ask one of your friends to hire him?" she'd asked. "If he's so adept at his tasks, surely he could find another position?"

He had to leave.

Must she be forced to be around him? Must she truly be subjected to his presence? He made her remember things she needed to forget. If she was to live in this new world of hers, she must put away all thoughts of the past, including those earthy pleasures she'd once enjoyed.

What man would have her?

Did men ever consider such things? Did an ugly man ever think that a woman wouldn't have him? Or was a man so blessed simply being a man that the thought never entered his mind?

In London, a fortune went a long way toward making a man attractive.

She had some money put by.

She stumbled to a halt, staring at the darkened window.

To do something like that would truly be forbidden. Scandalous was the word for it, or even wicked. She would be reverting to the foolish, improvident, outrageous girl she'd once been.

What would he say if she offered him money to love her?

Would he tell anyone? Would he send her away? Or take pity on her? She wouldn't accept his pity, but she'd pay for his passion.

Could she do such a thing?

The girl she'd been would have, and laughed at the idea of shocking the world. Now? She hadn't been that girl for a very long time. A year, perhaps, but it seemed like a decade, the distance measured by experience more than time.

Still, the thought beckoned her, taunting her to do the forbidden.

Andrew moved into position, the better to see Catriona on her walk. From where his house was located, he could only view a corner of the square, necessitating that he move to an area where someone might see him. His pulse raced, his stomach rolled, but his smile wouldn't be dampened.

Poor darling Catriona, veiled and hidden from the world. Had the accident ruined her face? He'd tried to find out in London, but no one would talk about her.

If she had been rendered ugly, killing her would be a mercy. She'd no longer have to mourn her looks, and he wouldn't have to endlessly recall her.

She'd be dead, one of those regrets of his life he remembered when he'd had a glass or two of wine. One of those memories that flitted into his life just before sleep. Whatever happened to . . . ? Oh, yes, Catriona. She died.

The rifle was barely concealed beneath his long coat. Anyone studying him would see he walked awkwardly. But no one, except for the two of them, were foolish enough to be in the square on a frigid midnight.

Correction, there were other people present, a laughing group that emerged from a town house on the other side of the square. Andrew kept his gun carefully hidden.

He wasn't entirely certain that he would be able to make a shot in the dark. He could hit a moving target, witness his success in London, but he needed to sight his target first. Only in two places was Catriona visible: at the far side of the square where she normally walked beneath the gaslight that was now dark, and once she'd left the shelter of the lower branches of a giant elm. The latter shot was impossible. The former, he thought he could make. If the gaslight had been lit.

He watched as Catriona kept to the shadows, out of sight of the partygoers.

Tonight was not going to be the night. But one night soon, he'd find a comfortable spot, perhaps on the steps of one of the town houses on this side of the square. He'd wait patiently, sight Catriona, and end the odd and relentless hold she had on him.

However long it took, he'd be patient.

He wasn't there.

Catriona stood in the doorway of the footman's room. She raised her veil to see the outlines of a long and narrow bed, a small bedside table, and a straight-back chair. Instead of an armoire, a line of pegs stretched along the wall near the door.

She went to the bedside table that held a small oil lamp and lit it, holding it high. What did she expect to find? A selection of reading materials, or a picture of a beloved?

No one lived here. Not one garment hung on the racks. Not one personal object was left behind.

Had she won, after all? Had the footman been dismissed?

Her throat tightened and she was ridiculously close to tears. She was tired, that was all. It was after midnight and she stood alone in a cold room with only thoughts of lust to warm her.

He was gone, and she regretted it more than she could say.

Chapter 14

"Where do you live?" Catriona asked when he entered her room the next day.

Afternoon had come and gone, and evening was fast approaching. His day had been filled with one emergency after another, and he'd come here for one reason—to put an end to this charade.

He put the tray down on the table. Their minds followed the same course, evidently.

Today would be the last day he served her. Today he would say good-bye to the woman who fascinated him to the exclusion of his common sense and even to his patients.

She stood at the window, her back to him. A black cloud against the green curtains.

"It's not here," she said, turning to face him.

"Does it matter?" he asked.

Now, he would tell her now, but the words didn't form.

"Are you my aunt's lover?"

The question so shocked him that he could only blink at her.

"Is that what you think?"

"What else is there to think?" she said. "I went to your

room, but you weren't there. At that hour of the night, where were you?"

"Why did you go to my room, Catriona?"

She didn't answer. Instead, she said, "At first I thought you'd been dismissed. I told myself that's what it was. I told myself that if you came today, it was something else. You had to have found another bed in which to sleep. Was it with my aunt?"

"Why did you come to my room?"

"Are you my aunt's lover?"

"I respect your aunt," he said. "But I'm not her lover."

"Artis?" she asked. "Isobel? Elspeth?"

He shook his head. "None of them."

Tell her, now.

Instead, he remained silent, trapped by curiosity and something else.

He took a step toward her.

"What were you doing in my room?"

She backed up one step. "It isn't your room. It belongs to Aunt Dina. Or, more properly, my brother-in-law."

"At the moment, however, it belongs to me."

He folded his arms, studying her. He wanted to strip the veil from her and look his fill. Not, however, as a physician, and that was just one reason why he should leave now.

"You're not living here," she said. "Why are you pretending to?"

"Why did you go to my room?"

She slapped her hands down on her skirts. "I was curious."

For the first time since he entered the room, he smiled. She was lying.

"Do I amuse you?" she asked.

"Every day," he said. "Why were you there?"

"Where were you sleeping?"

"You have a way of never answering a question, did you know that?"

"It's one I learned from you," she said, then shook her head. "You are not a good influence. I become a child around you."

"Do you?" He took another step. "Or do you revert to your true self?"

"Are you trying to insult me?"

He wanted to laugh. "Is that an insult?"

"What does my aunt have you doing that takes you away in the morning?"

"Does it matter?" he asked, reaching her.

He gripped the edge of her veil, and she pulled his hand free.

"Tell me, is your face red? Aren't you embarrassed to be asking all these personal questions of a simple footman?"

"There's nothing simple about you," she said. "I doubt you're a footman."

"Oh yes, you called me a confidence man. Have I gained your confidence, Catriona?"

She took another step backward.

"I'm not a virgin."

He stopped, startled. Of all the things she might have said, he hadn't expected that.

"I've known passion," she added.

He stayed where he was. She had squared her shoulders and looked as if she were preparing for battle.

"Is there a reason you're telling me this?"

"Have I shocked you?"

He was a physician; little shocked him.

"No," he said, "but in the last five minutes you've managed to confound and confuse me."

"You're a handsome man," she said. "Surely you've bedded your share of women."

"Are you asking for a list?"

She continued without answering. "I'm willing to make it worth your while."

No, she hadn't just confused him, she'd stripped the words from him. For a long moment he could only stare at her.

When she remained quiet as well, turning to peer between the curtains again, he moved closer.

"Are you asking what I think you're asking?"

She nodded. "I'm willing to pay you to bed me."

Every thought flew out of his mind. He remained silent, too fascinated by her proposition to move.

"You would have to keep it a secret, however, and leave Aunt Dina's employ soon after."

"You don't wish to be reminded of your mistake, is that it?"

She shook her head. "You aren't a mistake, footman. You're a temptation."

He had to leave now, before he took her up on her invitation. His body, long celibate, was warming at her words.

His mind was splitting into two divisions. One side whispered that if it was something she wanted, who was he to refuse? The other, nobler side, shouted at him to remember that this had originally been a ruse to help her. Not a masquerade to gain a bed partner.

She wasn't a virgin.

She wanted to pay him.

Who was to say she wouldn't solicit someone else, someone not as honorable? Someone who would talk of this episode?

Someone not him?

"What do you say?"

"I say I've never been offered such an interesting proposition."

"Are you going to rebuff me? If you are, I wish you'd do so quickly, before I humiliate myself further."

"Frankly, I don't know what I'm going to do," he said, spearing his hand through his hair.

"What do you want to do?"

"Take you to your bed and keep you there for a day or two."

There, more honesty than the situation warranted.

She turned again, clasping her hands in front of her.

"You see, we do have a problem," she said.

"Is that what this is?"

"We have some level of attraction for each other."

Was she asking if he lusted for her? What a damn difficult question to answer. It would certainly explain why he thought about her entirely too much, that he was here when he had other patients who needed him more.

She wasn't his patient, he reminded himself.

Slowly, she closed the distance between them and placed one hand flat against his shirt. He could feel the warmth of her palm even through his clothing. He was cold, or at least had been until a few moments ago.

"Yes or no?" she asked. "I won't beg."

What the hell was he going to say?

"Are you married? Have you taken a vow of celibacy?"

"No to both questions."

She turned and would've walked away had he not grabbed her by the upper arm. She froze, as if unfamiliar with another person's touch.

"Catriona," he said.

What else he might have said was lost in a surge of tenderness. She waited for him to repudiate her when it was the last thing he wanted to do.

She bent her head, her veil hanging low. Wreathed in black lace, she might've been anyone. If he hadn't seen her before, would he have been as fascinated?

"I've never been hired for the night before," he said.

"Nor have I ever hired anyone," she said, turning. "However, there are a few rules I must insist on."

"What would those be?"

"You are not to touch me above the neck. Nor are you to attempt to lift my veil at any time."

"I can't kiss you, then?"

She pulled free, standing with her back to him. "No," she said, after a full minute had passed. "No kisses. On my mouth."

"You realize that leaves myriad possibilities," he said. Was he seriously contemplating this?

"Are you a good lover?"

"I'd be a fool to say I wasn't."

"You'd be a braggart if you aren't."

"Are you sure you're not a virgin?"

"I'm certain," she said. "Does it matter?"

"Yes," he said, smiling. "It matters a great deal."

"You'd bed me if I was experienced, but not if I were a virgin?"

"I don't think I should bed you under any circumstances," he said.

"Do you want more money?" She named an amount, one that would have kept a family of four for a week, maybe two, in Old Town.

"The amount is enough," he said. "But why me? You've not hesitated to express your antipathy toward me."

"Nor you toward me. But is it necessary that I like you in order to bed you?"

"Then this is definitely not a transaction of the heart?"

"Don't be absurd," she said. "I have no fondness

toward you at all. In fact, I'm sure I dislike you intensely. However, you are well formed, and handsome. I've already admitted feeling attraction. Therefore, I believe you would give me a certain amount of pleasure."

"Is that so?"

"Unless, of course, you are inept at the act. If you are, it's best to confess that now, I think."

"Are you experienced enough," he asked, "that you would know the difference?"

"Why do you sound so Presbyterian?"

"Perhaps because I've never been purchased for the night."

"If you're good enough," she said, "you might consider that occupation rather than being a footman."

"I'll think about it," he said. "Only, of course, if I received a recommendation from you."

"I don't actually think people recommend other people, do you? For example, during one of Aunt Dina's teas, can you imagine Mrs. MacDonald standing up and saying, 'I truly do think you should try out dear old Mark. His stamina is amazing and he kisses like a devil.'"

"The stamina is true," he said, smiling again. "Pity you won't get a chance to try out my kisses."

"Are you amused?"

"Since I knocked on your door, I've been insulted, amazed, confounded, annoyed, and now? Yes, I'm amused."

She didn't say anything for a moment. When she did speak, he was surprised at her words.

"My bedroom is warmer."

Turning, she left the sitting room, leaving him two choices. The first would be to leave.

He followed her to the doorway.

She sat on the edge of the bed facing him.

"Very well," she said. "Where shall we begin?"

"I thought you said you've done this before."

"I have," she said. "However, I was not veiled at the time. I began with kisses, but since that isn't possible, we shall have to begin in a different way."

"What way is that?"

"Will you touch my breasts? They've always been sensitive."

By God, she was serious. Up until this second he'd half expected her ploy to be a trick, some type of feint to get him dismissed. Or, at the least, to hold him up to ridicule. But she was beginning to unfasten the jet buttons of her bodice.

He watched her unfasten the busk of her corset, then work on the waistband of her skirt, before moving to the tabs of her petticoat.

For the life of him, he couldn't move. Instead, he remained silent, watching.

When she was down to her shift, she stood, then turned her back. Slowly, she pulled the shift over her head, keeping the veil in place.

"You needn't wear your veil with me," he said.

She didn't answer, merely pulled down the sheets and two blankets on the bed, crawled inside, and tucked herself there, waiting.

He was a physician. He'd tried to be her physician, but she'd fought him at every turn. Therefore, she wasn't his patient. There, he'd assuaged his conscience enough.

He unbuttoned and then removed his shirt. His shoes were next, followed by his trousers. By the time he removed his socks, he was conscious of the cold air. He could see his breath, or was that only because he was panting at this point?

Naked, he stoked the fire, then crawled into bed with her. Reaching his arm under her, he gathered her to him.

Gently, he pulled the veil away from her shoulder. When she tensed, he smoothed the hem away from her skin, brushing his fingers over the curve of her arm. He murmured something conciliatory. He wasn't sure exactly what he said, being consumed by the feel of her, soft, warm, and womanly, curves in all the most glorious places.

She smelled of roses, which was impossible in wintry Edinburgh. Her breasts were full, the nipples hard against his chest like spears of desire.

The sight of her in the firelight, naked but for a coral glow, stilled his breath. He rolled her back on his arm, then bent to place a kiss gently between her breasts.

Although he wasn't as experienced as she probably wanted, he could muddle through well enough. First, he needed to contain his excitement, the heady surge of pure lust that hit him in that moment.

He was no longer cold.

He wanted to spend hours on her breasts. First, this pretty little nipple with its pebbly aureole. How tight it got when he licked it. Then the exquisite soft plumpness of her breast deserved a kiss and a nuzzle.

The sighs she made spurred him on, encouraged him to explore with lips and stroking fingertips. The flesh beneath her breasts received a kiss, as did the spot on each side of one breast. She rewarded him with a nearly inaudible gasp, but he was so close, so attuned to her, that he knew the exact second she began to tremble.

She was as he'd always imagined her, exquisitely and perfectly formed. He kissed the curve of her shoulder, trailing a line of kisses down her arm to her wrist. A part of him not awash in pleasure made note of the bulging scar near her elbow and the one on her leg. He put his observations away to study later, loath to do anything to change the pattern of her rapidly escalating breathing.

Raising up on his right arm, he used his left hand to measure the curve from breast to waist to hip. She must know how beautiful she was. Had other men praised her? Had her other lovers been as enthralled as he felt at this moment?

He was glad she wasn't a virgin, but there was one responsibility he still needed to assume.

"I would not have you bear a child from this night, Catriona."

She placed her hand on his shoulder. "I know how to protect myself," she said.

He remained still a moment, wondering at the sudden anger he felt. Was it because she'd freely admitted to being experienced? Or because he knew he was only an interlude, one she paid to have?

If that was the case, she was damn well going to get her money's worth.

He pulled back the blankets and sheet. Her arm lay on her hip, and for a moment, he just looked at the sight of Catriona's nude body in the faint light from the fire.

The veil added a forbidden tinge to the picture, as if she were incognito, a woman indulging in sex against all the rules and commandments she'd been taught.

He leaned over and kissed her breast, mouthing a nipple, pulling gently, then harder, until she made a sound at the back of her throat.

With one hand, he pushed her onto her back, rising over her.

"I want to make you moan," he whispered, the declaration almost a threat. "I want to make you scream."

"A battle joined, is that it, footman?" she asked with a quaver in her voice.

"My name is Mark," he said, bending to tease her breast. "Say it."

She remained stubbornly silent as he grazed her nipple with the edge of his teeth.

"Mark," she murmured, her body arching, demanding.

He smiled, satisfied.

She was his. Catriona Cameron, beauty, termagant, spoiled, willful, surprising, ever-changing, was his, if only for tonight.

His hand gently palmed her, fingers exploring that sweet spot between her legs. She made a soft moaning sound.

The flat of his hand pressed against her, one finger gliding through swollen folds. She widened her legs, her hands gripping his shoulders.

"Beautiful," he whispered.

Lust harnessed his breath, made his heart pound. When she gripped him tighter, he smiled.

She was wet for him.

He placed a kiss between her breasts and in a line down her belly to the nest of soft, curly hair. His fingers explored her, parted her, grew intimate with each fold and soft indentation.

Slowly, he slipped a finger inside her, paused, withdrew, and entered her again, each time taking minutes when his own body counseled that he mount her now.

Her legs widened still farther. He smiled into a kiss on her belly, his fingers leading the way for his mouth.

"Mark!"

He broke off his amorous attack to look at her. She was supported on both elbows, and although the veil shielded her expression, he knew she was shocked.

"I thought you said you've had lovers."

"I have."

"Then you've had staid lovers, Miss Cameron."

He pushed her back on the bed and went back to his task of driving her mad with passion.

Her fingers drummed a tattoo on his shoulders. Later, he would teach her to reciprocate, even though he had his suspicions she knew how to do that well enough.

Her fingernails were like talons. He spared a second of thought for the pain in his shoulder, then realized it was nothing compared to the discomfort his impatient erection was causing.

"Mark." Her voice had changed to liquid silk, giving his name two syllables.

Drawing back, he looked at her, legs spread, arms outstretched, a rosy flush encompassing her belly and chest, right up to those fiercely standing nipples. He rose up and kissed each, then entered her in one fluid motion.

She moaned a welcome, tightening and trembling around him. Pleasure coursed through his body and danced along his spine. His toes tingled and he smiled in a wordless expression of bliss.

He'd never considered himself a sensual person, but he rode it now, entering Catriona with deliberate slowness, pulling out with the same enforced delayed pace.

She arched beneath him, then pulled him closer, her breath harsh and rasping in his ear, her grip on his buttocks demanding.

When she shuddered around him, he waited, propping himself on his forearms, nearly insensate from her pulsing grip around his erection. He needed to kiss her, wanted to praise her. Instead, he leaned forward, kissed her breasts, and slowly began to move again.

Long minutes later she moaned again, a long, drawn-out sound that was accompanied by his release.

For a few moments his mind was deadened by pleasure, his senses reeling.

His conscience had been silenced by satisfaction until only a small and inconsequential remnant remained.

Chapter 15

Catriona awoke later than usual, the time between dreaming and full wakefulness spent in a haze of thoughts. What day was it? What time was it? What had she dreamed?

She stretched, feeling better than she could remember for a long time. Her breasts felt full, and between her legs there was an unaccustomed ache.

It wasn't a dream, though, was it?

Mark had left hours ago. She'd sat up, watched him dress, then reached into the drawer of her bedside table.

"Your payment," she'd said, handing him a small drawstring bag.

He'd looked as if he wanted to speak, but he only nodded, taking the bag from her and tucking it into his jacket.

After he left, closing the door of her sitting room, she'd removed her veil, put on her nightgown, and dozed for a while.

Now she sat up, feeling the chilled air on her face. These moments after first waking were always the most liberated of her day. For these precious minutes, she needn't don her veil and could pretend the accident hadn't happened, that she wasn't scarred, but the Catriona she'd always been.

The room was cold, the fire only a few orange and gray coals. Her thick flannel nightgown kept her warm, as did the memories of last night.

What a fool she'd been. What a silly, arrogant, idiotic fool. She'd played a child's game and received an adult's reward, enough shame to keep her cheeks hot for the whole of the day.

He'd been a magnificent lover. He touched her with delicacy, as if he'd rarely known a woman's body. He held himself back, ensuring that she reached her peak not once, but twice. The sensations were so exquisite she'd been reduced to tears.

Unfortunately, he'd noticed.

"Are you crying?" he asked, fitting himself next to her on the narrow bed.

"No," she said.

"You are crying," he said. "I can hear you."

She abruptly sat up, pushing him away when he reached for her.

"No," she said, carefully rearranging her veil. "I'm not crying. Don't be ridiculous."

"Did I please you?" he asked.

"Yes," she said. "I'd be happy to provide any recommendations, should you require them."

He'd placed his hand on the small of her back, trailing it up beneath the veil. His hand was so large and warm.

"Must your veil be so long? Couldn't you use a shorter version?"

"Are you offering advice on fashion now, footman?" she asked.

"You called me Mark earlier," he said.

She felt a tremor race through her.

"That was earlier."

"Why were you crying?"

She bent her head. She hadn't answered him then, and she wasn't sure she'd be able to now.

He wouldn't be bringing her breakfast tray, at least. She'd only have to worry about seeing him at noon and this evening. If she could make it through the day in her usual way, he'd understand that last night was an aberration, a foolish act by a woman who'd been desperately lonely.

He'd served a purpose, and one in which he performed magnificently. What a pity that she could never tell him. Or never express her gratitude toward him. He'd misunderstand, perhaps assume that she wanted to continue their liaison.

Of course she didn't.

She was wiser now. She'd learned that society can accept a philandering man with greater alacrity than it would a woman with loose morals.

Catriona Cameron, sister-in-law of the Earl of Denbleigh, would be a ripe target for the gossips. *Poor thing, she not only lost her looks, but her mind. She's having an affair with a footman, of all things. A footman!*

She could hear the tittering laughter now.

No, Mark must understand, immediately, that she had no intention of repeating last night. He must forget that she'd begun this liaison, as would she. Or perhaps she would store the memory of last night in a special spot. Where, though? In the place she put all indescribable wonders and delicious delights? Or in a spot marked "Caution, do not examine too closely"?

Last night had been truly wondrous, and she'd enjoyed every moment of her own debauchery. Enough to wish that she needn't deny herself the pleasure of his company.

Nevertheless, she must, and he had to understand that immediately.

If she felt a rush of eagerness, it was only because she wished to explain it to him as soon as possible.

That was all it was.

He had already called himself fifty kinds of a fool today. Brody hadn't said anything the last time he made that remark. Evidently, his driver agreed.

Because of his dislike for closed spaces, Mark lowered the windows, and even though the weather was bitterly cold, he bundled up against it, preferring a winter storm to the feeling of being buried alive.

Snow covered everything, and what wasn't covered with snow was iced over. Brody took the roads slowly, making the distance to the home of Catriona's sister seem interminable.

He fervently hoped the earl was in residence, and had been assured by Mrs. MacTavish that he would be.

However, people could be wrong, and since this journey had been an exercise in chaos, it wouldn't have surprised him to encounter frustration at its destination.

They'd lost a wheel this morning, and Brody was concerned about one of the horses. No doubt they would stay at an inn tonight, and he prayed for warmth and a lot of food.

He was hungry, mildly annoyed, and cold.

Why, then, was he here?

Perhaps it was because of the notes he'd received from Catriona's London physician. The barely legible scrawls were a masterpiece of obfuscation. Not one word about the initial injuries. Had the nerves in her arm been damaged? Why did she limp so badly? What was the extent of the injuries there? Had her leg been twisted beneath her? Or had broken glass severed a tendon or muscle? Instead, the man had whined on and on about Catriona's color, temperature, and attitude. Evidently, she'd vented her dislike for him and he'd been surprised by her complaints.

Over the years, Mark had discovered that a patient's will to live was as important as his physical recovery. He was treating one widow right now who concerned him greatly. Her two children had predeceased her, and she'd commented on numerous occasions how much she missed her husband. If anyone talked herself into the grave, it would be Mrs. MacRae.

He didn't want Catriona to do the same.

But he knew this journey had less to do with being a physician than being a man.

After loving her, he'd lain beside her, waiting for her cutting remarks. Instead, she wept, then denied it. Her grief had bothered him, and gnawed at him still.

He wanted to know her, to understand her, and perhaps that was the real reason he'd decided to come to Ballindair.

A person was known by those who surrounded him. A person's character was revealed by those he loved. What better source to learn about Catriona than her sister?

"I'm sorry, miss, but I haven't seen him. Mrs. MacTavish says he'll be gone several days."

"Thank you, Elspeth," she said.

The maid put her tray on the table, then stepped back.

"Is there anything I can do for you, miss?"

"No, thank you," she said.

The girl looked at her strangely before leaving, closing the door softly behind her.

Catriona walked into the bedroom and stood looking at her carefully made bed.

At Ballindair, Jean fussed about the pillows, wishing the earl had spent more money for the comfort of his servants. Now that her sister was a countess, had she thought of such things?

Where was he?

Had he quit?

Her stomach clenched.

Had he been so disgusted by bedding her that he'd left? Dear God, what if he had? What if she never saw him again?

Her life would be blessed by that fact.

She'd never again be bothered by that foolish man arguing with her at her meals. She wouldn't have to fuss with trying to eat while wearing her veil. Nor would she be distracted by his appearance.

She took a few steps toward the bed, reached out and smoothed the pillow with her left hand. He'd slept here for a few hours.

A man with his appearance had to have women lusting after him. How many women had he bedded? How many of them were foolish enough to yearn for him? How many were stupid enough to feel sadness at his absence?

Surely she wasn't the only one?

Andrew's secretary was an able-bodied and intelligent sort, who had the added benefit of being curiously uncurious. Not once had the man ever asked the reason for his whereabouts. His secretary merely forwarded his mail, performed his assigned duties, and kept his discreet mouth firmly shut.

Simply put, the man did as he was told.

Now, if he could only convince his wife to do the same, his life would be a great deal more enjoyable.

He studied Elizabeth's latest letter, the third he'd received in less than a fortnight. Any of his other correspondence was of more import than this missive of complaint. He'd never known Elizabeth to be so quarrelsome, and her pettiness couldn't come at a worse time.

The roof was leaking.

She needed a new gardener.

The children were misbehaving and neither the nurse nor the governess could discipline them.

The tutor for the oldest boy had unexpectedly quit.

Where was he? Why hadn't he answered her letters?

Had the silly woman forgotten their last parting? Perhaps another reminder of Morgan MacCraig's divorce might be adequate enough to silence her.

He contemplated that thought while staring through the front window of his bedroom, the only chamber he'd equipped to any degree. Since he'd be selling the house soon enough, there weren't any plans for more furnishings. The bed was comfortable, the fire adequate, the reading chair the equal of any of his furniture in London. The bench beside the window held his most prized possession, his rifle.

The fireplace was large enough to warm the room, and the wooden floors were polished to a shine. The town houses of Charlotte Square were in great demand. This house's only drawback was that it didn't provide a view of Catriona's home. Even so, he'd paid half again as much as the place was worth.

His plans were firming up, his knowledge of Catriona's schedule increasing each time he met with that insufferable maid. He knew, exactly, when the deed would be done. This time he wouldn't miss. This time he wouldn't have to contend with fog. This time he'd do what he set out to do nearly a year ago.

The knocking on the kitchen door was loud enough to set the neighbors to gossiping.

He bit back an oath and descended the stairs. His need for secrecy had resulted in only hiring one servant, a part-time maid with some culinary skill. She wasn't here now, so he was forced to open the door to the artless Artis.

She thrust herself into the kitchen with the grace of a lust-ridden bull.

"She's no better than she should be," Artis said. "That Miss Cameron pretends to be all ladylike, but she's in heat like the rest of the animals."

Andrew held himself still. "What do you mean?"

"Her and the footman. I saw her leave his room the other night. She, with her airs of being better than any of us. Telling me what to do and how to treat others."

He took a deep breath and walked across the room, the sound of his boots echoing against the floor.

"Tell me about the footman," he said casually, opening one of the shutters over the kitchen window.

"Him, he's as bad as she is. He comes and goes as he pleases, and Mrs. MacTavish thinks he's better than cream."

"He's new?"

"Aye," she said. "New and unskilled. I've yet to see him do anything around the house. All he does is talk to Mrs. MacTavish, spend time with her in her room, and he set Isobel's arm. He doesn't even sleep where the rest of us do. Instead, he has a room over the carriage house."

He turned to face Artis. The woman's face was twisted in an expression that mirrored her disgust with the world. Did she ever smile? He doubted it, and he didn't care.

"She goes to his room?"

She nodded.

"Saw her come out of it myself the other night. Sneaking around like the rest of us wouldn't know."

He tried for a smile and failed.

"They all watch me now after the accident." Her chin firmed and her eyes narrowed. "It wasn't my fault the stupid girl fell. I don't know how much longer I can stay there."

Returning to his bedroom, he opened the strongbox and retrieved some coins. Once back in the kitchen, he didn't drop the money into her extended hand until she was looking at him.

"I'd like you to stay for a few more weeks," he said. "As always, in a confidential capacity."

Her glance faltered at his look, but she nodded.

"A few weeks," she said.

Now his smile was genuine.

Chapter 16

Jean Cameron MacCraig arranged the throw around her lower body, hoping that she looked presentable enough to see Dr. Thorburn. As a physician, surely he was familiar with the sight of a female in the family way, even one as far along as she.

She'd read somewhere that an elephant carries her baby two years before it gives birth. Right now she felt an affinity for a female elephant. She lumbered when she walked, and when she sat in certain chairs, she required the services of two people to help her rise. She'd lost the ability to see her feet, but her ankles felt swollen. Each morning, Morgan helped her on with her slippers, and each morning, he teased her before bending to kiss her protruding belly.

The room in which she sat was called, prosaically, the Garden Parlor. She had nicknamed it the Yellow Room, for the abundance of yellow in every fabric, from the silk draperies on the tall windows to the flowered upholstery fabric. The yellow theme was even replicated in the large round carpet, with blowsy yellow flowers blooming along the edge.

All in all, it was a cheery room, and a warm one even in the depths of winter. Morgan had been profligate in insisting that a fire blaze in every room she occupied. For the sake of their finances, she remained in the Yellow Room, the library, or in the Countess's Suite.

Morgan had been foolish there, too, insisting they move out of the Laird's Tower and back into the main part of the castle, since he was concerned about drafts. She hadn't wanted to hurt his feelings by telling him that all of Ballindair was drafty to some degree. As long as he was with her, she agreed to reside in the Countess's Suite until their child was born.

After that, however, they were going to occupy the Laird's Tower again. To offset Morgan's complaints, she'd ordered new, heavier curtains and directed the carpenter to install shutters on all the windows of the tower.

Contrary to custom, she was going to raise their child herself, not turn him over to a nurse. She'd converted a corner of their bedchamber into a small nursery.

When she'd said as much, Morgan only kissed her and held her, making her once again think that the world was a great and wondrous place, as long as he was in it.

She wished he were there right now, but he was supervising the snow removal from the outer buildings. Otherwise, a few of the roofs might collapse.

Wiggling into a better position was difficult, but she managed it. For some reason, she couldn't remain in the same place for more than five minutes.

She couldn't pray that the time passed quickly, because such an entreaty might harm their child. She simply had to be patient. For that reason, when she learned that Dr. Thorburn had arrived last night, she'd been delighted.

Any diversion was welcome, even if it came from Edinburgh.

No, especially if it came from Edinburgh.

Dr. Thorburn had been given the famous Ballindair hospitality, installed in one of the guest suites, and warmed and fed. The same had been done for his driver, and the horses that bravely carried them through the snow.

This morning she'd sent word that she would like to speak to him, and Aunt Mary had arrived a moment ago, saying that he would attend them both soon.

"He gave me this," Mary said, handing her a letter from Dina MacTavish introducing the doctor.

Dr. Thorburn has been caring for Catriona, but has questions I cannot answer. I trust you will welcome him as he proceeds with his inquiries.

What questions did he have? What did he want to know?

Her letters from Catriona, although always eagerly welcomed, didn't tell her much. What Catriona decided to divulge to her was one thing; the truth was another.

When the knock came, she wiggled into another position, then nodded to her aunt, who went to the door and opened it, standing aside and ushering Dr. Thorburn into the sitting room.

"Dr. Thorburn," she said, holding out her hand. He took in her appearance in one glance and smiled as he approached her.

She had always thought Morgan was the most handsome man she'd ever seen. But this man was nearly so. She was to be excused if her heart beat faster. Even in her condition, she was female, and no female could ignore Dr. Thorburn's masculinity.

"This is my aunt, Mrs. MacDonald," she said. "Mrs. MacTavish says you have questions for us."

He nodded, smiling. "If you have the time."

"Of course. But first tell us about Catriona," she said. "Is she well?"

He waited until her aunt was seated, then took a chair opposite her.

"How is she?" Aunt Mary asked.

Dr. Thorburn looked as if he were struggling for words. They both waited. Was her aunt feeling as impatient? She wanted answers, and it was all too obvious the physician was attempting to be tactful rather than prompt in his response.

"I have seen improvement in her," he said.

"Is she eating?" Jean asked. "The letters from my husband's aunt were troubling. They made it sound as if Catriona had not only lost her appetite, but her spirit."

"She is eating," he said. "As well as regaining some of her spirit," he added with a smile. "Although I've never seen the lack of it."

"That is indeed good news," Aunt Mary said. She looked down at her hands, then back at the doctor. "But if she is improving, may I ask why you've come all this way?"

"I've discovered that sometimes the best way to learn about a patient is from his friends or family."

"I'm not sure Catriona has many friends," Jean said. "Other than me."

"Why is that?" he asked.

"Perhaps I misspoke," she said. "Catriona had a great many acquaintances. People wanted to be around her. She's personable when she wishes to be."

He didn't say anything, merely concentrated on his hands, draped in front of him.

"I take it Catriona has not shown her personable side to you, Dr. Thorburn?"

He smiled, the expression making her heart beat faster.

"Your sister and I have had a great many disagreements about a great many things," he said. "She hasn't had an opportunity to be charming."

That was surprising. Normally, Catriona charmed everyone, especially a handsome man.

"She's been a different person since London," she said. "It must be difficult for her. She has always been the most beautiful creature."

"Have you seen her since the accident?" he asked.

She nodded. "I traveled to London to be with her."

"Is there much scarring?"

Surprised, she asked, "Have you not examined her yourself?"

He smiled again. "That is only one of the points on which your sister and I disagree."

"To answer your question, I was so shocked when I first saw her that I was afraid of crying out. She saw my reaction anyway. I told her, then, and again in Edinburgh, that she was fortunate to be alive. I doubt she feels the same."

He looked away, toward the long line of windows framed by the bright yellow curtains. The yellow of the curtains against the gray day made Jean think about her own determined optimism against the despair that Catriona must be feeling.

"She is a spoiled and selfish creature," Aunt Mary said in the silence. "But she is a darling girl, for all of that. Catriona is a contradiction, and she always has been. She's lazy when it suits her and industrious when it pleases her. She can be charming or she can be cutting. She blows hot and cold, Dr. Thorburn, but rarely does she blow warm."

The sound of his laughter surprised Jean, but she couldn't help but smile in response to it.

"I have found her to be exactly that, Mrs. MacDonald.

She is passionate about what she likes and what she dislikes, and I suspect she would fight to the death for either."

"If only she felt the same way about her own survival, Dr. Thorburn," Jean said. "If she did, I would be more positive about her future."

"What future do you want for her?" he asked.

She moved to get comfortable, giving his question some thought.

"To know that people love her. That we love her no matter what. Yes, she sometimes behaves abominably when she feels cornered, but she's still my sister. I love her. Nothing she does will ever change that."

"What makes her feel cornered?" he asked.

"Ridicule," she said, startled that the answer came so quickly. "She doesn't like to be called names."

He nodded, and she had the oddest feeling that he was mentally noting all her comments. Would he put them to paper later?

"Do you think Catriona was affected by your parents' death?"

He did ask the most amazing questions.

A moment passed before Jean asked, "You know the story, then?"

He nodded but didn't comment further.

"At the time, we were both so desperate to survive that I didn't notice," she said. "It was only later that I realized something had broken inside Catriona. Perhaps it was hope, or the belief that things would always turn out right. Whatever it was, yes, I think our parents' death affected her greatly."

When he didn't speak, she continued. "We were labeled 'the Murderer's Girls,' and singled out on the street. Someone had made up a song about what our father had done, and children lost no opportunity to repeat it." In the silence, she repeated the words, never having been able to forget them.

> *"Old Doc Cameron went upstairs*
> *When everyone was unawares*
> *He gave poison to his wife*
> *And killed the love of his life.*
> *He was hanged for his crime*
> *Calling her name the whole time.*
> *Yet now they're parted, I've heard tell*
> *She's in Heaven and he's in Hell."*

Aunt Mary leaned over and patted her clasped hands in a wordless gesture of compassion.

Her tears were for her parents and perhaps her younger self and Catriona. "I'm sorry, Countess."

She nodded.

"So am I," Morgan said, striding into the room. "This meeting is done, I'm afraid, Doctor. My wife is tired."

Morgan wanted her to rest all the time, but at this moment she welcomed him with gratitude and a profound sense of relief.

As Mary MacDonald stood, Mark did as well. He understood, immediately, that the earl was protective of his wife. The man stood in front of Jean, a hand outstretched toward her. Jean clutched a throw that poorly concealed her condition, a look of embarrassment on her face.

"You and I will speak in my library," the earl said. Not a request as much as a command, and one he was tempted to refuse. However, he was the man's guest and had come to Ballindair for the express purpose of learning more about Catriona.

Or perhaps he was here to expunge his guilt.

As Mark followed the earl down the corridor, it oc-curred to him that Catriona's rooms in Edinburgh were smaller than the suite he'd been given at Ballindair, yet he'd never felt that sense of confinement there. Was it be-cause he was so fixated on her, rather than the size of the room? That was something he would need to explore later.

The earl entered a large, two-story library, marched to a massive carved desk, and turned to face him.

Morgan MacCraig was every inch a peer at the moment, as stuffy, Mark thought, as his father, and as arrogant. But Morgan didn't know that he wasn't intimi-dated by rank. When he faced death each day, what was a title?

"Why are you here, Dr. Thorburn? My wife is foolishly protective of Catriona. What has her sister done now?"

The Countess of Denbleigh wasn't the only one protec-tive of Catriona, if the surge of irritation he felt was to be believed. He pushed past it, wondered if he should tell the earl the truth, and settled for half measures.

"It's not what she's done," he said, "but what I've done." He told the earl of his pretense, carefully omitting the night he and Catriona had spent together. "I didn't know what else to do, since your aunt was adamant some-thing was wrong with her."

Morgan went and sat behind his desk, motioning for him to take an adjoining chair. "What did you find?"

"A woman desperately in need of purpose," he said. "Someone who'd decided to die, possibly. Or was simply wasting away."

To his credit, the earl looked disturbed. "After the accident, I never saw her," he said. "Catriona wouldn't allow it. My wife was shattered at her appearance and wouldn't stop crying for days." The earl glanced at him. "I won't have her upset."

"She's near her time."

"That's not why. I don't want her upset under any conditions or circumstances." Morgan concentrated on the tooled leather blotter before him, touching the small brass nails with a fingertip. "I can't abide seeing her weep."

He nodded, understanding.

"She was a beautiful girl. Catriona. She was, possibly, the most beautiful woman I've ever seen. Beauty, however, is not a mark of character, and Catriona's character was woefully lacking."

When Mark didn't comment, the earl smiled. "You've seen a different side of her, perhaps."

"I've seen a desperately unhappy woman," he said. "Angry at the world."

"She would be, though, wouldn't she? She was damn lucky to have survived the accident."

"How did it happen?"

The earl shot him a quick look. "I take it Catriona doesn't speak of it."

"I doubt she would, but I haven't asked."

"There's a mystery there, but I've never gotten to the bottom of it. I expect, in your ruse, that you'd be better suited."

He frowned, not understanding.

"The carriage driver in Edinburgh is the same one from London," the earl said.

"I didn't know. I'll make a point of speaking to him." He would, as soon as he returned to Edinburgh.

"I've never seen a man so distraught over the death of a horse. Had to put the horse down himself. Evidently, the animal was badly injured when the carriage turned over. A wretched accident, all in all. A girl died. But according to my wife, Catriona doesn't feel the least grateful for having survived."

"People don't, I've noticed," he said. "Not when they're in the throes of a crisis. They simply want to survive it. Later, they do, however. They begin to realize they're alive and look at their lives in a different way. I don't think your sister-in-law has reached that point."

"I wonder if she ever will. Catriona does not see the world like the rest of us. She has a way of getting exactly what she wants with the least amount of effort."

He couldn't help but think of Catriona paying him, offering the coins with an offhanded manner that had, frankly, shocked him.

"I wish you success with Catriona as a patient. Now that her beauty is gone, I wonder if there will be anything to her." He smiled. "My wife is certain of her own plainness," the earl said. "But I've never seen a more beautiful woman."

He stood, but before leaving the room, he turned to his host.

"You have a midwife for your wife's lying-in?"

The earl shook his head. "A physician from Inverness. I have faith in the man."

"I wasn't applying for the position," he said with a smile. "I have enough patients of my own. But I would recommend one thing. Have him use chloroform for the worst of it. It will spare your wife the greatest pain. I've used it with my patients, and women seem to endure childbirth easier."

The earl appeared to sag. He didn't say anything for a moment, being fixated on the surface of his desk. His fingers danced a pattern from one curlicue on the blotter to the next.

He looked up, the expression in his eyes one of misery.

"Thank you, I will. I don't know what I would do if anything happened to her," he said.

"Everything should go well. She's healthy, and that's what matters. I don't doubt you've been attentive."

The earl nodded. "Take care of Catriona, though, will you? I don't want Jean worried about her sister."

"I'll do the best I can," he said, feeling like a hypocrite as he said those words.

Chapter 17

"**Y**ou give him a great deal of latitude, Aunt," Catriona said.

Mark had been gone four days. Four days in which she'd wondered about his errand. Granted, she'd not been bedeviled once, but she was vastly annoyed, solely on Aunt Dina's behalf.

"Any other employer would have fired him for all his absences."

Aunt Dina only smiled.

She was not disappointed. She was only feeling overwhelmed by the seamstress and her assistant. Three extra people were in her suite when she was used to being alone.

Why was she eager to see Mark? He'd been a superlative lover, but even that judgment was suspect. She'd gone nearly a year without being intimate with a man. Perhaps the dearth of experience made her see him in a better light.

He mustn't presume upon the circumstances. If he was remotely disrespectful, she'd banish him from her room. Besides, he needed to mollify her with a decent explanation. Did he possibly think she'd missed him?

As far as that night, that had simply been expediency

on both their parts. She'd been lonely, and he was available. He mustn't think she'd ever repeat the experience.

But instead of being able to convey all of that to the man, she was greeted every morning with the news that he hadn't yet returned. This sensation she was feeling was merely elation that she wouldn't have to tolerate him any longer.

It was not disappointment.

It was not sadness.

She did not long for him. How utterly foolish to think *that* was the case.

"Will you lift your right arm, miss?" the seamstress asked.

She complied. Why had she agreed to change her wardrobe from black to dark blue? After all, the colors were similar. But Aunt Dina was adamant, and once the woman had decided upon a course of action, it was nearly impossible to change her mind.

As impossible as it had been to get her to reveal what errand had taken Mark away from the household.

"I do hope there wasn't a death in his family," she'd said this morning.

Aunt Dina only shook her head.

"He isn't ill, is he?" she asked, with what she hoped was a disinterested air.

Again Aunt Dina shook her head.

"How did you come to hire him?"

She didn't expect an answer, but Aunt Dina said, "I've known the man for some time. He's always impressed me a great deal. When the opportunity arose, of course I hired him."

That comment fostered more questions than it answered.

"I don't see what you admire in him," Catriona said airily. "He's insulting."

"Do you think so? Strange, but I've never thought that of him."

"How long will he be gone?"

"I honestly don't know," Dina said. "It all depends on the weather, I believe. If the roads are good, he'll make better time."

She fisted her right hand. "He's traveling, then?" In this weather? With winter storms buffeting Edinburgh? "Is he traveling far?"

Aunt Dina didn't answer.

The seamstress left the corner with her assistant, interrupting her thoughts. Both women halted in front of where she stood on a small riser. She couldn't stand in this position much longer. Her left knee was beginning to trouble her, and she wasn't going to make excuses or ask for special treatment. After all, she had her pride.

Had he known that he was going away for a time? Why hadn't he told her?

She wanted to stomp her feet on the riser, scream at all of them to leave the room, or simply vent her annoyance at Mark to anyone who would listen.

A lady, however, did not act in such a fashion. A mere footman should not cause her to behave in an improper manner. Even if offering him money to bed her was the height of impropriety.

In the past, she'd never had any difficulty dismissing a man when he was no longer of interest to her. She would simply have to do that with the footman. When he returned, she would ensure there was nothing for him to do.

As the seamstress measured her, albeit with some difficulty, given her refusal to remove her clothing, she turned to Aunt Dina.

"I think I shall discontinue taking a tray in my room,"

she said. "I believe it's time for me to join you in the dining room for our meals."

Dina clapped her hands together like a child given a long-awaited sweet. "Oh my dear, are you very certain? How wonderful."

She had already demonstrated she could eat with her full veil on. She would simply do that in the dining room, in case any of the maids came in. That way, the footman would not need to monitor her meals, and would not be required to come into her room at all. In fact, she needn't see him.

That was relief icing her stomach, that was all.

The apprentice knelt at her feet, working on the hem of a dress she certainly didn't need. Aunt Dina was relentless in victory, however. She'd ordered five day dresses and matching veils, all in a lovely deep blue. Not nearly as dark as she would have preferred.

This color blue would look lovely with her hair. No one would ever see the contrast, however.

He'd said she was beautiful. He'd kissed every inch of her. He'd been the most magnificent lover she'd ever had.

He was the most annoying man.

Where was he?

Bringing herself back to the present, she realized that her aunt and the seamstress were engaged in a fervent, yet polite, argument.

"We can't possibly finish by next Tuesday," the seamstress was saying. "It will be a month at least. I just lost my other apprentice and I don't even have time to replace her with all the orders I have."

The woman sounded on the verge of hysteria.

"I understand all that, Mrs. McPhee, and I am truly sorry for your predicament. But we must simply have two dresses ready within the week."

What was the need for haste? Especially since she was only going to show her new dresses to the trees in the square.

She might show Mark, if he ever returned.

Surely she wasn't longing for him?

"I can't possibly have two dresses ready in that time." Mrs. McPhee's voice was rising. Soon she would be at a screech.

"Well, you must," Aunt Dina said, standing there with her hands folded in front of her, a smile on her face, but an implacable glint in her eyes.

The seamstress might as well surrender now.

Mrs. McPhee, impeccably attired in white blouse and black skirt, an outfit that matched her apprentice, drew herself up to her not inconsiderable height and frowned down her long nose at Dina.

"It is impossible, madam," she said, each syllable carefully enunciated.

"Mrs. McPhee," her aunt said, in coaxing tones, "you will agree, will you not, that I have been exceedingly kind in telling all my friends about your skill?"

The seamstress nodded, her eyes never leaving Dina.

Was it her imagination, or had the seamstress paled, ever so slightly?

She ought to admit defeat now. Aunt Dina would use every weapon in her arsenal to win this dispute. Witness the fact that she was standing here being measured for dresses few people would see.

"I cannot provide two dresses in that time, madam. I do not have the staff, and we barely have time to sleep as it is."

"Then one," Aunt Dina said, smiling.

Mrs. McPhee sighed. "One, we can possibly do."

One dress was probably all Aunt Dina wanted from the beginning.

Perhaps she should be like her aunt, the master strategist, ask for twice what she wanted and be more than willing to settle for half.

The sound of running footsteps interrupted her thoughts. A second later Elspeth was at the door, breathless, her cap dislodged and hanging by a pin from her hair, her face red.

"Mrs. MacTavish, come quick! Oh, Mrs. MacTavish, you'll never guess."

Aunt Dina frowned at the girl.

"Have we another emergency?" she asked.

"No, ma'am, it's not a bad one at that. It's a duke."

She felt herself turn gradually to stone. First her feet, then her legs. By the time the sensation had traveled up her legs, Elspeth had calmed and was telling the tale.

"His footman, ma'am, announced the Duke of Linster was here." The maid glanced over at her. "To call on Miss Cameron, ma'am. He's getting out of his carriage right now!"

Yes, she had transformed into a statue. She should be placed in a garden, beside a path, perhaps. People would come and marvel at the depiction of a woman garbed in black, swathed in a veil, her hands clenched as if to hold back her emotions.

"Send him away," Aunt Dina was saying. "No, better not. I'll do it myself." Dina looked up at her. "Don't worry, my dear. It's a nuisance that will be dealt with all too soon."

"No," she heard herself say. "I'll see him."

The statue speaks.

Every woman in the room turned to look at her.

She glanced at Elspeth. "The Japanese screen in the corner," she said. "Could you move it in front of the flowered chair?"

Elspeth nodded rapidly.

"Are you sure, my dear?" Dina asked.

"I am."

She wasn't.

She was terrified. But she also knew Linster, having made a concerted study of him over the months in London. He was wealthy enough to command anyone in his corner of the world. Denying him only piqued his interest. If she didn't see him now, he'd simply return.

But why now? Why, after all this time?

The girl she'd been would have been ecstatic at this sign of Linster's interest. But that girl died on a foggy London street, and had been buried all these months, swathed in a black veil.

On the way back to Edinburgh, in a journey that blessedly took half the time as the one to Ballindair, Mark couldn't forget the Earl of Denbleigh's words. The man's antipathy toward Catriona was pronounced. He understood now why she'd stayed in Edinburgh, even if doing so meant she couldn't be with her sister.

Why bother to change when people didn't believe you capable of it?

The woman he knew, shrouded in a veil and silence, wasn't the epitome of all things decent, good, and kind. But neither was she evil. She was simply human, flawed and with failings.

So was he, because he wasn't going to confess his charade just yet.

He thanked Brody and walked from the stable into the house, his mind occupied with all the duties he needed to catch up on since he'd taken four days from his practice. With any luck he could call on a few patients this afternoon.

Sarah met him at the door, hands on her hips, her mouth pressed into a thin line.

"You have a problem," she said.

"I have many problems," he said. His father, Catriona, and his patient load, to mention a few. "Which one are you talking about?"

"Anne Ferguson is here, Doctor, and she's not a happy woman."

She was right. He had a problem.

"Why is she unhappy?" he asked, genuinely curious.

The last time he saw Anne had been at his grandfather's birthday party. When he said as much to Sarah, her mouth twitched up in a smile.

"You don't think that's reason enough for a few tears, Doctor?"

He shook his head, moving past her and down the hall to his apothecary, where he placed his bag on the broad oak table. Even though he hadn't used the contents on his visit to Ballindair, the bag was never far from his side.

Leaning his back against the table, he folded his arms and regarded Sarah.

"She's crying?" he asked, hoping Sarah had exaggerated.

The sound Sarah made was one he'd often heard in the stables when one of the horses was impatient at being harnessed.

"She was when she arrived here with her maid. I've given her tea and biscuits, so she's had time to compose herself."

Thank God Anne had the foresight to bring her maid. They both had their reputations to consider. A thought he should have had before posing as a footman.

Was that why she was here?

"How did she even know I was home?" he asked, frowning. "I could have been delayed at Ballindair."

"She's been here two hours, Doctor. She gave me to understand that she wasn't leaving until the two of you talked."

He did have a problem.

"Do you think she knows about my posing as a footman?"

"I've a mouth like a trap," Sarah said. "But what about the staff at Mrs. MacTavish's?"

"They don't know who I am."

"Are you sure about that? Servants know everything before anyone else, and some of them love to gossip."

"What do you suggest I do?"

She shook her head. "I've no idea. But must you pretend to be someone you're not? Can't you come out and tell the girl who you are?"

"That would be best, wouldn't it?" he asked, not mentioning that he'd meant to do that very thing more than once.

Never bedding Catriona would have been the best thing, a comment he wouldn't make to another living soul. The sight of her, naked and lit by firelight, standing there with her back turned to him, had been the single most erotic vision he'd ever seen.

Was he never to see her again?

Sarah sighed. "You'll do the right thing, I'm thinking. If you weren't that kind of man, I would never have come to work for you. Miss Ferguson evidently feels neglected, and you need to make it up to her."

She was more than his housekeeper. Sarah was also his nurse, and his friend. When he once said that to her, she beamed with pride. Now, if he could only keep her in those roles—and away from being a matchmaker—he'd be content.

Well, if not content, then at least not miserable.

"I'm not the type to tell you what to do," she said, a comment that had him smiling.

"But?"

"But you need to stop rescuing people," she said. "Especially if you're to be married. What would your wife think?"

He tried to envision himself explaining the circumstances to Anne, and realized it wasn't an image that came easily.

"Perhaps it would be better if I gave her time to compose herself."

She shook her head.

"Perhaps you could explain to her—"

Once again she shook her head. "Are you afraid of her, Doctor?"

The word wasn't afraid as much as cautious. Females who were given to overemotionality were also given to tantrums, hysteria, and unexpected behavior.

He knew better than to say that to Sarah, however.

His housekeeper was an eminently practical female. She wasn't given to hysterics or histrionics, and he'd never known her to be unreasonable.

But he'd once thought that about Anne, too.

Chapter 18

The sitting room was warm and comfortable. The best pieces had been reupholstered after he'd moved in, and the fireplace was large enough to offset the cold of the day.

The last time he'd been in here, he'd entertained some family members and friends. During that occasion, his grandfather had grumbled that the furniture was possessed. Pointing to an overstuffed chair with a frown, he'd said, "The damn thing has a spring with an arrow targeting my backside."

Because his grandfather was the Earl of Caithnern, his assembled guests only smiled. Because the earl was also wealthy, society labeled him an eccentric and excused behavior that would be considered coarse in another man.

Any pleasant memories in this room were soon going to be overlaid with other, weightier emotions. If Anne was weeping, that didn't auger well for a reasonable discussion.

What could he possibly say to excuse himself?

Catriona Cameron has held a fascination for me ever since I first saw her. Hardly something he could tell Anne. *Mrs. MacTavish wanted me to treat her niece.* But the woman didn't insist on his ruse as footman. That had been his idea alone.

He didn't have one idea of what to say, either to explain or excuse.

Anne occupied one end of the settee, her maid, Marjorie, opposite her in the chair his grandfather had sworn was possessed.

He wished he'd had the chance to bathe and change his clothes.

Would he be a better man if he was suffused with guilt? If he felt remorse for having been with Catriona? Each of them had entered into a sensual relationship as adults, with no expectations and no pretense.

Such things rarely happened in the world in which he lived.

The fact that it had meant more to him than a casual encounter would have to be examined later. He had a great deal of examining to do.

When Anne turned her head and followed his progress into the room, he forced a smile to his face.

Sarah had made his visitors feel comfortable, as she always did. A fire warmed the room; a tea tray, nearly empty, indicated that Anne and her maid had been fed.

All that was left was for the conversation to begin.

Anne made a quick gesture with her right hand, and Marjorie stood, bobbed her head at him, and skirted the tables to leave the room. Where would she go? The kitchen, where Sarah would no doubt ply her with more tarts and drain her of details? Or to the carriage, where she would wait in frozen anticipation? For her sake, he hoped it was the kitchen. For his sake, the carriage would be better, as long as she had a blanket for her lap and warm mittens.

He stood there, reluctant to approach Anne.

She believed him to be leaning toward marriage. Once, he might have felt the same way, but his sudden reluctance was a ten-foot brick wall. He might have been able to scale it if he truly wished, but he didn't.

Yet he needed to be honest to one woman, at least.

He'd fought his parents every day for years as he studied to be a physician. Although his father had been more verbal in his attacks, his mother also expressed her disapproval. Should he be so interested in disease? After he'd begun his visits to Old Town, he'd been questioned at length by some of his wealthier patients. Should he be spending his time in such a profitless and gruesome activity? He'd been assaulted twice in Old Town and acquitted himself well enough, only to be scolded by Sarah. What had he been thinking, to venture into that neighborhood?

In all those endeavors, he'd stood his ground, knowing that he was doing the right thing, both for his patients and himself.

This confrontation was different. He had no moral high ground on which to stand.

He sat in the chair Marjorie vacated, waiting. He'd seen the flash of anger in Anne's red-rimmed eyes. First, however, she'd weep some more, pressing her lace-trimmed handkerchief to the corner of each eye. Then she'd delicately dab at her nose and sigh. She'd look away, then back at him, to ensure he was paying enough attention.

Catriona would have lambasted him immediately, even in the presence of her maid.

Not a good idea, comparing two women.

"You're upset," he began, deciding the frontal approach was best.

She looked indignant. "Yes, I'm upset," she said. "I

planned the party with you in mind, Mark. I reminded you more than once. I wanted you there early to greet the guests with me."

He stared at her blankly.

"You don't remember?"

She allowed a few more tears to fall.

He shook his head.

"I told you at your grandfather's birthday. I told you that my parents were having a few friends over for dinner and wanted to introduce you. Except you didn't appear. How could you?"

"When was this?"

Her eyes narrowed. "Last night." She wadded up her handkerchief, realized what she was doing, and spread it out between her hands. "I've never been so embarrassed in my entire life."

"I wasn't here, Anne."

"I know that. Your housekeeper told me. Why didn't you tell me? Where were you? Why didn't you tell me you were leaving Edinburgh?"

"I didn't realize I was required to inform you of my whereabouts, Anne."

She frowned at him. Was she annoyed because he'd missed her party or because he wasn't apologizing to her?

He sat back in the chair, stretching his feet toward the fire. Sleet pinged against the windows. The wind was rising, the sighing becoming a presence in the silence of the room.

She blotted at her eyes.

"We aren't going to be married, Anne," he said.

Perhaps he should have regretted the bluntness of his statement, but she needed to realize the nature of their relationship. Once, he might have given some thought to marrying Anne. He wasn't sure exactly when his opinion had changed.

She fisted her hands, pulling on the handkerchief with such force that he was certain she was going to tear it in two.

"I'm certain I gave you that impression," he said, knowing he had. "I regret that."

"You regret that?" Somehow, she managed to instill intense loathing into those three words.

He nodded.

The two spots of color on her cheeks seemed oddly out of keeping with the overall paleness of the rest of her complexion. He wondered if she was feeling well, then realized his concern would not be welcome.

Her brown eyes were not flashing at him now. Instead, they seemed dull and flat, as if she were attempting to conceal what she was feeling. Or perhaps ladylike rage made them appear that way.

"I see you as a friend, nothing more." Was he making the situation worse with each word? From her look, it seemed he was. "I apologize for forgetting the event, but my patient came first."

"You were gone because of a patient?" she asked.

Perhaps it wouldn't be wise to continue that lie.

"I'm not going to explain where I was or why. The nature of our relationship does not mandate that I tell you my whereabouts or ask your permission."

"What is the nature of our relationship?" she asked, her voice brittle.

"I consider you a friend," he said.

She stood, impatiently twitching at her skirts.

"You are wrong, Mark. We are not friends. We are, from this moment on, no longer even acquaintances. I shall not greet you in public and I will tell my parents of this meeting, as well as your shameful behavior."

"Do what you think is best," he said, watching as she grabbed her cloak and made her way to the door.

Instead of following her, as a proper host and a gentleman, he sat back in the chair, staring at the fire. That was a relationship consigned to the bin.

He hadn't thought about Anne at all in the last four days. In fact, he'd rarely thought of Anne with any intensity in the last few weeks. Instead, his thoughts had been filled with Catriona.

Stretching out his feet again, he felt the languor that came from fatigue. He needed to go and check on a few patients who concerned him, see Christel, perhaps. If nothing else, he should go and mollify Sarah. Instead, he sat there thinking of his errand and what he'd learned.

Not as much as he wanted, to solve the enigma that was Catriona. Or maybe he was seeing this all wrong. Perhaps she wasn't the puzzle as much as his behavior was. He'd acted in a way that was alien to him. For the first time, he'd put medicine aside. He'd lost his dispassionate observation. He'd been a fool around her.

The time for his ruse was over. He needed to tell her who he was and get back to his practice full-time.

His reluctance to do so was curious and unsettling.

"It was nice for you to come to visit me, Your Grace," Catriona said. "Especially since the weather is brutal."

"I would have done so earlier had I known you were still convalescing. I am no stranger to injury, you know."

The duke had fallen off his horse once, a tale he'd embellished so much that the horse had been portrayed as a wild and unruly beast. Of course, he also explained that he'd been extraordinarily brave during the setting of his broken leg.

"When you didn't answer my letters, and wouldn't respond in any way to my man, I knew I had to see you myself."

"Your man?" she asked.

"I sent a footman to be my eyes. I gave him strict orders to see how you were doing. I even gave him a note to deliver into your own hands."

For a frozen second in time she wondered if Mark was the duke's spy. Then she immediately discounted that suspicion. Mark was so arrogant he would have told her. Or he might have even bragged about his position. Or, perhaps he was simply such a good spy that he was intent on discovering how injured she'd been in the accident.

Enough to bed her?

How convenient that Mark disappeared for a few days just before the duke's arrival.

Her stomach clenched.

"I apologize for not responding to your correspondence sooner, Your Grace."

"That is as it may be, my dear. We shan't talk about it any further. Instead, may I beseech you to come out from behind the screen so that I can see your lovely face once more?"

He was evidently under the belief that she was playing coy or not looking her best, and for that reason had chosen to address him from behind a screen.

If he only knew the truth.

"I have come all the way from London, you see."

"Have you? Is your footman from London as well?" Or was he blessed with a thick Scottish accent?

She could still feel his lips whispering against her skin.

"I regret, my dear, that the majority of my servants

are from London. I would have felt better with Irish servants, but my countrymen don't wish to be gone long from home."

"Yet you, yourself, do not have such territorial restrictions," she said.

He laughed merrily at that.

"I have missed you, my dear. When will you be returning to London?"

Never.

"Tell me about this footman of yours, Your Grace."

"My footman? Dismiss the man from your mind."

"I don't remember him calling on me," she said, determined to silence the little voice whispering in her mind.

"He called upon your aunt, I believe, who informed him that you were not receiving. He left and returned to my side, chagrined that he'd failed at his task."

"He's been at your side ever since?" she asked.

"I cannot say, for certain. I have a great many servants, you know."

Now he would tell her how wealthy he was, a conversation they'd had on numerous occasions. She'd been taken with him because of his wealth, yet now she knew that wealth could not turn time backward. Wealth could not make her beautiful again.

What good was money when it couldn't buy anything she wanted?

"I want to see you, my dear."

"Please honor my wishes, Your Grace. I would be more comfortable behind the screen."

"As you wish, but are you certain?"

"I am." Perhaps he would leave with memories of her from London, attired in a new frock, laughing at some old and tired jest. Perhaps he would remember the girl she'd been and carry that tale around Edinburgh.

"Are you in Scotland for long, Your Grace?"

She didn't for a minute believe that he'd come to Scotland simply to see her. The Duke of Linster was too selfish a personage. Once, however, it would have been easy to convince herself otherwise.

"I've friends in Edinburgh."

"It's hunting season, isn't it?"

"Is it? I believe you might be right, my dear."

She smiled.

Was she an afternoon's interlude? A mystery to solve, inserted into a blank space of time? Just what tale would he tell at the country party?

Just a short time ago she would have been thrilled to be an object of gossip. Now she cringed at the thought.

"Again, Your Grace, thank you for visiting."

The screen both shielded her from view and hid the doorway to the dining room. She would slip away before his curiosity grew. Aunt Dina would be the apologetic hostess, offer him whiskey, some biscuits, and perhaps even solicit a donation for one of her causes.

But she would not reveal herself to the Duke of Linster.

She could just imagine the tale he'd spread of the monster she'd become.

Chapter 19

It was early afternoon by the time Mark instructed Brody to pull in behind the MacTavish residence. Before he saw Catriona, he wanted to speak to the coachman.

He'd never paid much attention to the bay where the carriage was stored. Now, as he walked to the opening, the smell of paraffin oil and wax was heavy in the air.

Johnstone, the coachman, was short and stocky with broad shoulders, the type of physique that made him think the man would be an admirable opponent in a fight. His face was florid and full, with jowls that nearly obscured his neck. His eyes were brown and unfriendly, narrowing as Mark entered the bay.

In the time he'd been here, he'd seen the man twice, and both times they'd nodded to each other, neither going out of his way to further the acquaintance.

He regretted that lapse now.

The coachman stared at him for a long unblinking moment before returning to his work.

He moved around the carriage, inspecting it. The vehicle was in perfect condition, dust free, the body polished to a high shine. Brody maintained his own carriage with matching diligence.

"Is there only one of you here?"

The coachman looked over at him. "I've a stable boy to help me."

"Does Mrs. MacTavish attend a great many functions?"

"Enough."

"You drive her to Old Town, don't you?" He trailed his fingers over the leather of the guiding reins, an action that garnered him a frown.

"If I do?"

He shook his head. "I know a driver. He says that Old Town is dangerous, and he worries about his carriage."

"I've much the same worries."

"Mrs. MacTavish is a kind woman. Very generous."

The coachman frowned at him but nodded. "Aye, that she is," he said, continuing to rub down the driver's seat of the carriage, even though it was so well polished that he could see the reflection of the timbered ceiling of the carriage house.

"Is that why you came back to Edinburgh after the accident and continue to remain in her employ?"

"I work for the Earl of Denbleigh," the coachman said. "I came back to Edinburgh because it's my home. I'd no objection to taking them to London, but I wasn't going to live there."

"So you were driving the night of the accident involving Miss Cameron?"

"Aye, I was."

"How exactly did it happen? Have you any idea?"

"Why would you be wanting to know?"

"Because I'm curious," he said, giving the man the truth. "It seems to be a mystery to most people."

The coachman didn't speak for some moments. He balled up his rag and tossed it on top of a nearby barrel.

"You'll be solving a mystery for me first. Who are you? My nephew works as a footman for another house and he's never given the freedom you are."

Since he was on his way to tell Catriona the truth, he saw no reason why he shouldn't divulge it to Johnstone, which he did.

"So it's for Miss Cameron you're here, then?"

He nodded.

Johnstone's gaze moved to the left, then to the right, as if seeing the scene in his memory. A moment later his fleshy face firmed into an expression of resolve.

"I was told that I couldn't be right. That I'd imagined it. That what I'd seen with my own eyes couldn't possibly have happened. I learned to keep my mouth shut."

Mark moved to stand directly in front of the coachman. "Who told you that? The earl?"

Johnstone shook his head. "The authorities in London. Still, it kept me silent well enough."

"Tell me what you told them."

"You'll think me barmy, too."

He didn't respond, waiting.

Then, surprisingly, the coachman told him.

He was here.

He'd come back.

The most irritating man in the world was here, right at this moment, striding toward the kitchen door with his greatcoat open and his hair tossed by the blustery wind.

Catriona stepped back from the window, pressing her hand to her chest.

He looked angry.

What right did he have to be angry? He'd disappeared for four days, now he returned angry?

She would have him dismissed for certain.

Then she'd never see him again.

She'd never feel this pounding of her heart or the breathlessness that came from excitement.

She went into her bedroom, turned the mirror on top of the dresser, staring into it. She could see nothing but a veiled figure. Still, she wanted to be pretty. She wanted, desperately, to be beautiful at this moment.

Just once, to let him see what she had been.

When he entered the house, Elspeth greeted him. "Mrs. MacTavish wants to see you, Mark, the minute you arrive."

He removed his greatcoat and hung it on the peg near the door. He removed his jacket also, not saying anything when the maid looked at him wide-eyed. A moment later he looked like a footman in a casual household, dressed in white shirt and black trousers. He bent and wiped the rest of the snow from his boots and stood.

She picked up a tray and handed it to him. "She's in the parlor," she said, tittering in that way young girls have. At any other time the sound might've coaxed forth his own smile.

He carried the tea things into the parlor but couldn't find a place to put it. Every surface was filled with clothing of various types. Sitting in the middle of all the piles was Dina MacTavish, looking happier than he'd ever seen her.

"Isn't this wonderful?" she asked, pushing aside a neat stack of shirts so he could set the tray down on the low table before the settee. "People have been so generous."

"Is that all for Old Town?" he asked.

"It is. It couldn't have come at a better time, what with

the cold." She beamed brightly up at him. "But that's not all," she said, waving him into a nearby chair. "The Duke of Linster called on Catriona yesterday."

"Did he?" He sat and shook his head when she would have poured him a cup of tea.

"Yes, but that isn't the most wonderful thing. What is the most wonderful thing is that Catriona met with him."

"Did she?"

"Don't you see, my dear Dr. Thorburn? You've achieved everything I wanted you to do. Catriona isn't hiding in her room anymore, and the duke—the man who nearly offered for her in London—was sitting in my parlor. Imagine that."

She twinkled at him, clapping the tips of her fingers together. "Yes. Isn't it the most marvelous thing?"

He wasn't certain how marvelous it was.

The Duke of Linster was wealthy, but the man's reputation as a libertine was well known even in Edinburgh.

He didn't have a title. Nor did he want one. His father couldn't deny him the title of Lord Serridain when he advanced to the Earl of Caithnern, but that circumstance would be surrounded by the loss of his grandfather. Hardly cause for celebration.

Why the hell had Catriona met with the duke?

Every woman in his life was bedeviling him. Were they all corresponding with each other? Did they slip each other notes in the middle of the night? *I'll weep in front of Mark because he forgot a party. I'll lose all common sense and be happy that an Irish duke is visiting my niece.* Even his mother had joined the chorus, sending him a note that intimated he was in trouble on that front, too. *Surely the rumors I'm hearing couldn't possibly be true, Mark. I had always given you credit for having common sense.*

Common sense? He'd lost his mind ever since he'd decided to play footman to Catriona Cameron. Common sense? He had no sense at all.

"I think it's time we told her," Dina was saying.

He nodded. It was beyond time.

Why hadn't he told Catriona who he was before now? Did his reluctance have anything to do with the fact that she would have banished him the minute the words were out of his mouth? He knew how she felt about doctors. After having read the London idiot's letter, he couldn't blame her.

Today was the end to it all.

He stood. "I'll see to that right now," he said.

Mrs. MacTavish sent him a warm look, as if she knew just how difficult the next moments would be.

When Catriona answered the knock on the door, she was ready.

"I'm not hungry," she said, pulling the door open and facing Mark.

"I haven't brought your meal."

"Then why are you here?"

She stood back and he entered the room, closing the door behind him.

"I understand the Duke of Linster called on you. Did you enjoy his visit?"

"What does it matter to you?"

"He's old enough to be your father, and a lecher as well."

She turned, made her way back to the secretary. Sitting, she continued with her correspondence.

"Are you ignoring me?"

"I heard you," she said calmly. "I was just not paying any attention to you." She bent and began writing.

"He's a lecher. Don't you care?"

"The Duke of Linster's morals aren't your concern."

"Perhaps you're right," he said. "But yours are."

She didn't look at him. "Why? Because for one night I was your convenient? Perhaps the duke and I are perfect for each other." She placed her pen carefully on the blotter. Evidently, the letter to Jean would have to wait.

"Perhaps you are," he said. "Do you use passion as a weapon, Catriona? Do you use it to get what you want?"

Startled, she stood and approached him. "What did I want from you, footman?"

He smiled. "Perhaps you'll tell me."

"Do you work for the duke?"

He blinked at her in surprise, the expression real enough that she felt a weight being removed from her chest.

"Why would you ask that?"

"Why would you accuse me of using passion as a weapon?"

She desperately wanted to touch him. Or tell him the truth. That he'd overwhelmed her, that he flattened her so easily with words or that small smile he wore now.

"I've been talking to your coachman," he said.

"Next, you'll be conveying your conversation with the cook, and your quips with the maids."

"We were talking about the accident in London," he said.

Her breath suddenly stilled in her chest.

She looked down at the floor, now in shadow. She'd often measured the day by how shrouded the furniture and fixtures became. If she couldn't see the floor, afternoon was well advanced. If she wasn't able to make out the desk, night had fully descended.

When had that way of telling time become tedious?

"He told me that someone shot at the carriage, that it wasn't an accident after all, but deliberate."

A chill was spreading from her stomach to all of her limbs. Within seconds her fingers were icy.

She made her way to the table, but instead of sitting there, braced herself against it.

"Did you know?" he asked.

She couldn't answer him. What could she say?

"Catriona?"

Silence was evidently not going to be a recourse.

"Mr. Johnstone told me," she said. Before that she'd suspected. Why else would the windows have exploded as they did?

He advanced on her, one slow, stalking step at a time. She didn't move, even when he was close.

He smelled of linseed oil and leather. Could it be that the footman had done some work?

"It was an accident," she said firmly.

He reached out and touched her shoulder. Somehow, she could feel the warmth of his fingers through the fabric.

"Was it?"

"Of course it was."

She placed her right hand flat against his shirt, feeling the booming beat of his heart against her palm.

"Please leave, Mark."

"Take off your veil," he said.

"I've already told you I won't."

"I want to kiss you."

Her heart beat much too fast, and his was thundering as well. She dropped her hand and took a step back.

"That wouldn't be wise."

"Are you counseling people on wisdom now, Miss Cameron?"

When had she been wise where he was concerned? Was she expected to forget how he made her feel? Or what passion was like, especially when it had been so missing from her life?

No, what she'd experienced with him had been nothing like what she'd felt before. Not only passion, but more. Something tender and worrisome, that made her vulnerable. She was not given to tears, but he made her want to weep sometimes. Or to simply lay her head on his shoulder and ask for his protection.

Instead of saying anything, however, she backed up a few more feet. She was being wise at the moment, and she should be proud of herself.

"Is your damn duke coming back?"

"I don't know."

Linster had tended his farewells, albeit reluctantly. Deny Linster anything and he was suddenly captivated. Mystery, evidently, interested him more than beauty.

"What did the damn fool want?"

"Me," she said.

"Well, he can't have you."

"Are you commanding people now, footman?"

"I'm jealous," he said, "and I've never been jealous before. Forgive me if I'm irrational."

Suddenly, it was difficult to swallow, or to breathe. She forced herself to calm, clasped her hands in front of her, and concentrated on taking several deep breaths.

He circled the table, coming to stand beside her. Didn't he know that his proximity was disturbing? If he did, he was using it to his advantage.

Who was using passion as a weapon now?

"You've heard that before, haven't you? Catriona Cameron and all her suitors. I imagine you're adept at juggling all of them."

"Are you my suitor, footman?" she whispered.

"Take off your veil. I want to kiss you."

Heat flared through her body, reaching out to touch each separate finger, toe, and pool in the core of her. Her body wanted what he wanted and more. She wanted to kiss him, feel his mouth on hers, inhale his breath and taste him.

She moved away, going to stand behind a chair. A flimsy barricade, but at least it was something between them. Who was she shielding? Him or her?

"You need to leave."

"Yes," he said, surprising her. "I do."

He remained where he was.

"What I need to do and what I'm going to do are two different things, however."

She licked her dry lips.

"It's dark as the grave in here," he said. "Will you at least light a lamp?"

"No," she said. "I won't. Not if I'm going to remove my veil."

Chapter 20

Silence was another occupant in the room, breathing between them, a presence as solid as the table or the desk.

He took a cautious step toward her.

"What must I do?" he asked.

"Promise not to light the lamp," she said, wondering at her own courage. She'd agreed to change her attire, met a duke, and now? Now, she was thinking of doing the most foolish thing of all, just because she was desperate to kiss this irritating man.

"I promise."

"Do not build up the fire too high."

"I promise that as well."

She turned and walked into the bedroom. When he followed her, it was slowly.

He struck the chair, swore, then righted it.

When he entered her bedroom, closing the door behind him, she unclenched her trembling fingers and went to the vanity.

"How can you find your way in the dark?"

For months she had been as one blinded, growing gradually used to her heavy veil. She rarely lit the lamp even when alone, for fear of seeing her own scars. How did she tell him that?

"I learned where things were placed," she said. There, the truth, watered down and acceptable.

She stood with her back to him, her hands gripping the edge of the vanity.

Slowly, before she lost her courage, she withdrew three of the pins that fastened the veil to her hair. Before she withdrew the remaining two pins, she hesitated. Was this the wisest idea?

She'd gone a year without kissing. A year without the suffocating fullness of the veil in a man's presence.

She wanted to be naked, free, unadorned by anything but her own will and wishes.

For an hour, maybe two, she wanted to pretend. Not that she wasn't who she was, damaged and alone, but that she could have what other women had. Right now she'd have an interlude of magic. Not purchased, or arranged, but because each of them wanted it.

"Are you afraid?"

"Dear God, yes." An unwise admission, but one that escaped before she could censor herself.

He came and stood behind her, then enfolded his arms around her waist, bending to speak softly next to her ear.

"I have a reputation for kindness," he said. "For caring. For being gentle."

Tears spiked her eyes. How did he know that she desperately craved all three at this moment? Would he be understanding as well?

She turned in his arms, jerking on the veil. It clung to the remaining two pins before floating to the floor.

He didn't say anything, and the hollow feeling in her chest magnified. Could he see her? Please, don't let him be able to see her. Give her that, at least.

Lowering her face, she rested her forehead against his chest. Her pulse was racing and every muscle was tense. For several moments he didn't speak, move, or do anything but stand there with his arms linked around her loosely.

Other than her physicians, only two people had ever seen her: Jean and Aunt Dina. Both were generous and kind people, possessing good characters and capable of selfless love.

Mark was being kind because he wanted her body and her kisses. For that, she wanted to hold him close and thank him. For the gift of lust, she wanted to weep in joy. For passion, she wanted to respond in kind, praise his body and enjoy him.

Laughter was a strange thing to feel bubbling up from the fear.

She raised her head and kissed his shirt.

Slowly, she tilted her chin up, wishing she were taller. As it was, he would have to bend to reach her.

The hunger for kisses had been inside her for months. Now that it was soon to be appeased, she was impatient.

He lowered his head, finding her mouth with his. She sighed against his lips, feeling a flood of sensation when he opened his mouth and touched her bottom lip with his tongue. She did the same, reciprocity in seduction.

Fear had been replaced by heat.

She slid the tip of her tongue inside, touching his. He tasted of coffee and cinnamon. His mouth took hers as he pulled her to him. He kissed her as if he had her naked and on the bed. He kissed her as if the world would end in the next moment and he wanted the taste of her to last him for eternity.

Helplessly, she gripped his back, pressing him to her, standing on her tiptoes so all the places that ached and wept touched all his spots that were hard and hot.

She'd never wanted anyone as much as she wanted him now.

Without removing her lips from his, she walked him back to her bed. When the back of his legs hit the mattress, she pushed him with both hands. As soon as he landed, she was atop him and kissing him again.

Her skirts were too full; her bodice was too tight. She had entirely too many clothes on, and it seemed as if he agreed. His fingers flew over her clothing, undressing her with a skill that rang a far-off bell of warning in her mind.

Soon her bodice was off. Her left hand fumbled with his shirt. A second later he laughed into the kiss, pushing her hands away to unfasten the buttons and open his shirt.

Her fingernails scored his skin and his amusement vanished. He bucked and rolled with her until he was on top, his hands unfastening her busk, spreading the corset wide before ripping her shift with both hands.

He broke off the kiss to say, "I want you naked. If I can't see you, then I'll damn well feel you."

She writhed beneath him, but he pinned her by sitting astride, stripping her of her garments and her will at the same time.

She'd always dictated the pace of lovemaking, but he just pushed her hands aside, bent, and kissed her again.

Had she ever been kissed like this?

His tongue traced her bottom lip, coaxed open her mouth, played with her, teasing and taunting.

She could barely breathe, but if she lost consciousness, it would be because of bliss. Who would call a halt to that?

He was suddenly standing, stripping off the rest of her clothing. She didn't have time to marvel at the sensation of cold air on her heated body before he was covering her again.

"I'm naked," she said, "but you aren't."

"Give me a moment," he said in a raspy voice.

She smiled. At least she wasn't the only one affected by this suffocating passion.

He peeled off his shirt, and she rubbed her palms up his chest, marveling at the beauty of him felt through her hands. How magnificent he was. His duties had evidently been hard in the past, because his arms were roped with muscle. His chest was well defined, his stomach taut.

She reached out, suddenly bereft when he left her again. When he returned a moment later, she wrapped his arms around his naked shoulders to hold him there.

His body pressed against hers, warming her.

When she breathed, she inhaled his scent. His fingers skimmed along her skin, creating skeins of sensation. She felt as if he were stripping experience and knowledge from her, making her virginal, naive, and unsure at his touch.

Before, she'd tried to hold herself aloof. Now, when he bent his head to surround her nipple with his lips, she shuddered, adrift in feeling, lost but not alone. With his kiss and his hands, he urged her to come with him, as if he alone were familiar with the journey to pleasure.

No one had ever kissed her as softly and urgently. No one had ever worshiped her with his hands, or murmured praise because of the curve of her waist or the hollow of her navel. Not one man had ever spread her legs with gentleness and fervency, his fingers tenderly stroking.

"You're trembling," he said. "Are you afraid?"

"No." A word breathed on a sigh.

"Are you certain?"

How could he concentrate enough to speak? She could only think of him.

"Yes," she said. "I'm certain. I'm not afraid."

He pulled her up with one arm, lifting her to him as if she were a sacrifice. As he thrust his tongue into her mouth, he smoothed his hand over her body, touching her everywhere, learning her in long, heated seconds.

She was helpless and wanting. Out of breath and nearly dizzy with desire, she wrapped her arms around his neck, arching her back to get closer, to feel him.

He trailed kisses down her throat, then at her shoulder. A tremor tore through her body, and she shivered.

Slowly, he lowered her to the bed, spread his knees, and straddled her. For a moment that's all he did, as if he needed the time to calm himself. His breathing was hoarse, the match of hers. Was his heart beating as fiercely?

She pressed her palm against his chest, feeling the furious pounding. Slowly, she trailed her fingers down over his stomach to the nest of hair and below, reaching out both hands to cup him, sliding his shaft between her palms.

He groaned, a sound she'd forever remember, then kissed her again until she was light-headed.

A hand slid over her nipple, his palm gently abrading it. A burst of pleasure raced through her.

He bent and licked first one nipple then the other, leaving the cold air to pebble each. He mouthed them, gently sucking at first, then harder, until she arched off the bed, biting back her cry of surprise.

Her body trembled with her unexpected climax. Spent, she lay beneath him, as he slowly entered her.

Reaching up, she kissed him, then tasted his breath, inhaled it, and returned it. He filled her, causing her eyes to close with the piercing pleasure of it. Bliss started in her belly, wound through each limb, touching every inch with wonder. On a moan, she surrendered to him as he entered her again with long, slow, maddening thrusts.

He took her mouth as she came again, swallowing her cries.

For long minutes her body trembled. She lay with her eyes closed, her palm against his chest, feeling the thunderous beat of his heart slow to normal.

A small smile curved her lips.

Had she ever felt as wonderful?

He picked up her hand and kissed her fingers wordlessly.

A moment later the warmth of his palm on her cheek stopped her heart.

She was off the bed as quick as a thought, stumbling backward until she hit the wall. Naked and trembling, she wrapped her arms around her waist, holding herself silent when all she wanted to do was scream.

"What is it, Catriona?" he asked, sitting up and reaching for her.

She skittered out of his way.

"You promised," she said, hating the faint, frightened sound of her voice.

"What did I do?"

"You touched me."

"That wasn't one of the promises."

It should have been. It must have been. She wouldn't have been as foolish as to forget that. He would have felt the ridges of her scars, traced the path of them from chin to forehead. A river of remembered pain etched into her face.

If he left now, she could pretend it had never happened. Now, though, before any more time fixed this instant in her memory.

Suddenly, she was aloft, in his arms, and she'd never

seen him approach. She gasped in surprise as he held her
close, bending down to kiss her gently, tenderly, and so
softly that it was no deeper than a breath.

"Forgive me," he said against her lips. "Forgive me."
A chain of words he repeated as he returned to the bed,
lay her down and joined her, pulling her tight against him.

"Forgive me."

She shouldn't. She should banish him. Instead, she
raised her hand until she clutched his shoulder and rolled
closer, breathing against his chest, the soft hair tickling
her nose. He was so warm and she was so cold.

"Forgive me."

He should leave. But if he left, he'd take the warmth
with him, the arms surrounding her, and the wordless understanding. When had she become so attuned to him?
When had she begun to need him?

"It wasn't intentional," he said. "My only excuse is that
I forget everything around you."

"You do?"

He sighed. "I do. A decidedly odd reaction, one that
I'll need to study. I haven't been myself since the day I
met you."

She stilled, listening.

"I can see nothing of you, yet I find myself looking
toward you, watching you, as if you hold the answer to all
the questions I have."

She waited, but when he didn't continue, she trailed
her hand down his arm, then curled it into a fist, tucking
it against his chest.

"What questions do you have?"

"No," he said. "Not now. There's a time for that later."

He reached down and pulled the sheet and blanket over
both of them.

What had begun in passion muted to become something dear, a tenderness she'd rarely felt. She lay in his arms, feeling protected and cherished. Foolish emotions, and no doubt false ones, but she'd allow herself to pretend, just for a while.

"Where were you? All those days you were gone. Where did you go?"

"Did you miss me?"

"My meals were amazingly serene," she said, smiling when he bent and pretended to bite her shoulder.

"I had something I needed to do."

"A nonanswer."

"May I tell you later?"

"Will you?"

"Another promise?" he asked. "I promise to tell you everything. Later."

When he slept, she didn't pull away or demand he leave her room.

Just another sign of her foolishness.

Chapter 21

The smell woke him.

Mark left Catriona's bed, walking to the window naked. He parted the curtains, revealing a scene from Hell itself.

The carriage house was burning.

Noxious black clouds burst upward from the structure like orange-limned bubbles. Tongues of flames licked outward from the carriage bay. Soot clung to the window, as if wanting to render the scene as monochromatic as a daguerreotype.

A stable boy shouted at the others, while the far-off peal of the fire brigade brought hope that the fire wouldn't travel to the town houses of Charlotte Square.

The sight was bringing out spectators. A group of residents huddled at the end of the alley. Two of the maids, still attired in their nightclothes, were staring in horror at the blaze. As he watched, Dina MacTavish came into sight and, with a militaristic precision he'd previously admired, immediately began giving orders.

She was one of those people who performed admirably in a crisis.

Remembering the paraffin oil the coachman had used,

he wondered if the man was trapped now, and turned to gather up his clothes and dress.

"What is it?" Catriona asked, sitting on the edge of the bed and turning her back on him.

"The carriage house is burning."

The light from the fire illuminated the room as bright as day. She bent to retrieve her veil, and he didn't chastise her for doing so. He understood, in a way he hadn't last night.

As a physician, he touched his patients to discern the angle of a broken bone, the shape of a lump. His hands were tools, capable of conveying information from a patient's body to his mind.

The one touch on her face had given him a map of scars, of twisted flesh and distorted features.

He knew, in that one instant, how badly she'd been injured.

His heart expanded, filling with gratitude that she hadn't been killed.

One day she might feel the same, just as one day he might tell her that he didn't need to see her to know the truth.

She affixed her veil, grabbed the sheet and wrapped it around her.

Turning, she looked at him.

"Perhaps it's a good thing I seduced you," she said.

"Did you?" he asked, grateful that her voice held a note of humor.

"Will your room survive?" she asked.

He shook his head, just now realizing that the room he'd been given for his ruse was engulfed in flames.

"They may need me," he said, forgetting his role of footman for that of physician.

Thankfully, she only nodded.

The pretense must end. He should have spoken hours ago. Instead, he'd kissed Catriona and his conscience and his will had faded to nothing. However, now was not the time. People were shouting outside and the fire brigade was growing closer.

Yet it would be a simple matter to walk to the bed, help her stand, and look into her veiled face.

Catriona, I'm a physician, not a footman.

The words seemed more a betrayal than a revelation.

Regret infused him for all the things he should have done, and all his unwise acts. He felt uncomfortable, in a way that was alien to him. He was not given to such questioning. The lives of his patients depended on his ability to make decisions quickly. Yet everything he'd done with regard to Catriona Cameron had been second-guessed, even this moment when he stood in the doorway looking back at her.

The veil obscured everything but hints of her luscious body. Had there not been a fire, or if sense hadn't trumped lust, he might have returned to her bed.

His practice had suffered because of his fixation on her. He'd lost his focus, his single-minded pursuit of medicine.

He'd altered his relationship with Anne. Could he blame that on this ruse as well?

Without thinking, without censoring himself, he walked to the bed, grabbed her upper arms and pulled her, naked, up to him. Before she could say a word, he folded his arms around her, holding her. She stood stiff and unyielding for a moment, before her hands reached out and pressed against his back.

"Catriona," he said, his cheek pressed against the soft lace of her veil.

He couldn't thank her for last night. Doing so smacked

too much of making her a whore. He couldn't explain the truth, so he settled for repeating her name.

He dropped his arms and walked away, closing the door of the bedroom behind him.

Catriona dressed but she didn't hurry to join the melee in the alley. Her best vantage point was from her sitting room window, and she stood there, out of sight, intent on the drama.

She watched Mark, curious about him in a way that she couldn't remember ever being about a man. He was taller than most of the men in the fire brigade and, she would wager, more muscular as well.

All she had to do was close her eyes to see his physique as he'd stood at the window. Had she ever taken such delight in the sight of a man's body? He was all carved chest and taut stomach, muscled thighs and round buttocks. When he'd turned to look at her, a flame leapt to life inside her.

She'd wanted to stretch out her hand and urge him back to bed. Let her stroke her hands over his chest, lick his nipples, grip his backside with clenched fingers. Let her drive him mad with soft kisses over his cock until he strained not to erupt in her mouth.

Or let her feel his muscled chest tapering down to his waist, his thighs. His buttocks fascinated her, tight with muscle, they seemed ridiculously sensitive.

She'd run her fingers over him, and he'd twitched away from her touch.

"I'm not," he said, when she had accused him of being ticklish.

"Of course you are," she countered, and moved to the end of the bed to tickle the soles of his feet.

He was more intelligent than his position required. He was loyal, since he never spoke against Aunt Dina. He'd never divulged the mysterious errands her aunt had sent him on from time to time.

Why was she so fascinated with him? Was it because he was her lover, when other men would have shied away? Or because she was lonely, and he was kind, amusing, and as obstinate as she was?

Or was it simply something about Mark? He had a confidence that made her think he'd held a position of importance once, and a way of walking that decreed he was a man of power. Yet he was only a footman.

Did it truly matter what position he held? He was Mark, and she was too interested in him.

She'd never allowed a man to hold her as tenderly as he had last night. If she never saw another person in her hermitage, he would be enough, and wasn't that a frightening admission?

She suspected that she would have felt just as vulnerable around him with all her beauty as she did now. The yearning she felt, uncomfortable and new, was not due to her scarred face but for some other reason.

Attired in his black greatcoat—had an appreciative and wealthy woman given it to him?—she watched him hand off buckets. With two other men, he used a long forklike tool to poke at the remains of the stairway and the ceiling. As they walked away, the ceiling fell in a cloud of embers and ashes.

The bay was only a yawning black maw, and the windows above had been blown out, but the shell of the carriage house remained. The fire had not started from the outside, but from the inside.

Was it another improbable accident?

She wrapped her arms around her waist. She was seeing things that weren't there.

A carriage approached from the end of the street. She wondered if there were more onlookers, come to see the fire and the destruction.

People liked to view a tragedy.

Some kind people had attempted to help poor Millicent and her right after the accident in London. But just as many people had stood there, all agog about the carriage accident. No doubt they'd congratulated themselves on not being one of the occupants.

Below, Aunt Dina was scurrying everywhere. At one point she, Artis, and Elspeth emerged with trays of tea, coffee, and scones for the men in the fire brigade.

Aunt Dina turned and watched as a woman exited the carriage and strode up the alley as if she had a destination in mind. Without even greeting Dina, the woman walked right up to Mark.

He'd said he wasn't married, but had he lied?

Andrew hadn't bothered to lie. His marital status hadn't concerned him. He hadn't cared about his own adultery. In fact, he'd bragged that his wife was comfortable with it.

As long as I come home periodically, and always dole out the money, she doesn't care what I do.

She had a sickening feeling in her stomach as she watched Mark and the woman converse.

The woman appeared older than Mark, her cloak a plain serviceable brown. Her bonnet was the same, utilitarian rather than fashionable. She tilted her chin up at him, folded her arms, then made a wide sweeping gesture of her arm, her gloved hand pointing toward the square. A moment later she was shaking her head, then nodding.

Mark glanced up, his gaze on her bedroom window. She pulled back, but not so much that she lost sight of them.

He nodded again, and the woman looked mollified enough to step back and bury her hands in the pockets of her cloak.

Mark turned, escorted her to Aunt Dina's side, and the two women spoke.

Whatever secrets Mark possessed, Aunt Dina evidently knew them.

The feeling of betrayal felt like acid in her stomach.

From the window of his bedroom, Andrew could see the billowing black clouds of smoke over the tall roofs of Charlotte Square.

He smiled in satisfaction.

How strange, that of all his hobbies, murder might be the most fascinating.

His father had died and left him a fortune. He had no ancestral estates to manage and couldn't be bothered with the duties of husband and father. Although he liked a good whiskey and enjoyed port, he was adverse to being intoxicated on a daily basis. Gambling always seemed like a fool's occupation. Therefore, he'd had to come up with something to interest him, something on which to focus. This year it seemed to be killing Catriona Cameron.

Surprisingly, it had been easy to use the ladle, trailing a path of paraffin oil from the door of the room above the carriage bay all the way down the wooden stairs to the dirt floor below. The flames were hypnotic, but he'd escaped before being seen.

A crowd was gathering at the end of the alley now. He grabbed his coat and scarf and left the house, becoming one of many concerned neighbors. He mingled with the residents of Charlotte Square, listening to the comments.

"We're lucky it hasn't spread."

"The fire brigade won't let that happen. My nephew's a member, you know."

"Damned nuisance in this weather."

"Who lives there, do you know?"

"Was anyone hurt?" he asked a man standing at the front of the crowd. His vantage point was better than anyone's, and from the sprinkle of snow on the man's shoulders, he'd been standing there awhile.

"I've not seen any sign of it, praise God."

That was a disappointment.

"A miracle," he murmured, and the man said something Andrew didn't hear. His attention was suddenly on the window on the second floor, where a curtain fluttered. Someone stood there, wreathed in darkness, or a veil.

His stomach clenched.

Catriona was proving to be surprisingly difficult to kill.

A pity that he was going to need the maid's services one more time. She was the type to try and use her little bit of knowledge for her own personal gain. It couldn't be helped.

In the last five years, he'd learned how to paint passably well. His skills as a marksman had improved with his year of intense study of guns and his annual hunting expeditions. He'd grown proficient at French and Italian during his years studying languages.

He would have to learn to excel at murder.

Chapter 22

Sarah's lecture had been fervent and blistering, and Mark couldn't blame her. Brody had returned home last night, uncertain about what to do and nearly freezing. He'd forgotten about his driver and the fact shamed him.

As he moved through the chaotic scene, he was stopped by two members of the fire brigade. The first challenged his presence there, and when he explained that he was a physician and looking to see if he was needed, he was pressed into service by a second man, wanting him to see about one of his fellow firefighters. All of them wore long and scruffy beards, the better to protect their faces from smoke.

The man on the ground had a badly burned left arm, and he instructed that his jacket be cut away and a wet cloth placed on top of the burn. After giving instructions that he be transported to the hospital, Mark saw to two other people who were coughing badly, helping move them to an area with less smoke. He also was able to determine that the stable boy was not among the injured, that he had been away when the fire had broken out in the carriage house.

The fire brigade, one of the oldest in Scotland, had

managed to contain the fire. Luckily, all of the horses survived, having been led away by the stable boy to another stable on the other side of the square.

Dawn found the smoke turning to feeble gray plumes. Here and there heat blurred the air, but no more flames were visible.

His eyes hurt and he smelled of smoke, but rather than return home, he would make what calls he could in Old Town. He'd lost four days, and his patients were depending on him.

Sarah would be taken back to his house by Dina's driver. He was happy to discover that the man had been ferrying Dina to a meeting the night before, and away when the fire started.

He was making his way to his carriage when he heard a voice.

"Is that your wife?"

He turned to find a ghost standing there, one arrayed in black lace and wool. The hem of Catriona's veil blew about the shoulders of her cloak until she placed a gloved hand atop it.

He didn't comment on her being outside on what promised to be a blustery winter day. Instead, he focused on her question.

"Is who my wife?"

She nodded in the direction of the kitchen door, where Dina and Sarah had disappeared. The brigade was storing the hoses of the pump truck, each man's breath held in the air like puffs of smoke. Everyone else had sought a warmer place.

"No," he said, realizing the time, the moment, had come.

He could end it with words, and she'd never wish to see him again. He didn't want it to end that way. Or perhaps he didn't wish it to end at all. What he wanted to do was explain himself to her, have her understand. Perhaps then she could forgive him.

"Would you like to know what I do each morning?" he asked. "Discover where I go? I promised you other answers as well."

She glanced at the carriage, at Brody who sat atop the seat wrapped in enough wool to keep him warm. His scarf was over the lower half of his face, extending above his nose, and his hat was pulled down over his forehead. Even his eyes were half closed against the frigid air.

He owed the man an apology, perhaps even a bonus.

"Come with me," he said, holding out his hand. "The carriage is ours."

"Hardly proper, footman," she said.

He smiled. His position was such that it was doubtful gossip would attach itself to him. To other people, he would be Catriona Cameron's physician.

"I'll promise nothing will come of this."

Curiosity was evidently warring with prudence, because she looked at the carriage, then at him, then back at the carriage.

"What are you about, footman?" she asked, as if they hadn't spent the last night wrapped in each other's arms.

Catriona used that tone to push people away. He had neither the patience nor the time for either.

Turning, he opened the carriage door. "I have to leave now," he said. "If you're coming with me, then come."

"I've received more gracious invitations."

He didn't respond.

She took a step toward him, then hesitated before entering the carriage. She rearranged her skirts and the veil while he gave instructions to Brody.

"I'm sorry," he added to the coachman. "I should have sent word to you that I'd be delayed."

Brody only nodded, not quite meeting his eyes.

As much acceptance as he was going to get, and probably more than he deserved. For the first time in his life he wanted to be someone other than he was. Who, a footman?

A moment later he climbed into the carriage and sat with his back to the horses.

He opened the window to the right of him, moving closer to ease the tightness in his chest. The curtain was raised, yet the watery sun provided little illumination.

"Do you work for someone else? Is this their carriage?"

Instead of answering her, he asked, "Why do you dislike physicians so much?"

He hated the veil and the fact that he couldn't read her expression.

"Why do you want to know?" she asked.

"Call it my inveterate curiosity."

"You seem to have a great deal of curiosity about me," she said. "I would have thought you knew everything about me."

"I haven't even begun to know you," he said. "I believe there are many layers to Catriona Cameron, most of which are hidden from the casual observer."

"Do you think yourself a casual observer?" she asked, making an impatient movement with her hands.

Had he annoyed her?

If he had, he was glad of it. The entire situation was an irritant. He'd been a fool, shortsighted and optimistic. The word didn't exist that adequately described his stupidity.

Yet if he hadn't pretended to be a footman, he would

never have gotten to know her. He wouldn't have bedded her. Nor would he find himself at odds with his conscience now.

He didn't want to tell her who he was, but he'd already waited too long.

"We're going to see a woman with two children in Old Town," he said. There, the start of his confession.

"Does my aunt have you doing good works?"

He smiled. "No, this is my own doing."

"I've no wish to go to Old Town. I know about poverty, Mark. There's no need for me to wallow in it."

"Do you?" Surprised, his gaze never left her veil.

What had Mrs. MacDonald told him? That Jean and Catriona had come to Ballindair after their parents' death. He hadn't questioned the woman further, and he should have. One moment they were the beloved daughters of a physician, the next they were employed as maids.

Another layer of Catriona exposed.

Once again he wished that damnable veil wasn't in place.

She turned her head from one side of the carriage to the other as if measuring the interior dimensions. Did she think his vehicle lacking?

"This is the first time I've been in a carriage since the accident," she said.

How stupid of him not to have realized.

"Except for the one bringing me home, of course, but I think the doctor gave me something to make me sleep." She glanced at him. "That's why I don't like doctors," she said. "Because of the accident."

"Tell me about it," he said.

What would she say if he reached over and pulled her into his arms? Not a sensuous impulse as much as one of comfort. He wanted to hold her, press his lips against her hair, soothe her as she trembled. Now, she sat with her gloved hands tightly clasped, her voice thin and frail.

When had she stolen his heart along with his mind?

"They all said I was fortunate to have survived. They never told me how I was to live with this new face. They told me that the experience was to be endured, that it would strengthen my character. I didn't want character. I wanted to escape the pain."

She looked over at him again. "Time was the best doctor. Either the pain eased or I found a way of coping with it."

Glancing out of the window, she continued. "The physicians told me that there was nothing they could do for the scarring. Nothing they could do for the loss of feeling in my hand. Nothing they could do to cure the damage to my knee. They conferred in covens, and took my brother-in-law's money, but they never did anything except give me laudanum and tell me about the grace of God."

She took a deep breath. "That's why I dislike physicians."

"The reason we're going to Old Town is to see my patient," he said.

The truth, stark and unremarkable, except that the interior of the carriage became a bubble of silence.

"I'm a physician."

"You're a physician," she repeated slowly.

"Yes."

"That would explain why you're a lamentable footman."

For long moments she didn't say anything further. Should he try to explain? What could he say?

He'd been curious, then intrigued, then entranced. He'd been amused, interested, and too fascinated. What excuse could he give for being physically enthralled, for forgetting his ruse, for being intoxicated by her?

"Why?" she asked. "Why masquerade as a footman?"

"Would you have allowed me to treat you if I hadn't?"

"A spy, then. I thought better of Aunt Dina."

She made no movement, and to another observer her voice might seem calm and without inflection. He knew her well enough, however, that he caught the edge to her words, a faint hone to them as if they sliced as they were spoken.

"She was worried about you. So was your sister."

"Do you know Jean, too?"

"Yes," he said, deciding not to tell her about his visit to Ballindair yet.

"Are there any more secrets you wish me to know? Are you certain that woman wasn't your wife?"

"I'm not married," he said. "The woman was Sarah, my housekeeper."

"Was bedding me part of your treatment?"

He looked away. Was it the question or the confines of the carriage that disturbed him the most? He'd become accustomed to his dislike of closed spaces, enough to recognize the gnawing anxiety he felt. This, however, was more than that. Perhaps a touch of shame mixed in, along with regret.

"Being your lover was the worst thing I could have done as a physician."

She turned her head to study him.

"Yet as unwise as it was, I can't regret it," he said. "I don't regret it. Do you?"

"You'll pardon me if I don't answer that question," she said. "You've lost the right to hear any of my confidences."

He couldn't fault her reaction. Hadn't he expected it?

Her shoulders were squared and her hands clasped tightly over the hem of her veil.

"I want to go home," she said.

"To your suite of rooms," he said. "Avoiding the world, and pretending it doesn't exist. Do you know how dangerous that is?"

"I think the danger is venturing too much in society," she said.

"Will you forever measure your life against the carriage accident? Will you never get beyond it?"

She deliberately turned away, looking out the window.

"What has ever happened to you?" she asked. "Something so major that your life stopped because of it? Tell me what's happened to you, Dr. Mark . . .." Her words trailed off. "I don't even know your last name."

"Thorburn," he said. "Dr. Mark Thorburn."

"Very well, Dr. Mark Thorburn. What happened to you that was so bad that you had to stop yourself from thinking about it? Or have you led a charmed life? I suspect you have."

"My tutor used to lock me in the closet," he said. "I used to scream for hours to be let out. Once, when my father caught him, the tutor told him that he was trying to strengthen my character. My father allowed the punishment to continue."

She turned her head.

"What did you do that was so bad you were locked in a closet?"

"The first time, I didn't know the capital of Greece. It's Athens, by the way. I don't remember what I did all those other times."

"Your father allowed it?"

"My father was all for strengthening my character," he said calmly. "I was to be an example for my younger brothers. Besides, it was a way to discourage me from speaking of medicine." He glanced over at her. "I've wanted to be a doctor ever since I could remember."

She didn't say anything.

"I know it wasn't as physically taxing as your carriage accident," he said. "Nor the equal in trauma. But my life hasn't been charmed."

"So you test yourself by riding in a carriage with the window open?"

She'd noticed.

"A carriage is the easiest form of transportation, especially in the winter," he said. "Besides, it's something I need to overcome."

"What a paragon of virtue you are, Dr. Thorburn."

Her voice had become more cutting. At least it wasn't that calm demeanor she'd assumed sometimes, one socially acceptable but patently false.

What could he say to exonerate himself?

I was a fool, Catriona. He'd wanted her, and still wanted her, and wasn't that confession?

Chapter 23

The carriage rolled to a stop.

Catriona forced her hands to relax. Nothing was going to happen to her. Nothing had happened.

Only a betrayal so deep it felt carved into her bones.

He reached over and opened the door, leaving the carriage. For a moment she thought he meant to leave her there. She wasn't eager to venture out into the Old Town, but she wasn't going to remain here waiting to be robbed or worse.

"Wait," she said, slapping her hand against the door frame.

He turned back to look at her.

"Still giving orders, Princess?"

"As either a footman or a physician, you're insufferable."

He smiled, and she looked away. He shouldn't smile at her in such a way on a public street. Truly, he shouldn't smile at her at all after his deception.

"Will you not take me home?"

"We're nearly there," he said. "It won't be that much time out of your life."

He surprised her by reaching under the seat for a bag.

After retrieving several bottles from it, he placed them in his pockets, then left the carriage.

When he held out his hand, she stared at it, debated remaining behind again, and allowed him to help her down the steps.

"We're going to see Edeen and the children, Brody," he said, handing up his watch.

The driver nodded, barely visible in the layers of his wool.

The streets were narrow and dark. Only Mark's hand on her arm steadied her.

She'd heard of Old Town from Aunt Dina. From her words, she'd pictured the place as a labyrinth, a corkscrew of streets and alleys that led down into Hell. She hadn't considered that it might be worse than she'd imagined.

Twice, she wanted to turn and flee. Twice, she almost pleaded with Mark to take her back to the carriage. Pride and anger kept her silent, however, even as he led her down the steps, stopping before the dark rectangle of a door.

"We're descending into the vault," he said.

"We're going lower?" Were they truly going to Hell, then? Was this her punishment for all the selfish acts she'd ever committed?

She nodded, gathering up her courage.

"It would be easier for you if you removed your veil."

"Like I did last night?" she asked, hearing the bitterness of her voice. "When you continued to lie to me?"

He didn't answer, merely tightened his hand on her arm.

The steps were canted downward, narrow and slippery with something. Perhaps it would be better if she didn't investigate exactly what it was too closely. The smell of rotting vegetables and dank water hit the back of her throat and made her grateful for her veil. At least the heavy lace filtered the worst of the odors.

Thank God that Aunt Mary had saved her from a place like this. She hadn't liked being a maid, but at least she wasn't forced to live in a subterranean warren like a rat. But did Inverness have a section like Old Town?

The worst thing about Inverness was that the breeze blew over the river, bringing the scent of the sea with it. The smell of brine and fish was overpowering at times, but she'd gladly take that to what she was smelling now.

They traveled a good distance from the base of the steps, until the darkness was absolute. Just when she thought that this truly was Hell, a faint light gave her hope.

"What's that?"

"A fire," he said.

Suddenly, a redheaded lad with an engaging grin popped out of the darkness.

She jumped, startled.

"Doctor! I have a tiger!"

"A tiger, James?" Mark asked.

"Mam said I could keep her because she eats rats. Otherwise, she'd just be another mouth to feed." He grabbed Mark's hand and pulled him toward the firelight. "Come and see her."

Mark glanced back at her, then left to follow the boy.

She stood at the opening of the space, noting the shadowed vault above her. How could people live here, without sunlight or fresh air?

"A fine tiger, indeed," she heard Mark say as a striped cat emerged from beneath a pile of blankets, yawning and stretching. James immediately grabbed the cat and cradled her in his arms.

"How is your sister?"

"Better," a woman said, stepping into the light. "She's been coughing less this last week."

The woman was utterly beautiful, her red hair a flame in the shadows. Her eyes were tilted at the corners, giving her an exotic air. Her mouth, lush and inviting, was curved in a half smile as she looked at Mark.

"This is Edeen, Catriona," he said to her.

Jealousy cut through her.

The force of the emotion was so great that she took a step back, wanting to flee from the vault. She had always been the most beautiful woman in a room. Not now, with James's mother standing there silent and still, wearing her threadbare shawl over her shoulders as regally as an ermine-trimmed cape.

Then James appeared in front of her, staring up with a frown on his face.

"Are you the angel of death, come to take Christel?"

She was stunned into silence.

"No, James," Mark said. "She's a friend of mine. This is Miss Cameron."

To her amazement, James performed a lovely bow. She wondered how long it had taken his mother to teach him that.

The fire evidently served as a source of warmth, illumination, and where cooking was done. A small pot sat on a tripod, the contents bubbling.

Mark knelt beside a cot where a little girl lay. Gently, he helped the child sit up, then used his stethoscope to listen to her lungs.

Christel had bright red hair just like her mother. Her face was ashen, however, and she looked painfully thin bundled up in the narrow bed.

The little girl placed her hand on Mark's in a gesture of trust.

She'd felt the same for the physicians in London, at least at first.

They hadn't brought her anything but lies, couched in pretty phrases and spiritual entreaty. *God will decide, Miss Cameron . . . Only the good Lord knows . . . Providence will dictate.*

Did Mark dole out that advice to his patients? She doubted it. He would be direct and unflinching. He, no doubt, would have told her the truth.

You are scarred for life, Catriona. The glass cut through your skin and the scarring will always be with you. There will be no change.

She could have tolerated the truth with a great deal more acceptance than she had the lies. Or could she? Perhaps the doctors had told her what they needed to, in order to calm her. Perhaps she'd been so hysterical, and so desperate, that she wouldn't have accepted the truth.

Was she that shallow, that vain?

Edeen stepped closer to the cot, watching closely as Mark finished up his examination. He withdrew a bottle and handed it to the redhead, and she nodded several times.

The woman was poor, more destitute than anyone she'd ever met, but she'd not relinquished the responsibility of her two children. Why hadn't Edeen parlayed her looks into better opportunities for herself and her children?

Just like she herself had planned? Was she the only one who put such a high price on appearance?

Mark and the children's mother exchanged a wordless look and she immediately felt like an outsider. Had he been her lover, too?

Standing there in a space that offered no privacy, no comfort, and no light, she felt a curious sensation resembling shame. Her future, even scarred, was a great deal brighter than the one offered this family.

The child couldn't remain here. Didn't Mark see that? Why hadn't he demanded that she be taken from here immediately?

The situation reminded her too much of Inverness, and those black months following her parents' death. Without Aunt Mary's intervention, they probably wouldn't have survived. No one had come forward to offer food or money for coal. She and Jean had no one but each other and their aunt, and this woman didn't even have that.

"She can't stay here," she heard herself say.

The woman turned to look at her, her smile fading.

"If she's ill, she can't stay here," she said. "This is no place for a sick child."

"She's my daughter," the woman said. "I thank you for your interest, but this is our home."

"This isn't a home," she said, looking around. "It's a smoky pit. It's a cave."

Mark stared at her. "That will be all, Catriona," he said in a cutting voice.

How had she ever thought he was a footman? How had she ever believed him a servant?

The trip back to the carriage was faster than the descent into the Hell of the vault. She didn't speak and neither did Mark. Once in the carriage, she remained silent.

Only when their surroundings changed, becoming more amenable and less like Old Town, did she turn to look at him.

"Will the little girl live?"

"I hope so," he said. "Christel's looking better than she did last week."

"That's where you've been each morning?"

He nodded. "I try to visit Old Town first thing."

"What will you tell them?"

He turned his head and regarded her.

"What will you tell my aunt and my sister?"

He propped up one arm on the window and didn't move his gaze from her. She was disconcerted by his intense stare. He couldn't see through the veil, she knew that well enough, but he had a way of looking at her as if he could peer past the lace and directly into her soul.

"That I no longer need to see you," he said.

"You never did."

"You stopped eating."

She looked away, annoyed that she couldn't dispute that.

"I think you were troubled in spirit, Catriona."

"I wasn't."

"I think your world had narrowed, that it had probably always been narrow, accommodating only yourself and perhaps your sister."

She hadn't expected him to dissect her character in such a manner.

"You've allowed the accident and what happened to you to become a mirror, one you've wrapped around you. All you can see is what happened to you. Your wishes. Your wants. Your needs."

"I was concerned about the little girl."

He smiled. "A perfect example. Because *you* were concerned, *you* wanted action."

"How can you allow them to live that way?"

He didn't answer for a moment. When he spoke, his voice was somber with a touch of sadness. "Because I can't save them all."

Mark didn't speak again, even when the carriage stopped before the house. It was better that he didn't. Otherwise, he might say something cutting and cruel.

Or too honest for comfort.

Chapter 24

"**A**re you getting rid of your wardrobe?" Catriona asked, standing in the door of the parlor.

Aunt Dina looked up, smiling.

"It does look like that, doesn't it?"

All around her were piles of clothing. On the table before her were three stacks of what looked like aprons but on closer inspection were shifts and corset covers.

"I'm sorting our donations," she said. "People have been generous."

Catriona took a few steps inside the door. "Do you need any help?"

Aunt Dina smiled even brighter. "Oh, my dear, I would love some help."

The older woman patted the settee beside her, and she made her way around the piles. The minute she sat down, Dina thrust some shirts into her arms.

"There you go. Fold those, and we'll have one whole household done."

For several moments they were silent as she followed her aunt's lead. She didn't think she'd ever folded a man's shirt before this moment. At home, her mother had always handled her father's shirts, and then Jean, when her mother was too ill. At Ballindair, she had never been assigned to the laundry, which was only good fortune, since Aunt Mary often used laundry duty as punishment.

By the third shirt, she'd learned well enough that Dina was nodding in approval. That small nod gave her a glow, one that had been curiously absent in her life for a while.

The last shirt finished, she reached for a pile of shifts.

"Won't you take off your veil, my dear?" Dina asked. "It's just the two of us. Artis is off on errands. I've sent Isobel to rest, and Elspeth is cleaning my bedchamber."

Mark had gone, the role of footman no longer necessary. Blessedly, Dina didn't mention him.

Slowly, she raised the veil and pulled it back over her head. She closed her eyes at the touch of cool air on her skin.

"Oh, my dear, you've been crying," Dina said, reaching out and tapping the right side of her face with gentle fingers.

"I couldn't sleep," she said. "That's all."

Dina gently smiled. "We've had an eventful time of it, haven't we? But the fire didn't spread and we can rebuild the carriage house." The older woman sat quiet for a moment, her hands on the garments in her lap. "I do need to write dear Morgan, but I haven't yet."

"Why did you do it, Dina?" she asked, keeping her attention on her hands.

Dina, thankfully, did not pretend ignorance or confusion. "You weren't eating, my dear, and you refused to come out of your rooms." She glanced over at Catriona and smiled. "If you'd once offered to help me as you're doing now, I would not have been so concerned."

"So as long as I perform good works, you won't interfere in my life?"

Dina stilled, her busy hands resting in her lap. In those

moments, she wished she could retract what she'd said. Words were easily spoken and impossible to call back, yet they could wound as surely as a spear.

"I can't promise that," Dina said. "You see, I've become fond of you. When you first came to me," she added, "you were a haughty young woman. For a good two weeks I debated whether or not to write Morgan and tell him to come and get you. I despaired of ever being able to teach you anything. Then, one day, I saw you here, in this very room. You were walking back and forth. I was about to interrupt you when I realized that you weren't just walking, you were practicing walking. You got to the door and curtsied. Then you turned, walked the other way, and curtsied again. I realized that you weren't arrogant as much as afraid."

She felt embarrassment warm her cheeks. "I didn't know anyone had seen me."

"I began to feel affection for you," Dina said, glancing over at her. "You were so determined to change yourself, make yourself over. I admired your spirit and your courage."

"I doubt I was all that admirable," she said.

"Oh, but you were. A pity that girl died in London."

Shocked, she turned to the other woman. Dina didn't look away, but met her look squarely.

"Back then, you wanted to become someone different," Dina said, her words slow and measured, as if Catriona had difficulty understanding English. "You can do the same now."

"How?" she asked. "That girl was beautiful. You can hardly call me that."

Dina put the folded shift on the table before her.

"Very well, your face is scarred, horribly so. Very

well, some people will flinch. Very well, you might scare little children. But bitterness will strip beauty from you as fast."

She blinked at Dina. "You couldn't have said what you just did."

"Why are you so surprised? That someone would tell you the truth? Or that it wouldn't be so terrible once it was voiced?"

She looked away, feeling as if she were floating in thin air. She tried to take a deep breath but her lungs were tied tight by a ribbon of emotion.

People will flinch.

You might scare little children.

Your face is scarred, horribly so.

The girl she'd been, at both Ballindair and newly come to Edinburgh, might have been afraid, but she'd been confident in one thing—her appearance. If she didn't have that, what did she have?

Now, when she said as much to Dina, the older woman reached over and patted her hand.

"Even if the accident hadn't happened, you would have aged, my dear. Beauty is like an orange, Catriona. You enjoy it, you savor it, but you never expect it to last forever."

She had never considered such a thing.

Dina smiled. "You will have to discover who you are without your outward appearance. Who is Catriona Cameron?"

The person she'd been the past six months was a martyr, a hermit, an angry, bitter woman. Is that the identity she wanted for herself? Is that who she wanted to be until she died?

The bottle of laudanum sat in her vanity drawer, ready for her to end her life. Did she want to do that? Her mind veered from that thought so suddenly that she was certain she didn't. But if she lived, what kind of life would she have?

"You don't have to decide tonight," Dina said, as if privy to her chaotic thoughts. "You have the rest of your life to become the woman you wish to be."

"I don't want it to take that long," she said.

Dina smiled.

"I've often thought that the best way to help myself is to help others," Dina said, handing her another bundle of clothes.

She turned to look at her. "Am I very selfish?" she asked, and waited for the truth. Dina had always given her the truth, pleasant or not.

The older woman sighed. "Yes, my dear, you are. For a time, it was a good thing, because you needed to heal. Being so concerned about yourself was necessary. Your selfishness was like having a good coat in winter. Now, it's like wearing that same coat in the midst of summer, cumbersome and uncomfortable."

She gathered up her courage to ask another question. "Is it easy to live alone?"

Dina looked surprised.

"You've been a widow for some time," Catriona continued. "Is it bearable after a while not to have a man in your life?"

"Marriage isn't the only relationship, my dear. There is friendship as well."

Dina's cheeks were pink, and growing pinker. Did she have a friend or a lover? Could a lover be a friend? The questions were so fascinating that she studied the other woman for a long moment.

"Mark has left," she said, when it was obvious that Dina wasn't going to reveal any secrets.

"Yes, he has. A fine man, Dr. Thorburn. Too many times, people complain about the poor and do nothing to assist them. Dr. Thorburn puts his efforts into doing what he can, especially treating the children who most need his help."

"You like him."

"I do. I admire him as well."

Several minutes passed in companionable silence.

"Did he say anything to you about me?"

"A great many things," Dina said, smiling. "I'm to insist on fresh air and sunshine for you. I'm not to take any posturing from you. I'm to be my own woman and not allow you to run my household. I'm not," she said with a twinkling look, "to be afraid of you."

"Afraid of me?"

Dina nodded.

"Why would he say something like that?"

"I have no idea," Dina said.

"Annoying man," she said. "I can't imagine why you thought he'd do me any good."

Dina continued to smile.

Andrew sat in the parlor, empty but for one chair, a table, and a lamp that gave off a faint yellowish glow. He'd built a fire earlier but the room was still chilled.

He was feeling maudlin this afternoon, in a way that disturbed him. He'd not been himself since traveling to this godforsaken country a year ago. Once his mission was done, he'd turn his back on Scotland and never set foot across the border again.

As the fire spat and hissed, memories occupied him. All of his life, his enjoyable life, seemed compressed into a few short weeks. Before he met Catriona he'd felt asleep. Had he ever known pleasure until then, or even joy? He'd most certainly never known the insecurity that had blossomed in her presence.

He'd toyed with the idea of divorcing his wife in order to marry her. He'd made declarations of love to her, when he'd never said those words to another woman. He'd been willing to beggar himself for her, and she'd only laughed when she left him.

Her death would set him free, as nothing else would. Once Catriona was in her grave, he'd be released. He would no longer feel this damnable yearning, the pain that resided, not in his heart, but in his chest or perhaps in the whole of him.

At the knock on the door, he stood, consulted his pocket watch, and walked into the kitchen.

"You're late," he said as he opened the door for Artis.

"I couldn't get away. Mrs. MacTavish is watching my every move. Afraid I might make life miserable for her two little lambs, she is."

He waved his hand in the air, as if brushing away her words. He didn't have the patience or the time for her constant complaints.

She removed her cloak. He hadn't given her leave to do so, or to pull out the chair at the kitchen table. Short of banishing her, there was nothing he could do. She didn't look the type to listen to a lesson on deportment.

He hooked a chair leg with one boot, pulled it out, and sat opposite her.

"Miss Cameron? How is she?"

"Why you're so interested in the likes of her, I don't know, sir. She's an odd one, taking to going with Mrs. MacTavish on errands to Old Town in the last few days. They take their basket of clothes and food and dole them out to their particular friends."

"Does she?"

Artis nodded. "Mrs. MacTavish normally likes to take the minister with her, and a few other ladies. When Miss Cameron goes, however, it's just the two of them and Johnstone. Not safe enough, I'd think."

"Does the footman not accompany them?"

She shook her head. "Now him, that's the strangest story. After the fire, he stopped coming to work. When I asked Mrs. MacTavish, she told me it was none of my concern."

He felt a frisson of alarm. She could ruin everything with her talking.

"It's important that you not call attention to yourself," he said.

"I've done nothing wrong," she said, placing both elbows on the table. "Merely talked with a proper gentleman."

He couldn't wait until his task was done. If he had to deal with Artis much longer, he'd shoot her first.

Mark hadn't allowed his father to interfere with his love of medicine. He certainly wasn't going to allow a woman to do so.

Yet Catriona was occupying his thoughts. He woke thinking of her. When he traveled in his carriage, instead of having to concentrate on the passing scenery to tolerate the closeness, he thought of her. She'd cooked for him, and whenever he ate, he remembered that night. She'd made him smile, and he recalled those moments in quiet times. She'd wept in his arms, and at night he recalled the feel of her, loving her, and holding her before sleep claimed him.

His entire life seemed built around recollections of

her, even when he deliberately tried to banish her from his thoughts.

Even Sarah was conspiring against him. She lost no opportunity to ask questions about Catriona.

"Is she scarred?"

"I never saw her face," he said. He didn't tell her that he had an idea how extensive the damage was, however.

"What did you talk about?"

"How annoying I was, for the most part," he said, which won him a laugh from Sarah.

"What does she do all day?"

Sits and mulls over the unfairness of life, an occupation that will only make her bitter. That, too, he hadn't said aloud.

When Sarah wasn't being curious about Catriona, she was taking great pains to ridicule his days as a footman.

"You forget I employ you," he said one morning. For a quarter hour she'd indulged in a running dialogue with an imaginary servant, a footman of all things, with sidelong glances at him to ensure he was paying attention.

"I can fire you."

"You wouldn't," Sarah said. "No one else would do for you as well as I do."

She was right.

"Plus, who else would want to put up with you, all dour as you've been all week? Not to mention those medicines of yours. Scare a body to death."

"I'm sure I can find someone who would be overjoyed to work with a young, handsome doctor with an admirable disposition."

"Who is he? Will you introduce me to him, sir?" she asked cheekily.

He raised one eyebrow and stared at her over his cup.

"You might employ Edeen," she said. "But then, I dare

you to stop the gossips. I'm your mother's age, so no one thinks anything is amiss with me."

"You never used to be so verbal, Sarah."

"You never used to be so foolish, Dr. Thorburn."

He frowned at her.

"I'll wager you think about the lass in black all the time."

He set the cup down on the saucer with too much force. "Where did you come up with that name?"

"Isn't that what she is? Don't you?"

"Are you divining my thoughts now, Sarah?"

"I know the signs. You've been grumbling around here for days. You aren't eating properly, and you've not been sleeping well. I'm the one who makes your bed, Doctor. I see those sheets every morning. It's like you've fought a war in your bed."

"Very well, I haven't been sleeping all that much," he admitted.

But that was all.

"I could have Anne on my mind," he said.

She folded her arms and shook her head.

"No, you would have shown the signs earlier. It's her, the lass in black."

"Don't call her that."

She smiled.

Perhaps his conscience was warring with him. He remembered every cutting word he'd said to Catriona. She'd just sat there, absorbing his criticism, making no effort to protect herself.

Had he taken her to Old Town on purpose, to show her the other half of the world in which she resided? That question bit too close. Who was he to think he had that right? He healed the body, not the soul. Who was he to examine character?

He should look to himself first.

Perhaps Catriona was so much on his mind because of Johnstone's words.

After the visit to Old Town, he'd made his farewells to Mrs. MacTavish, informing her that Catriona now knew his true identity.

"Is she terribly unhappy?" she'd asked.

The truth won out. "Yes," he said, "but I doubt if it's at you as much as me."

She sighed, then perked up immediately. "I suppose it's worth it, if she's beginning to live again."

As he was leaving, Johnstone had motioned to him from the alley. He followed the man back to the charred ruin of the carriage house.

"The paraffin oil barrel was knocked over," the man said. Johnstone leaned against the door frame, pointing to the corner. "Someone knocked over the barrel. I've four horses in the stable there," he said. "They could have died."

The driver turned to look at him. Even though the man didn't speak, Mark could imagine what he was thinking.

Two accidents too many.

He glanced up at Catriona's window.

He depended on facts and the evidence before his eyes. The carriage fire might well be an accident and unconnected to what had happened in London.

A wise man observes. A comment Dr. Cameron had once made to him. He was going to do just that, and while he was at it, he was going to take other precautions.

Now, he stood and looked at Sarah. She knew him better than anyone and didn't hesitate to either lecture him or keep his occasional confidences. He gave her another one, not looking away from her steady regard.

"I shouldn't have deceived her."

She nodded. "No, you shouldn't have. The poor thing has been through enough. You added hurt to the mix."

How did he fix it? He couldn't bandage it, apply a compress, or give her an analgesic.

Absence would accomplish what he wanted, but it was the one solution against which he rebelled. Was he never to see her again? Was he never to talk to her? As a physician, he was concerned about her.

He was also a man who'd become surprisingly adept at lying to himself.

Chapter 25

Mrs. McPhee looked even more harried on this visit
than she had on the last.

Catriona stood on a riser in front of the seamstress
and her apprentice, enduring the final fitting for her new
dresses with hard-won patience.

Aunt Dina had encouraged her to use the drawing
room, where there was more daylight. Since only one
male was attached to their household, and Johnstone was
occupied with directing the rebuilding of the carriage
house, she was not adverse to the idea.

Nothing, however, seemed to please Mrs. McPhee.

The woman was a whirlwind in the parlor, bustling
around her, giving orders to the apprentice, consulting
her brooch watch more than once, and nodding her head
incessantly.

When Aunt Dina once again indicated a desire to have
the woman make a few more garments, she thought Mrs.
McPhee would cry.

"As I have mentioned before, Mrs. MacTavish, I've
enough to do. I've no idea how I can take on more.
There's the Moffat wedding, and the dresses for all the
Drummond girls. Not to mention the Farquharsons." She

twisted her hands together. "I don't know when I'll have time for the rest of it."

"Why do you not hire additional staff, Mrs. McPhee?" Dina said. "If your business is so good, I'd think that would be an option."

"I've no time!" The woman threw her hands up in the air. "How am I to judge a girl's talent when I don't even have time to sew on a button myself?"

"I truly doubt the situation is so dire," Dina said. "Besides, I might have a few candidates for you to consider. Good girls, with some talent with a needle."

Leave it to Dina to use the situation to advance one of her girls.

Mrs. McPhee, however, was not looking at all happy about the idea.

"Is there such a thing as a lighter veil?" she asked in an effort to diffuse the situation. Each woman looked as if she wouldn't give any ground. They could be here all day.

The seamstress was looking up at her, and so was the apprentice, both women wearing identical expressions of surprise.

Why were they acting as if she'd done something miraculous? It was a simple alteration, that was all.

"Would you truly agree to a lighter veil, Catriona?" Dina asked, her eyes wide.

She'd do anything if it hurried up the fitting. Standing in one place for so long was excessively wearisome on her left knee. Yet even that complaint seemed ridiculous to utter. At least she lived in a place of sunshine, where she could see the sky and have enough food to eat.

"Yes," she said. "Just something slightly lighter. Not transparent."

Mrs. McPhee nodded. "I've just the thing. I'll have to bring it next time."

She sighed inwardly. Why must there be a next time?

Dina strode forward, grabbed her hand, and squeezed it lightly.

"Oh, my dear, I'm so pleased," she said, looking as if she might cry.

What had she done? Nothing worth mention, yet it seemed to please Dina beyond measure.

Perhaps selfishness was a coat, and she'd worn it entirely too long. What had Mark said? Something about a world that narrowed to encompass only herself and perhaps her sister.

Sometimes, she'd even excluded Jean.

What would Jean have done, facing her circumstances?

She would have put a brave face on the situation. She would have allowed Dina to coax her from her room earlier or perhaps would never have become a hermit. She would have attempted to expand her narrowed world.

Even if she wasn't as good a person as Jean, perhaps she could accomplish something in her life. Something that would give her a purpose and take her thoughts away from her current situation and memories of a footman who wasn't what he seemed.

She would begin today. This moment, in fact. With Dina's help, she climbed down from the riser, made her farewells, and went to her room.

There, she sat and wrote her sister, only noticing after she was done that she'd lit the lamp.

"I do worry about my appetite, Dr. Thorburn. I haven't any for Sally's custard, and I always used to like it so. What could the matter be?"

Mark listened with half his attention, then carefully replaced his stethoscope back in the pouch inside his bag.

Mrs. Dalmahoy was forever lamenting about something or other. She was either too hungry or not enough. She wasn't sleeping well, but on his next visit she was worried that she might be sleeping too much.

Whether they paid him or not, he always wanted to give his patients his full attention and all of his skill. Lately, however, he was finding it difficult to tolerate patients like Mrs. Dalmahoy, especially since she, and several other matrons in New Town, were perfectly healthy.

Mrs. Dalmahoy's husband was not attentive to her complaints. Nor were her friends sympathetic when they were just like her, craving attention. Yet he couldn't afford to ignore her. One of her complaints might be a real disease.

How would she have fared with an injury like Catriona's? Would she have hidden from the world? Or would she have demanded pity as her due?

He told himself he shouldn't be thinking of Catriona.

"Appetite is sometimes transitory, Mrs. Dalmahoy," he said. "I wouldn't worry too much about it. If it persists in a week or so, we'll discuss it then."

"Then you don't think it's anything of concern?"

He forced a smile to his face. "I think it might be that you're simply thinking too much about it. You're quite healthy."

"I am?"

He nodded.

"Well, thank you, Dr. Thorburn."

His smile was more genuine this time. "You're welcome, Mrs. Dalmahoy."

He took his leave, giving Brody a wave, a signal that the next stop would be Kingairgen. Not only did he want to see his grandfather, but he needed some information.

At Kingairgen, he sent Brody to the kitchen to warm himself. He removed his greatcoat in the hall, smiled at one of the maids, and sought out his grandfather. He wasn't in his library but in his suite.

His knock resulted in a giggle. The sound kept him motionless, hand raised. He took a step back just as the door opened and a woman of middle years attired in maid's cap and apron scurried past him and down the hall, still giggling.

"Is that Mary?" he asked, turning back to the earl, who stood inside.

His grandfather looked down at the floor. "She was helping me with something."

He wasn't going to ask.

"Your father is angry at you," his grandfather said, moving back into the sitting room. "Said to tell you that he expects more loyalty from his own son."

He followed, setting his bag down on the table. When his grandfather sat on the settee and began unbuttoning a shirt that had been hastily buttoned—which Mark deduced from the wrong placement of buttons to buttonholes—he bit back his smile and took out his stethoscope.

"What have I done now?" he asked.

"No doubt failed to attend one of his entertainments," the earl said, grinning at him. Although his teeth were slightly discolored, they were all his and his grin was engaging. "Although he's not happy about the Ferguson girl. She's made no secret of the fact she thinks you're a scoundrel."

At least he didn't cavort with maids in his room, he thought. However, since he'd pretended to be a footman, he couldn't exactly claim to be virtuous.

"Have you taken to being the family messenger?"

"If I wasn't, neither of you would communicate with the other."

"I'm surprised that my father deigns to speak to you," he said.

"I know how damn stubborn each of you is," his grandfather said. "You've always been that way, the both of you."

"We've had this conversation before," he said, and it wasn't one he intended to repeat again.

He placed the disk of his stethoscope against his grandfather's chest and listened for a moment. When he was done, he stepped back and said, "I've taken to recommending the Banting diet for some of my patients. They seem to be prospering on it, just like you."

"Good for you," his grandfather said. "Knew you had sense. Can I put my shirt back on now?"

He nodded.

"A hell of a thing, when my grandson makes me undress and dress like I was an infant."

"I can recommend someone else, if you'd prefer a different physician."

His grandfather shook his head. "No, it's the only way I see you. I told your father, by the way, that he should become your patient."

"I doubt you met with much success. I've tried to give him medical advice in the past. He pretends not to hear."

"He seems to dote on those brothers of yours. I think it's because they're more like your mother in temperament, while you're just like him."

"I hope you won't mind if I disagree entirely."

His grandfather held out his cuffs for help in fixing the links. "I didn't expect you would agree, being as stubborn as you are."

He raised his eyebrows. "You're calling me stubborn?"

"You're used to people obeying your every word."

"Am I?"

His grandfather nodded. "It's being a physician, I think."

"Surely I'm not as autocratic as that," he said. Was he? "The reason my father enjoys the company of my brothers so much is because they want his money. They'll only say what he wants to hear and do what he wants them to do, at least until his back is turned."

His grandfather's eyes narrowed. "Your grandmother said much the same thing to me. She was disappointed in those two. Perhaps old age will give your father some measure of wisdom."

"Old age will give him arthritis, and liver spots," he said. "He'll have pain in his stomach and his heart will give him trouble from time to time. I doubt, sincerely, that he will ever grow wise."

"Do you hate him so much?"

Mark put his stethoscope back into his bag.

"I don't hate him at all," he said. "I love him, after my fashion. But I'm under no illusions as to his character. My father believes his title makes him better than other people. It doesn't."

"What makes the measure of a man, my boy? In your eyes?"

He closed up his bag and turned back to his grandfather. "What he does, I think. Who he is when no one is looking."

"So who are you when no one is looking?"

A failure, perhaps, or even worse: a hypocrite.

"Tell me about the Ferguson girl. What happened there? I hear she's telling everyone you deceived her."

He eyed his grandfather. "How do you hear all these things? You might as well live in the middle of Edinburgh."

"I've a penchant for gossip," the old man admitted with a smile. "People fascinate me."

"It's closer to the truth to say that she broke off the relationship with me. However, first you'd have to define relationship. We were friends, barely more."

His grandfather's laugh startled him.

"Oh, I suspect you were a great deal more than that, at least in Anne's eyes, and those of her parents, her siblings, and assorted cousins. I believe, my dear boy, that they were already planning a wedding."

"Were they? Wouldn't the bridegroom have to be involved?"

"You disappoint me, if you know so little of women as that. Once a woman has separated you from the flock, you might as well admit defeat."

"You make me sound like a sheep."

"As far as women are concerned, my boy, men *are* sheep. We may think we rule the world, but only until a woman has chosen one of us." He glanced over at a miniature of his wife on the bureau and smiled. "Most of us, I'm happy to say, follow after the ewe with the smell of her in our nostrils, content."

"Are you speaking of love?"

"What else? What else changes a decent man into such a docile creature?"

"That wasn't the relationship I had with Anne Ferguson."

His grandfather smiled again. "That's not what you felt for Anne. That doesn't mean she was similarly disposed. She probably thought herself deeply in love."

He considered that thought for a moment, remembering Anne's stricken look. "You might be right," he said.

"Is it another woman?"

He occupied himself putting his bag in order, taking

the minutes to organize his thoughts. No one saw through him as well as his grandfather, even though Sarah was a close second.

"Yes," he said. Perhaps honesty was best. "It is."

"Not well done of you, my boy. Always lead one woman out the back door before you open the front door to another."

He smiled. "It isn't that way," he said.

Catriona still occupied too much of his mind. He told himself, daily, to forget her, but the admonishment had no effect on his thoughts.

"It's always that way," his grandfather said.

"Even when you aren't aware it's happening?" he asked.

"Well, damn, boy, that's even worse."

He didn't want to discuss his relationship—or lack of one—with Catriona. Instead, he sat on the chair opposite his grandfather.

"I need your help," he said.

"Whatever it is, my boy, you know I'll help. Have you got her in the family way?"

He simply stared at the old man, who had a vivid and venal imagination. What he also had was a network of contacts that stretched throughout Scotland and England.

"I need help in a confidential matter."

His grandfather's eyebrows rose.

He shook his head. "No, I haven't got her in a family way."

Had he? He brushed that thought aside for the moment. "I need someone who can attend to a task and not speak of it."

"That sounds ominous, my boy."

"I need someone watched," he said. "A woman."

One of the old man's eyebrows disappeared into the thatch of his white hair.

"Let me tell you about Catriona Cameron," he said, realizing it was the only way he was going to get the information he needed.

For the next quarter hour he found himself divulging most of the story to the earl. He wasn't about to admit the physical relationship between himself and Catriona, but it seemed his grandfather could read well enough between the lines.

"So you're concerned about the girl, eh?"

He nodded.

"Go and see my solicitors, boy. They employ a few people. Some of them have done a great service for me in the past."

He looked at his grandfather quizzically, but the old man merely shook his head.

That afternoon he hired, by virtue of his grandfather's solicitor, a man by the name of Thomas MacLean.

Mr. MacLean wore a bowler hat and a garish plaid jacket, spoke little, nodded much, and kept taking notes in such a frenetic fashion that Mark wondered if he was recording their entire conversation, word by word.

The man also had a regrettably porcine appearance, with a round face, a short bulbous nose, and hair so light it appeared translucent.

"You think the girl is in danger?" the man asked.

He pushed back his impatience. "I don't know, Mr. MacLean. I just can't rid myself of this feeling that something's not right. I hope it's simply my imagination."

"It's an inkling, that's what it is," the man said, waving the hand holding the stubby pencil at him. "You're a wise man to be listening to it."

Was he?

Or was he simply overly concerned about Catriona to the exclusion of his common sense? She was constantly in his thoughts, and had started appearing in his dreams.

Something had to be done about that, too.

Chapter 26

Artis frowned at her from the opposite seat.

"Why are we going to Old Town?" she asked. From her tone, she was annoyed by the errand.

Catriona wasn't going to tell the maid that they were on a mission of mercy. Artis would make fun of the idea, and she wasn't in the mood to be ridiculed.

Perhaps she was being foolish, but she hadn't been able to get Edeen and her children out of her mind, especially the irrepressible James.

"Why did you insist I come with you?" Artis asked.

"Because you don't seem afraid of anything," she said.

The maid only frowned at her again. Thankfully, she didn't ask any further questions.

No one would understand, but was acceptance from other people all that important? She had to do what she felt was right, and this simply felt right.

She was only here because Mark had refused to aid the poor child.

No, she had to stop thinking of the man. Try as she might, however, he resided in her thoughts all too often.

Perhaps she could understand why he'd pretended to be a footman, especially if Aunt Dina had been that concerned. Perhaps she might have been intransigent about not seeing a physician. Perhaps she might have been teetering on the edge of despair. Very well, her behavior had concerned those who cared about her.

But he didn't have to bed her.

He didn't have to touch her with gentleness and tenderness.

Why were those moments in his arms so difficult to forget? That was the most unsettling thing of all. She was not an unschooled miss, adrift in the fog of her first passion. Why, then, couldn't she forget him?

She needed to find something about him that was despicable, a character flaw that was easy to hate.

He hadn't rescued the children, when it was all too evident they were in desperate need of saving.

I can't save them all.

There, a flaw worthy enough of being despised.

Yet he was kind, witness his treatment of Isobel. He'd chosen medicine as a vocation, which indicated he had a decent character, did it not? Or perhaps medicine had called him, as her father had often said.

No, she simply must look for his defects.

He'd complemented her cooking. He'd told her she was beautiful when she had been desperate for any kind word.

This would never do. She must find more faults. Either that or stop thinking about him, especially when doing so made her miserable.

When they arrived at the entrance to Heriot Close, she and Artis descended from the carriage. Mr. Johnstone, surprisingly, insisted on accompanying them. While she doubted the wisdom of leaving the vehicle unattended, she was heartily glad of his presence. She wasn't a fool, after all. Old Town was not a place for two women alone, however truculent and disagreeable Artis might be.

Even the maid was silenced by the scenes around them. Yawning maws of blackened doorways led to gin parlors. A prostitute leaned against a wall, her face turned away as they passed. Two boys, barely out of childhood, stood at the corner of one of the streets. She was sure that if Mr. Johnstone hadn't accompanied them, the boys would've waylaid her and Artis. As it was, they simply sneered and called out vile things as they passed.

Several minutes later she stood at the entrance to the steps to the vaults. She didn't want to go down there again. There was no choice, however. She couldn't simply stand here and wish Edeen and her children to come forward. Instead, they had to go in and get them.

The time of day evidently didn't matter in Old Town. Sounds of drunken revelry carried throughout the narrow passageways. The deeper they descended, the less light there was, until it was as dark as a tarnished soul. Mr. Johnstone held up the carriage lantern behind them, and once more she was grateful for his presence.

She counted the vaults beneath the bridge. At the third one she hesitated, wondering if she was wrong after all. There was no fire at the entrance, as there had been a few days earlier. The air was dank and cold.

Just when she thought she'd gone the wrong way, she heard the sound of a child's weak cough.

"Edeen." She called out the woman's name, then again.

A sound of footsteps came first, then a shadow. Edeen emerged into Mr. Johnstone's light, a scarf around her white face. In the faint light, she looked gaunt, as if she hadn't eaten for days.

In that instant Catriona felt justified for both the chance she'd taken and what she was about to do.

"I've come to take you away from here," she said. "To my home."

Artis glanced at her swiftly but didn't say anything.

"I am home," Edeen said, turning and vanishing into the shadows again.

There was nothing to do but follow her.

Her veil made it impossible for Catriona to see anything as she walked forward. She shuffled, her shoes sliding against the brick of the floor. She hated not being able to see where she walked or even her destination.

Mr. Johnstone's lantern was the only illumination in this part of Hell. He raised it directly behind her, revealing the high ceiling of the vault and the two children in the corner, as frightened looking as starving rats.

Despite the attempt to make the vault livable, it was a place of horror, hardly a home.

"Why wouldn't you want to leave this place?"

"I've no wish for your charity," Edeen said.

Why couldn't this be easier? Here she was, offering the woman a chance at a better life, and she refused to take it.

She'd never considered that Edeen might have other plans.

Is this how Aunt Dina had felt when faced with her own behavior? How odd to feel so disconcerted and irritated at the same time.

Edeen went to stand in front of her children, as if to protect them.

"You remind me of myself," she heard herself say. "Or what I would have become if people hadn't helped me."

Edeen's face stiffened. "Take your pity and leave us be."

She wasn't doing this well, was she?

"My sister is a countess," she said. "She lives in a place called Ballindair, a castle that's far off in the country, surrounded by hills, a river, and even a waterfall. If ever there was an enchanted place, it's Ballindair." If ever there was a place as far from Old Town as could be, Ballindair was it.

James peeped out from behind his mother's skirts. "Is your sister a princess?"

The question reminded her of Mark. For a moment she couldn't speak.

"Yes," she said. "I believe she is a princess."

She looked at Edeen. "It wouldn't be charity if you went to Ballindair. You'd be employed there and expected to do your job well. Everyone at Ballindair has a job."

"Even me?" James asked.

"Even you," she said, smiling. "Not a large one, because you would be expected to learn your letters."

"He would go to school?" Edeen asked.

"Yes," she said. Reaching into her pocket, she withdrew Jean's letter. Skipping over the part where her sister had expressed her pity for Edeen's plight, she read the most important part.

" 'We can offer her two positions, one as a maid-of-all-work, and one in the dairy shed. She needs to choose which she would prefer.'

"Now, I don't care which you pick," Catriona said. "I, myself, would rather work in the castle again than be a dairy maid, but it's your decision."

"You worked at Ballindair?" Artis asked from beside her. Until then she'd been silent.

"I was a maid," she said. "But not a good one." She looked at Edeen. "You would have to be better, but I don't think it would be all that hard."

Edeen didn't speak. What had she expected, that the woman would gush with gratitude?

"I'm not going to argue with you," Catriona said. "But I'm not leaving here without you."

She was not going to fail. This errand was more for

her sake than for Edeen's. She was going to perform her first truly unselfish act, and by God, Edeen was going to cooperate.

"If you come with me, it will be better for your children. If not for yourself, then do it for them." She looked around her. "Surely, you have no fondness for this place?"

"Why are you doing this?"

She decided to give the woman the truth.

"I'm here to be your savior, Edeen, and thereby save myself."

The woman didn't answer, merely stared at her long enough that she felt intensely uncomfortable. Should she say more? Or wish she'd said less?

Edeen abruptly turned and spoke to her children. James gathered up their clothing, while Christel looked wide-eyed at Catriona.

Without a word, Artis moved forward to help Edeen gather up their belongings. She took the lantern while Mr. Johnstone lifted Christel in his arms. Edeen and Artis carried a trunk. A single trunk, holding everything the three of them owned. She turned away from the sight of it.

She led the way through the warrenlike closes of Old Town. Artis surprised her by dropping the trunk and coming to her side at the base of the steps.

"The steps are steep," the maid said, offering a hand to her, "and your knee has been bothering you."

How did she know that? Instead of asking the other woman, she took her hand and slowly ascended the steps. The carriage was where they'd left it, the horses greeting them with a whinny that sounded like equine relief. Catriona felt the same way at the sight of the watery sun and the dreary winter day.

She promised herself that she would never again descend into the vaults of Old Town.

Mr. Johnstone deposited Christel carefully on the seat, tipping his hat as he left the carriage.

As she waited for the others to be seated, James tugged at her skirt.

"Are you very sad?" he asked.

She glanced down at him. "Why would I be sad?"

"Mam says that you're wearing mourning, for when someone dies."

"No one has died," she said. *I only lost part of myself.* Would a child understand that? Most adults didn't.

She helped him into the carriage, then moved to sit in the corner. Here, in the faint light, little Christel looked even more ill than in the vault. She hoped that living at Ballindair would heal her.

"I'm not wearing a veil because I'm sad," she said. "I don't wish for people to see me."

"Why?"

He tilted his head, looking at her as if she were the strangest creature he'd ever seen.

"I was in an accident," she said. "My face was disfigured. Scarred," she simplified.

There was that same inquiring gaze.

"Are you a monster?"

I might be.

With trembling hands, Catriona grabbed the hem of her veil.

What stupidity was this? Did she want to scare the child? Or was she simply tired of hiding?

Slowly, she drew up the lower part of the veil until her face was exposed. She draped it over the back of her head and sat there, her hands clasped together tightly on her lap.

"Did a dragon do that with his claws?" James asked.

She felt a smile begin deep inside.

"No dragon, I'm afraid. It was glass from a broken window."

James nodded. "I broke a cup once, and Mam was all worried I might cut myself."

He inspected her carefully, tilting his head one way and then another. Slowly, he reached out, his fingers out-stretched. With movement so slow she could easily have stopped him, he touched her cheek with warm and gentle fingers.

"Does it hurt?"

"Not anymore," she said.

"I fell once," he said. "Want to see my scar?"

She slowly nodded, permission for him to roll up one leg of his loose-fitting trousers.

He pointed to the faint mark with some pride. "See?"

"That's very impressive," she said, the words so dif-ficult to say they choked her. "Did it hurt?"

"I don't remember," he said. "I was probably very brave."

"I've no doubt you were."

She put her veil in place again, just in time to hide her tears.

Edeen reached over and touched her hand, a wordless gesture of comfort. Few people had extended such ef-fortless sympathy. When the other woman didn't speak, didn't offer her any platitudes, she was grateful.

Artis, however, had glanced at her face and turned away, a reaction for which she'd been prepared.

"I'll earn my keep at this castle of yours," Edeen said.

She only nodded. If she'd known all she needed for Edeen to capitulate was to remove her veil, she would have done it much earlier.

"Just don't, whatever you do," she said, giving her some advice from her own experience at Ballindair, "offer to work in the laundry."

She looked through the window at Old Town disappearing. If forced with having to choose, she'd return to being a maid at Ballindair and count herself fortunate, rather than live as Edeen and her children had.

Better to be in servitude to an employer than in bondage to poverty.

Because of Morgan, however, she was saved from either. Had she ever thanked him?

Another oversight on her part, another sin to lay at her feet.

Chapter 27

Within three days Edeen and her children had been outfitted in new clothing, fed well, bundled up securely, and loaded into the carriage.

"I don't like leaving you alone, miss," Mr. Johnstone said.

"I thank you for your concern, Mr. Johnstone," Catriona said. "But they need to get to Ballindair."

The town house was becoming crowded. Unbeknownst to her, James had hidden three kittens and a mother cat in the trunk they'd carried from Old Town. Between the kittens, the cat, Edeen, James, and Christel, they were up to their ears in noise.

She'd never appreciated the silence or the peace in the household until now.

"I can assure you, Mr. Johnstone," she said, "I will be fine in the time it takes for you to travel to Ballindair and return."

"I'll just make sure the doctor knows I'm gone," he said, his face set in mulish lines.

"What does Dr. Thorburn have to say about this?" she asked.

Mark had come to treat Christel in the last week, his

appearance necessitating that his identity be explained to the maids. All of them tittered about the masquerade, except for Artis, who looked at her strangely.

She'd managed to avoid him for three days. Now Mr. Johnstone considered him an ally of sorts?

"Neither of us believes the fire was an accident, Miss Cameron," Mr. Johnstone said. "You know how I feel about what happened in London."

Indeed she did. She was hard-pressed not to have him discuss the topic whenever they saw each other.

"I assure you," she said, "I'll be fine. There's no need to involve Dr. Thorburn."

She wasn't at all sure he had listened to her. No doubt he sent a message to Mark and she could expect him on her doorstep any moment.

Still, the two of them being so protective warmed her.

As they watched the carriage pull away, Catriona turned to Dina.

"You never told me that benevolence could be so exhausting," she said.

Dina's laughter brightened the gray day. "I don't adopt whole families, my dear," she said, her words creating small puffy clouds in the cold air. "Or such a precocious young boy." She sighed. "I wonder what will become of him?"

"At Ballindair, anything," Catriona said. Look what had happened to her.

"I do so love the castle," Dina said. "As soon as your sister has her child, we should arrange to visit her."

She nodded, but as much as she loved Jean, she wasn't in any hurry to witness her happiness with Morgan or see the newest member of the family. Until now she hadn't much experience with envy.

She hated feeling petty, hated being restrained in her

emotions. Most of all she hated the knowledge that she'd always had these flaws and ignored them until recently.

They entered the house together, standing in the small room off the kitchen to remove their coats.

Isobel entered the kitchen. "Dr. Thorburn just arrived," the maid said, her color high and her eyes twinkling.

"He's come for Christel," Catriona said.

Dina looked at her, a small smile on her lips. "He knew they were leaving this morning. In fact, he sent along his records for the physician who will be caring for her. He's a dedicated and talented doctor, you know."

"I'm sure," she said, moving toward the stairs.

"He's been asking about you."

She stopped and looked back at Dina.

"I don't want to see him," she said.

To her surprise, Dina shook her head. "Is that entirely wise? Perhaps if you wouldn't ignore him, he wouldn't be so curious about you."

He wasn't curious; he was intrusive, as well as irritating, annoying, and too unforgettable for her peace of mind.

Suddenly it was a moot point. He came through the hallway, large and tall, a wall of determination.

"Are you going to hide in your room?" he asked, frowning at her.

Dina stepped away with a murmured excuse. Cook and Elspeth likewise disappeared. Isobel would have remained behind if Aunt Dina hadn't pulled her away by her apron strings.

Wasn't she supposed to have a chaperone? Why had everyone left her alone with this man?

She couldn't go through him, and she doubted he would allow her to go around him. Inwardly, she sighed, resigning herself to yet another confrontation.

She feigned composure, all the while wishing she was up for the battle. For days now she'd been feeling weepy, a circumstance no doubt brought on by lack of sleep.

"Why are you here?" she asked. "Christel has left."

"You're shivering," he said.

Had his voice always been that deep, so filled with a Scottish burr? Mark would be a success in the drawing rooms of the ton. Women would flock to him, lean over him, brush against him. They'd engage him in conversation to simply hear him speak.

If he chanced to kiss a woman, she'd never forget it. She'd press her fingers against her lips wonderingly, recalling that exact moment.

Such a thing had never happened to her, of course.

"Yes, I'm shivering," she said, moving to pass him. "It's a cold day."

To her great delight, he moved aside. Should she try for the stairs?

Aunt Dina and the maids must be hiding somewhere, because none of them came to her aid.

"Your limp is worse."

Why had he noticed that?

"I haven't been walking lately," she said. She wouldn't make it up the stairs. He was directly behind her. So close, in fact, that it felt like he was herding her.

"You need a shawl," he said.

"I don't need fashion advice."

"Then use your common sense. You're shivering."

"As well as limping," she added, suddenly grateful for the absence of the servants. What would they have thought to hear such comments?

"Thank you for sending Edeen and the children to Ballindair," he said, startling her. "Your kindness will save Christel's life."

Had anyone ever been as concerned about her as Mark was about Christel? Perhaps her parents, before the bad times. Always Jean, but she'd never appreciated her sister's love and loyalty. Jean had always tried to protect her, even from herself.

Entering the parlor, she turned to face him.

"You'll be happy to note that I've taken to eating with Dina, and my meals are surprisingly tranquil."

He smiled at her, which would never do.

She'd missed him at meals and in her bed, but she wasn't going to say that, no matter how great the provocation.

"My days are remarkably serene without someone to argue with," he said, "or to challenge my every word."

"I doubt anyone ever challenges you as Dr. Thorburn," she said. "But I only knew the footman. You were an arrogant footman."

"I was your equal in arrogance," he said.

He was also her equal in passion, another comment she would not make.

"How impolite of you," she said.

His eyes twinkled when he smiled. What a waste of time to be mesmerized by such a sight. She must dust her room, change the linens, stare out the window, and pace the confines of her suite, all worthwhile chores.

"Have you been well?" he asked softly.

He placed his hand on her shoulder, and she shouldn't have been able to feel it, but she did.

"I am well," she said. "Exceedingly so. I am the picture of health. As soon as I stand before a fire, I'll be warm enough to stop shivering."

"Would you allow me to recommend a physician to you?"

"You think I'm ill?"

"No," he said. "I think you're the picture of health. But

I want to do everything I can to ensure you stay that way. I would be remiss if I did otherwise."

She nodded. "As a physician, of course."

"Or your lover."

Moving closer to the parlor fire, she took a few moments to remove her gloves, taking her time in order to compose herself. With only a few words he'd destroyed her day, and no doubt her night as well.

"Do you think to call upon me in such a role, Mark? Do you think Aunt Dina would accept if you said, 'Mrs. MacTavish, I'm here because passion brought me?'"

"Are you with child?" he asked softly.

"Is that why you're here? No."

He came to stand beside her, reaching for her hand. As her eyes widened, he bent and kissed her bare knuckles.

"That's not the only reason I'm here, Catriona."

Just when she thought he would leave, he moved both of the chairs until they were directly in front of the fire, then removed his coat and placed it on one chair. He led her to it and stood there until she had no choice but to sit, then pulled up his coat until it covered her shoulders.

"There, are you warm enough?"

She nodded, bemused.

"We've solved the problem of the shivers. Now we need to work on the limp. Why haven't you been walking?"

She didn't want to tell him, but she must. "My leg has been hurting too much," she said.

To her shock, he knelt before her.

"What are you about, Mark?"

He reached for his bag, opened it, and withdrew an amber-colored bottle with a cork stopper. He set it down on the floor, then raised her skirts.

She slapped his hands away, but he only smiled and continued with his explorations.

"You can't think to bed me here, in the middle of the day. What about the maids? Or Aunt Dina?"

"How adventuresome you are, Catriona," he said. "I've no intentions of bedding you on the settee." He leaned back, eyeing the furniture's dimensions. "First of all, it's much too short and too narrow. I'd never fit."

She knew exactly how large he was, but she wasn't going to say such a thing to him.

"Or the floor? Is that what you're thinking? That might be acceptable."

She frowned at him, and wished he could see her expression.

He pulled up her skirts again and rolled down her left stocking. She tried to roll it back up, but he held her hands with one of his and grabbed the bottle.

"What is that?"

"Liniment," he said. "It should take away some of the pain. Do you object to that?"

She sat back.

He poured the lotion on his palm. The pungent odor was strong enough that her eyes watered. She leaned back as he rubbed his hands together, then placed them on her knee. How large and warm his hands were.

Her heart thudded. Her mouth grew dry. Warmth traveled throughout her body, its origin not hard to decipher. He was warming her with his touch and the twinkle in his eyes as he knelt there.

Suddenly, it was difficult to breathe. Perhaps it was just the noxious odor of the liniment. Or was it Mark's slow and teasing smile?

She looked away but felt his fingers splay around her knee. Was she supposed to sit here meekly and be mauled? He pressed against her skin, the heels of his hands gently massaging away the pain. She closed her eyes, wished he were gone and, paradoxically, would never stop what he was doing.

If no one were at home, would he have seduced her? Or would she have urged him up the stairs and into her room again?

Dina deserved better than to be the subject of gossip.

Her own reputation hardly mattered anymore. She'd never be like the rest of society. She'd be Catriona Cameron, the woman wreathed in black or blue, an object of speculation and rumor. What did it matter if she indulged in hedonism from time to time?

She wanted to kiss him. She wanted to enfold her arms around him and lose herself in the feel of him, warm and smelling of medicine and wild, winter air. She wanted to press her lips against that spot on his temple, the place that would go to silver one day.

"How does that feel?" he asked, bursting her bubble of conjecture.

She opened her eyes and watched as his smile faded. Long moments later the twinkle in his eyes had disappeared, replaced by an expression she could only guess at. Was it hunger she saw?

They were so close she could reach out and touch him, trail her fingers through his hair. Her thumb would brush against that full lower lip, coax it into another teasing smile. Her knuckles would brush against his jaw, her palm against his cheek, feeling the hint of afternoon beard.

Her heart was so full she felt as if she wept inside. Tenderness was a dimension to passion she'd never experienced. Or perhaps what she was feeling had nothing to do with passion.

She clenched her hands into fists to keep from touching him.

He rolled up her stocking, patted her thigh, then lowered her skirt. She was the picture of propriety yet somehow could still feel his hands on her.

"Is that better?" he asked, his voice soft, low, and too seductive.

She nodded. "The pain has gone away."

He moved back, sitting on his heels. He hesitated, as if considering something and then thought better of it. A kiss? What would she do if he reached over and tried to remove her veil?

Standing, he picked up the bottle and placed it on the mantel.

"Perhaps it would be better if you used gloves when you applied it. It stings after a while, but my hands are tougher."

"What about the smell?" she asked. "What's in it?"

"Camphor, I imagine," he said. "Some herbs, perhaps some alcohol."

Her leg was still tingling where he touched her, and she doubted it had much to do with liniment.

Take me upstairs.

He took one step toward her then halted, stopping himself before he could reach her.

She stood, and unwisely walked to him, placing her hand on his jacket, above his heart. She felt the rapid cadence of it against her palm, closed her eyes and simply drew in the moment.

Mark, standing there silent and male.

She, wanting him so desperately that it was an ache.

"Take care, Catriona," he said, the words a benediction in a Scottish burr.

"You, too," she said, stepping back.

He nodded, bent to grab his bag, and retrieved his coat.

It would be wiser to simply send him away, forget all

that had happened between them. But, oh, how difficult that was proving to be.

He didn't move. Neither did she. Yet the yearning was there for that kiss. A farewell kiss, perhaps. Or a preface to something more?

She watched as he left the room, feeling as bereft as if she'd lost a loved one.

He was a confusing man in whatever role he played, footman or physician.

She wouldn't think about him anymore. Whenever he entered her mind, she would banish him. When Dina spoke of him, she would change the subject. If she saw him again she would simply treat him as a polite stranger.

Beginning this instant, she was determined not to think about him.

A decision that might prove to be her most difficult.

Chapter 28

A week had passed since Mark had seen Catriona. A week during which he was frenetically busy, yet visited by too many moments of daydreaming.

Worse, his patients weren't getting his best. He was distracted, his thoughts on other things. When he caught himself thinking of her, he'd pull himself back to the present.

Passion could bind two people more ably than chains.

Or was that all it was?

He recalled those times sitting at her table, feeling her annoyance and her irritation, wondering at her expression. He remembered her stinging comments and her arrogance masking fear.

What would she think of his grandfather? Of his father? That he wanted to know should have disturbed him.

"Where to now, Dr. Thorburn?"

He realized he had his hand on the door of the carriage, but he'd not given Brody any directions. He forced a smile to his face and gave his driver the next patient's address.

This had to end. He had to figure out what to do about

this situation, as quickly as possible. Either he had to banish Catriona Cameron from his memories or incorporate her into his life.

The thought of doing just that made him smile.

How dreary her prison had become in the last few days.

Catriona stood, walked to the window and parted the curtains. The afternoon was well advanced, the sun fading from the sky. Tonight would be warmer and she needed to walk.

Her leg hurt from her ankle to her thigh, a reminder that she hadn't been exercising properly. The liniment could only do so much.

From here she could just see the corner of the square. The carriage she'd seen for days was back again, in the same place. Did it belong to a neighbor?

A knock on the door interrupted her thoughts. When she called out, Elspeth entered.

"Miss Cameron, the duke is back," she said, her round face flushed with excitement.

Since only one duke had ever called on her, she assumed it was the Duke of Linster.

She raised her eyebrows. "Is he?"

Elspeth nodded. "He'd like to see you, miss. I'm to say whether or not you're at home to him."

She sent one more look toward the carriage at the corner before turning back to the maid.

"Tell him I'll see him," she said with a sigh of resignation.

"Shall I move the screen?"

She shook her head. "No, I'll see him without it."

A few moments later, attired in her new midnight blue dress and veil, she walked into the parlor to find the Duke

of Linster standing at the window, fingering one of the
lace curtains.

He was tall and lean like a sapling, with silver thread-
ing through his black hair. But it was his face that betrayed
his age, or his love of hedonism. Deep lines bracketed his
mouth and nose, while a sunburst radiated around each
eye. His lips were thin, and, with his long nose, it looked
as if he was forever smelling something foul.

Today he was dressed in black and white. She knew
how much expense and effort went into keeping a cravat
snowy and perfectly pressed. Did he have an army of servants? What would he say if he knew that she'd once been
a maid? The thought of such a revelation brought a smile
to her face.

"Why have you come to see me again, Your Grace?"
There, she'd dispensed with all the preliminaries. She
wouldn't call for tea. She wouldn't thank him for calling
on her. She wouldn't, whatever she said, comment on the
weather. She'd had enough of those conversations to last
her a lifetime.

"You whisked me from here so quickly last time, I
cannot help but believe there's something you're hiding
from me. Is there a mystery about you, my dear?" He
turned to face her, his eyes widening at her appearance.

"Are you in mourning, Catriona?"

"Perhaps I am," she said.

"Perhaps? Do you not know?"

She moved to sit on one of the chairs. The same chair
where she'd sat a few days ago and allowed Mark to pull
up her skirt.

What would he say to see her now, entertaining a duke?

The fire was burning well, and she stretched out her
hands toward it.

The day was another wan one, as if the city cringed

beneath the icy grip of winter. At least Edeen and the children would be safe and warm. But all those other children? Were all those other mothers as stubborn and resilient?

She couldn't save the world.

For the first time, she understood Mark's comment. He couldn't save them all. How did he stop from wanting to, though?

"Who do you mourn, my dear?" The duke sat beside her, extending his hand so she might put hers atop it. Instead, she clasped her hands together in her lap.

"I might have told you that I mourned myself just a short time ago," she said. "I don't know if I feel the same now."

"Then why wear that ridiculous veil? Show me that beautiful face of yours. You've occupied a great many of my dreams, you know."

Was he trying to be shocking? Or did being a duke give him carte blanche to say anything he wished? Yet being beautiful had allowed her to bend the rules as well, hadn't it? She could say anything and be forgiven. Or do anything and be understood. How arrogant she'd been. How foolish.

"Come, we're friends, are we not? Dispense with that silly thing."

Had they ever been friends? He'd wanted her because she was beautiful and for no other reason than that. She'd wanted him for his money and his title.

How shallow both of them had been.

The difference was that she'd changed.

"Come, Catriona."

She was becoming adept at removing her veil, and did so in less than a minute. She lay it down on the cushion beside her, looking up to meet his gaze.

She thought of James and his question. She doubted if the duke would ask if the damage to her face had been caused by dragon claws. No, the Duke of Linster would not be so kind.

"There, Duke, that's why I wear a veil."

His face froze in a pleasant expression, but his brown eyes turned flat and cold. His lips thinned, as if he were trying to contain words he otherwise might have said. His posture was rigid, his hand gripping the walking stick so tightly each knuckle was white.

"A little boy saw me the other day," she said. "He didn't seem frightened. Are you?"

"I am not frightened," he said, gathering up his dignity like a muddy cloak. "I am merely saddened by the loss of your beauty, my dear."

"As time goes by, I find I miss it less and less," she said, surprising herself. "I was once Catriona, the beautiful. Now I'm simply Catriona. I don't have to be anything but what I wish to be."

Who was that? That was a decision she'd have to make soon enough.

"I pity you, my dear. You were once a beautiful woman."

"I don't want your pity, Fitzgerald."

How strange that she'd once wanted him to offer for her. Now, she didn't think she had the temperament to be the wife of a lecher. He would always have mistresses, and why should she have to endure that?

He was looking everywhere but at her. The curtains again seemed to fascinate him, and the top of his walking stick seemed of immense interest.

She took pity on the man and stood, leading the way to the foyer, unsurprised when he followed her without a word. He didn't even bother to search his mind for polite words when she opened the door and stepped aside. He only nodded at her, tapped his walking stick on the floor, and donned his hat and coat.

She watched him descend the steps of the town house with a calm that surprised her.

Good riddance, Fitzgerald.

At the base of the steps he turned and looked up at her as if to ensure that the sight of her face was real and not some delusion. How soon would he spread the word about her? Within the hour, she had no doubt. The Duke of Linster was an inveterate gossip.

She closed the door on the sight of him and retreated to the parlor. At a sound outside the door, she reached for the veil.

Artis entered the room, holding a tea tray piled high with Cook's pastries. Aunt Dina had been more hospitable than she.

At the sight of her, Artis lowered the tray to the table.

"I've already seen you, miss," the maid said. "You needn't put the veil on for me."

Artis went to the front window overlooking the street. "You showed him, then?"

"Yes," she said. Where had her courage come from?

"There he goes like a dog frightened by an angry cat."

The idea of being likened to an angry cat made her smile.

"He's not worth it, you know. Most men aren't." Artis shrugged. "Oh, there are a few who might be, but not him. Not the duke."

"Society would disagree with you," she said. "He's wealthy."

Artis didn't respond to that.

"Have a great many men fallen in love with you?" Artis asked. "Before your accident, I mean."

She smiled again. "One or two."

The maid turned to look at her. "No one's ever loved me. Certainly not a duke."

"The duke isn't in love with me. If anyone, he's in love with himself. Or his title."

Artis didn't say anything further, merely turned and picked up the tea tray.

At the door, she hesitated. "Can I ask you something else?"

She nodded.

"Have you ever been in love?"

Unbidden, Mark's face flashed into her mind. She pushed it away. "No," she said. "I don't think I ever have."

"A man would go to great lengths to punish the woman he loved. Someone who didn't love him back."

"Why all this talk of love, Artis?" she asked.

Artis shook her head and looked down at the tray. "Here I am, taking the tray away. Would you like some tea, miss?"

"No," she said. "Thank you, Artis."

The woman looked surprised. Had she failed to thank her in the past?

Once alone, she lay her head back on the ornate mahogany carving of the settee. She wasn't eager to return to her suite. The rooms that had been a haven for the last two months now seemed a prison.

She stared down at the veil in her lap. What did it matter if she wore black or blue lace? Must she hide from the world? What difference did it make if everyone saw her?

She didn't want to be revolting to anyone, especially not to Mark. Wasn't that a surprising admission? Why couldn't she stop thinking about him, remembering his touch on her skin?

She'd been lonely, that's all. She'd been accustomed to the touch of a man, nothing more complicated than that. Never mind that she hadn't missed passion when she'd first come to Edinburgh or those months in London. Never mind that she could barely remember the face of her first lover, but she doubted she'd ever forget Mark.

He'd been the only man she'd ever truly missed, the only one who made her want something more than passion, the only one who'd held her tenderly as she'd wept in his arms. Perhaps she wanted gentleness, understanding, and even laughter.

Reason enough to banish him from her mind. Otherwise, she'd only invite despair, and she'd had enough of that to last her a lifetime.

Chapter 29

Catriona didn't care how many times she was in a carriage, the experience was unsettling, especially at night. Edinburgh wasn't as brightly lit as London. Nor was there a hint of fog. Traffic, however, was as bad.

Aunt Dina didn't seem to notice her anxiety, which was just as well. She wasn't a patient any longer, and she was going to have to find some way to cope. Either that or walk everywhere she needed to go.

The press of traffic ahead made them slow to a crawl. At this rate they'd never make it home.

"There's a party or some such," Dina said, craning her neck to see. "What a lovely event to have in the midst of snow and ice."

How could Aunt Dina sound so cheerful after the afternoon they had? Hungry little urchins gathered around them, eager to take one of the cast-off shirts or dresses home to their parents. After the last of the clothing was distributed, Dina had produced a sweet. For a moment she thought there'd be a riot. But somehow Dina managed to have one candy stick for each of the children.

She was tired, disheartened, and wished nothing more than the comfort of her suite of rooms. She didn't want to see another sad-looking woman standing in a doorway or hear the raucous laughter of another drunk. Most of all, she didn't want to see the naked yearning in the eyes of children who'd seen and learned too much in their tender years.

How could they help each one of them?

When she'd said as much to Dina, the older woman only smiled. "We can't, my dear. But we can touch one life, and then another. We can bring some beauty and joy to some, if only for a moment."

Now, Dina was looking like a child herself, peering out the window.

"Oh look, my dear. Isn't that Dr. Thorburn?" She waved Catriona over to see. "I swear, the man is one of the most handsome creatures I've ever seen. Oh, to be younger," she added.

The last person she wanted to see was Mark, but she barely had a choice. Dina grabbed the front of her cloak and nearly hauled her across the seat.

He was standing on the steps in front of a large building, each of the windows ablaze with light. The double doors were open, spilling enough illumination to see his attire of black coat and top hat. Beside him was an attractive older woman. As she watched, three other women gathered around him.

"He doesn't need me to look at him," she said. "It seems as if he has all the attention he needs."

She sat back, refusing to look in his direction.

"I would imagine he does most times, my dear. He's handsome and intelligent. Plus, he has a wonderful way of carrying himself, don't you think?"

Was one of those women his lover? Or was he engaged to be married? Would one of those beautiful women be his wife?

If she must survive on bannocks for the rest of her life, it would be better to forget the taste of plum pudding.

Blessedly, traffic eased so they could pull ahead, and she was spared the sight of him.

Mark stood on the steps, wishing himself anywhere but here. Anyplace would be preferable, even Old Town in the midst of an epidemic.

His brother was getting married, a surprise in itself. What was not unexpected was this lavish entertainment—a sign of his father's approval of the match. Anyone who was prominent in Edinburgh society had been invited, including his soon-to-be sister-in-law's three sisters, women who now congregated around him as if he were a wounded boar and they hungry hunters.

His mother laughed at some jest, an indication that he should have been paying more attention. Instead, he was considering the proportions of a new cough medicine that he'd like to give some of his patients in Old Town.

His presence tonight had been mandatory in his father's eyes, but he'd shown up for his mother's sake. His grandfather enjoyed these occasions when his son paraded him around like a trophy he was about to win. The old man had caught his attention several times during the night, the twinkle in the earl's eyes amusing him.

Now, however, he was done with being amused or bored. His quota of smiling, nodding, and pretending to listen attentively had been reached.

He could be home, working with Sarah to finish up his medications for the next week. Or he could be finalizing his patient notes. There was always correspondence to read and letters he needed to write. His days were full, and whenever one of these interminable social events occurred, it ate up time.

The three women in front of him smiled up as one. He'd endured their company the entire night, and not one of them had anything more than vacuous comments to utter. Did he like the color pink? Wasn't the snow pretty? Had he read the newest novel? Wasn't the music pleasant? The only time one of them had said something remotely interesting about politics, the other two had given her a look that quelled any further speech.

He missed Catriona.

Granted, they'd never discussed politics, but he didn't doubt she had an opinion about a great many things. Nor was she forever licking her lips or touching her temple, or spreading her fingers delicately across her bosom as if to make him look at her breasts.

Once, she'd been as flighty and frivolous as these women. Had it been the accident that changed her? Or what happened before that, when her father killed her mother and was hanged for the act?

Love shouldn't be that selfish.

"What are you thinking?" his mother asked. "You have the most off-putting frown on your face. You'll give us all a fright, I swear."

"I'm sorry, I've something on my mind."

His mother moved aside and he followed her.

"Anne?"

He shook his head. "No, not Anne."

She sighed. "Anne wasn't for you," she said. "Besides, it looks as if the girl has found another interest."

He didn't care enough to ask, but his mother furnished the information regardless.

"The son of a baron," she said, lowering her voice even further. "He's shorter than she, but much admired by her father."

"I wish her the best."

"I'm not entirely sure she feels the same for you." She sighed. "Never mind. She wasn't a good match. You need someone to make you forget medicine, if only for a while."

His carriage arrived and he bent to kiss his mother on the cheek. He wasn't about to tell her that someone had already done just that.

He smiled, exchanged pleasantries, and bid farewell to the three women. Did they realize how forgettable each one was? He wasn't certain he even remembered their names.

To his surprise, his brother raced down the steps toward him.

"I need to come and see you before the wedding," Jack said, leading him toward the carriage.

He turned his head to study his brother in the faint light. "The pox again?"

"How judgmental you sound, brother," Jack said. "Like Father. Tell me, are you going to withhold my allowance, too?"

Perhaps marriage would settle Jack, but he doubted it. He was the product of his father's influence. As long as he had the money to purchase women and whiskey, Jack wouldn't aspire to being more than a twenty-seven-year-old child.

To their father's discredit, he'd not encouraged any of his sons to do something with themselves. In fact, especially in his case, the less work, the less ambition he had, the better.

"I suggest you find yourself another physician," he said.

"That would be awkward. Who knows me better than my own brother?"

"Which is why you should get your own physician."

"What a prude you've turned out to be, brother. I'm ashamed to call you my kin."

Since his brother reeked of whiskey, he wasn't all that happy to claim him, either. He entered the carriage, settled into the seat, and looked out at his brother.

"I'm serious, Jack. You're not going to listen to any of my advice. I have enough patients who will to not waste time on you."

"Do you still get afraid in tight places, brother?" Jack asked, a sneer in his voice.

"Yes," he said. "I do. Do you still drink to excess?"

Jack slammed the carriage door, and Brody took off soon after.

He raised his hand in farewell to his mother and the gaggle of women he'd no doubt see at every event from this moment forward.

At times he felt like a changeling in his own family.

I don't belong anywhere. Hadn't Catriona said something similar?

Did she realize how alike they were?

He would call on her tomorrow and end this.

They'd done everything backward, hadn't they? Some situations couldn't be corrected, but as long as a man was alive, he could rectify certain mistakes.

He'd begin to court her in earnest. He'd be a suitor for once in his life. He'd bring flowers and presents to her. What presents were acceptable? He'd ask Sarah, she would know. No, this courtship should remain between the two of them.

She was going to be stubborn about it; he knew that much.

So was he.

Winter was the season of dying things. Yet perhaps winter needed to come occasionally, to rid life of the old, the unneeded, the out of date. Still, Catriona was tired of winter, both as a season and in her life.

She hadn't been walking for nearly a week, and her leg protested the absence of exercise. Perhaps she should walk longer than normal to make up for the lack. If her knee would allow her to continue.

Wind whistled through the branches, clicking them together like finger bones. She stopped where she was, listening.

She turned, looking out from the shelter of trees, clutching her arms beneath her cloak and gazing up at the cold cloudless night filled with stars.

Loneliness seeped into her bones, settled there to ache. In this wild night, it felt as if she were the only one awake in New Town, while the castle on the hill frowned down at her in censure.

She walked, shutting her mind to the pain. As she crossed the lawn, she saw the carriage on the other side of the square. Each time she passed, the driver looked away. Was he trying to conceal his identity?

The fourth time, she slowed, daring herself. The carriage could simply be waiting for a visitor to one of the town houses on the block. Or it could be the same carriage she'd seen every day this week.

She crossed the street, approaching the vehicle from the rear. Reaching up, she opened the carriage door.

A man sat there, a small carriage lamp at his feet. He

was bundled in a coat, his bowler hat pulled low over his ears, and even though he had a thick carriage robe over his lap, he looked remarkably chilled.

"Are you watching me?" she asked.

For a long moment the man didn't say anything. He folded his notebook, tucking a small pencil into the side. When he was done, he nodded to her, for all the world as if they'd just been introduced.

"Well?"

"Perhaps I was, miss."

She hadn't expected him to admit it. "Why?"

He shook his head. "Oh, that I can't say."

"Perhaps you'll tell the authorities when I summon them," she said.

He waved a hand at her. "Now, there's no need to do that. I'm just sitting here on a fine winter night, not bothering anyone."

"You're bothering me. I don't like being watched."

"Oh, I'm not exactly watching you, miss. You might say I'm watching after you."

"I beg your pardon?"

He sighed heavily. "Very well, miss. I've been commissioned to ensure your safety, if you will."

"My safety? Who, exactly, commissioned you?"

"That, I most assuredly must keep confidential."

"Tell Dr. Thorburn there is no reason to have me followed."

A pause, during which the man tried to hide his surprise.

"The doctor appears to be certain there is, begging your pardon, miss."

She stepped back and slammed the coach door shut.

It wasn't enough that he'd come into her room. It wasn't enough that he'd pretended to be a footman. It wasn't enough that he'd watched her eat. Now he was intruding into her life again.

How dare he set someone to follow her.

A guest of wind nearly tore her veil free. She grabbed at it with both hands, intent on reaching her warm room.

He must learn that he couldn't meddle in her life. She didn't need a protector, or if she did, she didn't need him.

The thought of their confrontation brought a smile to her lips.

Should she be so excited about seeing him again?

Chapter 30

To Catriona's great surprise, Dr. Mark Thorburn lived in a mansion.

The house was within an old, established area in Old Town called Parliamentary Square. She knew enough about the city to know that a great many wealthy and important personages had homes in this area.

The location was so different from what she expected that when Mr. Johnstone helped her from the carriage, she asked, "Are you certain this is Dr. Thorburn's house?"

"Oh yes, miss, this is the place right enough."

Boasting three floors, and nearly as wide as a block of Charlotte Square, the house was built of faded red brick. Two towers flanked the many chimneys on the roof. Each tower had a small window that gleamed in the afternoon sun. Although no doubt created for decoration only, the towers gave the house the appearance of a small castle.

Even the entrance was impressive, wide stone steps bordered on either side by two pedestals on which sat crouching lions.

Slowly, she mounted the steps, glancing back at the lions twice. The statues were weathered, as was the brick of the house, giving her the impression that this structure was similar in age to Edinburgh Castle, so close that it seemed directly overhead.

After using the knocker—another lion—she stood at the front door and waited for someone to answer. No doubt a stiff-necked majordomo would appear and ask, in a supercilious voice, what she wanted.

How foolish she was not to have brought her calling cards, or a chaperone for that matter.

Should she ask Mr. Johnstone to wait with her?

A park sat in front of the house, the remnants of last night's snowfall melting beneath a bright afternoon sun. Did the park belong to the house? Or was it shared like the residents of Charlotte Square shared their green lawn?

The door suddenly opened, and instead of a majordomo, a short, wizened woman looked up at her. Since she rarely towered over anyone, she couldn't help but be surprised.

The woman had bright white hair wound into a coronet at the top of her head, and a face crisscrossed by so many wrinkles it appeared to be a map of Edinburgh. Her smile, however, was welcoming.

"You're the lass in black, I'm thinking," the tiny woman said.

"Lass in black?"

"It's what you're being called." She leaned forward and whispered, "But I must admit, I started it. I think it's a lovely title, myself, don't you?" She frowned. "But you're wearing blue now, aren't you?"

She stood aside. "Come in, though. It's a cold day, isn't it? But still, there are touches of spring in the air." She peered beyond to where Mr. Johnstone stood by the carriage. "You go on in; I'll send your driver to the stables where they'll offer him something warm to drink."

"We're not staying long," she began, but the little

woman simply ignored her, grabbed her shawl, and trot-
ted down the stairs.

She entered Mark's castle and stood speechless.

Had the house once been used as a church? Or had the
builders wanted to create the atmosphere of a cathedral?

The ceiling soared above a winding stair, the but-
tresses creating shadows where statues lingered, looking down at the visitors. Cherubs held their wings close
to their bodies, women smiled while holding the hems
of their gossamer dresses. Men, dressed in togas, stood
either holding a tablet or pointing an accusing finger.

The statues, however, were not the only indication that
this was a unique home. At the landing, where the stair-
case split in two, each side going in opposite directions,
there was a massive, round stained-glass window. The
winter sunlight bathed the space in crimson, emerald, and
bright yellow.

She'd heard people discussing Notre Dame in Paris.
Had this window been designed with it in mind?

The foyer smelled of beeswax and lemon, and there
must be dishes of potpourri set in places she couldn't see,
because sandalwood perfumed the air.

"You'll be here to see Dr. Thorburn, of course," the
woman said, entering the house and closing the door
behind her.

She nodded.

The woman didn't say anything else, simply started
walking. She had no choice but to follow her.

"I can put you in the parlor," the woman said. "Or you
can sit with me in the kitchen, where it's warmer."

"The kitchen will be fine," she said.

She wasn't going to be here that long. She was simply
going to deliver her message and leave.

The aroma of baking biscuits, something made with

ginger and cinnamon, made her stomach grumble as they entered the kitchen.

"It's a grand home," she said, looking around. Even the kitchen was four times the size of the one at their town house. "Does Dr. Thorburn live here alone?"

The woman smiled at her as if the question was amusing.

"Are you thinking that he must have a family hiding here?"

"It's a large house for one person."

"That it is. We've one floor we don't even use," she said. "I put the kettle on, and you'll be having tea with me," the woman added.

Not a request as much as an order.

The woman pointed to a large square table surrounded by six sturdy chairs.

"You take your place; choose any chair you wish."

Was this a test?

She chose one with a view of the garden, a wide space with a high brick wall. She couldn't help but wonder how it would look come spring.

A good choice, or so it seemed, when the woman nodded her approval.

"I'm Sarah Donnelly," the other woman said, smiling. "I'm the housekeeper here. Although I'm more than that from time to time. When one of Dr. Thorburn's patients comes, I settle them down, give them some tea, and keep them calm until he arrives."

"I'm not one of Dr. Thorburn's patients," she said. "Is he here?"

Sarah smiled broadly. "He's not, but until he comes, you'll sit with me. I want to know the things he didn't tell me about you."

"He talked about me?"

She'd been here a scant few minutes and already the visit was a surprise.

"It was himself playing at being a footman," Sarah said. "I knew from the beginning that nothing good would come of it, but did he listen to me?"

Sarah's smile was so engaging that she felt her tension ease. "He's a stubborn man."

"Aye, you have the right of it. Burning the candle at both ends, he was. Tending to all his patients, and you, besides."

"I didn't know who he was. If I had, I would have sent him away."

"Och, didn't he need to do what he did, then? You, with your dislike of doctors." Sarah busied herself pouring hot water into the teapot. "Although how a body could think such a magnificent man was a footman, I'll never know."

Since she'd done exactly that, she remained silent.

Was Sarah this blunt with all her visitors? Or had she been singled out for a lecture?

"I've been doing for Dr. Thorburn for three years now. Of course, he was at university for years before that, but he didn't move here until he became a doctor."

Sarah looked around the walls and the ceiling of the kitchen, as if to encompass the whole of the house in her gaze.

"His grandmother gave it to him. Do you know about her?"

Feeling bemused, she shook her head, then realized Sarah might not be able to determine her answer through the veil.

"No," she said. "I don't."

"A daughter of a duke, she was. Pretty little thing. She had four children, all in all. Two of them died in infancy, but a daughter and a son survived. The son is Dr. Thorburn's father, a more intractable man I've never met. Have you had the pleasure of meeting him?"

"No," she said.

"You will," Sarah announced. "When you do, just remember, he hasn't many friends and a great many enemies. He's not a nice man, or a kind one. It's a miracle that Mark is such a good man. That, or good blood. His grandmother was a saint, I hear."

Her thoughts were reeling. All she'd wanted was to tell Mark Thorburn not to meddle in her life. In its stead, she was receiving a summation of his family, and an assurance that she would meet his father.

Sarah put the tea things on the table, returning a moment later to put a plate of biscuits before her.

She didn't see how she was going to drink in front of the woman who was watching her so carefully. However, she could manage a biscuit. She took one from the plate and nibbled on it beneath her veil.

"The whole time, his father was against Dr. Thorburn studying medicine," Sarah said, shaking her head. "But Mark was determined to be a physician, and his grandmother was determined to help him. When she died, she left him all her money and this great house. Her way of saying how much she approved of Mark, his drive, his ambition, and his talent."

Sarah took a sip of tea, sighing with obvious enjoyment.

She should stop the woman from divulging Mark's secrets. Instead, she nibbled on the biscuit and listened avidly.

"He was number one in his class in university, you know," Sarah said.

"No, I didn't."

"Will you take that thing off?" Sarah asked, nodding in the direction of her veil.

She hadn't expected the request. When she hesitated, Sarah said, "I imagine it's hard to breathe in that thing."

Slowly, she moved her gloves from her lap to the table. One by one she took out the pins holding the veil in place. When that was done, she removed the veil, revealing her hair arranged in a coronet not unlike Sarah's.

She placed the veil on her lap, moving her hands over the lace. She didn't look up for a few moments because she didn't want to see Sarah's interested study of her scars.

"You've had a time of it, haven't you?" Sarah said.

Finally, she raised her head to look at the other woman.

Sarah took another sip of her tea and studied her for a moment.

"I'm thinking that you were in a lot of pain for a long time. Pain does something to a body," she said. "I know, I've seen enough of Dr. Thorburn's patients. Some of them, pain makes angels. Some of them, it makes into devils. Which one were you?"

"I'm afraid I was a devil," she said softly.

Sarah nodded. "I'm thinking I'd be the same." She picked up a biscuit and ate it with relish.

The oak table bore scars that looked to be old. She trailed a finger down one particularly interesting gouge. Had someone sat here one night, bored and listless, and carved it out with a knife?

"Now, then," Sarah said, the biscuit finished, "you'll be telling me why you, a single woman, would be calling upon Dr. Thorburn all by yourself."

"My maid is feeling under the weather," she said.

Sarah nodded. "That might be true enough, but I think it's an excuse. What's the real reason you came alone?"

She felt her face flush. "Because I'm here to have a fit," she said. "I didn't want a witness to it."

Sarah sat back in the chair, both eyebrows raised. "Are you now? What are you going to have a fit about?"

"Dr. Thorburn has gone behind my back and arranged for someone to follow me. I don't like it, I don't appreciate it, and I want it to stop."

"He is a stubborn man, that's for sure. He does think he's right most of the time."

"Yes, he does."

"Am I to disappear?' Sarah asked. "When this fit begins?"

"If you could," she said, "I'd be grateful."

Sarah shook her head. "I'd prefer to listen."

"I've a feeling Mark's not the only stubborn person in this household," she said.

Sarah smiled. "That's the right of it. He's a fine man, Dr. Thorburn, but he hasn't had a good time of it lately. I'd rather be sure that you're not here to make him more miserable."

She missed Jean acutely at that moment. Her sister was the only person who'd ever been as protective of her.

"I won't make him more miserable," she said. "I wish he'd agree to do the same." She reached for her veil, but before she could fix it, a door closed somewhere in the house.

Panicked, she looked at Sarah.

The housekeeper nodded, answering the unspoken question.

Mark had returned.

She steadied herself, placed her hands back on the veil, and straightened her shoulders. Now was the best time for him to see her, to know what kind of monster she was.

They waited in silence, listening as Mark walked

through the house. A door closed, footfalls on the wood floor, another door.

"He's going into his apothecary," Sarah said. "He does that first when he comes home."

She nodded. Her stomach rolled; her feet felt damp in her shoes. She fisted the veil in her icy hands. Could she do this?

She stood, unable to sit and wait any longer. Her right hand was braced against the scarred oak table. The footsteps grew louder, each step drawing the chain around her chest tighter until she could barely breathe.

Dear God, please give me the courage I need.

Chapter 31

In the last three years, his life had taken on a frenzied energy, one that suited his personality. However, Mark couldn't remember being as tired as he was lately or as downhearted.

Despite being employed by the city of Edinburgh on a part-time basis, he had over three thousand patients in Old Town alone. Add those to the ten dozen or so paying patients, and his workload could have occupied a few men.

But it wasn't the sheer number of patients that was affecting him as much as Old Town itself. The unremitting poverty, the endless human degradation, the lack of hope, seemed to melt into his skin. The conversation he'd just had with Alex MacBain added to his mood and caused him to cut his day short. He needed to smile, and a smile seemed far away.

He'd had to tell the man that his wife would not live to see the spring. Even if they had come to him earlier about the lump in Mrs. MacBain's chest, there was nothing he could have done.

Medicine was making strides every year, but there were certain diseases he couldn't cure. Perhaps one day they'd be able to do so. Until then, however, he'd have conversations like the one he'd just had, and watch a woman with two little children die before his eyes.

He'd be damned if he had to like it.

This was what his father said was beneath him, the struggle between life and death. Lord Serridain's narrow-minded autocracy continued to amaze him.

As was his habit, he entered the room set aside as his storeroom and apothecary. Hanging his coat on one of the hooks by the door, he dropped off his bag on the work-bench and took a quick inventory.

He was concerned about the amount of morphine he'd need to ease Mrs. MacBain's pain in the coming months, as well as the medicine he mixed together for Harold Donaldson's ague. The medicines refilled, fatigue pressed down on his shoulders.

Tonight, surely he would sleep better.

Since Sarah hadn't joined him in the apothecary, he went in search of her, heading for the kitchen.

There, like the answer to a schoolboy's prayer, stood Catriona Cameron. She was in his kitchen waiting for him, standing there without her veil.

Her eyes were flat and expressionless, but how could he have ever forgotten their color? A greenish blue, reminiscent of a sunset over the Grampians. His mind furnished a picture of her laughing, her eyes sparkling with amusement.

She wasn't feeling joyful at the moment, however. Her hands clenched the veil in front of her. She was so still that she looked brittle.

He could almost feel her fear.

He approached the table and stood in front of her.

"Will you sit?" he asked. "Have some tea with me."

She sat without comment.

He pulled out a chair, sitting in front of her. Gently, he placed his hands beneath her chin, turning her head one way and then another, the better to see her in the afternoon light from the windows.

"Would you like me to bring the examination lamp?" Sarah asked.

"No," Catriona said.

"My patients normally don't get to tell me what to do," he said, turning her head to the left. He glanced at Sarah. "But I don't think I need it."

One long scar ran from the corner of her left eye nearly to her chin. Her skin had not knitted well, and the result was a thick red mass of tissue. In the middle of her cheek, the scar branched out like a tree of pain, stretching across her face in varying shades of pink. Over time the scars would fade in color, but they would forever be noticeable, stark reminders of how close she came to death.

The rest of her face was strangely untouched. She was two sides of a coin, beauty and its obverse.

He traced the path of one of the scars to where it ended above her ear.

"You were fortunate," he said, sitting back.

She blinked at him several times. "Fortunate?"

He nodded. "The glass could have easily severed your ear. Or cut right through your eye. Do you have any difficulty in your vision there?"

"Some," she admitted. "Sometimes it feels as if it tears too much."

"That's to be expected, I think. Any itching?"

She nodded once. A simple acquiescence to his question, and a reluctant one. Was she afraid that by acknowledging the damage to her face, she made it permanent?

He frowned at the worst of the scars, reaching out to trace the line of it with a gentle finger. "They didn't do a good job sewing you together," he said. "One day, perhaps, we'll have the ability to go back and rectify mistakes."

"They did the best they could," she said, her tone mocking.

"They might have," he said. "However, the best wasn't good enough."

"You're a physician. No doubt you're familiar with horrible sights."

He nodded. "Although I wouldn't categorize your face as a horrible sight," he said. "A regrettable fact, but not an insurmountable one."

"I doubt the rest of society would agree with you."

She was probably correct.

"The world is prejudiced against a great many things," he said. "The trick is to ignore what you can and endure the rest."

"So says an extraordinarily handsome man."

He felt a rush of warmth at her words.

Sarah pushed a cup toward him, and he nodded his thanks. When she added a plate of biscuits, he grinned at her.

She only shook her head at him, and he wondered if he was being chastised for his love of sweets or the fact that he wasn't acting with his usual professional detachment.

"You've examined me," she said, reaching for her veil. "Shall I hire you as my physician?"

"No," he said, reaching out and staying her hand. "We've gone beyond that, don't you think?"

Catriona frowned at him, but he didn't release her hand.

He sat back and ate a biscuit, thoroughly pleased with the world for this moment in time. He was warm, he was being fed biscuits and tea, and Catriona was in his kitchen.

"Why did you set someone to watching me?"

His good mood abruptly vanished.

"How do you know about that?"

"Your watcher isn't that subtle," she said. "I am not one of your patients, Dr. Thorburn. I'm not someone you have to guard."

"Do you refuse anyone the right to care for you?"

She looked surprised at the question.

He loved being able to see her expressions, to view those surprising eyes. If Sarah hadn't been sitting at the table, he would have leaned closer and kissed her.

"Are you that solicitous of all your patients?"

"You're not my patient," he said, deciding that Sarah was going to have to hear the truth. "You're my lover."

He glanced up to see his housekeeper leaving the room. Had he shocked her? No doubt he was going to be interrogated later.

He leaned forward, placing both hands on the arm of the chair. He dragged Catriona's chair closer, the legs making a loud screeching noise against the wood floor. Slowly, he framed her face with his hands. She didn't pull away, merely sat there looking at him with her wide, beautiful eyes.

"You knew," she said. "All this time, you knew."

"About your scars?" He shook his head. "It's your leg that concerns me more," he said.

Before she could speak, he placed his lips on hers, a gentle, teasing kiss.

When he drew back, she blinked up at him.

"I've missed kissing you," he said, tracing her bottom lip with a finger.

He wished he could explain to her what he felt, but he wasn't a poet. Besides, he wasn't certain he could put his emotions into words.

This room was changed by her sitting there. From this day forward, envisioning her in that chair in this exact spot, he would always smile. His house seemed a warmer place, too, simply because Catriona was here.

But it was more than a physical change. His life seemed to be enhanced by her presence in it. She warmed him from the inside out.

She made him smile.

He wanted to tell her about his patients, about his sorrow over Mrs. MacBain and the other patients in Old Town who refused to listen to his advice or whose health was compromised by their overuse of alcohol. There were so many things he wanted to talk to her about, and listen to her comments.

He lay his hand gently on her left knee.

"Have you used the liniment?"

She nodded.

"Does it always hurt?"

"It just aches," she said. "I think winter makes it worse."

He might battle death, and some of the time he won. He also battled life, wanting to heal every one of his patients, rid them of pain or discomfort or infirmity.

She wasn't his patient, but he wanted even more for Catriona. He wanted her to be able to walk without limping. Or for pain to only be a faint memory, one she need not recall on a daily basis. Yet at this moment he felt singularly defeated, wishing there was something he could do to help her and knowing there probably wasn't.

A minute passed, then another, and she was as quiet and still as a statue. The girl he remembered had flitted about like a butterfly.

She pushed back her chair and stood, before he could kiss her again.

"I must go," she said softly. "I have duties to attend to."

"Off with your aunt again?" he asked, standing now, too. She'd surprised and pleased him by her actions in Old Town.

"How did you know?" she asked, then answered her own question. "Your watcher."

"Why did you start accompanying her?"

"I've grown tired of my own company," she said, the truth shining in each of her words. "I find that I can pity myself for only so long. Either I have to change my life or end it."

He reached out and grabbed her shoulders with both hands, giving her a shake.

"Don't say things like that," he said. "Don't think things like that."

She reached up and put her hands over his.

"You heal," she said. "It's your calling in life, Mark. What do you do when you can't?"

"I keep trying."

She smiled, as if she'd expected that answer.

"Some causes are worthless."

He matched her smile. "Some aren't. You aren't."

"You can't heal me."

"Maybe I'm the one who needs to be healed," he said. "From you. Because of you. I've decided the only treatment is to be around you more than I have been. That way, I won't miss you so much."

Her eyes widened. "You shouldn't say such things."

"Marry me."

She took a step back, away from him.

"Are you mad?"

"Possibly," he said. "I know my life hasn't been the same since I walked into your room."

She blinked at him.

"Marry me."

She shook her head.

He'd expected her to be obstinate, and she didn't disappoint. He took a step closer, and she retreated.

He grinned, suddenly liking this chase. What she didn't understand was that he had every intention of catching her.

Before he could say something that linked them further, a chain of words he couldn't call back, she moved backward, away from him.

He couldn't do this to her. He couldn't push her past the boundaries she'd erected to protect herself.

He couldn't say things like that to her.

Marry me.

She wanted to weep.

If he understood who she truly was, he'd leave her alone. She wasn't good like he was. She definitely wasn't selfless. She had, in her past, been grasping, greedy, and mean.

Even if she'd changed, what did it matter? She would never be a saint. Nor did she truly wish to be, a confession that should shame her.

"Is there no one else who has caught your eye?" she asked. "No one who would be more acceptable to marry? A society miss, perhaps?"

"There was," he said. "Or perhaps it's more correct to say that I caught her eye."

She frowned at him. She was being perfectly serious, but he was smiling.

"What happened to her?"

"I decided that she wasn't as interesting as someone else I knew."

"Are you talking about me?"

Her heart began to beat too rapidly again. He needed to stop doing that to her. Surely it couldn't be a healthy phenomenon.

"I am."

"Well, you shouldn't," she said, suddenly annoyed.

What did he expect from her? That he would marry her out of pity? "Will you tell your man not to follow me?"

Instead of escorting her from the room, he walked toward her, one stalking step at a time. She backed up until there was nowhere else to go.

He braced himself with a hand on either side of her, leaning his head close. She could feel his breath against her forehead. He created a protective and warm bubble around her, whispering against her ear.

"What's the matter, Catriona? Passion is only acceptable if it's on your terms? Or if you instigate it?"

She could hardly breathe.

With one hand she grabbed his arm as he moved even closer, pressing against her, making her aware of every inch of his body.

"I seem to remember a time in my bedroom that wasn't at my instigation."

"No," he said, nipping at her neck. "It wasn't."

She closed her eyes, sighing as he moved his lips over her jaw, then kissed her again. This time the kiss demanded her cooperation and her surrender.

She willed herself to feel nothing, but her body recognized him, heated for him, and her lips—traitorous lips—softened for his mouth.

The man kissed like a demon; who was she to refuse him?

His tongue slid between her lips, touched hers before retreating to tease her bottom lip.

Somehow, she reached up and gripped his shoulders with both hands, and when he moved, she wished she were naked instead of protected by innumerable layers of cloth.

Where had her resolve gone?

She'd missed him so much. Not simply his touch, but his smile, and that twinkle that came into his eyes when he was being outrageous and knew it. She'd missed his kiss, and his acerbic comments, and the way he dared her and challenged everything she knew to be right.

He had not flinched at her face. He hadn't expressed his condolences once or made a hasty retreat from the sight of her. Instead, he'd examined her closely, separating the damage from the whole of her. To him, her scars had been nothing more than an afterthought, an accessory, a physical reminder of the accident but little more. Up until now, no man had been able to see her for the damage to her face. No man but Mark.

Now, he was kissing her as if he desired her. As if he wanted her as much as she wanted him.

Marry me.

She pulled back, pressing her hands against his chest. They were both breathing hard and his heart was booming against her palm.

"Is it because you're a physician?" she asked in a trembling voice. "Because you're familiar with deformity?"

He dropped his hands from her waist.

"Deformity?"

She nodded, not looking up at him. Instead, she concentrated on his shirtfront.

"Catriona, you have to be the most infuriating woman I've ever known."

She glanced up at him. He was frowning at her.

"Then you can't possibly want to marry me."

"Of course I do."

"Am I one of your good works?" she asked.

He drew back. "Good works?"

She nodded. "A project to prove that you're compassionate and kind."

"Marrying you is supposed to prove my compassion?"

It was her turn to frown at the amusement in his voice. "I am not being ridiculous."

"Yes, you are," he said.

"It was a perfectly valid question."

"Then let me give you a perfectly valid answer," he said. "No, you're not a pity project."

He kissed her again, and she came close to agreeing to marry him right then and there.

"No," he said, drawing back.

"No what?" she asked, trying to come back to the present.

"I'm not going to stop Mr. MacLean from following you. It's either him or me, and I doubt my patients would understand. Or you could accompany me on my calls."

She shook her head, not taking him seriously.

"You would be a good companion, I think. You'd be good with patients, and you've a great deal of compassion for others."

Was he talking about her?

She frowned at him.

He ran his finger down her nose, then tapped the end of it.

"Edeen liked you. Said you were bossy like Mrs. Mac-Tavish but that you had as good a heart."

"She did?" She slid along the wall until they weren't so close. "I'm not surprised. I'm likable."

He grinned at her.

"Very well, I haven't always been pleasant to you," she said. "But I was goaded."

His eyes were twinkling at her. He had to stop doing that.

"You threw a tray at me," he said.

She looked away. She'd forgotten about that.

"Very well," she said, pushing past him. "If you insist on spending your money on Mr. MacLean, do so."

She moved to the doorway, turning for one last glimpse of him. He looked tired, and she had the most absurd desire to tuck him up in bed, make him soup, and kiss him senseless.

Whatever was he doing to her?

"Catriona," he said, his voice making her name sound entirely too sensuous.

"Yes?"

"I won't give up," he said, smiling again.

She nodded, not entirely certain if he was talking about her watchdog or something else entirely.

"I can't do this no more, sir," Artis said, wringing her hands.

Andrew smiled and opened the back door wider. He was too close to success; she couldn't rabbit on him now. He led her to the table, took her raggedy cloak, and hung it on the peg beside the door.

"What is it now, Artis?" he asked, pretending a compassionate air.

He was glad he was almost quit of Scotland. He hated the country and would be glad to see the last of it—and this woman especially.

She slipped across the square every morning to report

on Catriona, and of late he'd had to reassure her that she was doing the right thing, the honorable thing, in assisting the course of true love.

He'd come close to gagging when he told her that.

Catriona Cameron was incapable of loving anyone but herself. He'd be doing the world a favor by eradicating her.

Did the maid see the rifle on the table behind her? He'd made no effort to hide it. He might well be going to the country over the weekend and needed to ensure it was in proper order. She wouldn't know that the only hunting in this part of the country was normally done with a shotgun.

Any fool could aim a shotgun and hope to hit something. The Pattern 1853 was a treasure of an instrument, a rifle possessing a deadly beauty. He'd become proficient with it in the last few years. It had become an extension of himself, an extra limb or a tool.

"Where is she going today?" Andrew asked, demonstrating a patience he didn't truly possess. He'd had years of practice feigning various emotions, however. With his amiable smile, the maid would have no reason to be nervous or afraid.

After all, she wasn't the one he was trying—unsuccessfully, so far—to kill.

Twice Catriona had foiled him. She wouldn't do so again.

"I'm sorry, sir, I don't know."

"I don't pay you not to know, Artis," he said, still affable. "I pay you to give me Miss Cameron's schedule."

"Why, sir?"

She stood before him, shoulders drooping, twisting her hands until they were red. Her brown eyes were flat with fear.

"Why?" he asked, not revealing his anger over such

a daring question. Who was she to question him? "I've told you that I'm a cast-off suitor. I'm seeking a way to convince her of my love."

She looked doubtful, but at least she'd ceased twisting her hands.

"I don't think she feels the same, sir."

He kept his smile anchored by sheer will.

"Why do you say that, Artis?"

She shook her head.

"Perhaps she doesn't know her own feelings, Artis. Perhaps she will change her mind once I plead my case. I need your help."

She nodded, which meant that she'd continue to be his eyes and ears as long as he paid her well.

He wondered if she'd ever know how close she came to dying first.

Chapter 32

Dina sat in the parlor, folding clothes once again. For
some reason, her smile wouldn't fade. Well, she certainly
had enough reason to smile, hadn't she? The donations for
the poor had been pouring in of late. She had witnessed
the transformation of Catriona's character, becoming as
sweet and kind as she'd always thought the girl could be.
One day, perhaps, she would rid herself of her veil entirely, and venture out into the world.

There would be times when Catriona would be rebuffed, no doubt. Although she believed in aiding her
fellow man, sometimes her fellow man left a great deal
to be desired. People would hurt the girl's feelings, but
Catriona must rise above that. The alternative was to
remain as cloistered as a nun, and Catriona, with her
loving personality, was not destined for dark corners
and silence.

The only thing she would have changed was that the
two of them—Dr. Thorburn and Catriona—would be
more intelligent in their secret courting. But people in
love rarely thought of the outside world. Foolish young
people to waste so much time on posturing.

Dr. Thorburn was a definite catch, and so was Catriona, as soon as she realized that her appearance was not all she had to offer the world.

"Mrs. MacTavish?"

She looked up to see Artis standing in the doorway. Even Artis had changed over the past few weeks. She wasn't nearly as surly as before, and had taken her punishment so well that it ended.

"Yes, Artis?"

"Have you a minute, ma'am?"

"Is anything wrong?"

"I need to speak to you," Artis said.

She frowned. Was the girl going to complain about either Elspeth or Isobel again? She had enough of Artis's complaints, and here the girl had been doing so well.

"I need to tell you something I've done, Mrs. MacTavish."

A strange request, but she nodded, moving a stack of clothing aside so Artis could sit beside her. Instead, the girl remained standing in front of her.

"You were kind to give me a position."

"I'd do it again, Artis." She sent a smile in the girl's direction, but Artis was still studying the floor.

She didn't have a good feeling about this.

Artis twisted her hands in her apron and bit her lip between words.

"I like having a roof over my head, and clothes to wear that smell good," she said. "I like that you don't tolerate drunkenness in your house."

The girl looked as if she were about to cry, and kept looking down at the floor other than at her.

"I like it here, ma'am. I just want you to know that, and if you give me another chance, I'll never do something like this again."

"Have you stolen the silver, Artis?" she asked, half in jest.

The girl's head rose, and Artis stared at her. "I haven't. I'd never steal from you, ma'am."

"Well, if it's not theft, what has you so worried? Your new duties?" She'd put Artis in charge of the inventory of all the linens. They had more sheets than they truly needed, but since they didn't belong to her, but to her nephew, all she could do was count them, launder them, and ensure they were kept in good repair.

"I've done a bad thing. She doesn't deserve it, I'm thinking. I've put her in danger, and myself, too. I've dealt with the devil, Mrs. MacTavish, and he won't be denied."

At the end of that impassioned speech, Artis burst out weeping.

She stood and enfolded the girl in her arms.

No, she really didn't have a good feeling about this.

Mark left his bag on the carriage seat and told Brody, "Go around to the kitchen. There's no need for you to freeze waiting for me."

"I'll do that, sir. Mrs. MacTavish's cook makes a fine scone, she does."

He grinned, since he and Brody shared a love of anything sweet.

He turned back to the steps, taking them two at a time. Today he was beginning his courtship in earnest. If he delayed, Catriona would have enough time to put up all sorts of objections to his suit. He wasn't going to be denied.

He'd wanted to be a physician and had overcome all objections. Perhaps the obstinacy he demonstrated then had only been preparation for this moment, his siege on Catriona Cameron.

After knocking on the door, he rocked back and forth on his heels. What mood would she be in today? Would she allow him to massage her leg again? Had she known that his pulse escalated when he'd touched her? Or that he'd had a hard time letting her leave him yesterday?

His house had seemed emptier without her.

Sarah, bless her, had decided not to comment on Catriona's arrival, his comment, or his sudden silence at her departure.

The door opened, and his smile immediately vanished.

"Thank God it's you," Mrs. MacTavish said, reaching out, grabbing the lapel of his coat and dragging him inside.

Would she always be frightened in a carriage? Would her heart always race? Would she always hear the shattering of glass, the screams of the horses?

Catriona's hands trembled and she clutched them together, the black leather feeling cold and constricting against her fingers.

She was on an errand for her aunt. That's what she needed to remember. Not that night in London. Not the fog outside the window, and Millicent's smile.

Did Mark feel the same way whenever he had to travel in a carriage? As if he were trapped, confined, and a prisoner?

How horrid to have had such a tutor and a father, too. She was not going to be polite to Mark's father when she met him.

Her thoughts stumbled to a halt.

She was not involved with Mark Thorburn. She was not paired with him. She would not be meeting his father. He'd pretended to be someone he wasn't and insisted on being a nuisance now, that's all, but there was nothing more to their relationship. His offer of marriage was just an act of kindness.

Marry me.

Her heart stuttered at the thought.

They'd been lovers.

Somehow, she was going to have to forget that. She shouldn't recall the shape of him, his beautiful, strong back, the column of his neck, or the angle of his stubborn chin.

Of course you're sad about your changed circumstances. How she'd disliked him when he'd said that.

You're only seeing a part of you.

How arrogant he was. Did he always get his way?

Why was she smiling?

Would she ever see him again? He would have no need to come and visit anymore. How foolish she was to feel pain at that thought.

So many people needed him, but she needed him in a different way. She needed the quick smile that lit his face and carried to his eyes. She needed to hear his voice with its rolling burr. She needed to feel the touch of his hand, to see that clear look in his eyes when he saw her ruined face. No pretense there. No pity or compassion, only understanding.

Marry me.

Perhaps it hadn't been an act of kindness after all.

Dear God, would she ever cease missing him?

Did Jean feel the same about her earl?

Perhaps she should go to Ballindair and nurse her wounds there. She'd hide at Ballindair for a while, then return when she was feeling stronger, more able to tolerate the absence of the most annoying man she'd ever met.

He had a quality about him that made her notice him immediately. When he entered a room, her body was suddenly alert. Yet he seemed unaware of his attractiveness, of the charming nature of his smile or the seductive twinkle in his eyes. Looking at him was dangerous; falling under his spell had been even more disastrous.

Her hands trembled and she clasped them more tightly together.

He couldn't have meant what he said yesterday.

She frowned at the carriage window. She couldn't stop thinking of him, no matter how often she told herself to concentrate on something else. Anything or anyone else other than Mark Thorburn.

She'd never been fixated on a man before in her entire life. But then, she'd never acted as foolish around one, either. What did that mean?

Isobel, sitting opposite her, ventured a tentative smile, then looked away.

No doubt the poor girl thought she was cross at her.

"How is your arm feeling?" she asked.

The girl smiled again and nodded. "Better, miss. It just aches from time to time, but Dr. Thorburn says that's to be expected."

"We need to ensure that he sees you again," she said. "Just to make sure you're well."

Truly, there was no need for that surge of excitement she suddenly felt. Did she intend to go around wounding the maids just to see him? How foolish she was.

"Thank you, miss."

She smiled in return.

Had people ever thanked her as much as they were doing recently? She couldn't get through the day without someone coming up to her and thanking her. She wasn't doing all that much. In fact, Dina was the example, the charitable one, the woman who did the most. She was just trailing after her, following her lead. But when people said thank you, they did so with genuine emotion. They smiled at her a lot more, even clad as she was in her veil.

How odd that she wasn't attracting their attention with her looks, but her actions.

She wasn't, however, being charitable or selfless in this errand. She'd been given a choice and picked the easiest one. Rather than visiting Old Town again, she chose to pick up donated clothing.

Instead of making her sad, Old Town angered her, and some of that anger was directed inward. For months she'd thought she was living in despair. She'd viewed her ruined face as an end to her life. She'd never seen the people who cared, the wealth around her, the three rooms dedicated to her comfort. She'd been worse than selfish. She'd been stupid.

In addition, she'd deliberately banished hope from her life.

Even those months in Inverness following her parents' death, she'd not been stripped of hope. Perhaps because Jean was with her then, and her sister would not allow her to dwell on their circumstances. The sun would always rise in Jean's world. The next day would always be better. They would persevere and succeed even when the odds were against them.

Somehow, they had.

Jean had believed in possibilities, and they'd come true. Now, if she could only do the same. What would she wish for? She'd wish for Mark, and wasn't that the most foolish answer?

"Tell him, girl," Mrs. MacTavish said, frowning at her maid. "Tell him exactly what you told me."

Mark stood listening to a tale of betrayal. For a few coins, Artis had divulged the inner workings of the household to a stranger.

"I think he means to hurt her, sir," Artis said, twisting her hands. "She's nicer than I thought," she added. "I'd not want anything to happen to her."

"You foolish girl," Dina said. "You should have thought of that before you started taking money from that man."

"I didn't know. I thought he only wanted a bit of gossip."

"Even after the fire?" he asked.

She looked away, staring at the floor.

"Artis? Do you know something about that?" Mrs. MacTavish grabbed the girl's arm.

"I told him I'd seen her." She glanced back at him. "I told him I'd seen her leaving your room. Back when I thought you were just a footman, sir."

He decided to change the subject at Mrs. MacTavish's quick look. "Why does he want to hurt Catriona?"

"He says he loves her, but I'm not sure," Artis said. "Sometimes, he talks about her like he loves her, but most of the time he sounds like he hates her."

"I can't believe you'd sell information about us, Artis," Mrs. MacTavish said, shaking her head. "I'm disappointed in you."

That lecture would have to wait until later.

"Where did Catriona go?" he asked, his mind racing, though he appeared outwardly calm. He treated emergencies in the same manner.

"To Reverend Michael's church," Mrs. MacTavish said, gripping her hands together. She glanced at the maid, then back at him. "He has more clothing donations, and she went to pick them up."

"How long ago did she leave?" he asked. "By what route? Was Mr. Johnstone driving her?"

"I'm not certain, I don't know, and yes," Mrs. MacTavish replied, her pallor nearly matching that of the maid.

He turned to leave, but glanced back at Artis.

"Why did you tell Mrs. MacTavish now?" he asked. "Why today?"

"He had a gun," she said. "This morning it was sitting there on the table."

If there had been time, he would have had a great deal to say to the woman who stood before him, head down, hands clasped together, a pitiful penitent. But time was the one commodity he didn't have.

Edinburgh wasn't as congested as London, but outside of New Town, the streets were winding, medieval, and hilly.

Andrew had made certain provisions for his task. First of all, he drove his own carriage. Horsemanship, in all its guises, had been a hobby of his a few years earlier. In addition, he'd had the seat modified so that he sat higher and farther to the front than normal.

Since it was a beautiful winter day, brisk yet bright, no one would think it odd that he was muffled, wrapped in a greatcoat large enough to hide his rifle and wearing a hat he pulled down low on his face.

The sooner he was done with this, the sooner he could return to England.

He hated everything about Scotland, from the indigestible food, to the unintelligible accent, to the god-awful notion each Scot seemed to possess that his backward country was somehow superior to England. More than once he'd heard the opinion that the only reason they were a united kingdom was because inhabitants of Scotland felt sorry for the English, and deigned to join their commonwealth. The better to show them how it was done, of course.

The last he saw of the arrogant Scots and their damnable country, the better.

He pulled behind the carriage, more than willing to
return to Charlotte Square if the occupant had been Mrs.
MacTavish or one of the maids. A quarter mile after leaving the house, however, the carriage turned onto a well-
traveled road, giving Andrew a sight of the veiled figure
inside the vehicle.

His heart nearly pounded out of his chest.

He would have liked to stand over her to deliver the
final coup de grace, but he wasn't a fool. He had no intention of ending his own life in this act of vengeance. No, he
would be an old man when he died in his bed.

Perhaps he would serve up the tale of a woman who'd
wronged him as an object lesson to his heirs. He'd allow
himself to remember her then, think of her glorious blond
hair wrapped around his body, how he felt when she
kissed him, praised him, and laughed with him.

He'd think of her just before he died.

Would Catriona think of him?

Chapter 33

As they turned a corner, Catriona peered out the window. The bright sunlight was directly in her eyes, and it took a moment before she could see the odd-looking vehicle directly behind them. But that wasn't what caught her attention.

Mark had told her the truth. He said he had no intention of dismissing Mr. MacLean, and the man was still following her. A few carriages back, granted, but he was still there.

Was he going to be a constant presence in her life?

She motioned Isobel over to sit beside her, exchanging places with the maid. Reaching up, she opened the grate and spoke to the driver.

"Would you please pull over, Mr. Johnstone? There's someone in a carriage behind us that I need to see."

Would the man Mark hired listen to her any better than he had a few nights ago? Or would he simply tip his hat to her, smile, and continue being a nuisance?

She had to at least try to rid herself of her shadow.

Andrew pulled out the rifle, placing it on the floor. One foot rested on the stock as he watched the carriage ahead of him.

When they turned the next corner, he'd have the perfect angle to see into the carriage. Catriona, in her veil, was nothing but a dark shadow now. He'd lift the rifle, sight it, and pull the trigger. She'd be as easy to pick off as a pheasant. Then he'd calmly hide the rifle, extricate himself from traffic, and make his way back to Charlotte Square. In a few days he'd depart for England, but not before the funeral. He might even make an appearance, somber and mournful, a friend from the past, devastated by the news.

Poor dear Catriona. To have left the earth so soon. To die so young, poor thing. To be taken by a random act of violence seemed the worst of all tragedies.

Yes, I knew her. I count her among my dearest friends. No, I hadn't seen her for a while. Yes, she will be missed.

The carriage abruptly pulled over to the side of the road.

Surprised, he could only follow suit.

What the hell was she doing?

As Catriona opened the carriage door, she was intent on the words she was going to say to convince Mr. MacLean to give up his task.

Mr. Johnstone shouted a command as the carriage horses jerked on the reins, impatient. Wagon wheels rumbled over cobblestones; a woman called to her child. Out of the corner of her eye she watched the fluttering wings of two birds engaged in mortal combat or flighted loving.

Her attention was caught when the driver of the carriage behind them placed his hat on the seat. His thick blond hair reminded her of Andrew. When he bent to retrieve something, she hesitated on the step, staring at him. When he straightened, she looked into Andrew Prender's eyes.

Slowly, he raised a gun, looked down the barrel, and smiled.

"Get down on the floor, Isobel," she said. "Now."

Thank God the maid didn't ask any questions.

The gunshot was so loud it seemed to split the air in two.

Mark knew Mr. Johnstone, of course, and even bundled against the weather, the man wouldn't be hard to miss. Yet as Brody drove down Prince's Street, there was no sign of Catriona's carriage. After he and Brody conferred, they decided to take one of the side streets. It was possible that Johnstone had taken an alternate route, knowing the traffic at this time of day.

Every inhabitant of Edinburgh appeared to be abroad, taking advantage of the clear blue winter sky and mild breeze. Even the castle on the hill seemed to sparkle in the sunlight.

The minutes ticked by, each screaming at him to hurry, but there wasn't much they could do in the press of vehicles.

Who was Andrew Prender and why did he want to kill Catriona? Both questions were equipped with a barbed tail, digging into his mind and remaining fixed there.

Pain speared through Catriona, a giant fist that threw her back against the carriage. Someone screamed. *Please God, don't let another maid die because of her. Please let Isobel be all right.* One more scream, but this one was only in her mind. *Don't let me die now.* Not now, when there were so many possibilities. Not at this moment, when she'd just begun to realize how wrong she'd been.

Her hand reached for the carriage door but faltered, her fingers spreading wide as she fell.

Agony raced through her, limned in crimson, lit by a bright afternoon sun.

She pressed her palm against the worst of the pain in her chest. Her fingers were rapidly covered in blood.

Regret, longing, even thought was thrust beneath the agony. She was no longer a person, a woman, a human, merely a repository for the pain. She reached out one hand to grasp something, anything, to hold onto life. Instead, a horrible hollowed-out darkness greeted her, a Hell not unlike Old Town.

After a distance of only two blocks, Brody pulled the carriage to the side of the street. Annoyed, Mark opened the door. Had Brody changed his mind and decided to take another route?

"Sir, it's Miss Cameron," Brody said, leaping from the driver's seat.

A few vehicles ahead the carriage was pulled to the curb. Catriona lay on the steps, her dress draped in folds to the street.

Blood was dripping down the carriage steps.

He ran, his heartbeat thudding in his ears.

Kneeling beside Catriona, he pressed his fingers to her wrist. After finding a faint pulse, he took a deep breath. She was alive.

All his training mattered at this moment. He wasn't a physician with thousands of patients and years of valuable experience. He was simply a student, being taught to heal, learning how to save lives.

He unbuttoned her cloak with steady fingers. The deep blue fabric of her dress glistened wetly. He ripped the bodice open, unfastened the busk of her corset, and pulled the material free from her chest. The bullet had struck her in the upper left quadrant of her chest, too close to her heart for his peace of mind.

He needed to get her home, to his surgery. If he was lucky enough, he could extract the bullet and stitch the wound before she lost any more blood. If he was skilled enough, he could save her.

A woman knelt in the doorway, one hand gripping the door frame. He knew her, recognized the sling she wore, but his frantic brain was trying to put a name to her white face. He had it—Isobel.

"Help me get her into the carriage," he said.

Isobel nodded, and the two of them raised her to the seat.

He knelt on the floor beside her and, with one hand on her wound, gently pulled the veil from her face.

Catriona moaned. He placed his knuckles tenderly against her cheek to soothe her.

Her eyelids fluttered open and, surprisingly, she smiled at him. "It hurts, Mark."

"I know, my love."

She smiled faintly, an expression that twisted his heart.

He called out for the driver, and seconds later Johnstone was in the doorway.

"We need to get her to my surgery," he said. "Do you know the way?"

"Aye, sir, I do at that."

Catriona's face was too pale and so were her lips. He

wanted to be able to take the pain from her, somehow magically remove it. If the bullet had been two inches lower, she would have died instantly.

He bent and kissed her on the forehead, frowning at the cool touch of her skin. *Please, give me the skill to save her.* She couldn't die. She couldn't die. She had come through so much. She deserved a chance at life, a chance to be herself. Catriona Cameron, intransigent, stubborn, willful, charming.

He closed his eyes. "I'll save you, love. I'll save you." A benediction to match the faith of his words.

He prayed he was right.

Andrew saw Catriona fall, smiled, and readied the rifle for another shot. Before he could raise the gun, however, someone grabbed his arm. His rifle clattered to the street as a stranger launched himself at him, jerking Andrew off the driver's seat.

The first impression he had was of a pig dressed in plaid. A short, beefy man with a round face and a flattened nose was pummeling him with fists like hammers, each blow accompanied by a verbal insult to his paternity.

Whenever he tried to jerk away, Pig Face hit him harder. He couldn't even get in an answering blow. All he could do was shield his head with his arms. Blood poured from a cut near his eye, and his lip was split.

Pig Face threw him on the ground facedown then knelt on his back while holding his wrists in a vise.

He couldn't breathe, but when he said as much, speaking with some difficulty from between rapidly swelling lips, Pig Face only grunted in satisfaction.

Not one damn Scot came to his aid. In fact, a tall savage

broke out of the crowd and helped Pig Face. Damned if he didn't hear cheering when the man rolled him over and hit him.

He shook his head to try to clear it, but his vision was obscured by blood. A moment later Pig Face had him by the scruff of his collar and was dragging him toward Catriona's carriage with the help of the other man.

"It's him, sir," the man said through the open door. "He's the one who shot Miss Cameron."

A stranger sat there, his bloody hands pressing against Catriona's bare chest.

She moaned, startling him. Did Catriona have nine lives? From the amount of blood pouring from her wound, she wouldn't have them for long.

The other man only glanced at him for a second before returning his attention to Catriona.

"Take him to the authorities, Brody. I've got to get her to my surgery."

Surgery? Who else but Catriona would have a physician on the scene?

"She should die," he said, in what he considered a rational tone, considering that his lip was nearly cleaved in two. "The world would be better off."

Before he could finish the thought, Pig Face struck him again. He fell to his knees. His assailant pushed him to the street and knelt on him once more as the carriage sped away.

Chapter 34

Time passed, during which Catriona's dreams were amorphous things, filaments of thoughts, memories of deep emotion. She wept for her mother, screamed in defiance over what they'd done to her father.

She was the Catriona of old, arrogant, haughty, secure in her beauty. Everyone else was simply a backdrop to her existence, moving scenery whose sole purpose was to be a foil to her.

I won't let you be a spider at Ballindair, Jean said, sitting there in her mind. *Trapping people in your web.*

When had she become a spider? When had she ceased to care for other people? Caring brought pain. Was that what it was?

Andrew smiled at her. *I do believe I've met my match. A thoroughly amoral woman. Have you always been that way?*

His smile changed, became less amused and more cruel. Andrew hated her, wanted her dead so much he'd tried to kill her more than once.

She couldn't die, not now. She had to do something, become something more.

The future carved a place in her mind, each separate

year etched in the acid of loneliness. There she goes, the Lass in Black, they'll say, pointing her out to the unknowing. She'll be known for her good deeds.

She wept for that, too.

She didn't want to be a saint. Let people declare her wicked. Let matrons whisper behind their fans about her actions and use her as an example to their wayward daughters. Who do you want to be like, Catriona Cameron? Wayward daughters would bow their heads and look pitiable while secretly wishing to be exactly like her.

But she didn't want to be as wicked as before. Nor as selfish and unkind and cruel as she'd been.

She wanted to be loved. She wanted to love like her father had loved her mother. She was no longer afraid of that type of devotion.

Love had crept up on her unawares. Mark was in her heart whether she wanted him there or not.

Was this her punishment? Was giving her a hint of happiness, then taking it away, how she was going to pay for all her sins?

"Do you think she'll wake up, Sarah?"

"Oh yes, ma'am. If Dr. Thorburn said so, then it's the truth."

"You have a great deal of fondness for my son, don't you?"

"I do, yes. He's the son I never had, if you'll be begging my pardon, ma'am."

"I do, indeed. Some people need more than one mother, I think. Mark is one of them. I suspect that the girl we're watching is another."

"She's had a hard time of it."

"I heard someone say that she'd been scarred by love. A strange way to put it, don't you think?"

"Is it love, though, ma'am, if only one person feels it?"

"It doesn't seem so, does it?"

He bent over her, kind and distant, lover and physician. She wanted to reach out to him but something stopped her. He'd saved her again—and always? Would he be there in the future as a bulwark against fate and her own foolishness? Because of him, she'd put the bottle of laudanum in the rubbish. Because of him, she'd emerged from her black cocoon into a world too impossibly bright.

Because of him, and what she felt for him.

"She's been more restless the last day, Dr. Thorburn. Is that a good sign?"

"I hope so, Sarah. I hope so."

"We'll watch over her, don't you worry. You go heal the world. Your mother and I will guard this corner of it."

"Thank you, Sarah."

"Go on, now."

The world changed again, and Andrew smiled at her, his teeth white and growing, then dripping with blood. Isobel sobbed aloud, cut from glass until there was nothing left of her face but ribbons of flesh. No, that was her.

Someone gave her water, changed the towels beneath her, rolled her to her side and made her cry aloud. The taste in her mouth was strange and she made a face. Gentle fingers patted her cheek, murmured to her that it was nearly time to wake up.

The pain waited for her, patient and steady.

Not so patient, after all. It used its claws to scrape against her skin, invade her mind with heated breath. Her chest burned. Her arm was on fire. When she tried to move it, the pain-beast pounced, digging its paws into her flesh.

She moaned, and a cool hand pressed against her forehead.

Jean? She wanted Jean. Jean had always been there.

"She's still so pale."

"My son says it's because she lost so much blood."

"She's an aunt. Pray God she'll live to see the child." Jean.

"The earl is a happy man. They've named the child after Catriona and Jean's mother. I'll not tell them about Catriona yet."

"Such a terrible thing. She's suffered enough, I think."

"She's a lovely girl. Not on the outside, of course. Not anymore. But inside, her heart is good and giving."

"Mark is taken with her."

"Is he?"

"Mrs. MacTavish, you needn't protect him. I know what I know."

The pain-beast stepped back, surprised. She mentally slapped it away and it reluctantly retreated.

Her eyelids flickered. She looked between her lashes, but everything was blurry, as if she hadn't opened her eyes in a while. She closed her eyes then tried again.

Two women sat on either side of a narrow bed. One was Aunt Dina, but she didn't recognize the other.

Where was she?

The light in the room was too strong and bright. A moment later she realized it was because the lamp was placed on a table beside the bed, as if they wished to view her every move or gesture.

She was not wearing her veil.

Closing her eyes again, she lifted her arm, but it didn't move. She concentrated, and the pain-beast padded out from its hiding place and struck again. Don't move that hand, then, or that arm. Could she move the right? She wiggled her fingers, and to her delight felt the texture of the sheet beneath them.

"I'm an aunt?" she said in a voice that sounded like a croaking frog.

Aunt Dina stood, bent over her, a rush of words escaping from her mouth so quickly that Catriona couldn't understand. Had she lost the ability to hear, as well?

Seconds later she realized it was a prayer, uttered in such a heartfelt voice that she wanted to weep. Once, she'd had only Jean to care about her.

"Yes, my darling girl, you're an aunt."

Why was Dina crying?

She tried to raise her hand to brush away her tears, but it was too heavy. So, too, were her eyelids. How strange. She'd just awakened, and now she had to sleep again.

"**Y**our father wouldn't approve of the girl being here," Rhona Thorburn said.

They sat in the parlor, the room warm, thanks to the blazing fire and the western-facing window. Everything was immaculately tended, from the bric-a-brac on the mantel to the velvet footstools. Not a smidgen of dust could be seen anywhere. She wished her own maids were as devoted to their tasks as Sarah appeared to be. She employed ten maids and one housekeeper, yet Sarah had no staff at all.

She shook her head in wonder.

"She's not 'the girl,' Mother. Her name is Catriona and she's well chaperoned," Mark said, accepting the cup she handed him.

Even the tea service was beautifully arranged. Would Mark hate her too much if she tried to steal Sarah away?

"Her aunt is here. Sarah is here. You're here."

"I wouldn't be, had it not been for Sarah, Mark. She was the one who let me know what was going on."

When had he grown so large? He sat in the twin of the chair in which she was sitting, and looked to overflow it. Had he always been that tall, and his shoulders as broad? For that matter, had he always had that air of mastery and command about him?

It wasn't difficult to understand why he and his father clashed. Kenneth was the same vital male as his son. Two rams on a hillside, that's what they were, and prepared to battle to the death.

"I'm not talking about her injury, Mark. I'm talking about how you feel about her. Your father will think that she isn't a proper wife to the future Lord Serridain and, eventually, the Earl of Caithnern."

He didn't say a word to that comment, which was as telling as a long speech. Mark might be a medical miracle worker, but he was still a male. One of her males, at that. She'd had a long education in the male of the species, and she knew a protective silence when she heard one.

She also knew the only way to counteract it was to remain mute as well. Sooner or later Mark would begin to chafe under the strain.

"What do you think?" he asked.

She took a sip of tea, hiding her smile in a porcelain cup. One of his grandmother's cups, she noted, grateful that her mother-in-law had cared enough about Mark to leave him this house, and a fortune as well.

"What do I think?"

She studied the delicate flower pattern on the edge of the cup, so tiny that she wondered how anyone had the skill to paint it. She put the cup and saucer down and looked over at her son.

"I think anyone who could make you forget medicine for a few days must be a remarkable woman. Is it true that you pretended to be a footman in order to get close to her?"

"Sarah talks too much," he said.

"Sarah talks just enough," she said.

He frowned at her, evidently feeling put upon.

"Sarah adores you," she said. "I've never seen a more loyal servant."

"Because I don't treat her like a servant."

She nodded. "Another thing your father would not approve of." She might be able to lure Sarah away, but would the woman be as happy around Kenneth as she was here? Rhona doubted it, and reluctantly dismissed the idea of poaching the housekeeper.

"Then I am destined to forever irritate my father," Mark said.

"Good," she said, smiling. "Otherwise, he could become quite the autocrat. It's good for one of his sons to disobey him. He doesn't like that you aren't dependent upon him for money."

"Pity," Mark said, in a tone that reminded her so much of her husband she could only smile. They were too much alike in certain ways, and different in others.

"How is she doing, Mark? Tell me the truth."

"She did well after the surgery. I've given her morphine to deaden the pain. If she hadn't moved at the last second, he would have killed her. As it was, the bullet just missed her heart."

"I hear he's mad," she said.

He shook his head. "I don't think he's mad at all. He's canny, which is different. I doubt that defense will work since there were a hundred witnesses to what he did."

"He would have escaped but for you. Very smart of you to hire a detective."

"Would you welcome her?" he asked, deftly changing the subject. "Into the family?"

"Is it that serious?" she asked, surprised.

"On my part it is," he said. "As for her, I'm not sure."

"Then I suggest you do your best to find out as quickly as possible," she said.

He looked surprised at her ferocity. Did he think her mother's heart changed to stone when he began his own life? On the contrary, it grew even larger, to accommodate children and in-laws.

She frowned at him. "I'm not disposed to like her if she's going to break your heart," she said. "So you'd better ensure that she doesn't."

He smiled, and she was transfixed by a mother's pride.

Truly, how could any woman resist him?

The next time Catriona awoke, she was alone and it was night.

She turned her head slowly on the pillow, realizing that while she'd been right about the time of day, she was wrong about being alone.

Mark sat there in a straight-back chair, his head leaning against the wall. His eyes were closed and his face tired, but she knew he wasn't asleep. His arms were crossed in front of him, his pose that of a man not relaxed so much as in contemplation.

What was he thinking about?

The left side of her chest was burning. She tried to raise her left hand to touch it, and to her surprise it obeyed her.

Mark's hand grabbed hers before she could touch the odd heaviness there.

She turned her head to meet his gaze.

"It's a bandage," he said. "You were shot."

Shot? She'd have to think about that. She closed her eyes but could still see his blue-eyed gaze.

"Did you save me?" she asked without opening her eyes.

"Yes."

She opened her eyes. "You sound arrogant."

"Would you rather I hadn't saved you?"

"No," she said. She would have smiled, but it seemed like too much effort.

He settled back in the chair. "Don't you want to know who shot you?"

She closed her eyes again. "No."

"Because you already know."

"Because I already know," she said, forcing her eyes open.

"Who is Prender?"

"A lover," she said. "A former lover."

He nodded as if he'd known that, too.

"He wanted you dead, Catriona. Why?"

How did she answer that? Only with the truth, she suspected.

"When I was at Ballindair," she said, speaking the words slowly, "I was desperate to find a way out. I didn't want to be a maid. I didn't want to be stuck at Ballindair for the rest of my life, dusting figurines or making beds."

He didn't interrupt her, merely sat there with his arms folded across his chest in the pose of judge and executioner. Surprisingly, she didn't want him to lose what good opinion he had of her.

She could hear Jean's voice. *You should have thought of that before you became Andrew's mistress.*

"Andrew was a guest at Ballindair," she went on. "We became lovers."

He didn't say a word.

"He offered to put me up in London, buy me a house, give me everything I wanted."

"Since you're not in London, what happened?"

She smiled, remembering. "My brother-in-law gave me a choice," she said. "Respectability or Andrew."

"You didn't choose Andrew."

"But I'm no longer respectable," she said, looking up at the ceiling.

"He tried to kill you in London, didn't he? You knew, all along."

She closed her eyes. She was so tired, but he needed to know.

"Yes," she said. "Ever since Mr. Johnstone visited me."

The coachman had come into her sickroom a few weeks after that accident, twisting his hat, his gaze on the floor.

She couldn't blame him for not wishing to look at her. Her face had been covered in bandages, the weight of them reminding her of what had happened each time she moved.

"Begging your pardon, miss," he'd said. "I wanted to know how you were doing."

"I am alive, Mr. Johnstone," she said slowly. "Beyond that, I can't say."

He waved his hand toward her bandages. "Will those be coming off soon, miss?"

She nodded. In truth, they were a blessing. She'd seen what she looked like before they'd applied the wrappings to her face.

"I wanted you to know, miss, that it weren't my fault. The accident, I mean."

What did he want her to say? Did he expect her to forgive him?

She remained silent.

"Maisie was a good horse, miss," he said, his deep

brown eyes the picture of grief. "She didn't deserve to be shot like that."

Surprise kept her staring at him.

"Who would deliberately shoot a horse, Mr. Johnstone?" she'd asked.

"I've been thinking about that, miss," he said. "I think it was because whoever done it wanted something to happen."

"Something like the carriage turning over?"

He nodded, his beefy face swaying with the gesture.

From that moment, she'd known.

Andrew would never have tolerated being rebuffed. He'd boasted that he was always the one to end a relationship. Yet she'd left him standing there with his hand outstretched, a declaration of love trembling on his lips.

Of course he wanted her dead.

She should have seen it in his eyes that night in London.

Did he simply want to kill her because he hated her? Or was his hatred a dog-in-the-manger attitude—if he couldn't have her, he'd be damned if anyone else did?

"'Heaven has no rage like love to hatred turned,'" Mark quoted now.

She turned her head slowly on the pillow.

"Shall I bear the responsibility for his actions, then, Mark? Shall I take the blame?"

"Perhaps he was mad. Perhaps loving you did that to him. I can understand that."

How could he try to heal her on one hand and wound her so quickly on the other?

Now, he would retract his offer of marriage. When he didn't speak, she stared up at the ceiling, faintly lit by the oil lamp in the far corner.

"The gossip must be swirling about the woman shot in the middle of Edinburgh."

"Why do you care so much about what other people say about you?"

She didn't truly care about what other people thought. Some people would rebuff her, but others would welcome her with a generous heart.

She cared about what Jean thought, of course. The only other person whose opinion she truly valued was sitting a few feet away, and it might as well be a thousand miles.

"Go to sleep, Catriona," he said, his voice gentle and soothing. "It's late and you need your rest. We'll talk later."

She closed her eyes like a child, sinking into slumber with a relaxed and relieved sigh. They would talk later. He hadn't marched out of the room. He hadn't left her without a word. Instead, he sat beside her, lulling her into sleep, caring for her, and watching out after her.

Yet he thought that loving her would make him mad. Did he know that she loved him as well?

That, too, she needed to think about later.

Chapter 35

"There you are, awake," a voice said.

Catriona opened her eyes to find a stranger peering into her face.

"I'm leaving but I wanted to have a talk with you first."

She knew that voice. It had occupied several of her dreams.

"I'm Rhona Thorburn," the woman said, taking the chair Mark had occupied earlier.

"Mark's sister?"

The woman laughed. "I'm disposed to like you already," she said. "I'm his mother."

That was a surprise. Rhona Thorburn looked much too young. Her hair was as black as Mark's and her eyes as clear a blue. Her face was on the long side, but she had a mole near her mouth on the right side, and a dimple on the other, as if nature wanted to balance out her features.

"Mark says you're making great progress," she said. "I'm afraid, however, that you're going to have another scar."

Catriona pressed her palm against her face. How could she have forgotten?

"What a pity such a thing had to happen to you," Rhona Thorburn said. "Because of love, do you think?"

She shook her head. "Not love," she said. "Obsession, perhaps, but nothing as fine as love."

"Is love fine?" Rhona asked. "Love makes you do odd things, doesn't it? Like right now. Here I am, sitting here talking to you, in direct violation of my son's orders, because I'm worried about him."

"Are you?"

Rhona nodded. "I am. You're not simply a patient to him, you know. Are you lovers?"

She would never have imagined a conversation like this with anyone, let alone Mark's mother.

"You think I shouldn't have asked that question, don't you?"

At her nod, Rhona smiled.

"I've seen the way he looks at you, as if you hold the answer to all his questions. Mark has always asked a great many questions, ever since he was a little boy. He's never been content to accept things. He had to figure out why they were as they were."

"I've never seen him look at me in that way, Mrs. Thorburn."

"Actually, it's Lady Serridain," she said. "Mark's father is Lord Serridain. His grandfather is the Earl of Caithnern. Didn't you know?"

Was she asleep? This conversation had all the signs of a dream.

She shook her head.

Rhona shrugged. "I'm not surprised," she said. "Mark has only preferred one title, that of physician. He does love medicine. He gives it his single-minded dedication. I've always thought that if he felt that way about a woman, he'd be a happy man, but only if she felt the same." Lady Serridain smiled brightly at her. "Do you?"

She doubted Mark felt that way about her after her revelations last night.

"I'm tired," she said, pulling the sheet up to cover the worst of her scars. She closed her eyes, hoping the woman would go away.

"Very well," Lady Serridain said, standing. "I do hope you'll consider my words, Miss Cameron. My son is a good man. He needs someone who recognizes his worth."

She opened her eyes. "You think I don't?" she asked.

To her surprise, Mark's mother smiled at her. "I have a feeling adventure follows you, my child. Mark tends to focus too much on medicine to the exclusion of all else. He needs a life of his own. I think you'd insist on it."

"You presume too much," she said. "There is no future for Mark and me."

"I think you ignore too much, Miss Cameron. Or, are you willfully blind?" With that, Lady Serridain turned and left the room as regally as any queen.

When Catriona had first come to live with Dina, a year and some months ago, no one knew that the woman would be pressed into service as a nurse not once, but on two separate occasions. This time Dina was proving just as superlative as she'd been in London.

Whenever Dina went to rest or eat, Artis was in attendance. The maid apologized whenever the two of them were alone. She was ready to forgive the girl anything if she'd only stop weeping.

"I can't fault you for making mistakes, Artis," she said. "Not when I've made enough of my own. Andrew is charming when he wishes to be. Shall we just forget it?"

The girl nodded as she blotted at her tears.

"Please, don't apologize anymore," she said. "It's not necessary."

She was healing quickly and soon could sit on the edge of the bed and dangle her feet over the side. The first day Catriona took a step, she nearly rejoiced, because it meant she would be able to leave Mark's home.

Between Dina, Artis, and Sarah, she was feted, fed, and nursed. Who wouldn't have healed with such care?

A fever in Old Town kept Mark away. So said Sarah, who changed her bandages every day. Catriona thought it might well have been an excuse not to see her. If that was the case, she couldn't blame him.

Without being asked, Sarah conveyed that Mark looked tired, that he was working twenty hours a day, that he'd inquired after her health. When the worst of the fever passed, she said, he'd call upon her himself.

Catriona only smiled in response, but privately doubted she'd see him again.

"Do you think that people truly reap what they sow?" she asked Sarah one day.

She was sitting by the window when Sarah walked into the room, carrying clean linen.

"If you're talking about that Mr. Prender," Sarah said, "it looks like he will. The man will be lucky to escape hanging for what he did."

She looked out the window feeling an odd compassion for Andrew.

"I didn't treat him well," she said.

Had she even thought of him after leaving his carriage? No, she'd been so fixated on reaching Edinburgh and the next stage of her life.

"Still, that's not a reason to go around murdering

people," Sarah said, beginning to change the sheets. "If you were disappointed in love, would you kill the object of your affections?"

"I might want to," she said. "If I was hurt enough."

Sarah made a sound of disapproval. "Then I think it best if you don't go being disappointed in love."

Perhaps it was best if she didn't think about love at all.

She wanted to go home so desperately that she begged Dina to bring something for her to wear.

At the older woman's doubtful look, she'd said, "You can't expect me to recuperate here forever. I think I would heal so much quicker in my own room."

The plan was born and carried out a few days later. She said farewell to the sickroom and was helped down the stairs not by Mark, but by Dina and Sarah. Artis led the way, her gaze intent on the ground as if searching for any impediments to her progress. The stairs were difficult but navigable.

She made it, and walked through the house to the front door with Dina on one side and Sarah on the other. Once out the front door, she stood on the top of the steps, looking down at the carriage.

Only ten more steps, and these were shallow. She could do this.

Mr. Johnstone got down from the driver's perch and came to stand in front of her, bowing slightly. "Miss," he said, surprising her by clamping his arm down on her uninjured shoulder. "You're well, then?"

"I am," she said, "thanks to you. I understand you got us here quickly."

"I did what I could, miss. It's glad I am to see you up and about."

She was up but certainly wasn't "about" at the moment. In fact, she felt as if she were going to fall over any second. Dina must've known, because she supported her around the shoulders, while Artis went ahead. Together, she and Mr. Johnstone opened the carriage door, lowered the steps, and moved aside.

No queen could have been treated more royally.

After Catriona was seated in the carriage, Sarah handed her a small twine-wrapped box.

"My sweet scones for a treat," she said. "I know how you like them."

What else had the woman discovered in the past weeks? That allowing people to help her made her grit her teeth? Or that she'd come to feel a fondness for her? Or that she rarely asked about Mark, for fear that she'd reveal something in her question?

She nodded, grateful for the veil that hid her emotions.

Surprisingly, the vehicle held little terror for her. Was it because she knew that Andrew had been imprisoned? Or simply because all the fear had been frightened from her?

"You needn't sit that way," she said to Dina. The older woman had angled herself so her back was to the window, blocking it. Artis had done the same on her side of the carriage.

She'd come to understand that terror existed mainly in the mind.

In the past weeks, whenever she closed her eyes she'd been able to relive those moments before the shooting, the feeling of regret she'd had, and the deep and bottomless sorrow.

Yet at the same time, she could recall Mark's kisses, his gentle touch, and the twinkle of amusement in his eyes when he'd teased her.

Which memories did she want most?

The answer wasn't even an answer, because it was rooted so deeply in her mind. When she indulged in recollections of the past, it wouldn't be fear she remembered, but love.

The days passed, during which Catriona slept, recuperated, and slept some more.

Her meals were brought to her on a tray, but by Artis, not a certain footman. When she felt better, she left her bed and began a slow pace of her living quarters, sometimes sitting beside the window and watching the construction of the new carriage house.

Everyone treated her like a well-loved patient. If she wanted company, Aunt Dina came and sat with her. If she wanted something to read, one of the maids was sent to the book shop. Chocolate? Her whim was instantly gratified. Whatever she wanted was only as far away as a wish.

But instead of being content, she was miserable.

She wrote to her sister, planned a visit to Ballindair when the weather was warmer. She wanted to see Jean and her new niece. First, however, she'd have to force her envy down into a secret place where no one could see it.

She wasn't recuperating as much as mourning. She didn't grieve for her lost beauty; she'd already done that for months. This was different, a type of sadness that was always with her. When she woke, it was the first thing she felt. During the day, when she didn't deliberately occupy herself in a task, it crept in and overwhelmed her. At night when she prayed to sleep, it crouched at the edge of her consciousness.

This was grief coupled with loneliness. Perhaps a future grief—for those things she could never have: a man to love her, who teased her and laughed at her, and made her heart stutter on seeing him.

A certain man who was as gloriously handsome as she was ugly. She never failed to appreciate that irony. In her days of beauty she would have shunned associating with an ugly man. Yet Mark had once offered her marriage. A sweet gesture, as well as an unexpected one, and something he no doubt regretted.

She would not remind him. She'd never see him again.

On the Monday of the third week she'd had enough. She lay in her bed and decided that she could still have a life that brought her happiness, as well as a sense of purpose, even if she was forever alone.

First, however, she would have to make some changes. Instead of remaining in her hermitage, the world was simply going to have to endure her presence in it. People could call her the Lass in Black or the Lass in Blue or the Veiled Lady, or Ugly Catriona. Let them say anything they wished, but she wasn't going to hide any longer.

Another change—she wasn't going to wear her veil in the house. Everyone had already seen her scars. They would just have to accustom themselves to what she looked like, beginning this morning.

She heard the soft knock, and instead of reaching for her veil, sat up in bed.

But it wasn't Artis with her breakfast.

Mark stood at the doorway, holding a tray.

Her heart stopped, then madly began to race. She placed her hand against her chest to keep it inside her body.

"What are you doing here?"

The sheet had dropped to her waist, and she noted that he was looking at her chest.

"Have you come to examine me?" she asked. "I'm healing well, and Aunt Dina changes my bandages every morning."

We don't need you.

"You still require the services of a physician."

"Not necessarily you," she said.

"I agree."

She frowned at him.

"However, I'm here, so it would be remiss of me not to check your wound."

"It's no longer a wound. It's a scar." Another one, but this scar didn't bother her as much. Perhaps because it was a testament to being a survivor.

"I've come to make sure you eat," he said, setting the tray on the edge of the bed.

"I'm eating. I'm eating well."

"I've heard differently," he said, coming around the end of the bed.

She scooted up until her back was against the headboard. "From whom?"

He didn't answer, merely picked up her hand, his fingers against her wrist. Her pulse was racing; he must feel it. He smiled, dropped her wrist, and slowly unbuttoned the placket of her flannel nightgown. His gaze wasn't on the buttons but her hair.

"I think your hair has grown lighter," he said. "Do you always braid it like that?"

She nodded. Who was he to comment on the color of her hair, however she fashioned it? If he was going to be her physician, then let him examine her and be gone.

He parted the fabric wide enough that her shoulder was exposed. Gently, he fingered the edge of the bandage, then unwrapped it to examine the wound.

"You heal fast," he said. "Good."

She nodded again.

"Next week we'll remove the bandage. Until then, be careful not to lift anything or otherwise strain yourself."

Once more she nodded.

"You're angry at me."

"Angry? Why should I be angry at you, Dr. Thorburn?"

"There was an epidemic in Old Town. I couldn't take the chance of spreading any disease to you," he said. "Otherwise, I would have been here sooner."

"As you see," she said tightly, "I've been just fine without you."

"Have you?"

Another nod.

He slowly buttoned her nightgown. "I haven't," he said.

She glanced at him, startled by his words.

"All my patients have noticed. 'Are you feeling well, Dr. Thorburn?' 'Is anything amiss, Dr. Thorburn? You seem distracted.' I am distracted," he added. "My life hasn't been the same since I met you."

She didn't know whether to be insulted or pleased.

Bending down, he shocked her by scooping her up in his arms and depositing her in the middle of the bed. Before she could question him, he climbed in beside her.

She looked away, but he reached out, placed his fingers on her chin, and gently turned her to face him.

"I didn't feel it was right to pounce on you when you were a patient in my house."

"But it's acceptable to pounce on me now?"

"I couldn't wait any longer."

He bent and kissed her. Despite all the warnings that suddenly bloomed in her mind, she sighed into his kiss, opened her mouth, and was lost.

Moments—or hours—later, she pulled back.

"My father was a doctor," she said.

"I know."

Startled, she looked at him.

"I knew him. He was one of my mentors when I was training."

"Did you?" she asked. "I don't remember you."

"I don't think you ever saw me," he said. Reaching out, he pushed back a tendril of hair from her face. "I thought you were both the most exquisite beauty I'd ever seen and the most spoiled creature I'd ever met."

"You did?" Was she supposed to apologize for the foolish, self-centered girl she'd been?

"I much prefer you as you are now."

"Ugly?"

"I doubt you could ever truly be ugly, Catriona, although your character has leaned in that direction in the past."

She frowned at him.

"Footman, have you come here to be annoying?" she asked.

"No, I've come to give you fair warning."

"What kind of warning?" she asked, her eyes widening.

Had Andrew been set free?

"I'm going to marry you, Catriona Cameron, and we're going to begin this courtship today. It's been long enough."

Astonished, she stared at him.

"You're going to meet my family, such as they are. My grandfather will adore you. My mother already does. You'll despise my father, and the emotion will probably be mutual, I'm sorry to say. My brothers are worthless, but I'm interested to know your opinion of both of them."

She'd lost the power of speech.

"When all that is done and a proper time has passed— but not all that long, by the way—I'm going to marry you, take you back to my house, and stay in bed with you for a month. Or however long my patients allow us."

He raised her hand to his lips, kissing her knuckles tenderly.

"That's my warning."

"I don't want your pity, Mark," she said.

His laughter startled her.

"Of all the people in the world I might pity, I think I'd label you last. You're a fighter, Catriona, and one of the most stubborn, obstinate, and hard-headed people I've ever had the privilege to meet. You stand your ground regardless of where you are or what circumstance you're facing."

"I do?" she asked, her voice sounding distressingly faint.

He nodded.

Yet, for all his words, he deserved someone better, someone who had no ghosts in her past. Someone who had been chaste and sweet. Someone unlike her.

How could she bear to send him away? How could she live without him? For weeks now she'd told herself that she could, and all she had to do was see him again to prove that resolve foolish.

"But I truly can't marry you," she said, determined to be honest.

"Why not?" he asked, kissing her cheek. She pressed her fingers against his lips, wishing he wasn't so kind, so honorable.

"I've made a great many mistakes in my life," she said. "But between London and Andrew shooting me again, I've learned a valuable lesson."

"That life is short?"

She shook her head. "That I have to make up for those mistakes. I have to be a better person."

"You can't be a better person married to me?"

She frowned at him again.

"I only care about who you are now. I like this Catriona. I admire you. I like talking to you. I like being with you."

"Are you certain you're not infatuated with the girl I was?" she asked. "Perhaps you see the memory of her instead of me." She looked away. "She was beautiful."

"I'm not infatuated," he said. "I'm afraid it's gone beyond that." He cupped her cheek, gently turning her face. "I see your beauty, Catriona."

For several long minutes he studied her scars, never once flinching. When the agony of inspection was finished, he smiled down into her face.

"I see your beauty," he said again. "Perhaps one day you will, too."

"I'm not a good person, Mark," she said, shaking her head. "Not like you. I've been selfish and mean. I've hurt people and ridiculed them. I've been deliberately unkind. I've been shocking."

She placed her fingers over her scars, wishing she were beautiful for him. He smiled at her, reached over, and peeled her hand away.

"I don't like one of my patients," he said. "She complains constantly. I think she's vain and shallow. All her ailments are between her ears."

He bent to kiss her temple.

"I could go the rest of my life without seeing my father again. He's ruthlessly pompous."

Her frown was having no effect on his smile.

"I put a frog in my tutor's bed once and castor oil in my father's port. He figured it out, eventually, but not before he had a fitful night."

A strangled giggle escaped her.

"I confess to wishing I was paid more for all the work I do in Old Town, and there are times when mankind disgusts me."

"All in all," she said, "those flaws make you a better person."

"While yours make you human. Neither of us is perfect. Together, we can help each other be better, don't you think?"

"I don't deserve you," she said.

He pulled back and smiled at her.

"Pardon me, but where have you put Catriona Cameron? The woman who called me an irritating boor?"

"She was truly arrogant, was she not?"

He traced her bottom lip. "She was afraid," he said. "Everything she knew as certain and sure had disappeared, and she was trying to find herself."

She studied him. "You knew about Andrew," she said, the thought having occurred to her after the shooting. "That's why you set Mr. MacLean to follow me."

"I didn't know about him specifically," he said. "I suspected the same person was responsible for both events."

"You never said anything."

"Would you have told me about Andrew if I had?"

She wasn't entirely sure.

"He belongs to the past, don't you think?"

She nodded.

"So do all your sins, real or imagined."

When he smiled, she frowned at him once more. "You are a stubborn man, Mark Thorburn."

"Your perfect match, Miss Cameron," he said, laughing. He bent closer and kissed her again.

"This is love, isn't it?" she asked a few minutes later. "This feeling of being miserable all the time?"

"Are you miserable?"

She nodded. "I only feel right when I'm around you. As if you belong to me and I'm not whole without you. It's bothersome."

"Have you any other symptoms?" he asked, brushing his knuckles against her chin.

He smelled so wonderful. She lay her head on his shoulder, content to stay there forever.

"I can't sleep well."

"Very disturbing. I shall have to find a treatment," he said.

"I lied," she said softly. "I haven't been eating well. I find that I have no appetite."

"That's a troubling symptom as well."

She raised her head and cupped his cheek tenderly, smiling into his eyes.

"What do you think I should do, Dr. Thorburn?"

"Put yourself in my hands," he said.

"Will this situation last long?"

"Being in love? I think it will."

She sighed heavily. "Then I shall have to become accustomed to it." Closing her eyes, she smiled as he pulled her into his arms.

Did love blind people to the truth? When he looked at her, he saw someone better than she knew herself to be.

Loving him in return was both exhilarating and frightening. Loving someone deeply changed a person, didn't it?

She might even become a better person. One who charmed others. One who made them smile or made their days pleasant. Instead of complaints, she would deal in hope and thankfulness, exactly the emotions she felt right now.

How odd that because of the accident, she'd been made over. Or maybe it wasn't the accident at all. Perhaps it was Mark, and because she'd fallen in love.

"Share my life with me, Catriona," he said, kissing her temple.

"You just want me in your bed," she said, tilting her head back to smile at him.

"Well, yes," he said, grinning at her. *"Byde weill, betyde weill."*

"Everything comes to him who waits?"

"I'm a patient man, within reason."

Wouldn't that be a delight? To retire each night with this handsome man? To wake to feel his hands, his lips, on her? To laugh with him, talk with him, and love him? To share her insecurities, and her doubts, with the one person who knew her better than anyone?

"Don't you want me in your bed, in your life? In your heart?"

"Oh yes," she said, leaning forward to kiss him again. A moment later she pulled back. "What did you say?"

He grinned at her. "Baa."

" 'Baa'? As in the sound a sheep makes?"

"Something my grandfather said," he admitted. "I'll tell you in a moment," he added. "But right now I'm more interested in kissing you."

Explanations would have to wait, because he was right, a kiss was vastly more important than anything else.

Author's Notes

The Edinburgh Fire Brigade is one of the oldest in the UK.

William Banting's diet, published in a pamphlet entitled *Letter on Corpulence Addressed to the Public* in 1863, is considered by many to be the first low-carbohydrate diet.

In the middle- to late-nineteenth century, medical care was available to the poor in Scotland, but only if they applied for poor relief. Those who hadn't applied, or couldn't qualify, had to be treated as charity patients.

Those on poor relief had the services of a parish doctor—if they could see him. In the city of Glasgow in 1875, for example, only one doctor existed for every twenty thousand inhabitants.

Charlotte Square does exist in Edinburgh's New Town. Built in the nineteenth century, it was an address for the wealthy. I took the original layout of the square and expanded it.

The Lass Wore Black

Third in line for an important earldom, Mark Thorburn is expected to idly wait to take up his position. Instead, he devotes himself to medicine, a life's work that leads him to the door of famous beauty Catriona Cameron.

The victim of a terrible accident, Catriona has refused to admit even the most illustrious physicians to her lush Edinburgh apartments. But what if a doctor were to pose as a mere footman, pretending to serve her every need . . . would she see through such a ruse?

Entwined in the masquerade, Mark manages to gain Catriona's trust, only to find that somehow she has captured his heart at the same time. But when their passion becomes the target of a madman bent on revenge, Mark will have to do more than heal her body and win her love . . . he'll have to save her life as well.

A Scandalous Scot

One scandal was never enough . . .
After four long years, Morgan MacCraig has finally returned to the Highlands of his birth . . . with his honor
in shreds. After a scandal, all he wants now is solace—
yet peace is impossible to find with the castle's outspoken
new maid trying his patience, challenging his manhood
. . . and winning his love, body and soul.

Jean MacDonald wants to leave her past behind and
start anew, but Ballindair Castle, a Scottish estate rumored to be haunted, hasn't been the safe haven she envi-
sioned. Ballindair's ancestral ghosts aren't as fascinating
as Morgan, the most magnificent man she's ever seen.
Though their passion triggers a fresh scandal that could
force them to wed, Jean must first share the secrets of
her own past—secrets that could force them apart, or be
the beginning of a love and redemption unlike anything
they've ever known.

A Scottish Love

Shona Imrie should have agreed to Gordon MacDermond's proposal of marriage seven years ago—before he went off to war and returned a national hero—but the proud Scottish lass would accept no man's charity. The dashing soldier would never truly share her love and the passion that left her weak and breathless—or so she believed—so instead she gave herself to another. Now she faces disgrace, poverty, and a life spent alone for her steadfast refusal to follow her heart.

Honored with a baronetcy for his courage under fire, Gordon has everything he could ever want—except for the one thing he most fervently desires: the headstrong beauty he foolishly let slip through his fingers. Conquering Shona's stubborn pride, however, will prove his most difficult battle—though it is the one for which he is most willing to risk his life, his heart, and his soul.